THE PRICE OF LOYALTY: SERVING ADELA OF BLOIS

MALVE VON HASSELL

HISTORIUM PRESS

Library of Congress Registration Number on file

HARDCOVER ISBN: 978-1-964700-25-0
PAPERBACK ISBN: 978-1-964700-26-7
EBOOK ISBN: 978-1-964700-27-4

Published by Historium Press 2025

Contents

PART I - TAPESTRY OF CONQUEST: FRAYED THREADS

Marcigny Abbey

1132

"Hold it straight, girl."

"Yes, Sister," Adelaide muttered. It was the first time that she had to bring the tray upstairs. It seemed to weigh as much as a barrel of apples. And yet it held no more than a beaker of ale, a bowl of gruel, and a smaller bowl of stewed pears. "Why doesn't Lady Adela come downstairs to eat in the refectory with everyone else?"

"If you needed to know that, we would have told you." Sister Louisa's wimple had slipped, and her cheeks were reddened from the heat of the hearth. She brushed her hands over the girl's kirtle, adjusting the folds. "Now go. And remember to be quiet. Lady Adela doesn't care for gibble-gabble from the likes of you."

The stone steps of the narrow staircase leading to the tower room were uneven. Adelaide had to tread carefully so she wouldn't spill anything. Her sandals pinched.

"You have to stop growing," her grandmother would say, her voice always a bit higher than usual when frustrated. "I can't keep up with you." She had sent Adelaide to Marcigny even though she didn't want to go. "It will be good for you. You will learn more than I ever had a chance to learn."

"But do you want me to become a nun?" Adelaide had asked despairingly.

"That is your decision," her grandmother had responded. There had to be some other reason why she wanted her granddaughter to be at Marcigny Abbey, but she refused to talk about it. Adelaide gave up asking.

Petra, the other novice, had told her about Lady Adela. "I think she gave a lot of money to the convent, and now she lives out her days here."

"Is she a nun?"

"I think so." Petra shrugged and wrinkled her nose disdainfully. "What does it matter? She won't talk to you anyway."

The heavy oak door to the room was open, and a breeze came through the narrow window that fronted onto the street. It smelled of spring, mixed with the odors from the road, moist, pungent, evoking night soil tossed out of windows. It was quiet. The room was as large as that belonging to the abbess. The carpet with its warm colors of dark red, blue, and brown looked soft and inviting; Adelaide made a face when she thought of the cold stone flooring in the dormitory she shared with the other novices. To the left of the door, there was a tall screen, covered with a tapestry of flowers. A broad oak table near the window was buried under piles of manuscripts, leaving hardly enough room for the inkwell and a pile of quills. One had fallen onto the floor. Adelaide felt a pang of homesickness. She always loved watching her grandmother sharpen the long points of the goose feathers she used.

"Of course, I'd prefer swan feathers, but they are very dear."

"Why do I have to write on a wax tablet?"

"When you are older and have learned your letters, you'll write with quills," her grandmother told her.

Adelaide hesitated at the door, unsure whether to call out. Then she tiptoed forward, clutching the tray. *What am I going to do with you?* her grandmother's voice echoed in her mind, chiding her. "Stop being so nosy." The lady must have started writing a letter. The girl could make out the date on top and the word Chartres.

A rustle to the side startled her, and some of the ale spilled out of the beaker. Quickly she nudged one manuscript aside and put the tray down on the corner of the table.

"Who are you?" The voice was sharp and imperious. "What happened to the other girl?"

A woman emerged from behind the screen, her hands adjusting her wimple and tucking a gray curl away. While her tunic was in a somber tone of dark gray as befitting a lay sister, the embroidered bands edging the sleeves hinted at elegance.

Adelaide dropped into a curtsy, feeling oddly tongue-tied. She was taller than the lady by about a head, but it didn't make her feel any less intimidated by this woman, whose round bosom and plump body were in curious contrast with her piercing blue eyes and slightly aquiline nose. "Sister Louisa had a chore for the other novice."

"What is your name?" The lady gazed at her intently. "You look familiar."

"Adelaide, my lady."

"Indeed?" The lady smiled. "Then we share part of the same name."

"My grandmother named me in honor of a lady with that name."

"Your grandmother? What is she called?"

"Giselle, my lady."

Lady Adela stared at her. "And your grandfather?"

"Cerdic."

"Your grandfather was Cerdic of Wessex?"

"Yes." Adelaide was puzzled by the reaction. "You knew him?"

The lady moved toward the chair. Her hand held on to the edge of the table when she sat down. It was as if she had forgotten the girl in her room. She turned her face to the window, seemingly absorbed in the play of the late afternoon sunlight on the windowsill.

"Oh, yes," she whispered. "I knew him."

THE LITTLE DRAGON

"What's the story with the runt over there?" One of King William's men nodded toward a small boy in the stern of the cog. "Is the king so desperate for men that he's taking on children?"

The boy wore a thin jerkin and a hose too short for his legs. His feet, encased in threadbare sandals, were grimy and tinged with blue. His reddish-blond hair, damp from the spray of the sea, fell into his face, so one could only see the childish cheeks and curiously adult-looking hook nose.

"That runt?" Another man laughed. "You should have been there. The king rode into Southampton on Sunday on his way to mass and to inspect the progress of the new church—you know the one that's being dedicated to St. Michael. He and his retinue were traveling along a crowded road, when a beam from a building came crashing down. A horse threw his rider and started stampeding. Several people got hurt. This little fellow ran out from behind some of the townspeople and somehow stopped the horse. When he led the horse back to the knights, he was talking to it as if they were old friends."

"That doesn't explain why he's on this ship. He doesn't look happy, does he?"

"The king talked to the boy's mother and offered to take him to Normandy. Apparently his father died at Hastings, and the mother is poor."

The man grinned. "Well, if he picks up every kid orphaned at the battle of Hastings, he can set up more than a few nurseries."

"He just signed the Accord of Winchester, didn't he? Now he's got the Archbishop of Canterbury in his pocket. Maybe it put him in a good mood, and he wanted to do something nice for the runt."

The boy stared toward the shoreline, oblivious to everything around him. Why did he have to run into the road to stop that horse? He shivered in his thin jerkin. The wind made him sway. Squinting to keep the spray out of his eyes, he tightened his grip on the railing.

He kept seeing it over and over in his mind. "Horses aren't very smart," his uncle had told him. "They scare easily; but remember, they don't like to trample people." So he had stepped out into the road and spread his arms, calling to the horse as if they were alone in a pleasant meadow. The horse swerved and then came to a stop, his flanks dripping with sweat. He flicked his ears, lowered his head, and allowed him to pick up the rein trailing on the ground.

Several men came running up; one took the rein out of his hand, and the other dragged him toward a group of people standing at the top of the road.

His mother pushed her way through the crowd and, ignoring the men, grabbed him by the arm. "What have you done?" she hissed.

One of the men spoke; his voice was deep and hoarse sounding.

He couldn't understand a word. Were they going to punish him?

Another man said words to his mother that he understood, but he couldn't make any sense of it. Caen? They wanted to take him to Caen? Was that a jail?

His mother said nothing at all; she held him close to her. He tried to look out from under her sheltering arm. The man who was speaking wore armor. He was broad and stout; his pointy beard made his face appear long. Yellow hair, tinged with red, stuck out at the edges of his helmet. These men would punish him for touching the horse. He would get whipped for walking into the road like that. He kept his eyes on his mother's skirts. They smelled damp and musty, he thought, distracted for a moment. They hadn't made a fire in their house in the last days. All he could hear was something about his mother's name. Orva. He knew what that meant. Brave friend. More words he couldn't understand from the big man, followed by urgent whispers into his mother's ears from the other one.

His mother's grip on his shoulder tightened painfully. Then she took him by the hand and turned him around so that the others couldn't see their faces. "You will go with this lord," she said, speaking in a low tone. "He is the king of England, and he is taking you to his home in Normandy. He wants to raise you in his household and train you to be a page. Maybe you will become a knight."

"A knight? Like my papa?" It was as if the world had turned golden. Then he realized what she had said. He was supposed to go with these men. He stared up at her. She was pale, only her cheeks were flushed just like when she was angry with him.

"Don't send me away," he pleaded. "I'll be good. I want to stay with you."

"You must." Her voice sounded gruff. "Can't you see that this is your chance? There is nothing here for you." She brushed her calloused hands over his shoulders. "Remember who you are. You are Cerdic, son of Osbeorn."

His eyes blurry, Cerdic could hardly see his mother's face. "When can I come home?"

"Not for a while." His mother rubbed the sleeve of her gown over a spot on his face. "I'll pray for you every day."

"I have to go right now?"

"Yes." She stroked his head, smoothing down his hair. "It's better that way."

He couldn't let her see how frightened he was. He couldn't tell her how upset he was she would send him away. Worst of all, he couldn't let her know that for a glorious moment he had been thrilled. He pressed his lips together and lowered his head. Again he felt his mother's hand on his head.

"Go, my brave boy," she whispered. "And don't forget, you are named for Cerdic of Wessex. You are my little dragon. God will protect you."

Everything happened so quickly that Cerdic had no time to think.

One of the king's men lifted him up onto his horse. He gripped him as if he were a sack of oats. It was a brief ride to the harbor where three cogs were riding at anchor. Men were already lugging sea chests on board. Dizzy and winded, Cerdic watched the loading of the horses and for a moment forgot what was happening to him. Men shouted and struggled with the horses, trying to coax them up a broad plank and dragging them into a pen set up on the ship. They snorted, shaking their heads, dancing sideways and kicking, their necks and flanks shiny with sweat.

The king and his retinue went on board one of the cogs. Still held in a near stranglehold, Cerdic was lifted onto the deck where the man dropped him unceremoniously. The swell of the sea underneath the ship's planks made Cerdic lose his balance. No one paid any attention to him.

Crowded into a narrow pen on the stern side of the ship, the horses stamped and whinnied when the waves lifted up the vessel and then let it down again with a thud. Cerdic was oblivious to everything. He stood on his toes, his hands clutching the slippery wood of the railing, and stared at the pier. He couldn't see his mother amid all the people there, but he raised his arm to wave anyway. The cog lurched and moved with increasing speed. The harbor of Southampton receded, and soon the shoreline was no more than a blur. His eyes burned.

Then he flinched. A heavy, coarse blanket settled on his shoulders. He whipped his head around.

A man stood behind him. "It gets windy here," he muttered.

"Thank you," Cerdic whispered and tried to smile. He hadn't understood the words, but he realized the man wanted to help. He felt as if his face was frozen. *Keep smiling. Don't show what you feel.*

He could no longer see land. His home was gone, and he was adrift in a gray black sea of churning angry waves. The snapping of the giant sail above his head was like words slamming into his head. "Go," his mother had said. "There is nothing here for you." He could still feel her hand on his head and her whisper, "Don't forget." *I must not cry. I am Cerdic son of Osbeorn and Orva, and I will go home one day.*

Adela

Where Harold, duke of the Angles and his soldiers, ride to Bosham. Church. --- Here Harold has sailed the sea, and with sails filled with wind has come into Count Guy's territory. Bayeux Tapestry

1077 Caen

"Tell my daughter to make haste," the queen said to one of her ladies. "We are going to be late." Flustered, the lady rushed inside the house.

A few moments later, a girl's pink face appeared at the window. "I am coming, Mother," she called out. "I have been searching for the *cote* you wanted me to wear."

Matilda frowned. She'd have to have words with that girl later. She should know better than to raise her voice like that. With her finger, she pushed a damp lock back underneath her wimple. She felt uncomfortable in her heavy red gown, with the sleeves and collar trimmed with bands of gold brocade. Her girdle repeated the colors red and golden in its embroidery. It was hot, and it hadn't rained in weeks; everything was covered in dust. At least her gown wouldn't have to drag along a muddy road to the cathedral. Why did they have to choose July 14th for the consecration? They had ridden from Caen the day before, and she was tired. The manor in which they were staying near the cathedral was damp and uncomfortable. It belonged to one of Bayeux's leading nobles who was beside himself with the honor of hosting the king and queen. He kept bowing whenever she asked him a question, practically falling over his feet in his eagerness to fetch whatever they needed. Matilda sighed. It would be a long day.

The courtyard was bustling with knights, squires, and servants running around, getting everything ready for the procession to the cathedral. The flag bearers stood at the front, the long poles swaying in the wind so that the two golden lions on the red background seemed to ripple and move in the sunlight. The pages were lined up near the gate, each outfitted in red tunics over dark hoses. Cerdic, straight and proud, stood at the end, his face schooled into studied calm as befitting a twelve-year-old page. He was taller than the other pages.

For a moment, Matilda thought of the little waif from five years ago. He had been so pale and skinny when her husband had brought him back from England. "We could put him in with the other pages," he said after briefly explaining how he had come upon the boy. Perhaps that was William's attempt to make up for some of the awful things that have happened at the battle of Hastings and after. Conquest with a carrot.

Matilda opened her mouth to protest. Then she shrugged. She told a servant to take him to be bathed. Of course, at first, the boy hadn't understood a word of anything. Matilda had always rued the fact that her husband had dismissed any notion of trying to learn English.

"Why should I?" He had frowned in irritation. "That's what scribes and interpreters are for."

Matilda had made a point of learning some English during her frequent sojourns there when accompanying the king. So she addressed Cerdic in his own language, trying to show him that the world was not as alien and unfriendly as he seemed to think. But the child flinched like a spooked horse. Perhaps that was his last bastion of the world he remembered, and her heavily accented words felt like another invasion. So she let him be.

Matilda smiled when she looked at Cerdic's gangly frame and his oddly unbalanced face, with thin lips, long jutting nose, and a shock of blond hair that flopped over his forehead, hiding his gray eyes. In the first months after his arrival, he had maintained a smile on his face like a determined little soldier. He didn't realize that she watched him sometimes when he thought he was alone and the mask lifted, leaving behind an expression of deep sadness. His almost desperate cheerfulness of the early days eventually gave way to a secretive attitude; he withdrew into his shell, and she didn't hear him talk at all until one day, when she discovered that he had begun chatting with Adela and later with Henry. For a while, he was running wild. In the end, Cerdic was handed over to one of the retainers for training as a page and future squire and also was allowed to sit in on Henry's lessons with his tutor. He was shaping up well.

Her two older sons, Robert and William Rufus, would be joining them at the cathedral. Matilda sighed when she thought of Robert. He had been at loose ends ever since he lost the County of Maine in 1069, when the county revolted against his leadership.

"It wasn't my fault," Robert told his father when he returned to Caen after the County of Maine had chosen a new count to lead them, Hugh, son of Azzo d'Este. Disheveled and bewildered, he stood in the great hall, his legs apart and his shoulders slightly hunched, as if in his fear of his father's snide comments. His stance made him appear even shorter than he already was. Matilda loved him—perhaps because he was her eldest. When he was a little boy, other children had teased him. William Rufus, who soon towered over his older brother, was merciless. When she tried to intervene, her husband had told her that to leave the boys alone. "They need to learn." Robert's dour expression was dear to her because she knew what was behind it. His rare smile he seemed to reserve for his mother and sometimes his sister Adela. He was always gentle with his mother even when he walked around most of the time with a surly expression on his face, impatient and quick to anger. She loved all her children, but Robert was closest to her heart.

William Rufus, Robert's younger brother, always had been a stranger to her for all that she loved him. Sometimes it seemed as if he wasn't even her son—so little did he care for anything to do with faith or good taste for that matter, always ready to break every rule and to offend every convention. Taller than his brothers and stout, with a bit of a paunch, even though only in his late twenties, he looked ruddy and cheerful, with his shock of reddish hair and a twinkle in his odd eyes, one hazel and the other brown.

Cecilia was at the Abbey of the Holy Trinity in Caen, where she had been since 1066. She seemed content there. Matilda made a quick sign of the cross in gratitude for her gentle and gracious daughter, who had never complained at having been entered in the convent when she was ten years old.

Her husband had insisted that Adela and Henry attend the ceremony at Bayeux.

"They are too young," Matilda protested. Henry was just nine and Adela ten.

"That's irrelevant," William said. "They need to learn. This is an important moment for us and for the future of the kingdom."

Perhaps he was right. It was time that both Henry and Adela learned some decorum. Henry was bright and absorbed new information easily, more so than his older brothers. Matilda sighed. Henry liked to boast of the things he had heard, announcing them proudly in his high treble voice at mealtimes. His tutor would try to shush him, but not quickly enough. Henry was cheeky with his tutors and on occasion with herself and his father.

A horn sounded. It was almost time to begin. Where was her daughter? Frustrated, Matilda glanced up at the window to the room where they had been sleeping.

"I am coming, Mother." Adela's high, clear voice boomed across the courtyard. Followed by an aggravated looking governess, Adela tripped on the stone blocks of the front steps and then righted herself. Beaming at her mother, she adjusted her wimple with an impetuous tug and flicked her expensive new long gown away from her feet. Matilda had to suppress a smile in return. Infuriating as that child was, willful and always challenging her superiors, she was a source of secret pride for her mother. Already Adela spoke several languages and had absorbed far more information than most at her age. Sometimes when she was not at her school in Caen and her father was at home—a rare occurrence—she would talk to him and even start arguing with him about current affairs. Most likely, she wouldn't grow up to be a beauty. Her nose was too long, and her thick eyebrows made her appear fierce. But she was strong and bright. She would need to be.

Matilda didn't show any of her thoughts as she brusquely brushed her hands over Adela's gown and adjusted her wimple. "We must start. Stay next to Henry." She nodded to the senior knight at the head of the procession.

The horn sounded again, and they filed out of the courtyard.

Bayeux Cathedral

Here Harold has sailed the sea, and with sails filled with wind has come into Count Guy's territory. --- Here they have given Harold the king's crown. Here sits Harold as King of the Angles. --- Here Angles and Franks have fallen together in battle. Here Bishop Odo holding his staff encourages the younger soldiers. Bayeux Tapestry

1077 Bayeux

Adela's feet itched. She was tired of standing still. "Stop wiggling," she murmured, kicking Henry in the side with her elbow.

"You are wiggling too," he hissed.

At least they stood in the front row on one side of the cathedral. Adela craned her head to watch her father and mother with her father's closest advisors on the opposite side.

The new cathedral was massive. Despite the hot summer day, the cavernous expanse felt damp and chilly. There was only one large round opening and several smaller ones allowing sunlight into the interior. Candlesticks set up along the perimeter made the stone pillars and niches and the high ceiling appear even more imposing. Gilded candelabras illuminated the dais. The cathedral wasn't finished; there was still scaffolding in some areas. The workers had set up temporary wooden stakes all along the outer wall for displaying the tapestry, one segment on the left, another segment on the right, and two others flanking the entrance.

"I expect you to be still and to refrain from talking," Adela's mother had told Henry and Adela, fixing them with a stern look. "Bishop Odo will bless the church with holy water on the outside. He must walk around the entire building three times and then repeat the blessing inside."

A loud knock reverberated through the hall. Nobody moved. Another knock. Silence. At the third knock, the wide double doors opened, and the procession filed in, the monks chanting as they moved along. The chanting grew louder, drowning out all sounds from the people inside the church. "Let this temple be sanctified and consecrated," the monks intoned. The bishop circled the interior three times, followed by other priests and monks. He sprinkled holy water on each section of the wall. After that, he anointed each of the crosses along the walls with oil.

Adela pressed her lips together to keep from giggling. It made her think of maids at home wandering around with dusters and polishing the silver. Then she sobered as the chanting of the Benedictus washed over her. "O how fearful is this place; truly this is no other than the house of God, and the gate of Heaven."

She glanced at her father, tall and heavy next to her mother. His reddish curls were hidden under his crown; his beard had lately acquired a new shade of gray and yellow. He was frowning, his lips pursed as if something about this ceremony irritated him.

Maybe her father was annoyed with his brother, the bishop. She'd worm it out of him later. When he was in a good mood, he liked to explain things to her. Only, when he went on too long, sounding just like her tutor, her mind wandered. Noticing her abstraction, he'd laugh and pull on her hair as if she were a horse. "I'm glad you are asking questions, but run along now."

Bishop Odo held his head and chin high, glancing down his nose at the scene in front of him as he made his circuit around the interior of the church, resplendent in his vestments and miter. The gold threads along his long sleeves glinted as he continued to sprinkle holy water on the walls. He certainly appeared prominently on the tapestry. In one scene during the battle of Hastings, he wore full armor and a helmet and held a huge mace in his hand. Adela hadn't thought that bishops would go to war. But it did look impressive.

"Your uncle supported the production of the tapestry; most of the work was done at the embroidery school of Canterbury," her mother had told Adela the day before. "So he deserves a place on it."

She had taken Henry and Adela to a visit to the cathedral for a private viewing of the tapestry. "Tomorrow, during the ceremony there won't be time." She told them how much work it took to create all these scenes. "Just imagine how many women had to sit there for many hours over many days placing the individual stitches in accordance with a drawing."

"If women did all this work, why aren't there more women shown in the tapestry?" Adela asked.

"War is fought by men." Matilda studied her daughter from the side. "You should know that by now. Women act on another stage."

Adela had stopped listening. "Look, there is a woman next to someone on a bed. Who is that?"

Matilda stepped closer and peered at the lettering. "Oh, that's Edith, the wife of King Edward, at his deathbed."

Adela pursed her lips. She loved all the animals along the edges, some unlike any she had ever seen. There were wild beasts from Africa and from the East, lots of horses, dogs, and all manner of birds.

"What's that?" she asked, mesmerized by a bright blue bird with a huge multicolored long tail that fanned out like a carpet.

"That's a *paon*. The English say 'peacock,'" her mother explained.

"Oh, a paon," Adela said dismissively, as if she had known that all along while she repeated the strange word to herself.

"Why isn't that man wearing any clothes?" Adela pointed and then quickly pulled her hand back. She had been chewing her nails again, and her mother would scold her.

"No clothes?" Matilda peered at the edge of the tapestry. Then she laughed. "I suspect someone might have put this in as a joke." She pondered the skillful embroidery. "Come to think of it, there are several scenes here where I am not sure of the intended meaning."

"Look, mother!" Henry pointed at another section. "Here they are cooking!"

"Well, soldiers need to be fed."

"Why did that house get burned down?"

"It's a battle, silly." Adela poked him in the side. "Things get burned."

"You wouldn't like it if it happened to you." Henry made a face at his sister, while poking her back.

"Remember where you are. You shouldn't argue inside a house of God." Matilda led them to the end of the tapestry. "Any battle is hard and full of bitter loss for many. But that doesn't mean these battles shouldn't be fought."

Here the French are fighting and have killed those who were with Harold. Adela whispered the Latin words on the edge of the tapestry underneath the last sections. *Here King Harold is slain and the English have turned in flight.*

"Remember that this is only one story told about the Battle of Hastings," her mother said drily. "There are many ways to tell a story."

Adela glanced at her mother's face. Maybe she didn't like the way the tapestry told this story.

The monks were singing again. Adela stopped thinking about the tapestry. Her father discreetly scratched his neck underneath the stiff robe he was wearing. Bishop Odo had finally reached the end of his prayers, and the procession out of the cathedral began.

Once the clergy and her father with his wife had filed out, the others were allowed to follow. The pages framed the entrance, standing stiffly in their festive tunics.

"There is Cerdic," Henry muttered.

Indeed, there he was, one of the tallest of the pages. His face was an expressionless mask.

Adela grinned at him. "You are very dapper in your page outfit," she murmured as she walked by.

Cerdic didn't move a muscle, his eyes staring right above her head into an invisible world, his lips firmly pressed together and a line on his forehead.

What was he thinking about? Adela puzzled over this as she walked out into the sunshine and then followed her mother back to the castle, where they were going to stay for the night.

Return to Caen

One of the English, lying hidden close to a sea-rock, perceived how the countless ranks spread far and wide and saw the fields glittering, full of glancing arms. He saw the people, their homes ravaged by flames for their perfidy, perish by the raging sword, and what tears the children shed for their fathers' slaughter. The Carmen of Hastingae Proelio. Bishop Guy of Amiens, approx. 1067.

1077 Caen

Early the next morning, King William and his followers set out to return to Château de Caen.

Impatiently, he glanced around at the bustle in the courtyard. It had rained during the night, and the flagstones steamed in the July heat. He wanted to get home. Caen was the one place where the pressures of his daily life lifted. Already when riding up the hill, he felt happier. From the ramparts, he had an unobstructed view of the surrounding area. Matilda had started a garden, sheltered from the wind by the surrounding tower walls. When he leaned out, he sometimes glimpsed her flowing gowns as she moved around the flower beds. At Caen, he made his plans and commissioned buildings and dictated orders to his scribes for the governance of

Normandy and England. He loved welcoming musicians, storytellers, and scholars whom his wife invited. Matilda enjoyed reading and often relayed to him what she had learned, sometimes making him laugh out loud at some of the curious tales of foreign lands. He scoffed at her when she insisted that all the children learn to read and write.

"Even Adela?" he had asked doubtfully.

"All of them. Especially the girls," Matilda said firmly. "They need it more."

William had shaken his head, but had let it be. In these matters, it was easier to give Matilda as much leeway as possible. Besides, he had learned to value her advice.

"You need to work with what you've got," she'd told him when they talked about how to administer their conquered lands. "Don't knock down all the local laws and customs. Use them."

Soon he would have to go back to England, always on the alert for yet another rebellion. Matilda had suggested that he retain the local sheriffs. "It will help to quell dissatisfaction," she had pointed out. He had to admit the wisdom of that.

Meanwhile, he worried about his brother Odo. While William had granted positions and land to several of his Norman supporters in England, he had resisted giving his brother more power. Well, that was over and done with now. He frowned, his lips pressed firmly together. That trial in 1076, when Odo had been accused of defrauding the Crown and the Diocese of Canterbury, still left a bad taste in his mouth. At least, Odo had been forced to return some of his properties. He certainly had become much too powerful.

For an instant, William smirked as he remembered one of the scenes on the tapestry. *Here Bishop Odo holding his staff encourages the younger soldiers.* It sounded impressive, only he couldn't for the life of him remember his brother acting like that in the middle of the battle. Perhaps it was wiser to let it go. At least, Odo had paid for the tapestry. William would have to keep a close watch on him.

But first he wanted to spend some time at home. He wanted to go hawking; maybe he could take Adela along before she had to return to her school. All he had ever known in his life was struggle and violence; life at Caen seemed a haven of calm and serenity by comparison. And yet, there was his worry about his eldest son. But this he could not share with Matilda. She was blind to all of Robert's faults. William frowned. He remembered a conversation with his son many years ago. "The Normans are a restless people," he had told Robert in trying to explain something about his inheritance to him. "And they seek out disorder." Perhaps Robert had taken this to heart in a way his father had never intended. Such a restless and angry young man, with no sense of proportion, no judgement. The king sighed.

"Oh, there you are." William watched his wife walk toward him, followed by a servant leading her horse. She moved with her usual swift step; her short stature belied by her poise. She had born him seven children. Her figure had filled out, but it hadn't taken away any of her vitality. They had had such fights in the early years. It pained him to remember how he had to chastise her for infidelity. Even in the beginning, they fought; she didn't want to marry him. He had to teach her to accept him. Now he couldn't imagine life without her.

Her expression was calm and friendly. "You look troubled, my lord."

He smiled at her fondly, touched by her ability to read his moods, but he didn't respond to this. "We need to get going." Before the servant could act, he bowed to his lady and then lifted her onto the horse.

"Thank you." Matilda arranged her gown to her satisfaction. "Ah, there is Adela finally."

As always, her daughter was late; the band with which she had fastened the hood had slipped, and her hair stuck out. Another servant helped her mount; even though she was small, she showed no sign of discomfort as she sat on her horse. Her father had taught her as soon as she was old enough.

Matilda glanced across the courtyard. The other pages chatted and laughed while they checked their gear and helped to load bags into the carts. Cerdic stood alone along the wall, holding his horse, oblivious to the activity around him. His shoulders were hunched and his head bent as if the flagstones, glinting with damp, absorbed all his interest.

"Adela," Matilda called. "Come over here for a moment."

Adela obediently pulled on her horse's reins and rode across the courtyard to where her parents were.

"Yes, Mother."

"Keep an eye on Henry today."

"Why?" Adela asked. "He is going to spend all day with Cerdic. And Cerdic has been a grouch. He didn't even speak to me yesterday."

"I don't remember asking for your opinion," Matilda responded, her voice even.

"Oh, very well." Adela sniffed and pulled her horse around.

The entire train moved out of the courtyard and started on the road to Caen.

William raised his eyebrows at his wife as they rode side by side through the gate. "Is that wise?"

Matilda looked at him, her expression unruffled. "You mean encouraging the friendship between Adela and Cerdic?"

The king nodded.

"What worries you more? That Cerdic might get confused, or that Adela might forget her status and her future responsibilities as your daughter?"

William hesitated, but as always comforted by Matilda's frankness. "Both, I suppose."

"Well, I think you can quit worrying. Adela understands her future responsibilities perfectly well."

"If anything, she is too smart for her own good." Her husband laughed. "And Cerdic?"

"Cerdic would never do anything to hurt Adela. You know that as well as I do. But I think he just remembered that he is English, and he is struggling with it."

William scoffed at that. "If he still were English, he'd probably be dead of starvation."

"Perhaps," his wife conceded. "But regardless, he needs a friend. And to be honest, there might come a time when Adela will need a friend as well."

William frowned. He remembered when his wife had remonstrated with him several years ago. She had heard the stories of women being abused in the early days after the conquest. "You have to do something about this." She had never spoken to him quite so sharply. "It won't help in ruling England if women are afraid and angry." Perhaps she had a point, especially since she had made it a political matter rather than a personal one. After some thought, he acted upon it, warning his fighters to restrain themselves toward their victims, and toward women.

But this was different. Anyway, it wasn't likely that Adela would ever be in such a position of vulnerability. Then again, perhaps Matilda was right. William looked at the tall young page he had brought back from England and shrugged. Having friends could only help.

FRIENDS

Adela bit her lips while she watched her parents ride through the gate. Then she nudged her horse across the courtyard to where her brother was fussing with his horse. The pages had already mounted. Henry was still too short to mount by himself; a servant came over and helped him. Gruffly, Henry pushed him away when he tried to adjust the saddle blanket.

"Say thank you," Adela admonished her little brother.

"You are not my mother," he snapped.

Adela sighed. It would be a long ride home, and then in a few weeks, she'd have to return to school at the Sainte-Trinité Abbey in Caen. She cheered up as the entire train moved out of the town of Bayeux, clattering along the cobblestones, and out onto the dusty road, edged by fields and woods. It wasn't so often that she got to travel such distances, and she relished the novelty. Her parents rode in front, surrounded by some of her father's knights, their armor glinting in the sunlight. The servants and pages followed, with a few more armed knights in the rear.

Henry rode ahead of her, sticking close to Cerdic. He kept asking questions, but Cerdic seemed unwilling to respond. Adela could hear him grunt reluctant answers occasionally. What was wrong with him?

Usually, he was cheerful and patient, treating Henry like a little brother. He even joined Henry in pranks. During one of these occasions, Adela had been at home and studying with a tutor. Henry had been giggling with Cerdic all day, and Adela knew they were plotting something, but of course, they wouldn't tell her. The next morning, the awful truth came out early in the morning in the form of a deafening screech. Henry, with Cerdic's help, had caught a rooster and hidden it in Robert's room.

After calming Robert down, Matilda had both Henry and Cerdic come to her private room. It was not a comfortable meeting. Adela, crouching outside the room, could hear her mother's raised voice right through the heavy wooden door. "You clearly don't have enough to do. Well, that's going to end right now."

The next day, both boys started their training as pages and also had lengthy sessions with the tutor. They groaned, but they also were secretly proud of their new status.

Initially Adela had disliked the thin little waif. She couldn't understand why her father had brought him to Caen. He couldn't even speak French.

She remembered the day when he arrived. Her mother had taken one look at him and sent him to be bathed. He screamed when her mother's servants pushed him into a wooden tub and didn't stop until they were done scrubbing him. He was so small that Adela didn't realize he was older than her by almost three years. It seemed so long ago.

But she was intrigued by him. He smiled all the time, and when he thought no one was watching it was as if his face melted. A few times, she had seen him rub his eyes as if he had been crying. One day, she followed him. She had noticed that he liked to sneak off and climb up the stairs to the top of the tower. The children weren't allowed up there. She had crept up the steps to the top of the tower and peered around the corner.

And there he was, sitting at the opening and staring north. Perhaps he was thinking of the sea and the coast of England far away across the water. Adela's feet slipped on a pebble on the flagstones, and Cerdic whipped around.

"What you want?" he asked in his heavily accented and ungrammatical French.

"That's rude," Adela answered. Then she grinned; she realized she had tried to sound like her mother. Besides, he probably hadn't understood her. She crouched on the ground next to the boy. "What's wrong?"

Cerdic raised his head; his face was streaked with tears. But he was already rubbing them away and tried to smile as if everything was fine.

"I brought you some honey bread."

The boy hesitated, but took it from her. He held it in his hand and then stuffed it into his belt.

Adela watched him, perplexed. He seemed so sad and lost. Then she had an idea. "Here, look at this." She held out the leather hood her father had given her.

"What that?" His voice was thick with tears.

"That's for my kestrel." She flapped her arms to indicate wings. "Do you want to come and see him?" Adela pointed toward the mews.

The boy followed her down the stairs and into the mews. They had been friends ever since.

First it was just the two of them, spending time in the mews and playing with the hounds. Later Henry started tagging along.

Soon, his French was so good that nobody could tell anymore that he hadn't spoken it until a few years ago. When her father had decreed that Cerdic could sit in on Henry's lessons with his tutor, he had no problem following. He even began to help Henry with his Latin exercises.

Sometimes Adela wondered why her father hadn't learned any English. Cerdic tried to teach her some words. But then he got upset. "I don't remember." He sounded close to tears. "I am forgetting my language." Did Cerdic still remember those days?

The road was dusty, and it was getting hot. Wistfully, Adela eyed the blackberry brambles that edged the fields. Ahead of her, Henry was getting bored. He rode closer to the brambles, reaching for the large, shiny berries with his hands.

"Stop that, Henry," Adela said automatically. She was tired of having to keep an eye on her little brother. She nudged her horse forward so that she was next to Cerdic.

The road to Caen meandered along the shoreline. Occasionally, they got close enough to feel the wind sweeping over the waves. Adela licked her lips; the brisk air with a hint of salt made her wish they could go down toward the water. Her mother had taken her to the shore once when she was little. She remembered watching breakers wash up on the cliffs and the beach. It made her feel excited and small at the same time.

"That's where Cerdic came from. That's England." Her mother had pointed north across the endless gray expanse.

"Maybe he misses it."

"Perhaps he does," Adela's mother had said curtly. "But he has a good life here."

In the blazing July sun, the sheaves of grain in the fields glowed like a golden sea. They passed orchards of apple trees. The branches on the trees already were bending under their load, promising a fall perfumed with the sweet-sour smell of ripened apples. Henry lagged behind, using his whip to flick away the flies.

Adela moved her horse closer to Cerdic. "You are awfully quiet today," she said, when she couldn't bear his morose silence any longer. "You look as sulky as a cat that fell into the pig trough."

FRAGILE MEMORIES

Cerdic was lost in thought. He kept his face on his horse's mane as he trotted along, oblivious to Henry's fidgeting and Adela's attempts to engage him.

Sometimes, when they caught glimpses of the North Sea, Cerdic imagined looking all the way across the water toward his home. Several lines from the tapestry kept running through his head. *Here Duke William in a large ship has crossed the sea and come to Pevensey. Here the horses debark from the ships, and here the soldiers have rushed to Hastings… Here a house is being burnt. Here the soldiers have left from Hastings, and entered into battle against Harold the king.* His father had been there, at that battle. Cerdic didn't remember him even though he had come back to his family for a short while before dying.

The king hadn't paid any attention to Cerdic in the first years after bringing him to Caen. Perhaps that was just as well. Cerdic didn't know how he felt about this man. His father had died from his battle wounds because of the war started by the king, and his homeland was now controlled by the Normans. And yet, William had taken him in and given him a home. Still, how could he go on serving the man responsible for his father's death and that of so many?

Lately he had taken Cerdic along on hunts, showing him how to handle his kestrel and even the precious falcons from the king's mews. "The most important thing for a hunter is patience," he told him. "You need to learn how to wait for the right moment to release your bird in chase of prey."

Cerdic trusted Matilda almost immediately. Stern and uncompromising, she was like a cold stream—clear and brisk. She made sure he had everything he needed, giving thought to all the details of his life from the beginning rather than simply handing him off to Squire Matthias. Oh, how he had hated that first bath. And then she had come to the room where several maids had forced him into a tub and scrubbed him. "Here, these belonged to Henry." She held up a clean cotton tunic and a proper belt. "He is younger than you, but for now they might fit you." And those clothes, the nicest he had ever owned, did fit him for a while, until he started growing from all the food he got.

But Adela was the first to befriend him when he was lost and homesick and couldn't even understand what people were saying to him. He remembered how she would stand in front of him, a short and stout little girl with laughing blue eyes, her hands sticky with the sweet pasties she'd bring him. She'd grab his hand and drag him all over the castle grounds showing him her favorite spots. When one of the king's dogs had a litter, she and Cerdic played with them. In the first years, when she was not yet at school, she and Henry had spent a lot of time with him. William Rufus and Robert had been far out of their reach, much older and uninterested in the ragtag of children running around. Cecilia, Adela's older sister, had already entered her convent in 1066, and another sister, Constance, was married.

Cerdic couldn't remember his mother's face. It tortured him. All he remembered was that overwhelming sense of comfort when she held him, a comfort that was present even when she scolded him. Missing her was a big black void inside his head. To his despair, he had forgotten almost all his mother's Anglo-Saxon; sometimes, a few words came to him and made him feel homesick all over again.

After he had been in Caen for a while, Matilda decreed that Henry and Cerdic both start their training as pages, even though

Henry was two years younger. A tutor taught them reading, writing, arithmetic, and Latin. They spent their days with lessons in wrestling, throwing javelins, the tack and care of horses, handling swords and lances, axes and maces, crossbows, longbows, and daggers. He loved training as a page and hated himself for being proud of it. Would he ever return to Wessex? But then he would be surrounded by those who had burned and pillaged and raped and killed his people. And he would be a stranger among his own people.

"Are you listening to me at all?" Adela shouted. "What's wrong with you?"

Startled, Cerdic looked up. He tried to shake his thoughts. He shrugged. "You wouldn't understand."

"I am sick of you telling me I wouldn't understand. How can I understand if you don't say anything?" Adela sniffed, raising her nose high in the air. "Anyway, I think you are rude. You can't talk to me like that. You forget who I am."

Cerdic pursed his lips. Then he turned towards her, taking in her small, sturdy form on the horse that was too big for her, her hair coming undone underneath her cowl, her thick eyebrows pulled together over her blue eyes, and her mouth pouting. She was just a little girl.

"How can I forget?" He smiled at her. "You remind me every day, my lady."

"Now you are laughing at me." She glowered at him, but her lips twitched in response.

Giselle

1077 County of Blois

"Giselle!"

A woman with a stained apron wrapped around her bulk rushed out of the door of a run-down manor house. Pigs and chicken scattered in all directions. "Where is that dratted girl?" The woman's face was flushed. "The master can't expect me to run after his brat all the time."

"Look what I found, Jehanne."

Following the voice, the woman stepped behind the cart near the stables. "There you are," she said, exasperated.

A small girl with a mop of dark curls sat on a pile of hay with three kittens climbing all over her. One kitten put a paw into the neck of her tunic, tugging on it, and the girl giggled. Bits of hay had gotten stuck in her hair. She blinked in the sunlight. "Aren't they sweet?"

"Leave those kittens alone and come inside. Your father wants to talk to you." Jehanne ran her hands over the girl's tunic, brushing off hay and dirt. "You are like a wild child."

The girl wiggled to get away from Jehanne's ministrations and walked across the yard toward the house. Inside, she pushed on the wooden door to the great hall.

"Ah, Giselle, come in." Her father was sitting at his desk, a tankard of ale next to him. He had been studying a roll of parchment. He put it down with a sigh. "Sit." He pointed at a chair with faded covering. "Let me take a look at you."

Giselle sat down. She folded her hands in her lap.

"You haven't grown much." He stared at her dirty bare feet, brown from the sun. "What happened to your sandals?"

"Oh, I forgot." Giselle wiggled her toes. "They itched, and I took them off."

Her father sighed again. "Listen, my dear, you are still young, but it is time that you understood some things." He gazed at the little girl with affection. His hair hadn't been trimmed for a long time, and his clothes were unkempt. His face was puffy, with bags under his eyes. "Times are hard, and I can't afford to hire a tutor for you, much less provide you with a dowry. If your dear mother hadn't died too early and if you had brothers, things might be different."

"But Father, I know," Giselle exclaimed. "Don't worry. I am happy as things are. Jehanne is good to me. And I don't want a tutor."

"Do you know what your name means? It means a pledge or a hostage. We meant it to symbolize our pledge to you to keep you safe and well. But now you are a hostage to our misfortune." He ran his hands over her head and then dropped them again with a sigh.

Giselle loved her father's long slender hands and loved watching him work with them, deftly bending grape vines, skillfully tying them so that they would not break in the wind, and gently testing the firmness of the new fruit. Today, she didn't think about that. His despondency frightened her. "Truly, I know, Father." She stood up and stepped closer to his desk. "Jehanne told me about the drought and other misfortunes that destroyed the harvest. Let me help," she said. "Please. Jehanne has started teaching me things around the house. I want to learn everything. I can help you more, and we can be happy. Maybe the springs will start flowing again."

The landholding where they lived was called the *La Vallée des Sources*, the Valley of the Springs, but the last years had been unusually dry, affecting everyone in the region.

"Anyway, dry seasons are good for our wine," Giselle added, her voice prim and adult sounding.

"How do you know that?" Her father looked at his daughter with amazement.

"Raoul says that every morning." Giselle laughed at her father, no longer so adult sounding. "He shows me how to tie up the vines and when to prune them."

A Game Of Dice

Chowder with pike
Roast your fish. Take bread, puree of peas or boiled water, wine,
verjuice, ginger and saffron, sieve, and boil. Throw onto your fish
with (if you wish) just a bit of vinegar. It should be yellowish.
Le Viandier de Taillevent.

1077 Caen

"Tell us a ghost story," Cerdic pleaded.

There were three of them, Cerdic, Henry, and his brother William Rufus. They sat on the flagstones in a corner of the mews, a leather cloth between them held flat by boots at each corner.

Without responding to Cerdic, William threw the dice. Sitting next to his small brother, William's maturity as a 23-year-old was evident. Of middling height and heavyset, he was, for the most part, affable and easy-going. He had stretched out his legs and was leaning back against a pile of hay, his expression partially hidden by the reddish blond hair hanging into his face.

"Three threes!" Henry groaned. "Not again."

"My game." William chuckled. "You know what that means."

"Yes, yes, I'll have to clean your blasted gear for three days."

"I am sure you'll do that beautifully, like the good little page you are supposed to be."

"So, how about a story?" Cerdic interjected. "How about the one about the priest visiting the hot springs?"

An apricot-colored cat pawed at William's satchel. Without moving from his comfortable position, he picked up a pebble and threw it. The cat yowled and ran off.

"I don't know if that appeals to me right now. We just attended mass, remember?" William's face was bland and unreadable as usual. "Anyway, it has too much of a whiff of a priest doing godly things, being rewarded for being kind and caring. Likely story. Let's talk about something else." He eyed his brother. "What's griping you? Was it that you lost the game? Or did the potage at the midday meal not agree with you?"

Henry frowned, running his hands back and forth over the leather cloth on the ground.

Cerdic wanted to tell William, but he stopped himself. These were not his brothers, and it wasn't his place to interfere. Besides, he wasn't sure how he felt about William. The young knight never said what he was thinking. Instead, his shrewd and watchful expression made it seem as if he was constantly planning something. Occasionally, he lost his temper, and another side of him emerged—he could be extremely cutting and harsh. Robert frequently was at the receiving end of that. Yet William was kind to Henry, who was so much younger than his two brothers.

"Well?"

"Robert," Henry mumbled after a moment.

"Ah, our dear brother." William picked up a stalk of hay and poked in his teeth. "What's he done now?"

"We were practicing shooting—Cerdic and me and the other pages." It all spilled out. Henry was talking fast, while rubbing his face with his hands. "Robert walked through the courtyard and then stayed to watch. I got nervous and kept missing. Then Robert came over and took the bow from me. 'That's how you do it,' he said, shooting and hitting the target five times in a row." Henry sniffed. "Why does he do this? I could hear the other pages whispering."

Robert was the oldest, born seventeen years before Henry. Despite his short stature, he was an outstanding athlete. Everybody knew that. Hardly anyone felt like challenging him in the field or on the tilting grounds. But his father treated him with disdain, even ridiculing him for being short.

"You are too impatient and too lazy to put in the hard work necessary in order to do something really well," the king had once told Robert when Cerdic happened to be close enough so he could hear every word.

"Ignore him," Cerdic said now, trying to console Henry. "Of course, Robert is a great archer. So what? Besides, you are the youngest of the pages, and you just started working with bow and arrow."

"Cerdic is right," William said. "Anyway, you'd better get used to this. He's jealous. After all, you are the only one of our father's sons born into the purple."

"What does that mean?"

"Father had become king of England when you made your entry into the world."

"Oh." Henry frowned. "But you don't act like that."

"No, I hide it better." William picked up the dice. "Besides, I am not about to let a scrub like you bother me."

"Remember the time when we filled his boots with snails?" Henry was looking more cheerful. "We should come up with something else."

Cerdic laughed.

"I thought the rooster you hid in his chamber was inspired." William rolled the dice back and forth. "He hates water, you know," he added casually.

Both Henry and Cerdic had learned to swim in a side arm of the Orne river. Squire Matthias insisted that all pages learned this skill. Cerdic loved it and even taught himself to dive.

"I have an idea." Henry's eyes were glinting with excitement.

"Well, I need to go. No more fun and games." William got up. "Father is sending me on an errand to Rouen. Try not to get into too much trouble, little brother."

Cerdic and Henry were whispering and giggling when Adela walked into the mews a short while later, proudly holding her hooded kestrel on her gloved wrist. Her cheeks were flushed.

"What are you two doing? Aren't you supposed to be working with Squire Matthias?"

"What about you?" Henry snapped. "Aren't you supposed to be working with your tutor before you return to school?"

"Father said I didn't have to do that today." Adela beamed at the boys, too pleased with her day to be provoked into a fight. "He praised me and said I was getting good at handling my kestrel. I wish I didn't have to go back to school. So, what were you laughing about?"

Cerdic chuckled. "Oh, just men talk."

"Men?" Adela wrinkled her nose. "Huh!" Shaking her head, she walked off to take her kestrel to its perch.

A few days later, while William hadn't yet returned from Rouen, Robert tried once again to convince his father to give him more power.

Robert had forgotten to close the door, and Cerdic and Henry, in a room above the great hall, could hear every word.

"What do you want me to do?" Robert asked. "You never let me act on my own, and you control my every move. You had me witness a charter for the first time when I was fifteen. But now you treat me like a child."

"Let me remind you that you are the one who lost the county of Maine. The barons revolted against you because you were unwilling to do the work of administering the county. True, they weren't overly fond of Norman rule, but still it needn't have gone that way. It's sad that they replaced you with someone equally incompetent, moreover described as an imbecile, a coward, and an idler. Whatever, you have given me no reason to date to entrust you with more responsibilities."

"You should return to England," Robert shouted. "And let me rule Normandy. I'll show you what I can do."

"Normandy is mine by hereditary descent!" The king's voice boomed. "I will not relinquish the government while I live."

The kitchen staff, joking and laughing while cutting vegetables, salting fish, kneading dough, and stirring the potage, fell silent when they heard the raised voices.

Finally, the door of the great hall banged shut, and there were hurried steps out into the courtyard. A resounding crash followed by a scream of shock and rage.

"Get back here," the cook yelled as the servants rushed outside.

Robert sat on the ground, his head and shoulders drenched. A wooden tub lay next to him, upended.

From the banister above the courtyard, the sound of two boys laughing hysterically filtered down. Robert stood up, almost toppling over in his hurry. Dripping and leaving behind the pungent stink of urine, he rushed back inside and up the stairs. A few moments later, he reappeared, dragging Cerdic and Henry outside with a firm hold on their necks. Both of them were still laughing.

"You think this is funny?" Robert bellowed. "I'll teach you to treat your elders with more respect." He threw them onto the flagstones. And he kicked and hit them, as if they were wild beasts that had devoured his favorite falcon.

Dogs barked, and inspired by the frenzy, started fighting among each other. A servant, walking toward the stables with a bucket of feed for the chicken, stumbled over a dog, and spilled the feed. A flock of chattering pigeons settled down to this unexpected feast.

"Bravo," a mellow voice from above bounced off the flagstones. William was leaning out of a window and clapping his hands.

"Who's making this infernal racket?" The king came through the doors and stepped into the courtyard.

At the sound of the king's harsh loud voice, some servants quietly disappeared while others stopped cheering on the combatants.

Robert was so intent on chastising the boys that he was oblivious to what was going on around him.

The king raised his sword and hit his son on the back with the flat side.

Shocked, Robert straightened up and stared at his father.

Henry was already on his feet. He was bleeding from his nose, and his right eye was beginning to swell. Cerdic was still on the ground, his arms folded around his stomach. He struggled to get up. His face was bruised and smeared with grime and blood.

The king gazed at the three in silence and then glanced at the window above where William was still leaning out the window, his expression of amusement giving way to mild consternation.

"William, I see that you enjoyed the view. I expect you to attend me shortly."

Cerdic and Henry gazed at the king, trying not to move.

"And you two." The king frowned at the boys. "You can take a message to Squire Matthias that he is supposed to give you extra work for a week. Now get cleaned up." Then he turned to his eldest son. "Robert. This is unacceptable."

"You are not even going to punish them properly," Robert exclaimed. He was furious. "You call my behavior unacceptable. What about those two?"

"Don't raise your voice. I don't know what those boys did to provoke you, and I don't want to know. It is irrelevant. Henry is barely ten, and Cerdic hardly much older. Your actions are unchivalrous and unworthy of a man in your position." The king was red in the face, and he was breathing quickly. "Now, get out of my sight."

Robert glared at his father. Then, without another word, he turned and walked off. A few hours later, he was gone.

Fathers And Sons

Fresh Lamprey in a Hot Sauce
The lamprey should be bled by its mouth, and its tongue removed;
you should shove a skewer into it to help bleed it, and keep the
blood because that is the grease and scrape the inside of the mouth
with a knife, then scald it as you would an eel and roast it on a very
slender spit inserted through it sideways once or twice.
Then grind ginger, cloves, grains of paradise, nutmegs and a little
burnt toast moistened in the blood together with vinegar, and if you
wish, a little wine; infuse all of this together and bring it to the boil
and then put the lamprey whole into it. The sauce should not be too
dark—that is, when the sauce is thin, but when the sauce is thick,
and it is called 'mud', it should be dark. Le Viandier de Taillevent.

The main meal in the hall that day was the quietest meal ever. The usual chatter up and down the long table was missing.

Cerdic spooned fish broth into his mouth, trying to focus on the clunking sound it made when the wood hit the bowl rather than on the oppressive silence in the hall. The cook had added too much pepper. He knew it was supposed to counter bad humors, but that didn't mean he had to like it. Out of the corner of his eye, he watched Matilda absentmindedly take a pinch of salt from the saltcellar in front of her and dropping it into her bowl. She whispered something to her husband.

Cerdic strained to hear the king's response. He was shaking his head and frowning. Matilda stared at him in dismay.

"He is not a child," the king muttered, shrugging. Generally abstemious in his habits, today he ate almost nothing. He pushed his bowl away.

"Robert didn't say goodbye," Adela whispered to Cerdic. "And I have to go back to school tomorrow, so I might not see him for a long time."

Cerdic didn't know what to say.

He respected the king's eldest son for his skills with weapons and his evident courage. But Robert had never been kind to him, and he treated Henry as if his brother were no more than one of a litter of puppies in the stable. He liked to show off and to wander around restlessly, while complaining to anyone willing to listen about being unfairly treated by his father. But most of all, he never laughed. Humorless, pugnacious, and quick to pick quarrels with everyone, Robert only relaxed when around his mother and Adela.

Adela was clearly upset, even though Henry was closest to her. Cerdic honored her for having an affectionate heart. It made him miss his mother all over again. He didn't know what it was like to have siblings. Maybe his mother had married again. Maybe there was a little boy or girl running around his mother's house in Southampton.

Over the next days, everything seemed to return to normal. Adela went back to her school at the abbey. Her brother William left for England, entrusted with a mission by his father. Robert was gone. Nobody talked about him, at least not in the king's hearing.

Cerdic and Henry resumed their training.

"Pay attention!" Squire Matthias was acerbic and relentless as ever. "You act like rotting mushrooms, one-legged and impotent," he shouted. "What are you? A tub of sour herring? You are young men. Soon you will be called upon to serve your lord. Act like it."

"Rotting mushrooms?" Cerdic muttered. "Of all things to yell at us."

"What's impotent?" Henry asked in a whisper, trying not to giggle.

"Oh, you know, without power. Weak." Cerdic knew there was another meaning but refrained from elaborating. Henry was two years younger, after all.

Mostly, the pages practiced shooting with a bow and arrow, spear throwing, and sword fighting. They were introduced to the crossbow, but the squire scoffed at this weapon.

"You don't need a lot of skill to use this," he said dismissively, "even though they pack quite a punch."

"What about battle axes?" Henry eyed the long wooden handles topped by sharp metal blades. The handles of some axes in the armory were reinforced with metal plates.

"Yes, we will work with those. But you need upper body strength to handle these effectively." He glanced at Cerdic. "Your people did us quite a bit of damage in the battle at Hastings." There was a curious mix of admiration and regret in his voice. "Now, let's get back to work."

A few weeks later, a messenger rode into the courtyard of Caen. He was disheveled, and his horse's legs were streaked with caked mud.

"I need to see the king urgently."

Within an hour, messengers left Caen in all directions. The castle hummed with tension. Rumors spread almost immediately.

"What happened?" Cerdic asked Squire Matthias.

"Aren't we nosy?" The squire frowned at the young page. Then he relented. "You are getting too tall for your tunic. We'll have to get you outfitted, and you need a sword and spear that's right for your size."

"Why?" Cerdic gaped at him. "Are we going into battle? What's going on?"

"Count Robert has assembled some of his followers and is raiding into Normandy."

"Who would follow him?"

"Oh, those young idiots—Robert of Bellême, William de Breteuil, and Roger of Clare, among others. What makes it worse is that these are all sons of supporters of the king. Fathers against sons." Matthias sighed.

"What about me?" Henry asked. "I need a sword and a spear as well."

"I don't think so," the squire responded with a regretful smile. "You are too small. I doubt the king will give his permission."

"He will too!" Henry threw down his bow and ran off.

It took a few days until the king had assembled a troop of three hundred knights. More were to join him later. The courtyard was bustling with activity; squires and pages rushed back and forth to get their knights' gear ready. In the gray of the morning, when they were ready to set out, Matilda stood on the steps in front of the main entrance to the castle. Even though it was warm and humid, she had wrapped a shawl around her, her hands hidden and a pinched expression on her face.

Cerdic fumbled as he tried to tighten the girth of his saddle. The horse danced away from him. "Stop that." Cerdic yanked on the rein. Finally, he was done, and he mounted. The king bowed from the saddle toward Matilda.

Henry stood at the entrance to the mews, his thick shock of black hair sticking up as if he had just woken up. He was scowling. When he saw Cerdic, he raised his hand and waved. Cerdic waved back.

Then Cerdic forgot about Henry.

Quivering with excitement, he moved along with the squires in the back of the troupe. This would be his first battle. He glanced down at his sword. He liked how it flapped against his leg as he rode. The day before, he had polished the sheath and pommel until Matthias had stopped him. "It's good enough." The squire laughed. "You are not about to ride in a victory march through Paris."

Cerdic wanted to sing and shout, echoing the clip clop of the hooves and the sounds of weapons clanking against each other. Oblivious to the dust kicked up by hundreds of horses ahead of him, Cerdic thought the air smelled fresh, promising a new day. Everything was bright; even the apple trees with their red and yellow fruit alongside the road seemed cheerful.

The knights looked splendid in their armor, riding proudly on their sturdy steeds. Then he noticed a tall young knight, who wore his long pale blond hair tied like a horse's tail behind his back, and for a moment it was as if the early morning sun had dimmed.

Toki was the son of an English lord called Wigod of Wallingsford, a kinsman of the last king of the House of Wessex, King Edward. In 1066, Wigod had chosen to support William when he invaded England, and his son had continued to be loyal to the king.

During his last visit to the king in Caen, Toki rode into the courtyard as if he owned it. He tossed Cerdic the reins of his horse. "Take care of my steed," he said curtly. "Make sure you don't give him water that's too cold."

Later, when he came outside again, he shouted, "Boy, fetch my horse."

Cerdic brought out the horse and held it while Toki mounted. "What's your name, boy?"

He answered, his voice cracking in his nervousness.

"Cerdic?" Toking laughed. "You need to grow quite a bit until that name fits you."

Cerdic chewed on his lip. What right did Toki have to be so arrogant? Toki's father had betrayed his own king and kinsman in favor of a Norman invader. And now Toki rode along with King William as one of his trusted supporters. Cerdic felt all twisted inside. What about himself? He had accepted the king's shelter and protection, eaten from the king's board, played with the king's children, and enjoyed the training that was offered.

Then he shook his head, dismissing Toki and all thoughts about him. He was off on the most exciting adventure of his life.

They rode toward Rouen. According to the messenger, Robert and his followers were camped in a field on the eastern side of Rouen, where they weren't trapped by the snake-like loops of the Seine. So far, their forays into the town had been repulsed, and the town's mayor had managed to send a messenger to the king in Caen.

Approaching from the west, the king's army moved toward the northern end of the town. Here, the king called for a halt. Squires and pages watered and fed the horses, and the men drank and ate. Sitting inside his tent, the king conferred with his closest advisors while others stretched and checked their gear.

Cerdic ran back and forth, bringing water for the horses. When a squire offered him a piece of bread, he shook his head. He couldn't possibly eat anything.

"Time to mount!" came the call. Those who had been sitting on the ground dozing rose hastily, while others came rushing out of the bushes, pulling up their breeches.

Cerdic turned toward his horse.

"Not you." A squire placed a hand on his shoulder. "You and two others are supposed to stay here, guarding the spare horses, and to serve as messengers if need be."

Cerdic stared at the man. He wasn't sure what he felt; chagrin at not getting to participate and relief were mixed up in his mind. He looked down. "I understand."

"You better get some rest; you may have to carry a message back all the way to Caen." The squire sighed. "How old are you, anyway?"

"Old enough to fight," Cerdic muttered.

The squire shook his head. "There'll be time enough for you to fight."

Cerdic watched them ride off toward the south. The other two men had already curled up to sleep in the shade of a gnarly apple tree.

He wandered around. What was he supposed to do now? He had hobbled the spare horses and given them water. He picked up an apple that the storm had knocked out of the tree and bit into it. The sour juice filled his mouth. Unripe. He spat on the ground and tossed the apple away. Why did they treat him like a child? Enviously, he stared at the sleeping men. One was snoring.

For a while, he sat on a tree stump and used his knife to whittle away at a piece of wood. The shadows were already getting longer when he heard hoofbeats. A knight rode up, his horse sweating but not appearing unduly stressed.

"Time to pack up," he shouted.

The two men sleeping on the ground lifted their heads. "What happened?"

"Oh, nothing at all." The knight laughed. "Duke Robert saw us coming across the hills and decided to decamp."

"Where are they going?"

"South toward Rémalard." He held out a flask. "They left a barrel of wine behind. Here, take a swig."

"Oh, that's good stuff." The man's Adam's apple moved up and down as he drank in hurried gulps.

He passed the flask to Cerdic. It was warm and tangy. Then they quickly packed up the king's tent and everything else, and leading the spare horses, they set out to catch up with the pursuing army.

"Why Rémalard?" Cerdic asked the knight when they followed the path around the town of Rouen toward the south.

"Duke Robert is using the castle of Rémalard as a base for his raids into Normandy. The king wants to put a stop to this."

They caught up with the king in a valley south of Rouen. The king had called a halt for the night. The squires and servants were already setting up camp.

Cerdic dismounted.

"Cerdic," a familiar voice shouted. The king was sitting on a tree stump, dictating to his scribe. He waved Cerdic over. "I need you to do something for me."

Cerdic nodded. "Of course, my Lord."

"It is important that this message reaches the queen." He waved toward the scribe, who was folding up a small piece of parchment. "Tonight you rest, and tomorrow morning I want you to ride back to Caen and deliver this."

Cerdic clenched his fists and tried to keep his eyes focused on the king's hands. He was being sent away just when it got exciting. Then he bit his lip, swallowing his disappointment, and nodded. He could hardly argue with the king about a direct order like that. "I will do so, my Lord."

He set out at first light.

THE ART OF HUNTING WITH BIRDS OF PREY

And in September, O what keen delight!
Falcons and astors; merlins, sparrow hawks;
Decoy birds that shall lure your game in flocks;
And hounds with bells; and gauntlets stout and tight.
Folgore da San Geminiano (12th century)

Usually, Adela loved September.

During harvest season, the air was rich with the scent of ripened apples. Other fruits were swelling on the trees. Her favorite were the fragrant golden green pears. She didn't care for the drink that the monks made from pears called *poiré*, but stewed pears were wonderful. Best of all was eating the pears fresh so that the sweet juice would run down her chin. From the window in the room where they had their lessons, she could see carters trundle oak barrels through the town on their way to the cider mills. The sight of the well-worn oak encased in bands of iron made her think of the dense, pungent odor of wet leaves in the forest during a hunt.

When the sisters allowed the girls to walk into the town on market days, they would marvel at the stalls overflowing with apples —red, golden, even green. At the abbey, some Benedictine monks, mostly occupied with brewing ale, worked on fermenting apple cider. The nuns complained that the monks spent too much time experimenting, using different types of barrels and extending the time of fermentation. Then, when they were finished, they tried out the fruits of their labor and would get drunk. The nuns locked the girls away during those days. Adela had to pinch herself from laughing at them. She had watched them sing and sway with abandon in the cloister hallway, their habits slipping and smelling strongly of spilled cider. Evidently, they enjoyed it as much as the monks did.

September meant crisp mornings and clear days warmed by the sun. On days when she was not at the abbey and her father was at home in Caen, he allowed her to come along on hunts. Her father showed her how to fly her merlin. While everyone in the castle feared his harsh, grating voice when he lost his temper—and this happened frequently—he never once raised his voice when teaching Adela during a hunt. He was always patient when showing her how to handle her bird, when to remove the hood, and how to use the lure.

"Why can't I fly a falcon?" Adela asked, enviously eying the peregrine falcon her father was training for Henry. She liked the bird's nearly white throat above the mottled black and white belly and its stark yellow-ringed eyes. Her kestrel looked less dramatic, with its soft golden-brown plumage with black spots and black-tipped tail; she had named it Doucette for her best friend at school.

"Children fly kestrels," her father responded. "Falcons are for kings and emperors. When you are a lady, you can fly a merlin. That's the order of the world. You should know this by now. Repeat the list for me."

"How often do I have to do this?" Adela protested.

"Until you remember."

Adela sighed and rolled her eyes, but recited obediently:

| King | Gyr Falcon |
| Prince | Peregrine Falcon |

Duke	Rock Falcon
Earl	Tiercel Peregrine
Baron	Bastarde Hawk
Knight	Saker
Squire	Lanner
Lady	Female Merlin
Yeoman	Goshawk
Priest	Female Sparrowhawk
Holy water clerk	Male Sparrowhawk
Knaves, servants, and children	Kestrel

The last time she had been home, Cerdic hadn't come out to hunt with them. He was spending more time training with Henry and the other pages. She missed him. But lately, things had felt awkward. It was as if there was a new veil of formality between them and they had both taken on new roles. Remembering his stiffness made her feel even more irritated now.

Yes, she loved September. But not today. It had been a hot and dry summer, and the nights hadn't yet begun to cool down. The room where the three girls at the abbey had their lessons was stifling. There was no breeze at all. The only sounds came from the scraping of wooden styluses on wax tablets, where the girls were laboriously forming their letters over and over again.

"Why? Why do I have to do this?" Adela had repeatedly protested when her mother insisted that she learn to read and write from the nuns at the abbey.

"This is important."

"But you don't write, and Father doesn't read or write, and he doesn't speak any English." Adela argued.

"I was only taught how to read. You should count yourself lucky to have this opportunity. Your father can do many things you can't do. It is not your place to question this," Matilda said, her tone sharp and forbidding.

Adela flushed and pressed her lips together.

"Your sister Cecilia has studied the arts, Latin, rhetoric, and logic. I want the same for you." Her mother had hired tutors for her sons; her daughters she sent to the abbey for their lessons in reading, writing, Latin, French, and even some English.

"What good will Latin do me?"

"I want all of my children to be educated," her mother snapped. After a moment she spoke again, her voice gentler. "I want to give you as many tools as possible for the position you might occupy later in life."

Somehow, the thought of whatever position she might occupy later in life didn't make Adela feel any better about attending lessons. In fact, right now, she felt distinctly uncomfortable, as if something at last night's meal had disagreed with her.

Adela had to copy the short Latin phrase that Sister Leona had written on the top of her tablet–*dum vivimus servimus*, which meant "while we live, we serve."

"Dum, dum, dum," she wrote before she realized what she was doing. Surreptitiously she turned around her stylus and scratched at the letters on the wax with the flat end of the stylus and then tried to smooth the edges with her finger. She had managed to copy out the phrase several times when Sister Leona clapped her hands.

"You may go outside for a while until it is time for *None* prayers," she told the girls.

Relieved, the three girls left quickly and quietly, afraid of being reprimanded if they talked too loudly inside the abbey. They walked down the stone hallway into the cloister walk that framed the garden.

"Look at the prunes," Douce exclaimed. A tree planted against the garden wall beckoned with its heavily laden branches.

"They are too high," Petronella said.

"Hah!" Adela raised her head. "We'll see about that." After a quick look around to make sure they were alone, Adela grabbed onto the lowest branch, and using the trunk to support her feet, worked herself higher until she could sit in the tree. She reached for as many plums as she could reach. She stuffed some into her mouth, chewing happily and then spitting the pits out over the wall onto the road.

"Hey," Petronella shouted. "What about us?"

Adela grinned at her friends, Petronella with her dark curls that never stayed underneath her cap, her pert little nose, and her fun-loving nature, and Douce with her pale face and sweet smile. Adela sometimes wondered what her friends would do. Like her parents, theirs had wanted to provide their daughters with an education prior to marriage. But she didn't think Douce would ever marry. She could imagine her joining the abbey and even becoming an abbess in her own right, with her gentle manner that belied her strength of character. "Here you go." Adela grabbed more plums and tossed them down.

Just one more. Adela bit into the purple blue fruit in her hand. The tart, sour taste somehow fitted her mood these days. She raised herself to spit the pit over the wall and then winced, almost losing her balance on the branch. Oh, that hurt. Her belly cramped like it never had before. And she had an awkward sense of something having come loose in her nether regions. Perhaps the plums weren't ripe enough, and that's why she was feeling so ill. She lowered herself and let go of the branch at the end to jump onto the walkway below.

"Oh, Adela, you have started." Petronella pointed at her legs.

"What do you mean?" She looked down; blood trickled down her leg. Dismayed, she stared at her friends.

Petronella laughed. "You don't know?"

Just then, Sister Leona walked up to the girls. "Why is it always the three of you doing something you shouldn't be doing?" she asked, but with a laugh in her voice, swiftly scrutinizing the three friends and barely lingering on the blood dripping onto Adela's ankle. "I hope you won't have a bellyache from all those plums. But now, Adela, I want you to come with me."

Sister Leona didn't wait for Adela to respond and walked off, her wide black skirt swishing. Numbly Adela followed her. Was she ill? What did it mean? Petronella had laughed, and Sister Leona certainly didn't appear disturbed at all.

Maybe Adela was in for yet another lecture. Just the other day, Mother Superior had called Adela to attend her in her office. "Sister Leona tells me that you are impatient and prone to anger. Is it true that you hit another student with your wax tablet?"

"Yes, Mother," Adela had whispered. "I am sorry."

"I don't want to hear of any other occurrence like that. I would hate to have write to your mother."

Adela maintained a penitent expression, but it was hard not to smile. Mother Superior would certainly not be writing to the queen about her daughter's behavior. It would reflect too badly on her management of the students; besides, Adela knew perfectly well how much the abbey relied on the queen's support.

Outside the room Adela shared with her friends, Sister Leona said curtly, "Go inside and wait for me. I will be back. I need to get something for you."

Adela didn't want to sit down, afraid to get blood all over the blankets.

Sister Leona returned a few moments later, carrying a wash bowl filled with water and a bundle of rags. "Well, my dear. I see you have finally started your courses," she said.

"Is something wrong with me?" Adela's voice was scratchy.

"No, of course not," Sister Leona responded with a sigh. "Didn't anybody explain this to you?"

Adela shook her head.

"It means you are a woman now. This will happen every month until you are too old to bear children. It's a way for the body to clean itself and prepare for a baby in the womb." She helped the girl clean herself up and put on another shift. She also showed her how to bind herself with a bunch of clean rags secured with a strip around her waist.

"I will have to wear this always?" Adela studied the rags with intense dislike.

Sister Leona laughed. "No, of course not, only for a few days until you stop bleeding." She got up, ready to take the bowl out. "Remember to rinse out the rags when you are done. It gets easier. The first time is the worst."

At supper Adela didn't feel like eating the onion soup. Something about it, especially the foamy cheese floating on top, put her off. She nibbled on the bread instead. They weren't supposed to talk under the rules of the order. She was glad when the abbess stood up, nodding at them in dismissal.

Later, Adela told her friends what Sister Leona had said.

"Is that all she said?" Petronella grinned at her friend.

"What do you mean? Isn't it bad enough? Every single month, I have to go through this. At least, we don't have to use moss. She told me that's what they used in her village when she grew up."

"No, I can see why she wouldn't tell you more. She is a nun, after all." Petronella laughed again. "This means you can now lie with a man, and that's how you become pregnant."

"Oh." Both Adela and Douce looked appalled.

"You two make me laugh," Petronella said. "Listen, it's going to be fine. It can even be enjoyable. My sister told me all about it." She glanced around to see whether anybody was close by. "She said it's important to understand exactly how it all works so you can relax and enjoy it."

A new expression appeared on Adela's face. "I wonder whether my mother enjoys it."

"I'll tell you everything I know from my sister, but perhaps not here where others might hear us."

"I certainly couldn't ask my sister," Adela said wistfully. Her sister Cecilia had been in the abbey since 1066 and was already wearing the veil. "She is sure to be the abbess here, eventually."

Rebellion

1078 Caen

King William returned to Caen several weeks later.

It was a mild September day, and the flagstones were warm from the sun. Cerdic was cleaning his tack. An orange cat sat next to him, diligently licking her paws. Cerdic hummed as he rubbed tallow into all the seams and corners of the leather saddle on his lap. Tallow kept the leather supple and would make it shiny once he started polishing it. The work helped to settle his thoughts.

He hadn't enjoyed that long, lonely ride back to Caen. He had failed somehow and had been sent home as if he were a child. At least he was carrying a message for the king. Matilda had opened it in front of him and read it in silence. Then she had looked at him with red-rimmed strained eyes. "Thank you, Cerdic." That was all. Dismissed, he returned to the courtyard.

Henry had been spending more time with his tutor, and Cerdic was increasingly relegated to his duties as a page. Only rarely now did they share in lessons. Adela had been home a few times, but here as well, there had been a noticeable change. She was stiffer with Cerdic, more formal, as if trying to emphasize their difference in status. He missed the easy bantering between him and Henry and Adela. He was restless and frustrated without knowing why. Worst of all, he didn't know where he belonged. Caen had become home, and he could barely remember anything about England or his home there or even his mother's face. And yet, he always felt like an outsider, the boy from Wessex with a grand name belonging to an ancient king. He was bound to obey orders from the king. The sound of hooves clattering over the flagstones made him look up. It was the king, riding in with some of his knights.

Servants ran across to take the horses. The king dismounted. He glanced around as if momentarily confused where he was. Cerdic stood up and bowed. The king nodded and then turned to walk into the castle.

What had happened? Cerdic abandoned his tack and followed to see whether he could hear anything from the great hall. He heard voices, the king's low and subdued, and Matilda responding. He couldn't make out the words. Then Matilda's voice, normally deep and warm, rose to a shriek. "Exile!"

Just then, someone pulled the large oaken doors closed, and Cerdic stood outside. Frustrated, he walked back outside.

He didn't get to satisfy his curiosity for several days. But eventually, the news trickled down, and squires and pages talked about what had happened.

Robert had been using the castle of Rémalard for his raiding activities. The villages and towns around Rémalard were torn, some supporting the duke and others loyal to his father. The king hadn't bothered to besiege the well-fortified castle; instead, he had simply waited at a distance for one of these sorties. When Robert and his men finally emerged, the king attacked. Robert's small army was no match for the king and his 200 knights, and they knew it. When the king came thundering down the hill, Robert made a quick decision. Before the opposing parties could even come to blows, Robert signaled to his men to abandon the field. They rode off, with no loss of life to any of them. The king pursued them for a while and then decided to return to Caen.

"So, where did Duke Robert go?" Cerdic asked Squire Matthias.

"Toward Vexin. King Philip granted the duke the use of his castle Gerberoy."

"Why?"

"Why?" Matthias glanced around to see whether his pages were paying attention. "What do you think the king of France would prefer? A unified Normandy under the rule of the king of England, or a weakened Normandy with a duke who would be in his debt?"

Cerdic chewed on his lip. It made it sound as if this was all a board game like fox and geese or mill. But people died as a result.

"Anyway, King Philip is shrewd," Matthias added. "Where he can't win people over by force, he buys their allegiance by handing out lavish benefices. Dividing father and son is par for the course."

"And what will King William do now?" another page asked.

"Well, he has done it already. He exiled the duke."

The king had exiled his eldest son and heir. Cerdic was shocked. What would Henry and Adela think when they heard this? He could picture their brother William's smirk of amusement.

In fact, when William heard the news, he chuckled. "Oh, brother dear is in trouble," he said. "That's going to be interesting."

"What do you think about your brother being exiled?" Cerdic asked Adela when she had returned to Caen for a few weeks. They stood next to each other on the bridge over the stream leading to the fishpond. They had been tossing bits of bread to the ducks floating beneath the bridge.

He felt Adela stiffen; her face closed. She shrugged. "My father had to do this," she responded, her tone cold and uncompromising.

"And Samson?" Cerdic asked. "Did your father have to do that?"

Adela pursed her lips and didn't respond.

Samson, an older retainer of Matilda, who had served the queen before her marriage to the king, had been caught carrying messages and money from the queen to Robert in Gerberoy. Incensed, the king had several of his men administer a brutal beating to the man in the courtyard.

"Stop this," Matilda shouted. When she heard the commotion, she rushed outside to intervene. "Stop this at once. This man acted on my orders. He is not to be blamed."

The king made a brief sign to the men, and they stepped back. Samson lay on the ground, bruised and battered, and his face covered in blood. The king turned to his wife. "This was an act of betrayal, and he deserved his punishment. No one may go behind my back with impunity." He bowed cursorily, his face a cold mask, and walked off.

"Who will help me carry this man to the infirmary?" Matilda asked.

Several servants scurried over and picked up the sodden mess that had been a stout man a few minutes earlier. The flagstones were smeared with blood. Two dogs started licking at the stones.

That night, Cerdic tossed and turned on his pallet. The image of Samson, his face swollen to the point of being unrecognizable and dripping blood and pus, haunted him. He didn't sleep for a long time. He couldn't make sense of it, especially after having overheard two knights talking about the king the other day.

"Did you hear what he did on his only visit to Wales?"

"Indeed, I did. He freed hundreds of people who had been slaves. This will hardly have endeared him to the powerful lords of Wales." The two men laughed.

All this came back to him now as he stared at Adela's face. It reminded him of her father. Adela had the same expression— unyielding, unforgiving. Would Adela ever impose such harsh punishment on someone in the future? He shivered.

Adela tossed another piece of bread into the water. Then she brushed off her hands. "Don't look so grim." Her face had softened again. "And it's easy to judge when you are not in a position to assume responsibility."

SIEGE

1079

"Get your gear ready," Matthias shouted at Cerdic.

"Why?"

"You'll ride along with the king's army."

"Where?"

"Where?" Matthias spit on the ground. "You have your head in the clouds again. The king is riding to Gerberoy where his son is holed up."

"I am supposed to ride with the king!" Cerdic's face was flushed.

"Now, don't get any ideas." Matthias frowned. "You'll help with setting up camp and transporting the gear and taking care of the horses. So don't get silly and think you are going into battle."

Cerdic bit his lip and didn't reply.

The next day, the king and his army set out from Caen. The trees were rimmed with frost, and the sky was gray and somber. But so far, the roads were not unmanageable. The king set a rapid pace, intent on reaching his goal before any winter storms could delay them.

At first, Cerdic was feverish with excitement, riding in the back of the long train of knights, squires, and foot soldiers. This time, he wasn't going to be left behind or sent home. He wanted to be out on the field fighting with the others. He kept his eyes on the king's helmet.

Cerdic wondered how William Rufus felt about going into battle against his brother. But it was impossible to tell. The heavy-set young man rode along, relaxed on his large horse, and occasionally chatting with the other knights as if on a pleasant outing.

It took several days to reach Gerberoy. Even in the chilly, damp days of winter, the hills and woods around the village seemed lush and rich. The village, nestled in the shadow of the castle on the hill, felt inviting, with its narrow winding lanes lined by half-timbered houses. The king's troops camped on a field beneath the castle.

Sieges were boring, Cerdic concluded. Initially, the knights and their retinue were of good cheer, eager to teach young Robert and his followers a lesson. But soon the mood turned sour.

For one, it was cold. While this January was mild, and there were only a few days of heavy snow and ice, the damp seeped into everything. Cerdic had blisters on his feet; his socks never got a chance to dry out. During the long nights, the tents smelled of unwashed men and wet gear, and Cerdic looked forward to those times when he had guard duty and could march around on the field.

Sieges meant endless waiting and endless stories told at night and stupid accidents.

A horse had slipped and broken his leg during a night excursion to explore the land around Rémalard. Groaning and screaming in pain, it lay in a ditch on the other side of the field. Eventually, a squire stood up, cursing, and went across the field toward the poor beast. A few moments later, silence returned to the night sky.

Several knights got sick; and the hastily dug latrines near their encampment stank.

The older men gave Cerdic cider to drink. It tasted faintly rotten and prickled when it went down his throat. He gulped down several beakers of it and smacked his lips to show that he liked it. It made him woozy. The men laughed uproariously when he tried to stand up to go piss in the bushes. Then he threw up, and his head ached for a day.

The stories he heard were something else. He didn't know what to think. One described another siege by the king. He had besieged the fortress of Alençon. The defenders waved animal hides from the castle walls to mock William for his mother's humble origins. Enraged, William took thirty-two townspeople and cut off their hands and feet. The castle's defenders surrendered, as did two other neighboring towns when they found out. Cerdic shivered. Would the king do the same now that they were besieging Gerberoy?

"Have you heard about Mabel de Bellême?" one of the men asked him.

"No," Cerdic responded hesitantly. He wasn't sure whether they were laughing at him. "What about her?"

It turned out that Mabel was a bad person. To begin with, her father William Talvas was awful in his own right, killing his wife just because she disagreed with him. He also enjoyed blinding and mutilating his enemies. You would think his daughter would be revolted; quite the contrary, she stayed by his side. Hedging his bets, he had promised his favorite daughter a huge inheritance provided she marry Roger de Montgomerie. She did, and they had a lot of children. But motherhood didn't soften her in any way. She was ruthless and cunning in her treatment of those who got in her way. There was poor Arnold d'Échauffour whose estates she coveted. First, she tried to convince the king to confiscate Arnold's lands. This didn't bring the desired outcome, so she resorted to poison. But alas, it didn't go as planned; the wrong person, in fact, her husband's brother, drank the poisoned wine and died. Undaunted by this failure, she bribed Arnold's chamberlain and provided him with poison. That time, she was successful.

Cerdic was appalled. He could hardly believe that someone like this existed and that the king seemed to tolerate and even support her.

An older knight looked at Cerdic with pity. "You have to understand, her husband is a supporter of the king, and has even acted as a co-regent with Matilda while the king was in England for the battle of Hastings."

"It won't end well for her," a squire said, shaking his head.

A few days later, one of the younger knights, after a whispered conference with some others, walked over to where Cerdic was sitting on the ground, repairing a saddle. "Are you up for a little excursion? We are planning to ride to the village for some warm food and entertainment."

"You want me to come?" Cerdic stumbled over the words, excited to be included.

"Well, don't take all evening to make up your mind. We'll leave shortly."

"It's not exactly an inn," a squire explained to Cerdic when they trotted along the road toward the village. "It's not as if there is a large town nearby and hardly any need for a hostelry. But the mistress obliges with meals and some other conveniences," he added cryptically.

"What if we meet supporters of Duke Robert?" It seemed a foolhardy undertaking at best. Nobody bothered to respond. Cerdic wondered whether the king knew about this. No, he was probably sleeping in his tent.

It was dark by the time they rode into the village, through narrow streets lined with half-timbered houses, finally stopping at one where there was a torch lit at the wooden door. A blast of warm air hit Cerdic when he walked inside in the wake of the others. At first, the noise overwhelmed him, and his eyes had trouble to adjust to the dark interior. The smoke from the fire in a large hearth mingled with the scents of a rich soup in a cast-iron pot over the fire. The room was crowded. A man, his hood thrown back, sat in a corner, singing to the riotous applause of the people around him. To keep the rhythm, he beat on a drum that hung around his neck. Between verses, he would pick up the pipe and blow a few notes.

Drink up and be merry.
Live now and sing when you are young and in fine fettle.
Soon enough, it will be cold and dark.
Your teeth will crumble, and your bones will be brittle,
And the earth will embrace you.

Someone had placed a tankard of ale in front of Cerdic. Laughter and giggling from above made him look up. A door closed on the landing above, and a man, slightly disheveled, came down the rickety staircase. He grinned when he reached the bottom.

"Now it's your turn," the men jeered. Hands on Cerdic's back and shoulders pushed him up the stairs. "Go ahead. Live a little."

"Your first time?" A short plump woman, framed by a doorway, studied him, her face a mixture of resignation and amusement. She smelled of sweat and ale and something musky and pungent.

Cerdic blinked at her in confusion.

"Well, come in. We'll take care of you." She grabbed his hand and pulled him inside. As she pushed the door shut behind him, he could hear the men downstairs laughing and knocking their tankards on the tables. But then the woman, her expression resigned and business-like, tugged on his tunic with one hand, while reaching inside his hose with the other. The bed was lumpy, but Cerdic barely noticed. "That's right," the woman murmured as she pulled him down with her, guiding his movements. For a few moments, Cerdic felt invincible, glorious, more powerful than he had ever felt in his entire life, and then it was as if his entire body were going up in flames. There was a roaring in his ears, and he no longer heard anything at all outside the room. Winded and unable to focus, he lay there as the woman slid out from underneath him and straightened her skirts.

"Did I do it right?" Cerdic asked shyly.

"Not too bad for a start." The woman chuckled. "Well, go on with you. Time's wasting."

When he emerged from the room, the men below cheered. Cerdic's face was red, but he didn't mind. He was elated, and part of him wanted to go right back up. Would he have to go to confession? It had never occurred to him that he could feel so many things all at once—fear, shame, pride, and joy.

Much later, when the men left the tavern, it had begun to snow. The snow muffled all sounds. Cerdic raised his face and tasted the fresh snowflakes on his lips, and it seemed as if nothing had ever tasted as sweet. Back at the camp, he crawled under his blanket and fell asleep.

"Wake up!"

Cerdic blinked at a disheveled looking squire. He was disoriented, still caught in a dream after last night. "What?"

"We are being attacked. Duke Robert and his supporters have staged a sortie."

Now Cerdic was wide awake. He jumped up. "I'll get ready."

"We are supposed to join the king. You are to guard the camp."

Cerdic scowled. Not again. This time, he would be part of the battle. The squire had already turned and was mounting his horse.

Cerdic pulled on his hauberk; it was heavy even though made of leather, and it was damp and stiff from having lain on the ground. He tightened the belt over it and grabbed his helmet. It was a raw chilly morning, and snow covered the ground. The camp was a mess —cook pots knocked over, tents tilting, blankets flung onto the ground. But Cerdic didn't notice any of this. His horse whickered when he approached, apparently restless, his ears flicking back and forth as if to catch sounds of the battle.

Cerdic mounted and cantered out toward the meadow beneath the castle. As he got closer, he could hear shouting and clashing of swords. He pulled up his horse. At first, he couldn't make sense of what was in front of him—it all blurred into a single raging mass of men and horses.

Gritting his teeth, he spurred his horse and galloped toward the battle. His helmet slid back on his head, because he had forgotten to tighten the chin strap. A squire, taking a breather on the edge of the chaos, yelled at him, "Pull down your nose guard, you idiot."

"What's happening?" Cerdic pushed his horse closer to the man.

"We have been taken by surprise. The king must have misjudged how many supporters Duke Robert managed to marshal. William Rufus got a broken arm and is back there." The squire pointed to the edge of the field. "I suppose he is lucky that it's no worse than that."

"Where is the king?"

"Oh, he is right there in the middle. Toki is sticking close to him."

At first, Cerdic couldn't distinguish anyone in the heaving mass of horses and men; then he saw a conical helmet with a red and blue ribbon tied to the top. He spurred his horse forward.

"Stop. Where are you going? Get back here, boy."

Cerdic gripped his sword in his hand. It slipped in his sweating palm, and he tightened his hold as he pushed between several men, intent on fighting each other. His bowels cramped, and he felt an urge to pee. Then he forgot about everything, and even the screams and shouts and groans had blended into a distant roaring.

There was the king with Toki right next to him, their horses dancing sideways and turning in a circle to evade attackers while slashing out at others. Toki had lost his shield. Guiding his horse with his knees, he swung his sword with one arm while pointing a lance with the other. He wasn't wearing his knee-length mail hauberk. He must not have had time; besides, Cerdic suspected that he was too arrogant to take Robert and his supporters seriously.

A knight on a bay launched his spear directly at Toki's unprotected side. With a groan he slid off, his foot caught in the stirrup. His horse reared up in panic and leaped backward on its haunches before it fell, rolling over Toki as it came down. The king swayed in his saddle, his shield arm was down, and he struggled with his sword. Another knight pushed his horse closer and swung his heavy mace. Cerdic kicked his horse forward, barreling into the knight just as the mace came down. His horse took the brunt of the impact on his neck, and it sank to its knees. Cerdic made a desperate grab for his sword; he lifted it up and caught the knight in his side, before tumbling down. Grunting in pain, the knight collapsed on the back of his horse. Another knight, his face completely concealed by his nose guard, spurred his horse toward the king, ramming his horse. The king lost his seating and landed on the ground. He cursed, trying to raise himself with one arm.

The knight steadied his prancing horse and lifted his helmet. It was Duke Robert, eyeing his father with a curious mixture of chagrin and triumph. The king stared at his son, his lips pressed together.

"There are more of us," Robert said calmly. "Call for a retreat."

Cerdic had managed to get back on his feet and stood next to the king.

Robert dismounted. "Here, Cerdic, hold my horse." He went over to his father and helped him to mount.

Without glancing at his son, the king raised himself in his stirrups and shouted across the field. "Retreat! All the king's men, retreat!" Then he pulled the horse around and rode off.

Cerdic's horse had gotten back on its feet. Cerdic dragged it along by the reins and followed the king. His ears were ringing, and he shivered. He was alive. Why was he still alive?

Robert and his small army had already wheeled and withdrawn back into the castle. Foot soldiers and servants worked their way across the field, gathering the dead and the wounded.

The king was bruised but otherwise unhurt. Toki was dead; so were nineteen others.

The next morning, the king's army abandoned the siege and rode east toward Rouen and from there, home to Caen.

Later, when Henry asked him to describe the battle, his eyes shining with anticipation, Cerdic shook his head helplessly. "It wasn't like the jousting in the castle grounds."

"But what was it like?" Henry prodded.

"Very loud," Cerdic said reluctantly. "Everybody screaming." He glanced at the boy, taking in his round shiny cheeks and bright eyes. "I don't really remember much; it's all a blur now. Your time will come soon enough." He couldn't tell Henry about any of it, not about the horse with its broken back groaning in agony, while the knight who had ridden it, lay still underneath its bulk, or the foot soldier whose head had been ripped off, or the man holding his side where a lance had pierced him, spilling his guts onto the muddy ground.

"Father told me that you were very brave."

Cerdic flushed. "You would have done the same thing."

Parsnip, Onions, and Bitter Herbs

Soringue of Eels
Skin and then cut up your eels; then have onions cooked in slices
and parsley leaves and set it all to fry in oil; then bray ginger,
cinnamon, clove, grain [of Paradise] and saffron, and moisten with
veruice and take them out of the mortar. Then have toasted bread
brayed and moistened with pur6e and run it through the strainer,
then put in the purse and set all to boil together and flavour with
wine, verjuice and vinegar; and it must be clear.
The French Medieval Household Book *Le Ménagier de Paris*
(The Goodman of Paris)

I *hate onions.* Adela adjusted the basket in her arms, trying to avoid the scent of the freshly picked green bulbs.

"Ah, Mistress Adela," Madame Nénotte exclaimed when Adela came to the kitchen. "Are you going to the garden? Please get me some purslane. Snip some, leaving enough of the plants so that they grow back. Also, onions and some parsley. And you might look for a few stalks of celery." The cook handed Adela a basket.

Adela had begun to make regular trips to the kitchen garden because her mother had insisted.

"Why?" Adela asked. "It's not as if I'll be grubbing around in the dirt looking for cabbage," she complained and then added in an undertone, "especially not once you marry me off to some important count so and so."

"It won't hurt you to do this work." Matilda frowned at her daughter. "But that's not the point. You need to know what feeds the people in a castle and understand the work that goes into it. I want you to go every day when you are not in school. Ask Madame Nénotte whether she needs anything for the kitchen and bring it back. That's the best way to start learning."

Adela found it frustrating. She couldn't tell a turnip cabbage from a parsnip, and in the spring she found it hard to gather enough peas, since they tasted so sweet directly out of their shells. She confused coriander and dill, especially when in bloom, but chewing on the leaves or rolling the seed pods between her fingers for the scent helped. The cook added parsley leaves to almost everything she prepared. Madame Nénotte told her about the healing properties of many plants and explained about the need for hops for brewing ale.

Her mother insisted on planting flowers along the edges and throughout the garden. The roses were coming into bloom, and Adela was breathing in their scent when she walked through the gate.

"Ouff," she exclaimed.

"Whoa, slow down." Cerdic stood in front of her, rubbing his side. She had barreled into him, and her greens had spilled onto the ground.

"Oh, sorry."

Cerdic bent down to gather up the basket's contents. "What's this?" He held up a bunch of small leaves.

"That's purslane."

Cerdic put a leaf between his teeth. "Sour." He grimaced. "Which part of it do you eat?"

"Oh, everything, leaves, stems, flowers, even the seeds. Cook wanted me to get to get some for the stew; there isn't much else ready yet this early in the season. The cook says purslane gives a nice tangy flavor in the stew." Adela stopped. She realized that she was babbling.

"So you are becoming a gardener now?" Cerdic laughed at her.

Adela laughed back; for a moment, her discomfort and sense of awkwardness were gone. It was as if they were children again, playing in the castle courtyard.

Cerdic plucked the last onion from the ground and straightened up to drop them in her basket. With a shock, Adela realized he now was taller than her by a head. His long reddish blond hair had fallen forward and hid part of his forehead, but not his aquiline nose or his wide mobile mouth. It was no longer the face of a boy.

His eyes slid over the new gown Adela was wearing at the insistence of her mother. His eyes clung to hers for a moment. Then something in his expression changed. "Well, I better go on. The squire will be looking for me."

"You saved Father's life," she said before he could turn and walk away.

"Toki did," Cerdic responded. "I just got in the way."

"No, I heard what you did." She shifted the basket in her arms. "And I won't forget."

Exile

1080 Caen

"My Lady?" Cerdic stared at the queen.

"Yes, you heard me. I need you to ride to Gerberoy with a letter and this bag for my son." She pointed toward a leather satchel on the table. Matilda's face was blanched. Despite the warmth from the brazier, she had draped a shawl around her shoulders. "No one must know."

Cerdic took the bag gingerly. He remembered Samson lying on the ground, beaten to a pulp, his face swollen beyond recognition.

"Here are the directions." Matilda held out a small piece of parchment.

"My Lady," Cerdic blurted out. "Where is Samson?"

Matilda turned away to look at the pile of abandoned needlework on her chair. "Samson is in a monastery; he is well taken care of." Then she faced him again, her back straightened, and her voice hard. "Don't ask me anything else. I will protect you as best I can, but be careful. Don't let anyone see you."

"What should I say to Squire Matthias?"

"Don't tell him anything; just ride out early. I will tell him I sent you to the Holy Trinity Abbey with a message for Lady Cecilia if he asks."

"But that's right here."

"He probably will forget all about you or think that my daughter needed you for something."

By the time Cerdic returned from Gerberoy several days later, he was dusty, tired, and sad. It had been a long ride on muddy roads through slush and remnants of snow. At least the days were getting longer. It was March.

Robert had treated him as if he were a stranger. He perused the letter quickly as if it was of no more importance than a list of provisions. "Tell my lady mother that I will consider her thoughts carefully." He glanced at Cerdic for a moment. "Wait, I'll write a note to her; it will be ready for you when you leave." He rang a bell and curtly gave his order to the servant. "Ask the steward to arrange for a place to sleep for this messenger. He'll resume his journey in the morning."

The courtyard of Caen was quiet when Cerdic rode in. The guards recognized him and waved him on. He dismounted and led his horse to the stable. Once he had settled it in an empty stall, he went inside. Cerdic didn't want to wait to get rid of the letter Robert had given him and walked toward the stairs that led to the queen's apartments.

"Where are you going?" The king's voice boomed behind him. He was coming out of the great hall. "You have no business upstairs."

"Sorry," Cerdic stammered. "I was going …" His voice petered out. He tried to hold his hand with the letter out of sight.

"What's that?" The king reached out and grabbed his hand, taking the letter from him. "Who wrote this?"

Cerdic flushed. What could he say? He knew the king didn't read; he usually had a scribe read messages to him.

The king had turned over the folded parchment with its seal prominently displayed. His face got red.

"My lord, that is for me." The queen's voice was clear and firm. She was coming down the stairs, her long gown sweeping behind her.

"You?" A vein on the king's temple was beating.

The queen glanced at Cerdic. "You may go."

Cerdic didn't hesitate. He backed away as quickly as he could and walked back outside into the courtyard. It had begun to rain, and the flagstones were slippery, but he didn't notice. He ran toward the stables and into an empty box at the end. The smell of old hay, horse piss, and dried horse apples was comforting.

"You saved my father's life," Adela had said in her soft voice when they had met at the garden gate after the battle at Gerberoy.

Cerdic couldn't remember what he said to her in response. It wasn't true. He had gazed at her large blue eyes, glowing and filled with affection, and was lost in the tangle of thoughts that haunted him. He didn't know why he had gone to the king's aid. Ever since he had seen the Bayeux tapestry, he had been dreaming about the battle of Hastings and had been picturing how his father had met his end at the hands of the Normans, even though his mother hadn't told him anything beyond the bare facts. He resented the king and was angry about having been taken away from England and his mother. And yet, this same king had been kind to him, had sheltered him, and let him study with his sons. He couldn't possibly tell Adela about all that. In the battle, he had acted without thought, nearly blinded by his fear and deafened by the roaring around him and caught in a frenzy of terror that pushed him to charge forward into that heaving, groaning, screaming mass of men and horses.

The king wasn't known for being merciful in dealing with those who crossed him. Cerdic shivered as he burrowed into a pile of hay in the corner. What was going to happen to him? Would he be beaten to a bloody pulp like Samson?

Husbands and Wives

Urge your husband, do not cease to suggest useful things to his soul. For it is certain that, if the infidel husband is saved by a believing wife, as the apostle says, a believing husband can be made better by a believing wife. Pope Gregory VII, letter to Matilda of Flanders, Duchess of Normandy and Queen of England, 1074.

Adela heard them arguing when she walked toward her mother's room.

The king was never particularly concerned with who could hear him when he started shouting. And her mother might have forgotten how much voices carried and echoed in the stone halls of the castle. Years of time spent at the abbey school in Caen had taught Adela the advantages of listening in on conversations not meant for her. She put her ears closer to the door.

"He did this on my orders." Her mother sounded as she always did, calm and in control.

"It's unacceptable," her father shouted. Adela could hear him pacing back and forth. "It was my wish that no one should contact Robert."

"Well, are you going to punish me, then?"

She knew that tone. She could picture her mother standing there, with her hands pushed into her hips, her eyes narrowed, as she used to look when Henry and Adela had tried to get away with something.

"Cerdic will be severely punished." Her father banged a fist against the door frame. "I was too lenient when this happened before. Samson got off easy."

"No, Father, you can't do that." Adela burst into her mother's room.

Shocked, her parents turned around.

"What are you doing here? You should be working with your tutor." Her mother sounded exasperated. "Let me handle this."

"No one will 'handle' this but me," her father snapped, his face red. "You forget yourself. And you, young lady, have no business here. Go."

"I won't go," Adela yelled. "He saved your life!"

The king glared at her, at a loss for words.

"Do you want to be known as a king who doesn't honor loyalty?" Adela said, sensing an opening.

"Strictly speaking, it was Toki who gave his life for you," Matilda commented drily. "But yes, Cerdic certainly tried to serve you bravely, if foolishly. Might I offer a suggestion?"

The king's angry flush had receded. "Could I ever stop you from making suggestions?"

"You can punish him and also do right by him. How about sending him to Count Stephen-Henry to serve him as a squire?"

The king narrowed his eyes. Then he remembered his daughter's presence. "Adela, you are done here. Go."

Adela nodded. She knew better than to protest now. Her mother had things well in hand. She curtsied and went out.

In the afternoon, she joined her mother in the Great Hall. Reluctantly, Adela picked up her needlework.

Matilda was reading. She glanced at her daughter. "You should read this as well," she said. "It is a treatise by Anselm of Bec. He talks about atonement."

Adela wasn't interested in Anselm of Bec. She glanced looking around to make sure her father wasn't nearby. "What will happen with Cerdic?"

"Your father has made an excellent decision."

Adela almost burst out laughing. This was how her mother operated. First, she would tell her father what she wanted him to do, and then she would make it sound as if it was his idea to begin with. "Will he stay here?"

"No, that's not possible. He's sending him to become a squire in the service of Count Stephen-Henry of Blois."

"Oh," Adela said. She was relieved and sad at the same time. She would miss Cerdic.

"As exiles go, this will be an easy one—perhaps the making of him. It's a good opportunity," her mother said. "Besides, it might be nice for you if Cerdic were with Count Stephen-Henry," she added offhandedly.

"Why?"

"Well, my dear, your father and the count have had a conversation about a possible alliance. He is coming here soon to meet you."

Adela for once didn't know what to say. She hadn't expected this. Her belly was cramping again. She lowered her eyes, pretending to be absorbed in the colors of her needlepoint work. "What if I don't care for him?" she whispered after a long silence. "What if I want what you have wanted?"

Her mother stared at her, her brows drawn together in a frown.

"You tried to make your own arrangements," Adela blurted out. She had heard two court ladies whisper about her mother. Apparently, she had become enamored of a young man sent to the court by King Edward, one Brithric Mau. She had actually sent him a message offering herself in marriage. It hadn't ended well, and her reputation had been shaky for years. But Adela was impressed by her mother's spirit.

Matilda pursed her lips; there were red blotches on her cheeks. "Now, young lady, what did I tell about paying attention to gossip?"

"But you did, didn't you?" Adela was surprised at not getting a harsher reprimand. "Was he handsome?"

For an instant, her mother's face softened. "Things are different now. That was a long time ago. Also, my heedless act made me an object of derision for a long time." For a moment she sat quietly, her hands rubbing the brocade border of her gown. Then she sat up straight. "We have talked about this, Adela," she said firmly. "You had no trouble understanding the concept of alliances earlier. This is your role; it is an alliance that would be good for your father, for Normandy, and ultimately for all of us."

"I understand, I think," Adela said. "But what about what I want?"

"What you want doesn't come into it." Her mother sighed. "Anyway, I have heard that he is an amiable and kind man."

Adela said nothing. What could she say to her mother to stop this? She was afraid. Was this what it felt like for a bird of prey to have the hood placed over her head?

"Listen to me," her mother said, speaking more gently than before. "Do you want to be able to do things in your life? Important things? To help make life better for people? Then you need the position and the wealth to do it. That's what an alliance can offer. It need not be a hindrance. Think of all that I am able to do at your father's side. As the wife of a man as important and may I add as wealthy as Count Stephen-Henry, you could do a lot."

The next day, Adela went in search of Cerdic. It was raining, and Adela thought of the long ride to Blois in the cold March weather. She wanted to talk to Cerdic before he left. Everything was changing, and she would miss him. He had been a part of her life, almost more so than Henry. And yet she was angry with herself for feeling that way.

He wasn't in the stable. In the courtyard, Squire Matthias was standing in front of a few pages and demonstrated the working of a catapult. The pages seemed to be getting smaller every year. Cerdic wasn't among them. Where could he have gone?

Then she had an idea. Grabbing the folds of her gown so she could walk faster, she went back inside and climbed the stone steps to the north tower. It was cool in the stairwell. She could feel the breeze through the air slits. The small room at the top used to be their favorite hiding hole. It was nothing more than a carved-out space with a tall, narrow opening that allowed light to flood in. In the event of an attack on Caen, an archer would sit here, ready with his crossbow to shoot through the opening, also known as the arrow loop.

This was where she would find him, looking north toward England. When she entered the cavern-like space, cooled by the breeze from the narrow window, Cerdic didn't move at all, even though he must have heard her.

"It's all going to work out." She was speaking to his back. "Mother got what she wanted, and Robert is coming to Caen to meet with our father."

"And I'm being sent away." Cerdic didn't turn around.

"I know," Adela said. "But it could be worse. Mother told me where you are going. Count Stephen-Henry will treat you well. Soon you'll be a squire."

"I wish I could go back to England."

"Well, you can't; at least not now."

"No, you are right." Cerdic still didn't look at her, his face turned north. "But it feels as I am going to lose my home all over again."

"You might come back soon." Adela felt a lump in her throat. "Mother told me that the count has been invited to come here in the fall."

Cerdic stood up and brushed the dust off his hose. He flicked his long hair out of his face with a motion that stung Adela with its familiarity. "Why?" His voice was flat. He wasn't interested.

"Oh, I don't know." Adela regretted saying anything. "Anyway, I suppose you better get ready."

Cerdic looked at her oddly. It was as if he had just noticed her new gown and cap hiding her hair. He stiffened. Then he gave her a formal bow. "Thank you."

"I am returning to the abbey today. Safe journey." Adela turned to go back down the stone steps. She didn't wait for Cerdic to follow her. Her eyes burned.

UNKNOWN ROADS

Cerdic had never traveled this far south.

In the first days, he hardly paid any attention to the world around him. He kept going over his last conversations with Adela. At least her voice hadn't changed.

He felt more alone than he ever had.

For a moment in the north tower, it was as if they were small children again, sitting together on the cold stone floor and eating honey bread. Then he turned around and knew that time was long gone. Still small in stature, she stood there with her head held high. Her dark green gown, with its wide sleeves edged with embroidery, and a fine shawl, shimmering in shades of gray and green and scented with lavender, were the trappings of the daughter of a king. And he was nothing but a page and one about to be exiled at that.

He was going to miss her. She had been central to his life since he first arrived from England. She had been his friend.

He would even miss Matilda. The queen had written a letter he was to give to Count Stephen-Henry and had given him money for the journey to Blois.

"Remember, you need to rest your horse occasionally before you continue," she said, frowning in her concern. "It's a long journey. It will take you at least 8 days." It was funny; it was as if she was talking to young Henry. "Be careful with the money. Don't trust anyone."

Cerdic nodded. He didn't want to seem ungrateful, but he could figure all this out for himself. After all, he had made his way back to Caen by himself after Gerberoy.

"And try to stay in safe houses or inns. The roads are full of dangers."

"It will be fine." Cerdic smiled at her. "And thank you." He was filled with affection for this short stout woman with her graying hair and the deepening lines around her mouth. She had treated him almost as one of her children. He bowed more deeply than he would normally have.

Despite all of Matilda's warnings, he slept on the side of the road during the first nights. It was summer. He would hide in the bushes. Besides, the other travelers—merchants and pilgrims—seemed peaceful. They wouldn't bother him. He wanted to keep as much of the coin he had gotten from the queen as he could. Most of the time, the road was nothing but dust and deep ruts where carts had gotten stuck. Often, he had to stop and pick pebbles out of his horse's hooves. Near Falaise and Argentan, there were stretches of road covered with paving stones. Everywhere else, there was nothing but dirt and mud.

His thoughts wandered. He loosened the reins and let his horse amble along in the warm sun. What had Adela meant by that last cryptic remark that he would see her soon?

Once he had passed through the town of Sées, he gazed around in wonder. It was as if he had entered another world. This was nothing like the wooded hills around Caen and the luscious rolling fields with the hint of the sea in the distance. He stared at enormous cliffs rising like white-limbed giants out of steep green mountain sides. Waterfalls had carved deep grooves into the rock walls. It was as if he had moved back in time by hundreds of years.

As Cerdic continued riding south, it occurred to him that he was free for the first time in his life. It was exhilarating. He was going to see new lands and meet new people.

After days of traveling on the road, he was tired. The names of the towns he had passed through got blurred in his mind. But he knew he was getting closer to his goal. He had already entered the County of Blois. He slowed his horse to a walk. Suddenly, he felt a curious reluctance to reach his goal. What if Count Stephen-Henry rejected him? What if the count was a hateful man? Cerdic had reached a wooded area, and he welcomed the shade.

Ping. Cerdic winced and reached for his neck. His horse shied. Another ping. He was being pelted with something. His horse danced as he peered up through the branches above him. Two slender bare feet poked through the leaves. Ping. His horse bucked.

Thoroughly angry now, he pulled up, dismounted, and advanced upon the tree. "Come down from that tree," he shouted. "Otherwise I will come and get you."

The branches swayed, and with a rustling sound, a slight and diminutive person slid down onto the ground.

Cerdic stared. It was a girl, in a brown tunic, tied around her waist with a cord. Her short, curly hair was full of leaves and twigs. "I made your horse jump." The girl was laughing at him, completely unafraid. "It's only cherry pits," she added, holding up a small bag.

"You can't do that. You can't sit in a tree and spit cherry pits at strangers."

"Do you want some?" The girl held out her bag. "I picked them this morning." Then she shrank back as if regretting her temerity and studied her toes.

Cerdic considered her. She seemed sad. Strangely, a long-forgotten moment came back to him. Nine years ago, he had been standing at the railing of King William's ship, desperately staring back at the coast in the hopes of another glimpse of his mother. Something about this little waif touched him. "I still have some bread and cheese in my saddlebag," he said. "Do you want to join me for my midday meal?"

Pushing her tongue out between her teeth, the girl watched as he pulled a blanket from behind his saddle and spread it on the ground.

"I bought this bread two days ago." He dug in his pack and took out the bread and cheese wrapped in a towel. "But if you chew it, it's fine."

The girl rubbed her hands on her tunic. "Give me that. Do you have a knife?"

Surprised, Cerdic handed her a knife he carried in his boot.

Deftly, she broke off a few pieces and cut chunks of cheese that she placed on the bread. "Here."

For a few minutes, they munched the bread.

"Where are you going?"

"To Blois."

"Oh, that's not so far from here. Do you think you'll come back?"

"I don't know." Cerdic hesitated. "Maybe. Anyway, I have a flask with some cider. Would you like a sip?"

He watched his strange hostess lift the flask and dribble a bit of cider into her mouth. Her feet were grimy, and her tunic was worn, and yet she didn't look like a farm girl.

"Do you sit in this tree often?"

"Yes, it's my favorite tree." The girl picked a cherry and chewed on it thoughtfully before spitting out the pit. "You like wood cherries? They are tart, but not bad." She offered the bag again. "I can see far along the fields if I climb to the top. I saw you coming."

"Where do you live, anyway?"

"You must have ridden right past my home." The girl pointed the way he had come. "It's called *La Vallée des Sources*, the valley of the springs. Isn't that pretty?"

"And what's your name?

"Giselle."

"I like that. Mine is Cerdic."

"What an odd name." The girl wrinkled her nose. "Cer…dic… bah, I can't say that. People should call you Cid."

"Who lives at La Vallée des Sources with you?"

"My father. It's his vineyard. He works hard. He has been teaching me." Abruptly, she jumped up. "I'd better go home. Jehanne will be looking for me. Thank you for the bread and cheese." She poured out the last cherries onto the blanket. "Here, finish them." Then she ran off.

Perplexed, Cerdic watched her until she was out of sight. What a strange, self-possessed little girl.

The next day, Cerdic rode into Blois. He was amazed at his first glimpse of the stone bridge spanning the Loire. Someone had come up with the notion of placing mills underneath the bridge's sheltering arches. Slowing down his horse, Cerdic stared at the chapel, the houses, and the gate tower on the bridge. The bridge was a town unto itself. He shook his head and continued on. The castle was in the town's center. A massive stone wall, dominated by a tower, surrounded the entire edifice.

"Right now, Count Stephen-Henry only manages Blois, Châteaudun, and Chartres for his father, Theobald," Matilda had explained to Cerdic before he left. "But make no mistake; this is an important man. Eventually his holdings will include Champagne, Provins, Sancerre, Meaux, and Reims. So his patronage means a lot. This is your chance."

With some trepidation, Cerdic patted his bag as if to reassure himself that the letter from Matilda was still there. Then he squared his shoulders and spurred his horse forward.

The courtyard was humming with activity. A farrier was working on a horse. "Hold still, dammit," he shouted, narrowly avoiding a kick. A group of knights chatted near a well. Servants ran back and forth. On a bench in the back, a man sat in the shade, gently plucking the strings on his lute and singing softly. No one appeared to pay any attention to Cerdic. The place seemed much more cheerful than Caen had ever been.

He dismounted and approached a woman who was carrying a pile of soiled linens in her arms. "Can you tell me where to find Count Stephen-Henry? I have a message for him."

The woman smiled at him. "He is right there." She pointed at a man coming out of the main entrance.

His future employer was a big man, portly and with a ruddy face. He had to be around forty years old. He was beaming all over his round face as he walked over to the knights. "Perhaps you already heard the good news!" Everyone in the courtyard could hear him. "I have a daughter. And she is beautiful."

Behind him, Cerdic heard a man whisper. "I wonder how his mistress will feel when he finally marries a lady of rank?"

Another laughed. "Since when has that mattered? Anyway, I'm sure the count will see to it that his mistress will be well provided for."

The count was shaking hands and getting slapped on his back by a few people near the well. Then he saw Cerdic, who was holding his horse and debating how to approach the count. "Well, young man, you look like you have come a long way. What is your business?"

Cerdic hastily opened his bag, dropping it in his confusion. Then he fumbled until he found the sealed packet from Matilda and handed it to the count with a bow.

The count glanced at the seal, raising his eyebrows. "Come, let me offer you something to drink while I peruse this letter." He beckoned a servant to take Cerdic's horse.

In the great hall, he invited Cerdic to sit and offered him some wine. "This comes from our own holdings at Sancerre." He smiled at Cerdic over the rim of the pale green translucent goblet, sniffing at the wine before drinking and smacking his lips appreciatively. "Now let me take a look at this."

Cerdic studied the count in bemusement. He couldn't imagine the king being so affable to a young stranger. The count didn't call for a clerk to read the letter to him. The table behind him near the fireplace was covered with manuscripts and a psalter. There were even a few quill pens and a jar of ink; apparently, he did some of his own writing. There was a small pile of something that didn't look like parchment. It was finer than that. Cerdic's fingers itched to touch it.

The count raised his head from the letter.

"What is this?" Cerdic blurted out, unable to stop himself. He pointed at the pile.

"Nice, isn't it?" The count beamed. "It's paper. It comes from Toledo where they are experimenting with paper making. I understand that they use linen and hemp rags to create the surface. Of course, it's very dear. Not like this heavy stuff we have to use." The count flattened out the parchment and perused it once more. "Well, young man, you come highly recommended. Now tell me, the queen mentions that you read and write."

"Yes, I was permitted to sit in when the tutor worked with her youngest son."

"Ah, I see. The queen always felt strongly about education. And I understand you have proven your loyalty repeatedly." The count took another sip of wine. "Very well, I will take you on as a squire. As it happens, I haven't had a personal squire for the last year. You'll have the usual duties of a squire; but I also want you to assume some clerking functions in connection with the management of my holdings. Now let me show you around and introduce you to the steward and the marshal." The count put down his goblet and stood. Cerdic immediately got up, stunned by the rapidity with which everything was happening. "The marshal will also arrange quarters for you and instruct you in some of your duties."

And so Cerdic began his second apprenticeship.

BLOIS

1081 BLOIS

Cerdic quickly felt comfortable in Blois.

For the first time in his life, he had his own quarters. They were in the wing where other squires and some knights were housed. He didn't spend much time in the small room; often, his duties included sleeping in front of his lord's chamber or riding around the county on his behalf. But he cherished it, and he enjoyed the unfamiliar sense of being alone.

One of his first acts to put his mark on the room was to hang a small piece of tapestry over his bed. Adela had given it to him when she was still a little girl.

"I made this," she had said proudly, holding out a slightly crooked bit of fabric with multiple threads pulled through. "See, there are flowers and a rabbit." She pointed at some blobs of color. He remembered peering at the blobs and nodding gravely, as if he could see the rabbit perfectly. Now, the threads were coming out, and the colors were faded, but he loved it.

He also hung a small leather bag with a braided string over the back of the chair. Matilda had presented him with it. "Young men like to keep their various treasures in a bag. I hope you will find this useful."

Count Stephen-Henry kept him busy. Cerdic copied letters and often spent hours making entries in a large leather-bound ledger. Everything was recorded. Purchases for the estate, wine production, trades with merchants, payments to churches, revenues from transport tolls paid by merchants, and fees paid by market stall holders had to be noted down to the last denarius. Of course, most things needed for day-to-day life were produced on the estate, and tenants did all the woodworking, smithing, tanning, cloth making, spinning, and weaving that was called for. But Blois was a vibrant town at the crossroads of France, and trade was central to its power. Sometimes Cerdic would find the count absorbed in studying the ledger. Then he'd look up at him and smile. "You have no idea how satisfying it is to see the signs of growing trade."

Cerdic wasn't sure how to respond. This was all so different from everything he had learned at Caen. There, life was ruled by the king's soldiery preference for sparseness and austerity in style and habits, only partially relieved by the furnishings in the queen's quarters and her insistence on culture and music. The joyous opulence in Blois was surprising.

"I know the Lord favors warriors," the count said, with a rueful grin as if he had read Cerdic's mind. "And you have certainly served one of the supreme warrior kings of this time. But I believe that this," he patted the ledger, "is the future. Go to the fair and walk around town. Tell me what you see," he commanded.

And so Cerdic went.

"Watch where you're going," a woman yelled at him as he blundered against her cages filled with chickens and quail. He walked past fruit and vegetable sellers. There was salted meat and fresh bread, eggs, cheeses, and ale. The smell of fish was so strong in one area that he veered off and tried another direction. Fur traders and merchants with fabrics screamed over each other to get his attention.

"Look at these sables. Caught in the wilds of the north. Keep your lady warm in the winter."

"Check out the finest marten!" What was marten? The brown yellowish pieces piled up on a table didn't look attractive at all.

"Genuine woad dyed fabric. These colors won't wash out. Look at the deep blue."

"Amber. Finest amber, crafted by artists along the Baltic shore."

When Cerdic got tired of this maelstrom of trade, he wandered toward the river. Flat-bottomed boats traveled slowly along on the broad stream. "Where do they come from?" he asked a man on shore.

"Those boats?" The man spit on the ground. "They come from Orleans, and they'll end up in Nantes." The boats transported sand used for building, and the wood used to build the boats would be taken for building construction in Nantes. Their shipmen traveled back to Orleans on horseback. The boats carried other goods as well, including precious salt.

"That's why it's called the *route du sel*," the man told him. Apparently, he had taken it upon himself to lecture this uninformed youngster. "And guess what happens to those boats when they reach Nantes?" Cerdic shook his head. "They get cut up, and the wood is used for building. The boatmen make their way back to Orleans on horseback."

Cerdic was dizzy with all the new sights and sounds. When he got back to the castle, Count Stephen-Henry insisted on peppering him with questions about what he had seen. "Look, this is where the amber comes from." He pulled out a map. At first, Cerdic couldn't make out anything on the large parchment, confused by the colors and the strange shapes and images.

"It's hard at first to learn to read a map. Here. This is where we are." The count put his finger on an area left of the center. His finger moved on. "See that shoreline up in the high north? That's where they find amber. And if you travel all the way to the east, you get to the Holy Land. Here is Iberia, and that is the ancient city of Rome." He rolled it up. "But enough for now."

Cerdic listened with wonder and tried to absorb everything he could.

"Would you like some of this?" The count held up a flask of wine. "The latest vintage from Sancerre. We should be able to get a good price for it." He poured some of the pale golden liquid into a goblet and offered it to Cerdic, who sipped it carefully. It was still disorienting to be treated as if he were an honored guest. He didn't know what to make of it. He tried to picture King William offering him a drink in his study and failed. Too often had he seen how the king would abruptly dismiss men of high rank as if they were nothing but lowly servants. Perhaps one day the count would show his true colors.

But for now, he liked the count. He seemed to be an amiable man, jovial and tolerant, who enjoyed the comforts of life—good wine, delicious meals, a comfortable seat near a crackling fire, and enough candles for reading. He rarely spent time in the tilting yard or watched his knights practice sword play and work with lances and maces or other weapons of war, preferring to sit in his study and studying manuscripts and maps and discussing the most recent political developments with his visitors. Often, he insisted that Cerdic would sit in on those. "I want you to listen and learn." Rarely irritated, he was unfailingly courteous and averse to conflict, suavely withdrawing from heated exchanges. Sometimes he sat in meetings with his little daughter Emma in his arms, tickling her and pulling on her pudgy fingers before handing her back to her nurse. Cerdic never saw Emma's mother. He wasn't even sure whether she was still living in the household.

One aspect of his new life at Blois was utterly unexpected. At first, he thought it was an accident. A soft body lurched into him as he passed by on the way to the great hall. A scented piece of fine linen dropped on the flagstones, so he had to bend down to pick it up and hand it to its owner. A husky voice whispered as he passed by. Then it was clearly not so accidental. A hand casually resting on his sleeve when nobody was watching. A face turned toward him with a suggestive smile. Finally, an invitation.

Cerdic found himself being seduced by several women who were bored and whose husbands were conveniently abroad. At first, he was thrilled. He also enjoyed the new sense of control and knowledge as these women whispered instructions and showed him unsuspected mysteries of the human body. "Slow down," one said, chuckled and guiding his hands. "You have all the time in the world."

Then one day, while watching a knight arrive in the courtyard and being greeted by his wife, who went into a deep curtsy in front of him and then raised her face for a kiss, Cerdic felt cheapened and sick of what he had been doing. That same day, he asked Count Stephen-Henry for an assignment away from Blois.

VALLEY OF THE SPRINGS

"I need you to ride to Angers." Count Stephen-Henry handed Cerdic a packet of letters.

Angers was an important town along the Loire, and in the last decades it had begun to thrive and to grow in importance. There was still an occasional whiff of resentment against the Normans. But now, the House of Anjou in Angers was emerging as a leading center of power in France.

"I am interested in repairing relations with the House of Anjou. My great-great-grandfather and my father, among others, have fought with Anjou repeatedly. King William as well has been aligned against Anjou, though they made their peace in 1054. Admittedly, Fulk of Anjou is a difficult man to put it mildly and with a less than stellar reputation, but it doesn't hurt to try. Fulk keeps picking quarrels with both the king of France and with Normandy. I want to see whether I can entice him with the sweet sounds of commerce traveling past his castle on the Loire."

Fulk had indeed been surly. He barely acknowledged Cerdic, scowling as he glanced at the packet. "No need to wait for my response. My steward will show you where you can rest before you return to Blois."

It rained hard all the way back. The Loire swelled, threatening to overflow its banks. Crossing some of the small tributaries on his way east was fraught with peril, and several times, Cerdic had to ride north to find another crossing that wasn't washed out. The small wooden bridges, especially those that hadn't been maintained, were at the mercy of severe storms.

Cerdic was tired and disgruntled. This was already the third time that he had to make a detour north and then head back toward the south and Blois. He was riding slowly, nervous about the many holes created by the flooding. His hose and shoes were soaked.

Aside from the physical discomfort, Cerdic was feeling unsettled. He was so tired of doing someone else's bidding. There were days when he felt he was no more able to choose than those pieces of wood bobbing up and down in the current.

Of course, Cerdic knew how much he owed Count Stephen-Henry. The count had been acting like a tutor and even like an older friend. And yet, dissatisfaction was eating at him. Did he want to be an errand boy and a plaything for bored court ladies for the next years of his life? But what choice did he really have? He was nobody. He had no land or title. He didn't even have a home, not anymore. Ruefully, he thought of his mother, her pallid face, her hand gripping the folds of her gown like a lifeline, staring at him for the last time as he rode away on the ship. Then again, what choice did anyone have? You did your duty, said your prayers, and hoped you would find your heavenly reward. Part of the difficulty was that he didn't know what he wanted. It had all been so easy when serving as a page together with Henry. For all that he and Henry had liked to complain, he had enjoyed the drills and the practice sessions and the reprimands of Squire Matthias, spurring them on and forcing them to perfect their skills. He never doubted that one day he would be a knight and charge forth into battle at the side of his king. Now it appeared as if he was going to be a penniless clerk for the rest of his dying days.

Count Stephen-Henry had opened another world to him. The count was unlike any of the warrior knights of Cerdic's childhood. The count seemed the most content when working on the management of his holdings. Perhaps he would have been happier as a merchant or even as a trader traveling to the farthest reaches of the known world.

Screaming and shouting ahead of him knocked Cerdic out of his reverie. He raised his head and noticed a commotion a few hundred yards ahead of him alongside the stream. People ran up and down along the embankment, yelling and pointing. He spurred his horse forward.

"What's going on here?" he asked a burly set man who was lounging on the shore and chewing on a twig, evidently not interested in helping or running around like the others.

The man took the twig out of his mouth and spit on the ground. "The mill wheel got stuck."

Cerdic dismounted.

"Don't do that," several women shouted. "Don't. Jean is fetching the steward."

"If we wait for Jean to get the steward, we'll be here all day, and no grain will get ground," a young voice flung back at the women. "We have to find out what's causing the blockage." Amazed, Cerdic watched a girl kick off her shoes and pull off her tunic, leaving just a shift. Then she stood on her toes, lifted her arms, and leaped into the stream in as neat a dive as any he had ever seen.

Everybody fell silent, watching as the girl disappeared in the murky water next to the mill wheel.

Hastily, Cerdic stripped down to his hose and leaped into the stream. He came up sputtering and cursing. He had forgotten to close his mouth and nose, and scum and mud along with water had washed into every orifice. Then he took a gulp of air and dove again near the wheel. Blindly, he fumbled for it and encountered a soft body that struggled when he tried to grab it. Frustrated and afraid of running out of breath, he resurfaced, only to see a head pop up next to him. He could hardly see her face because her hair had come loose and was obscuring it like floating weeds. Behind them, the wheel was groaning and beginning to turn.

The girl spit out water and flicked her hair away from her face. "What were you trying to do?" she screamed. "Are you insane?" She waded to the shore and scrambled up the steep embankment, dragging a large rag-like thing after her. Several hands from above reached out to pull her up.

"I was only trying to help," Cerdic grumbled, feeling thoroughly disgruntled as he made his way onto dry land.

On top, the girl held up a piece of sacking. "This was stuck in the gears of the wheel," she announced to all who had watched. She shivered. "I told you we shouldn't wait for Jean. Now everybody can get back to work."

Cerdic shook himself to dry off. Nobody paid any attention to him. He pulled on his tunic and then sat on the ground, waiting for his feet to dry. The mill wheel was turning steadily. Water dripped off its spokes as it came up and went back down; after a while, he found the sound of it soothing, and his sense of disgruntlement lifted.

"I am sorry I shouted at you." A small voice behind him made him look around. "I know you were trying to help. I got frightened, and when I get frightened, I get angry." The girl stood there, with an apron wrapped around her shoulders like a blanket. She had tied her wet hair back so he could see her face.

"Cherry pits," Cerdic exclaimed. "I recognize you. Your name is Giselle. You spit cherry pits at me when I rode through here last summer."

The girl flushed. "Well, I don't do that anymore. I was still a child then." She sat down next to Cerdic on the embankment. Together they studied the wheel's progress, inexorably going round and round. In the distance, they heard shouts of farmers eager to have their grain ground.

Cerdic studied her from the side. He wondered how old she was. Eleven or twelve? She still was slight and not much taller than the waif he remembered, but she acted as if she were a fully grown woman. "So why didn't you want to wait for the steward?"

"Wait for the steward? Are you joking?" Giselle shook her head. "He spends most of his time sleeping or drinking ale. Besides, he curses at me when I ask him to do something. Often it's easier if I handle it myself."

"But what about your father?"

"He isn't well," Giselle responded curtly.

"And your mother?"

"She's gone. She died when I was five."

"Oh, I am sorry."

"Don't be. I don't remember her." The girl jumped up, clearly uncomfortable now and unwilling to talk. "I better go. I have things to do."

Cerdic was watching her run off when a woman came up to him with a hunk of *meslin*, bread made from wheat and rye.

"Here, eat this before you continue on your way."

"Thank you." Cerdic was suddenly ravenous. He broke off a piece and chewed on it while he pondered whether to ask this woman about Giselle. Why would someone so young be doing the work of taking care of an estate? But he let it go. It wasn't any of his business. He'd better be on his way. He looked forward to getting back to Blois.

Then everything changed.

MARRIAGE

All these are goods, on account of which marriage is a good; offspring, faith, sacrament. Saint Augustine, *De Bono Conjugali (Of The Good Of Marriage).*

1132 MARCIGNY ABBEY

"How do you know all this?" Adelaide was amazed at these revelations. "How do you know what Cerdic was thinking?"

The young novice had become fond of Lady Adela in the last months and looked forward to the time spent with her. Today she had brought up a tray of bunches of dried lavender. To her delight, Lady Adela had told her to bring her work to her cell. They sat near the open window and stripped the flower heads of the twigs. The scent enveloped everything, and Adelaide loved the dusty feel on her fingers.

"Oh, he told me later when we were friends again."

"Why? What do you mean? I thought you had been friends." Surprised, Adelaide watched the lady strip the lavender twigs with calm efficiency, as if she had worked with her hands all her life.

"Yes, but after my marriage, everything changed for a while, and we were like strangers."

"Did you like being married?" Adelaide asked shyly.

"Oh, yes," the lady said. "Perhaps not at first. My mother had given me some treatises to read about marriage and about my responsibilities to my husband that I found upsetting. Initially, I thought marriage would be like being sent from the confinement of the abbey school in Caen to another kind of confinement. I felt trammeled. Also, I didn't care much for what St. Augustine had to say about marriage and about bringing children into the world as one of its main goals. My mother explained what he meant by attempts to end a pregnancy and how evil that was. So, I was frightened. But that changed soon."

The lady had a dreamy expression on her face.

Adelaide was silent. This diminutive, elderly woman, sitting contentedly by the open window, a bowl of fragrant lavender in front of her and gently rubbing bits of flower heads between her fingers, was the daughter of a king and the sister of two kings. In her own right, she had managed a huge dominion for years when her husband was away and then again after his death.

Could I ask her to tell me more about her marriage? She couldn't possibly ask what it was like to be married to a man so much older than herself, almost forty by the time he brought home his young bride. She shivered. Would her grandmother arrange for her to marry an old man if she refused to become a nun? Adelaide shook herself. Until now, it hadn't occurred to her to question why she had sent her here. She had obeyed, thinking her grandmother would want her to take the veil. Now she wasn't sure anymore.

The lady gazed at the dust motes lit up by the afternoon sunlight and resumed her tale.

1082 BLOIS

Cerdic watched Adela ride into Blois at the side of her husband in the spring of 1082.

She rode confidently, her hands steady on the reins, and her head held high, her dark blue long woolen mantle sweeping behind her like a flag. She nodded graciously at people waving as they moved through the street toward the castle gate. Inside the courtyard, the women sank into deep curtsies, and the men bowed.

Frozen, his face blank, Cerdic forgot to bow. Then Adela saw him. She inclined her head, glancing at him from beneath her lowered eyelids with an odd, secretive little smile.

Count Stephen-Henry frowned, evidently surprised by his young assistant's impolite behavior.

Hastily, Cerdic bowed, and the moment passed. The young bride and her husband entered the castle.

At Blois under Count Stephen-Henry's informal tutelage, Cerdic had learned so much, not least about a whole world far beyond the borders of Count Stephen-Henry's holdings. He knew that.

However, being there and watching Adela day in and day out was a peculiar form of torture. He hadn't realized how important she had become for him until she appeared in Blois. As the wife of one of the most important men in France, she should have been as far from his thoughts as if she were across the seas in another land. In Blois, he saw her almost every day, certainly more often than during their childhood in Caen. He heard her voice in the hall and wanted to turn around and make his escape. Of course, when she smiled at him, he was drawn back in.

Over the next months, Cerdic avoided Adela as much as he could. He was glad of any assignments that took him away from

Blois. Of course, he couldn't avoid her altogether. Often, when he entered the great hall to speak to Count Stephen-Henry, she was there, sitting in a comfortable chair near the fire. He heard her when she came running down the wide stone stairs, calling for her husband. He marveled at the ease with which she had settled into her new role, given orders to her lady's maid and servants in a clear, firm voice. Perhaps she enjoyed being able to do so; at Caen, the only ones giving orders were her father and her mother.

She was happy. It puzzled him. Count Stephen-Henry was so much older. But he was delighted with his young wife. Of course, for a woman of Adela's status, marriage was all about alliances. Cerdic knew that, but it didn't help at all.

Sometimes, when he watched Adela's enthusiasm and interest, he remembered her in Caen, with her high voice challenging everyone with constant questions. Her father showed remarkable patience with the little girl. "Why can't I have a peregrine?" Adela had complained to Cerdic in her high, sibilant voice. "And you are training with a lanner. It's not right." She had stamped her feet. Her father, who had overheard this, said sternly, "Peregrines are for princes, dukes, and earls, not for cheeky young girls like you."

Her glowing eyes when the count pulled out his maps and precious manuscripts made Cerdic forget her altered status. She was curious about everything from the king of France to the role of the local clergy, trade, and even wine making. She wanted to know about the holdings that were part of his estate, tracing them on the map: Châteaudun, Provins, Sancerre, Meaux, and Reims. Eventually, Count Stephen-Henry would also be Count of Chartres and Blois. For now, his father, Theobald III, held those titles even though he had passed the administration of these holdings on to his son already in 1074, preferring to spend his final years in prayer and contemplation.

"Why do you need to know all this?" Count Stephen-Henry rubbed his eyes, pushing a stack of documents away from him and tossing the quill onto the desk. He and Cerdic had been working all morning, trying to work out a solution to an unpleasant dispute with a metals merchant who had been complaining about the new bridge duties and had threatened to take his goods elsewhere.

"How can I learn if I don't ask?" Adela stared at him as if surprised by the question. "Anyway, I like it. You want me to worry about wall hangings and how to keep moths out of our bedding and what to do with overripe medlars?" She laughed. "But I better go and see about some of those moths. I will see you at the midday meal, my lord." She sketched an exaggerated curtsy and ran off, still laughing.

Count Stephen smiled at Cerdic. "Women," he said with a sigh, but he beamed. He sniffed the air, redolent of the smells from the kitchen. "Ah, stuffed swan with yellow pepper sauce," he muttered appreciatively.

For an instant, Cerdic was flooded with affection for this man, so kind and loving and generous and with such childlike enjoyment of the pleasures of life.

"Would you believe what happened the other day?"

Cerdic shook his head, uncomfortable and unhappy once again. If only this man weren't married to Adela.

"Well, my young bride came to me and told me something about the Abbey of St. Laumer that I hadn't known. It took her no more than a few weeks to worm it out of a couple of clerics who had visited Blois."

It involved a piece of land that the abbey had claimed. The abbey had used it as an orchard, but for reasons they couldn't understand, the fruit trees failed to thrive. Some people claimed it was bewitched. Nobody knew what to do. Rumors were already beginning to spread, but nobody had bothered to tell the count.

"I think they were ashamed to tell me. But my lady immediately saw through the fog of this story. 'Find out how the abbey acquired the land,' she told me. 'Maybe they need to do something for the original owner. Once that is settled, all will be well.' She was right; the abbey had not been fair to the owner. She has an uncanny ability to learn about people; this was not the first time that she presented me with a problem to be solved."

"My lord, would you excuse me?" Cerdic found he could no longer listen to this. "I want to get on the road."

"Oh, yes, of course. I forgot. You are leaving for Paris today. God speed."

Mothers And Daughters

You should know, dearest daughter, with what love we receive this and whatever gifts we may obtain from you. What more are gold or gems, the precious things of this world that I might expect from you, than a chaste life, the distribution of your things to the poor, the love of God and your fellows? We pray your nobility that we shall obtain these and similar gifts from you, that you love simply and wholly, that you obtain what you love and never lose what you have. With these and similar weapons arm your husband, when God gives you the opportunity, and do not cease to do so.
A letter from Pope Gregory VII to Matilda, Duchess of Normandy and Queen of England, 1080.

1083 Blois

The fire in the large hearth of the great hall had been lit, and Adela was glad of it even though it was summer.

It had been thundering and raining all day. She shivered and drew her shawl firmly around her.

She missed Stephen-Henry. He had told her that he would be in Paris for a few weeks. She could not have imagined two years ago that it would be like this. Matilda had told her all about the sanctity of marriage but hadn't said anything about it being enjoyable. Of course, the first night had been strange and uncomfortable, but Stephen-Henry had been gentle and patient. But then, soon, Adela had begun to relax. *I enjoy it*, she thought with amazement, not entirely sure whether she was committing a sin in doing so. *Oh, how I miss Stephen-Henry coming to me from a long ride into the country, sweaty and smelling of horse and full of energy. I crave his arms around me in the mornings when the first gray dawn rises over the ramparts. I don't think this was what Augustine meant when he talked of the infusion of the soul that was a mystery known to God alone. But it is wonderful.*

Adela thought of her mother's words shortly before her marriage. *Do you want to be able to do things in your life? Important things? To help make life better for people? Then you need the position and the wealth to do it.*

Her mother had been right. Adela was determined to do everything in her power to make these words come true. There was so much she needed to learn, but oh, how she enjoyed her new freedom. Here, she could give orders when she didn't like something. At first, Stephen-Henry had laughed when she asked him questions. *Now he even listens to me. Sometimes I hear more about what is going on than he does. I knew full well that for my husband, the alliance with the Norman king was an enhancement of his own power. For me, it opened up a new world.*

But then, why did she feel so restless lately? Why did she feel like weeping?

Adela eyed the bowl of soup that a servant had brought for her with misgiving. "Try it, my lady," the servant said. "You haven't been eating much in the last few days."

"Thank you, Cateline." Adela tried to smile at the older woman. She dipped her spoon into the broth. It was her favorite—leeks and fish, flavored with ginger. The pungent steam rose into her nostrils. Then she dropped the spoon into the bowl and gagged. Almost falling over, she lurched toward the hearth and found herself throwing up right into the flames.

Exhausted, she wiped her mouth on her sleeve and turned around to find the older woman looking at her with an expression of satisfaction on her face.

"What?" Adela snapped, enraged at this lack of sympathy.

"Have you felt like this before?"

"Yes, a few times, and I have been so tired. I don't know what's wrong with me. But I am fine now."

"Yes, indeed, you are, my lady. You are expecting."

"Expecting?"

"Yes. You are going to have a baby."

"A baby?" Adela sank into the chair. Her mother hadn't told her about this or what to expect. She smiled. "My lord will be so pleased."

Now that she knew what was happening, the nausea of the last weeks began to disappear. At times, she was flooded with pure elation and a sense of pride that made her want to sing out loud, and then, in an instant, fear of the future overwhelmed her. She dreaded the childbirth, and she feared for the baby's health. Even worse, she worried whether she would be a good mother. But gradually her fears faded and her happiness warmed her when she stitched small clothes, had a carpenter prepare a cradle, and thought of names for her son, because, of course, her first-born would be a son.

Adela had written to her mother, but hadn't heard back from her. Maybe she had gone to England with the king, and the news of the baby hadn't reached her yet.

Several months later, when the messenger from Caen rode into the castle of Blois, tired and dusty after the long ride, he had to wait in the courtyard for a long time. A servant finally led him to the great hall where Count Stephen-Henry took the message from him without a word. The count's eyes were bloodshot, and his hands shook when he opened the sealed packet and perused the contents. "Get some rest before you head back," he said to the messenger. "I will give you a letter to take back tomorrow."

Adela didn't know a messenger had come until he was already gone. She was lying on her bed, surrounded by servants and a healer who had been called in during the night. She hardly moved, while a girl kept placing fresh wet rags on her forehead. Her belly was flat under the sheet. Everything hurt. A pile of sodden sheets and towels lay on the floor. Candles lit the room, but they could not hide the metallic scent of blood.

"Where is the baby?" a weak voice from the bed startled the healer who had turned to leave the room.

"Oh, my lady, we have taken it to the chapel."

"Was it a girl?" Adela asked in a whisper.

"No, a son." The old woman sighed. She straightened the blanket that covered Adela. "You are strong. You'll have many more."

Adela didn't respond. Her eyes were closed.

"Now you must rest. You had a bad fever. But you'll feel better soon."

"Can I see my lady?" Count Stephen-Henry stood at the door.

"Yes, my lord. But remember, she needs her rest."

The old woman withdrew, taking a bundle of soiled linen with her. Stephen-Henry glanced at the wreck of the room, not entirely disguised by the dim light from the candles. Adela was propped up on pillows. He sat down next to her and took her hand.

"My dear, you have been ill. But they tell me you will recover quickly."

Adela squeezed her eyes shut, but couldn't prevent the tears rolling down her cheeks.

"Oh, my dear." Stephen-Henry sighed. "The Lord gives and the Lord takes. I am sure you'll have many healthy children." He still held her hand securely in his own. "But now I must tell you some news that will grieve you. A messenger has come from Caen."

Adela raised her head. She clung to her husband's hands as he told her.

Her mother had died. The only one of her children who got there in time was Sister Cecilia. As a sister in the Abbey of Sainte-Trinité at Caen, Cecilia didn't have to contend with arduous travel.

"I am glad my sister was with her. She will have comforted her," Adela whispered. She put her head down again and closed her eyes. Stephen looked at her wan face and then quietly left the room.

Adela recovered quickly, just as the old woman healer had predicted. But she was quieter than before.

It snowed early in December, and Emma ran around in the courtyard, raising her hands to the sky to catch snowflakes. When she slipped on the flagstones and fell onto a mound of snow, she giggled. Count Stephen-Henry, who was walking past on his way to the stables, picked the girl up and tickled her until she shrieked with laughter.

Adela watched from the door and then quietly walked back inside.

That's when Cerdic came upon her when he entered the great hall. Perched on a bench near the fireplace, Adela was hunched over, her face obscured, and her shoulders shaking.

Cerdic sat down next to her and slung an arm around her shoulders.

Adela leaned into him, comforted by his warmth and glad that the feeling of distance that had grown between them in the last years since her marriage had lifted. He didn't say anything.

After a while, Adela stopped sobbing. She sat up and dried her face with a scrap of linen stuck in her belt. "Normally, that little girl doesn't bother me," she muttered. "But right now, when I see Stephen-Henry give her leather leads used for his hounds to chew, it makes me want to scream."

"I am sorry about the queen," Cerdic said. "She was always kind to me." He still had his arm around her shoulder.

"I heard that my father swore to give up hunting to express his grief." Adela placed the linen scrap on her knee, flattened it, turned it around, and flattened it again. Without looking at Cerdic, she whispered, "I wonder whether Stephen-Henry would give up anything if I were to die."

"When you were lying in bed with a fever, everything stopped in the castle," Cerdic said in a low tone. "Count Stephen-Henry spent all the time in his room, constantly sending servants up to ask after you. When he called me in to take care of the messenger from Caen, his eyes were bloodshot, and he hadn't slept in days."

Adela tilted her head and glanced at him from underneath her half-closed eyelids. Then she sat up straight, and Cerdic lowered his arm. With that small shift, she reasserted her position as lady of the manor, reestablishing some distance between them. Then she grinned at him. "So, what do I hear about certain ladies chasing you?"

"It's nothing," Cerdic mumbled, his face red. He rose. "I need to go."

Adela watched him walk out and smiled. His lanky frame and unruly hair that curled over his collar made her think of home and those easy days when he and Henry had been laughing with her in the mews.

She resumed her regular visits to the chapel, something that she had neglected during her illness. She prayed for her father. When she could bear thinking about it, she prayed for the baby now buried in the cemetery of the Abbaye Saint-Laumer de Blois. Stephen-Henry told her that he had placed a small wooden toy horse alongside the tiny body to keep it company. She cried when she heard this.

Now that she was well again, she returned to reading, reviewing reports, and writing letters. Shortly before her mother died, she had sent Adela yet another packet of texts for her to read, never tiring of trying to educate her daughter. Adela read the accompanying letter her mother had written to her and laughed and cried at the same time. *She is still lecturing me from beyond the grave. Really? What do I care about this monk Reichenau and his astrolabe? Or about the Benedictine Anselm of Bec?*

Adela remembered a time in her mother's chamber when Matilda had tried to convince her to read the good abbot's writings. Adela had nodded obediently and glanced at the treatise her mother had pressed into her hand. Then she shook her head in frustration. "But I don't even understand the title." She pointed at the word *Proslogion*. "Do you want me to read this?"

Matilda smiled at her daughter. "Don't worry; you will eventually understand." She leafed through the other manuscripts on her desk. "Actually, I prefer this one; it's called *Monologian*, and he argues that the existence of God can be demonstrated not only through faith but through reason. I like that; I like reason."

Adela blinked and grimaced when she heard this. It had never occurred to her to question the existence of God. She shivered, wondering whether she would have to mention this during her next confession.

Now, three years after this conversation, Adela remembered and laughed at herself. Then she sighed. Oh, how she wished she could talk to her mother once more. What would Matilda have said about

Anselm's arguments about free will as a choice to do good, not to gain a benefit from it, but for its own sake? Did she, Adela, have free will? Would her mother have talked to her father about this? Unlikely. Her father didn't read, and he wasn't prone to reflection. Would Stephen be willing to talk to her about these writings? Sometimes her husband laughed at her, but less frequently of late, and he listened to her.

She ran a hand over her sides and her belly and then sat up with a frown on her face, thinking hard. She had been feeling queasy and tired. Yes, she was pregnant again. She kneeled in her quiet room, her eyes on the crucifix above her blanket chest. *Please, keep him safe*. It was a boy. She was sure of it. She bowed her head in supplication. *Please, dear God, keep him safe*.

Brothers, Betrayals, And Intrigues

1084

"Where is Count Stephen-Henry?"

The messenger was out of breath and disheveled. He swayed and held onto the mantle above the fireplace to keep himself from falling. "Excuse me." He sketched a bow. "I have ridden for two days to reach Blois in time."

"I see." Adela frowned. "I am sorry to tell you that my lord is away." Adela leaned back, unable to suppress a sigh. She was close to her time, and it was hard to find a comfortable position. "How can we help you?" She waited expectantly. Clearly, his manners had gotten lost along the way. What did that young man see when he looked at her? Since her marriage, she had begun to enjoy her new status and had acquired many elegant gowns. Today she wore a dove-gray robe over her underdress, trimmed with dark-blue velvet. Her hair was coiled in a braid underneath her wimple. Perhaps all he saw was a young woman and a pregnant one at that. He seemed reluctant to speak, and yet evidently his message was urgent. How could she reassure him? "And you are…" she added delicately, raising her eyebrows.

"Oh, pardon. François de Bourcq. I come from Châteauneuf-en-Thymerais."

Adela kept her face blank. Her brother Robert had sought refuge with Hugh of Châteauneuf-en-Thymerais during the time of his rebellion against their father.

"It is urgent that I speak to Count Stephen-Henry," the messenger repeated.

"I regret that this won't be possible. My lord is in consultation with King Phillip. He won't be returning until next week. He left me with full authority to act on his behalf." Adela spoke sharply. "Who sent you?"

The messenger bit his lip. "My lady, I have been asked to deliver this message without revealing the sender's name. Meanwhile, it is of utmost importance also to your brother, Duke Robert."

Adela frowned. "And this mysterious message pertains to what?" She wasn't particularly inclined to listen to anyone who supported Robert in his conflict with her father, but decided to wait to hear what this man would tell her.

"The sender has become aware of a plot against your two brothers, Lord Henry and Lord William. If it were to succeed, Duke Robert would be the first to be accused, even though he is blameless."

"Why has my father not been apprised of this?"

"The king is currently in England to collect the Danegeld that had been assessed for the defense of the realm."

"So, you are telling me that people hostile to my father and his heirs are planning to act on this by killing two and discrediting the other?"

"Exactly, my lady." The messenger straightened his posture and tried to brush back the hair that had fallen over his brow.

"Let me call in one of my husband's advisors." Adela rang a bell and directed a servant to fetch Cerdic. "I suggest that we wait to discuss the details until Sir Cerdic is with us. Allow me to offer you some wine."

Within minutes, the messenger found himself answering many questions about his home.

Adela tried to hide her amusement at his evident discomfort with her familiarity with matters of trade. Prodded by her comments, he reluctantly confirmed that in several parts of Thymerais there were efforts to clear the forests so that the land could be used for growing grain. "Of course, we also import fine wood for building from northern regions and ship it south."

"Yes, we received some of that timber being transported along the Loire." Adela wrinkled her brow. "You might want to have a talk with your suppliers. The quality of the wood left a lot to be desired. Meanwhile, I believe the region also has a source of iron."

"Indeed." The messenger coughed, having gulped down the wine too hastily. Just then, a tall man entered the hall.

"Allow me to introduce Sir Cerdic of Wessex, one of my husband's trusted advisors," Adela said.

The messenger quickly turned to Cerdic.

Adela had to suppress a sigh. This man hadn't only mislaid his manners; he also exhibited the typical demeanor of men in situations like this, relieved when there was a man he could talk to. Would it be always thus whenever she was acting without her husband by her side? "Sir Cerdic," she said loudly, secretly gratified by Cerdic's impeccable deep bow. "This man," she stopped briefly to show that she didn't intend any unnecessary politeness, "has come with a message for us of some urgency." Quickly and succinctly, she told Cerdic the gist of the message.

"You don't have much time," François de Bourcq now interjected. "Lord William and Lord Henry are on their way to Rouen, and from there, they plan to travel to Le Havre."

"Why didn't you go directly to Rouen?" Cerdic asked. "Why waste time coming here to Blois?"

"They would not have believed a message coming from a supporter of Robert." The man frowned; he clearly thought Cerdic was a fool. "They would have assumed it was a trap."

"And you are telling me it's not a trap?" Cerdic raised his eyebrows. "Someone unnamed found out about a plot planned by someone else unnamed to damage a ship in such a way that it would sink while making the journey to England. And all this trouble to eliminate two sons of King William and discredit the third? Likely story. Besides, even if it's just talk, sharing it with William and Henry will hardly help to endear Robert to them any further."

François de Bourcq stood up, glaring at him. "I rode through the night to get here," he hissed. "I am not here to deceive anyone."

"This is not the time for further debate," Adela interjected. "Sir Cerdic, we owe Sir de Bourcq our gratitude, and if this warning comes to us in a roundabout way from a supporter of my brother Robert, we owe our gratitude to that man as well. And now, we need to act and not waste any more time."

ON THE ROAD AGAIN

A few hours later, Cerdic was on the road north.

He had chosen the fittest horse he could find. If he pushed, alternating between trotting and cantering, he might cover much of the distance in two days. In Chartres, he could change horses. It was summer, and it was warm. He rode into the evening and through the night. His sword was in his sheath, tied behind his saddle, but he could reach it quickly if someone was foolish enough to attack him.

As the dark settled around him and the crickets kept him company, his thoughts went around and around. Once again, here he was tasked with something on behalf of King William, even if only indirectly. He kept getting drawn into the affairs of the Normans. All his life. For a while, he had felt a sense of release when serving Count Stephen-Henry. No longer the little urchin, dragged across the water and treated with charity by the same people at whose hands his father had died. No, here in Blois, he had become a trusted advisor.

Then Adela had appeared, a glowing young bride, and Cerdic's contentment vanished. He thought that with time, it would get easier. Instead, with every passing day, it was harder. He asked the count for as many assignments away from Blois as was possible. It didn't help.

When he watched her give orders and query people far older than her about their actions, he didn't know her at all anymore. Then again, maybe that's who she'd always been. He had just been blind to it.

Now Adela wanted him to do this. How could he say no? The trap had closed upon him once more.

That day in the great hall, when he had come upon Adela crying, her face still pale and thin after her illness, he thought there would be nothing he wouldn't do for her. Would it always be like that? Would he ever get used to this lurching from estrangement and resentment to complete familiarity and friendship to the wrenching feeling of fierce protectiveness?

By the time he reached Rouen, he was too tired to think. A wild boar that appeared on the path in the dusk had spooked his horse. Now it limped, and he had to walk it for several miles until he reached Dreux. He left the horse there so that it might rest, and he had to beg and plead for another; that one turned out to be a plodding old nag, a bay gelding that liked to turn his head to bite his rider's feet. It took a while to establish a modicum of peace between horse and rider, but this did little for their speed. A night and a day and most of the next night had passed by the time he arrived at the castle, where he hoped to find William and Henry.

"Oh, no, they left already about two hours ago," a servant told him.

Cerdic cursed. "Let me have a fit and fast horse. It is of utmost importance that I reach them."

Within minutes, a horse was being readied, while Cerdic downed some ale and a piece of bread. The raw-boned gelding looked at him balefully, clearly not pleased at being dragged out of his stall. "He doesn't like things come at him from the left," the servant warned him. "But he is sturdy and fast."

Fortunately, the roads between Rouen and Le Havre were good. Some stretches were stone paved and cambered for drainage. It was not as exhausting as riding along muddy roads with holes and ruts horses could easily trip over and hurt their legs. He decided to stay north of the Seine and head for Lillebonne. Part of that road led through a densely wooded region, where he cantered, pushing his horse as much as he dared.

Cerdic had been in Lillebonne once when King William had asked him to come along on a visit to the town. During Roman times, it had been an administrative, military, and commercial center, well connected to the surrounding region by an extensive network of Roman roads. Then it had fallen into neglect, and the king had done much to restore it to its former glory. Proudly, he had pointed out the remnants of the Roman baths and the amphitheater to Cerdic, who was more interested in the many watermills along the river Bolbec that flowed through the town.

In Lillebonne, Cerdic caught up with William and Henry. When he reached the cobblestones of the road leading into town, a group of knights were riding ahead of him, with a few squires in attendance, and he spurred his horse forward.

One turned around at the sound of a horse thundering behind them. "William, look," he shouted. "It's Cerdic."

Cerdic was badly winded when he reached them and pulled up his horse.

William hadn't changed much since he last saw him. Now a young man of about 27 years, he was heavier, but he still had the same lanky reddish shock of hair that escaped from underneath his helmet and a reserved, almost supercilious expression on his face, as if bored with life. Cerdic recognized that look; he had seen it often enough when he watched the brothers interact.

Henry had been a boy when Cerdic left Caen. Now, he was a young man, slightly stocky and strong. Henry had spent some time at the Salisbury Cathedral to further his education. He sat on his horse with ease, holding the reins loosely in one hand and guiding the horse with his legs as he waved at Cerdic. His face still had the narrow cast and intent look of a young monk. The other pages had sometimes teased him, calling him 'master scholar' or 'master abbot.' But now he was beaming. "What are you doing here, Cerdic? I thought you were in Blois."

"I was until the day before yesterday." Cerdic glanced around; the other knights and squires had pulled up. "Could we talk in private?"

William narrowed his eyes. Then he nodded and dismounted. A few moments later, the two brothers and Cerdic stood in the shade of a large willow tree at the shore of the river; its branches drooped over the embankment into the water. Henry was flicking the brown capsules into the water.

"Well, Cerdic? What's so important?" William asked brusquely. "We are supposed to reach Le Havre by midday. Ships and tides wait for no man."

"That's exactly why I am here. Your sister sent me." Cerdic then recounted the tale told by François de Bourcq. First, he rushed his words, irked by the quizzical expression on William's face. Then he slowed down. They would listen to him if he spoke calmly and firmly.

"So, let me see if I got this right," William drawled. "An unnamed person sent an equally unnamed messenger—yes, I noticed that you didn't name him—to warn us about an unknown person trying to sabotage the ship on which Henry and I are planning to travel to England. And to add spice to this tale, the unnamed individual is doing so because successful sabotage would not only remove us as possible contenders for the throne, but it would also damage our dear brother Robert's reputation even further." He glanced at his brother. "It sounds convoluted to me. Does it sound convoluted to you, Henry?"

"Yes, indeed." Henry picked up a dry branch from the ground and chucked it into the stream. "Actually, too convoluted for someone to have simply made it up. I think we should take this warning seriously."

"Well, now it gets interesting. Cerdic tells us there is someone on the ship who has arranged for its foundering and for a rescue boat to show up in time to rescue said individual, but alas, no one else. So, Henry, can you apply your undoubted acumen to this puzzle. Who among our people might do this?"

Henry grimaced. "With any certainty? No. I am afraid that there are quite a few who might welcome such an accident. It won't be easy to find out who in this case." He pondered and then added: "How about the one who seems most eager to get us 'to church', so to speak, most eager to make sure we don't miss the tide?"

William clapped his younger brother on the shoulder. "Excellent suggestion. Let's do that. And what about you, Cerdic?"

"I will return to Blois." He had done his duty. The brothers had been warned and seemed well-prepared to meet the challenge. It was not his place to learn on whom their suspicion had landed. After a brief rest, he began the return journey south.

Lime Trees

Faith, hope, charity, justice, strength, moderation, and loyalty.
Virtues of a knight as per Ramon Llull,
The Order of Chivalry, 13th century.

1085

"He looks small." Cerdic peered at the bundle in Adela's arms from a cautious distance. The tiny face in its nest of white linens was red and scrunched up as if about to explode. He wrinkled his nose at the baby scent, a mix of milk and something faintly putrid, pungent, and sweet all at once.

"Well, of course, he is small." Adela smiled at the red face. "He is a baby." The little creature was now making spitting noises. She had named him William in honor of her father. Would he take after his namesake?

Cerdic gazed down at Adela. This latest transformation from ripe young woman to mother was disconcerting.

"Excuse me, my lady. My lord is awaiting me in the courtyard." Cerdic sketched a bow and walked out of the great hall.

"Isn't she gorgeous?" Count Stephen-Henry asked Cerdic when he joined him in the courtyard. The count was inspecting a young gray mare. "I think my lady will love her." He was beaming.

Cerdic smiled. That's all the count had been doing over the last weeks. Every single visitor had to listen to him brag about his infant son. And he showered Adela with gifts that seemed to arrive at the castle almost by the hour. It was a good thing that he was one of the wealthiest men in France. Otherwise, his coffers would be empty in no time.

"But come, Cerdic. I want to talk to you." The count walked across the courtyard toward the shade along the wall leading to the kitchen garden. "My lady and I have been giving some thought to how to do right by you in gratitude for your service."

Cerdic stood straighter. "I am honored to serve you, my lord."

"Now, we have learned that the king is planning to knight his son Henry early next year, once he has completed his military training with Robert Achard." The count scrutinized his young protégé to make sure he was listening. "So, your time has come as well, and we will do the ceremony after mass on Sunday."

"Thank you, my lord." Cerdic felt his cheeks burn.

"There is something else," Count Stephen-Henry said. "There is some land in my holding that's been vacant and neglected for years. I had granted the holding to a knight who sadly fell ill and died without issue."

Cerdic was breathing faster; he clenched his hands behind his back.

"This land is close to Blois. You will have your work cut out to make it profitable again and to turn the manor into a habitable place. But it gives you a start." The count paused and waited for Cerdic to say something, but Cerdic had temporarily lost his power of speech.

"Of course, we don't want to lose you." The count smiled at him. "I rely on you to continue your duties here."

Cerdic no longer heard anything at all. His own land. And he would be a knight.

A few weeks later, he rode north. The count had granted him some time. "It borders on land that belongs to a friend of mine," the count had told him when he handed some documents with his signature, testifying to the land grant, the so-called *beneficium*. "It's called Les Tilleuls, but that's about all I know."

"Les Tilleuls," Cerdic kept repeating, trying to picture stands of lime trees.

"Their sweet blossoms are wonderful for honey." A cleric in Blois had told him about these trees. "They are good trees, with sturdy branches, so pleasantly rounded that they look as if they had been pruned."

Cerdic rode through the luscious landscape, lost in a dream. He imagined sitting on a stone bench in front of the manor and sipping honey wine made from his own honey.

Then his horse stumbled on the badly maintained path, and he sobered up. The last wisps of his fanciful vision fled when he reached the manor. Half of it was blackened, and the roof of that section had caved in. The courtyard was filled with debris. Several piglets sat in the corner near a trough filled with kitchen waste, blinking in the sunshine. Shouldn't pigs be in pens? The stable entrance appeared in better shape than the house.

"Anybody here?" Cerdic shouted.

A man walked out into the courtyard, rubbing his hands on his apron and blinking in the sunlight. "Sir," he said. "How can I serve you?"

Cerdic gazed at the man. He was perhaps not as old as he had thought at first, but thin and tired. Cerdic had worried about how to introduce himself. He wanted to assert his authority but not make enemies from the start. "My name is Cerdic of Wessex. I come from Blois. Count Stephen-Henry has given me a land grant. I have come to see what is needed most urgently."

The man stared at him. Then he smiled. "Finally."

"Finally?" Cerdic asked. "Were you expecting me?"

"Well, not exactly. Just someone. Someone to get things going again."

"And you are?"

"Auberi. I have been acting as a steward after the master died and the previous steward left." Auberi turned toward the stable and shouted, "Jacques." A boy with a tunic that was too short for his skinny frame came running out of the stable. "Leave your horse here. Jacques will see to it. Come inside."

For the next weeks, Cerdic and Auberi worked without a break, going over the books, riding through the fields and woods, meeting with the villeins and cottars on the estate, inspecting the manor for urgent repairs, and trying to establish a budget based on incoming rents and levies. Auberi also warned him about a free peasant whose land bordered on Les Tilleuls. "The disputes go back to the father of the previous lord."

Cerdic winced. While freshly knighted, he was hardly a lord, but he let it slide. "What disputes?"

"Oh, the usual," Auberi said. "One involved a girl raised by this peasant's family. She became *enceinte*. While there was a settlement to ensure that the young woman and her baby would be taken care of, it left a bad feeling. And then there is a large fishpond that straddles the border."

"Ah, murky borders." Cerdic sighed. "Well, I will have to pay him a visit eventually, but not now. Tread lightly for the time being. Who owns the vineyards to the south of this land?"

"Oh, Artus. He is a good man, but he isn't well. He received the land as a deed from Theobald, the father of the current count of Blois, in return for a service he performed for Count Stephen-Henry."

"Oh, I see." Someone else with whom he would have to establish good relations. Then Cerdic remembered something else. "What about beehives?"

At this, Auberi beamed. "Several villeins keep hives. I might add that our hives produce the best honey."

One of Cerdic's first decisions was to ask Auberi to serve as his steward. "Let's make it official, shall we?" he asked with a smile. "I will try to return as soon as my duties in Blois permit."

Cerdic was smiling as he rode south toward Blois. The thought of Les Tilleuls, blackened by soot and with a caved-in roof, made him happier than anything had in a long time. Skills he had acquired in Count Stephen-Henry's service had come in handy in his discussions with his steward. Auberi hadn't disguised his surprise at his new young master's incisive questions and apt suggestions for the continued management of the land. He would have to do something about the man. Would he stay with him if he gave him his freedom? Auberi was steadfast and reliable, and he had done his best in the years of uncertainty.

Les Tilleuls offered Cerdic what he had missed at Blois—a certain independence and the opportunity to work at something productive. The mere thought of the long alley lined by venerable old lime trees took away some of his sense of feeling fragmented and lost. He could build a life there. Between his duties at Blois, he knew no greater contentment than to plan all the things he wanted to do in order to bring the estate into good shape.

He couldn't wait to learn all he could about beekeeping, honey production, and the wax trade. If only his mother could see him now. One day soon, he'd go back and search for her. He'd bring her honey from Les Tilleuls. She'd caress his face with her warm, calloused hands. "I am so proud of you," she'd say. "Your father would be so proud of you, my little dragon."

PART II - TAPESTRY OF LOVE: KNOTS AND TANGLES

Sanctuary

1086 Blois

"What's going on here?"

Cerdic had been on his way to the great hall when he heard the commotion in the courtyard and rushed outside.

In front of the gate, several servants and pages surrounded a rider on a small mare. One was trying to pull the rider down.

With a vicious grunt and a clearly audible curse, the rider kicked at the page, her long braid whipping around as she pulled herself away from the grasping hands. "Get your filthy hands off me," she shouted in a surprisingly deep voice.

Cerdic knew this girl. The last time he had seen her, she had been dripping wet from diving into the stream. She didn't seem much taller, but she had clearly filled out over the last two years.

"Stop this brawling at once. Leave the lady alone," he shouted, finally jolted out of his surprise.

Several pages chuckled. "Some lady," someone muttered.

Cerdic hastened across. The servants and pages backed away and let Cerdic through. "Mistress Giselle, how can I be of assistance?" he asked, looking up at the girl's overheated face.

She frowned at him, her grip on the reins relaxed slightly. "I remember you. Cid, right?"

"Close enough." Cerdic laughed. He glanced at the roll, inexpertly tied behind the girl's saddle, and her clothes, clearly meant to hide her shape, a dark cloak with a hood, a rough brown tunic, severely belted, and serviceable boots over a dark hose. Now that the girl's flush of anger and fear was waning, her exhaustion was evident. He held out his hand to help her dismount. "Come, Giselle, you are safe here." He felt oddly protective of this strange, fierce little person. "Let's hand your horse to a servant and get you inside."

"I have come to seek succor and protection from my lord Stephen-Henry." Giselle straightened up.

"Very well. I'll take you to him."

Cerdic led the young woman to the great hall. "My lord, my lady," he said. "This is Mistress Giselle. She is asking for your aid."

"Mistress Giselle?" The count stood up and walked toward her.

"Yes, my lord." Giselle curtsied. "From the Valley of the Springs."

Cerdic's lips twitched. Given that she wasn't wearing a long gown, it looked funny.

"But of course, you are the daughter of my old friend, Artus. How is your father?"

"My lord, my father is dead." Giselle spoke with a tremor in her husky, deep voice. Her wrap had slipped down, revealing a disheveled head of dark curly hair and a thick long braid. All color had fled from her face. "That is why I am here."

"I am grieved to hear this." Count Stephen asked a servant to bring a goblet of warm spiced wine. "Come sit with us and tell us your story."

Giselle's story tumbled out of her as she gulped down the wine. Her father Artus had died several months ago in an accident. A tree limb had crashed down on him as he rode around during a storm to check on his vineyard. "He had been tired and worried about the vines, you see," she explained. "That's why he wasn't paying enough attention." Unfortunately, he had made no provisions for his daughter. As sole heir and without any protection, she was vulnerable. A neighboring landowner by the name of Clement had begun to pressure Giselle into marriage.

"Oh, I have heard of this Clement." Stephen-Henry snorted. "He doesn't have a good reputation in the county."

"Yes, he is cruel to the people on his estate. My father had warned me."

Apparently, Lord Clement had begun to be impatient and thought of ways to force the issue. Alerted by a servant that he was about to descend on her in the company of a priest, Giselle made her escape, riding without stopping until she reached Blois. "My father always spoke of you and your friendship."

"Well, of course, we are delighted to welcome you." The count patted her hand and poured more wine into her goblet.

Unexpected Peril

1132 Marcigny Abbey

"I hated her, you know," Adela told the young novice.

"You hated her? But you didn't know her at all," Adelaide exclaimed. Over the last months, she had become fond of the lady. She couldn't believe that this pious woman would have felt something like hate for anyone.

"Indeed, I did," Adela said.

Blois 1086

Adela had her needlepoint work on her lap and was struggling with a thread that had gotten entangled when Cerdic entered the great hall in the wake of a strange young woman.

Puzzled, she gazed at the small person, dressed like a man, with an old tunic and worn boots, splattered with mud. The hood of her cloak had slipped down, revealing her unkempt dark hair and a thick long braid.

But that wasn't what had caught Adela's eye. Cerdic stood next to this stranger, his tall frame sheltering her, and his hand holding on to her arm supportively. Adela narrowed her eyes.

Cerdic belonged to her. He was her friend. Of course, she knew about the court ladies' interest in him. Her maid told her all the gossip. But it hadn't bothered her. Court ladies come and go. So why was she bothered by this waif?

Then there was Stephen-Henry's cordial reception of this odd guest. True, he knew the girl's father, but did he have to be so charming? She shook her head to clear the thoughts from her mind and stood. It was time to take control of this situation.

"Come, Mistress Giselle, I'll show you where you can rest. You must be weary from your journey."

After Adela got the young girl settled, she returned to her own chamber. Gratefully, she sank into her favorite chair. Her last pregnancy had worn her out more than she had anticipated. A maid had straightened her bed and laid a tray with wine and some bread on the table. *Why do I feel so sad?* The young woman's arrival and Cerdic's apparent familiarity with her had unsettled Adela as if it augured the end of something.

Just the other day, Count Stephen-Henry had berated her about Cerdic. She still got angry when she remembered his words.

"Your father, the king, sent Cerdic to me to become my squire, and he has served admirably in that role, I might add." Her husband looked at her sternly. He had never spoken to her like that before. "That doesn't give you the right to send him here and there as if he were your personal servant."

"It was in your interest that I sent him. You know how important Lavardin will be in the future. It is important to send someone in person to talk to them." Adela sat straight, her voice raised slightly. "I certainly don't employ anyone as 'my personal servant.' But I see your point and will check with you in the future."

"Very well, my dear."

Count Stephen-Henry was loath to fight. Adela knew this. But she was angry. Her father, acting upon her mother's advice, had sent Cerdic here so she would have a friend nearby, someone from her childhood, someone she could trust. She hadn't done anything wrong. Still, she would need to be more careful in the future.

A New World

"Here is your apartment. It's not much, but it will have to do for now." Adela waved casually at the large chamber. "Of course, you'll stay with us for the time being. You can tell me all about your home tomorrow." And then she left, cool and composed, very much the lady of the manor for all that she looked hardly older than Giselle.

Left alone, Giselle gazed at the platform on which rested a large featherbed with a bolster and a soft woolen coverlet. A heavy, deep red fabric hanging from the bed frame on three sides made the bed look like a separate chamber. There was a stool, covered with needlepoint. Someone had brought up her roll with her belongings, leaving it on top of an oak trunk. Stained and worn after years of use by her father, it didn't belong in this elegant setting.

At home, her bed was a pallet on the floor, with the stuffing flattened from long use and a threadbare covering. Giselle sighed. She missed the familiar sounds from the stable and the farmyard. Most of all, she missed her hound. She had left him with Thomas and Maria. They promised to take good care of him. She missed the snorting sounds he made when he slept. She even missed his musty scent when he was warm and dry and comfortably rolled up on his old blanket in the kitchen. When would she go home again? How would Thomas handle the harvest? She had promoted him to steward after his perennially drunk predecessor had died. She could trust him, but still she worried. Then she pictured Count Clement, large and corpulent, stomping through the manor, raging and fuming at her absence, his bloated red face with spittle in the corners of his mouth. She shivered. He had left her no choice.

Suddenly, Giselle was overcome with exhaustion. At least, here she didn't have to be afraid of Count Clement bearing down on her. And her father's steward had promised that he would look after everything while she was away.

Over the next days, she became more familiar with the castle.

Count Stephen-Henry spent some time with her going over details of the estate. He also advised her about instructions she should send to her steward. "For the time being, you'll stay here," he reassured her. "You are safe here and among friends. Don't worry about Count Clement. Of course, there is nothing wrong with that marriage per se," he added, evidently not particularly interested in Giselle's feelings about the matter. "But I wouldn't relish this man having control of that land. Let's see if we can find a better solution."

Of course. Giselle translated this to mean her marriage down the road. She understood that. Marriages were arranged for women. This was the way of the world. Eventually, she would have to submit and be grateful. But this gave her some breathing space, and she appreciated the count's kindness.

She wasn't as comfortable with Lady Adela, a young woman hardly much older than herself, elegant, self-assured, and with a note of authority in her voice that clashed oddly with her youthful appearance. Several times when sitting in the great hall, Giselle noticed Adela studying her with a curiously intent gaze, cool and faintly hostile, for all that she was unfailingly polite.

Restlessly, Giselle wandered through the sprawling complex. People stared at her. She knew her cote was simple, but they didn't need to stare so. Ladies, elegant and scented, whispered when she passed by. She walked toward the castle kitchen, yearning for the comfortable warmth of the kitchen at home and the cheerful presence of Thomas' wife Maria, her arms covered in flour as she kneaded the day's bread. Maria would nod at her and point at the big pot over the fire. "Give that a stir, would you?" But when Giselle reached the kitchen and looked inside, she stopped. There were at least four servant girls and several boys, supervised by a small man, who screeched at them with a high voice. A wooden table, almost the length of the manor's great hall at home, was covered with bowls and piles of vegetables. The front part of the hearth itself was large enough for a short person to stand up in. Long iron racks with hooks along the walls supported more pots and pans that Giselle had ever seen in one place. Steam rose from several large pots, and the noise from the voices and the clattering of instruments was deafening. She backed up. No comfort here. A cool voice spoke into her ear.

"I must admit things were simpler in Caen."

Giselle spun around to find Adela standing close by, a small boy next to her, one pudgy hand wrapped around a wooden toy horse.

"You might be surprised, but my father never cared much for maintaining a large kitchen staff or elaborate cooking." Adela smirked. "Though you wouldn't know it if you look at him. He has become quite portly."

Giselle had to suppress a grin. It wouldn't do to laugh about the king. But perhaps it wouldn't be so bad here. "Who is this?"

"This is William." Adela put her hands on the boy's back so that he was forced to bow. He held out his toy horse. "Horse," he mumbled.

"I can see that." Giselle smiled at him. "It's a fine horse."

"Come, join us in the great hall," Adela said.

At first, Giselle felt awkward. But gradually she relaxed with her hostess.

Adela was only a few years older than Giselle, for all that she had already lost her first baby in the womb, had given birth to her son, and was pregnant again. Underneath her learning, her worldly experience, her poise, and the veneer of a wealthy lady who happened to be the daughter of a king and the wife of one of the most powerful men in the county, she was still a young woman who was apparently happy to have a younger companion.

"Why exactly did you object to getting married to this count?" Adela asked several months after Giselle's arrival.

Startled, she raised her head from her needlework.

Adela was looking at her intently. Until then, she had refrained from asking direct questions.

"I know I will have to marry," Giselle said after a pause. "But not someone like Count Clement. He is …" She hesitated, reluctant to use a crude word that came to mind. "Unpleasant. He smells bad, and all the maids are afraid of him. Besides, he is almost as old as my father." Then she blushed. She had forgotten that Count Stephen-Henry was considerably older than Adela. "But that's not all," she added, still flustered. "He is awful to the people working on his estate. And his estate is badly managed. I wouldn't want someone like that to take over my father's vineyards."

Adela was silent, her head bent over the threads of her needlework.

Just then, the large doors of the great hall opened, and Count Stephen-Henry entered. He moved fast as he approached Adela, unlike his usual calm and stately demeanor, and kneeled in front of her.

Giselle shrank back, trying to make herself less noticeable. This was evidently a private matter.

"My dear." The count took Adela's hands. "I am afraid I have bad news."

Clean Kill

1087 Blois

"I don't understand." Adela stared at her husband. He was clasping her hands in his. "My father is dead?" Her voice trembled. "I just received a letter from Henry, who told me that our father was on his way to Mantes to chastise the French in Vexin."

"I am afraid it's true. He got hurt in Vexin in late July. I am not sure how. His servants brought him to the priory at Saint Gervase in Rouen, where he died on September 9."

"He lingered on for weeks?" Tears were running down her cheeks. "He always prayed for a clean death. He told me over and over that a good hunter must try for a clean kill as the most important form of mercy." She pulled her hands away from her husband's and rubbed her eyes. "But why Saint Gervase? He wouldn't want to be buried there." Adela shook her head in disbelief. "He wanted to be laid to rest in Caen."

"I am certain this will all be arranged," Count Stephen-Henry said gently. "I will send a messenger. We will know more soon."

"And what happens now?" Adela sat up. Some color had come back into her face. "Where is Robert? Where are William Rufus and Henry?"

Count Stephen-Henry stood up and extended his hand to his wife. "We will know more soon. Right now, let's go to the chapel and pray for your father's soul."

Giselle left the great hall quietly. She felt out of place, and she was flooded with a vivid memory of the anguish and sense of desolation after her father's death.

But this was different. It wasn't only Adela's father. It was the ruler of Normandy and England.

Over the next weeks, Blois was a beehive of messengers rushing back and forth and heated discussions between Stephen-Henry, Adela, Cerdic, and other advisors. Giselle heard from ladies in the castle that the king's brothers were at each other's throats over the inheritance.

"Why?" she asked, perplexed and painfully aware of her ignorance.

"Isn't it obvious?" The lady sneered at her. "Don't you know anything? His eldest, Robert, has been feuding with the king for years. It's no wonder that the king cut him out of the succession. Besides, I heard he is lazy and a spendthrift to boot."

"But at least he is now ruler of Normandy, another lady said and laughed. "I heard that Henry is left with nothing at all."

"True. And William Rufus wasted no time rushing off to England to be crowned. He didn't even bother to wait for his father to be buried."

"Did you hear about that burial?" The ladies tittered, covering their mouths with their hands. One whispered to the other, but loud enough for Giselle to hear, "They say that the king didn't fit into the tomb they'd made for him? They had to break his bones. And apparently his guts burst. It stank up the entire church."

"Is that true, Cid?" Giselle asked Cerdic later when they met in the courtyard. Giselle wanted to see the market, and Cerdic offered to come along.

"People say the cruelest things," Cerdic said. "Someone might have made it up out of spite. King William certainly didn't deserve that."

"You liked him."

"He was kind to me. He was never as harsh with me as he was with his sons. Even though sometimes I got some of that treatment, since I spent so much time with Henry. But mostly he was good to me."

Together, they passed through the gate and toward the market. Cerdic walked next to her like a large protective crane, angular and slightly awkward.

Giselle looked at Cerdic from the side. His long, dark blond hair partly hid his face, but his prominent nose stuck out. It was a mild day in November, and he hadn't bothered with a cloak over his tunic. He smelled of sweat and horses. Perhaps they were both strangers here. She was like a fish out of water; none of her experiences had prepared her for life at the court of Blois. And Cerdic, for all the years of living in Normandy and then Blois, still had an air of a stranger about him.

"Do you sometimes miss England?" she asked.

"It's been a long time. I don't even know what I would find there." He frowned and shook his head, clearly not wanting to talk about this. "What about you?"

"Every day." Giselle sighed. "I miss home terribly. If I weren't so afraid of Count Clement, I'd go back today. Here, I don't have anything to do but sit around in the great hall and hope my steward is doing what he is supposed to."

"I am supposed to ride in that direction on behalf of a request by my lord. I can check on your steward."

"Oh, that would be such a comfort." Giselle beamed at him.

They had reached the market, and the sights and sounds of the merchants and customers distracted her. It seemed like everyone was shouting and arguing at the same time.

"That smells delicious," she exclaimed when they walked past a seller of pies and bread. Cerdic bought two hot pasties. They ate them as they continued on, savoring the sweet treat stuffed with fruits. The vendors with their cages of chicken and rabbits didn't surprise Giselle as much as the stall with the strange spices.

Fascinated, Giselle studied the open clay bowls, filled with powders in many colors from bright orange to dark gray. "Where do these spices come from?"

"Count Stephen-Henry told me traders bring them from the east. They are expensive," Cerdic muttered.

"Well, I doubt Count Stephen-Henry's cook is worried about the expense. He prepares the most exquisite meals every day."

Cerdic laughed.

"I have no idea what any of this is." She bent forward and sniffed the bowls' contents, pungent, sweet, and musky. One made her sneeze, and the vendor frowned at her.

"Be careful," he said sharply. "That's the finest pepper from the east,"

"Sorry." Giselle backed away. "What's this?" She pointed at a small bowl filled with a dusky red powder.

"Saffron." The vendor whisked the bowl out of her reach as if afraid she might sneeze into it. "And if you are not going to purchase anything, you better let me serve other customers."

Giselle glanced around. Several well-dressed women stood behind her, frowning and twitching impatiently. Cerdic had wandered off to the next stall. He waved her over.

"Look at these gloves."

"Oh, they are so soft." Giselle ran her fingers over the fawn-colored leather.

Children were playing tag amidst the stalls. A woman selling sausages shouted at them. At the corner of the market square, a man with an unkempt long mop of hair and tattered clothing stood on a barrel and gesticulated as he talked loudly.

"What is he saying?" Giselle whispered.

"I have no idea. He certainly thinks it's important. Probably he is talking about the end of days and divine retribution."

Giselle shivered. Then she realized that Cerdic was grinning at her.

"You know that there are preachers like this in every single town from here to the coast in Normandy? They are harmless." He took her arm and dragged her to another stand. The scent of the roasted chestnuts was intoxicating. He bought a handful, tucking them into the leather pouch he had tied to his waist.

"How do you eat them?"

Cerdic took his knife and pressed the blade on the shell of a nut, and it split open, revealing the white inside. "Here," he said, handing it to her. "Now you can peel off the skin and eat it."

The chestnut tasted sweet.

They kept walking, past the vendor of linens and woolens and on to a stall where there were a few precious carpets on display. A wealthy lady with an attendant waiting patiently behind her was haggling with the carpet seller. "No, I won't drop the price," he exclaimed. "I am the only merchant who has these. Ask anyone. They've come all the way from the east. They are very rare."

Giselle liked the rug on top of the pile. She wanted to run her hands over the warm colors from dark red to blue and brown. Wistfully, she thought of the rush mats in her father's study. He would have loved this. But she missed those days in spring at home when the old, dry and musty smelling rushes were taken up and fresh rushes spread all over the house, with herbs sprinkled onto them.

Giselle was filled with a sense of wellbeing. She hadn't felt this content for years. She lengthened her stride to keep up with Cerdic's long legs. Cerdic turned his head and looked down at her with a sweet smile on his face, the one he seemed to reserve only for Adela. Something tugged at her heart.

Stricken, she hardly noticed how they got back to the castle. She excused herself and sought refuge in her room. What was she going to do? She had heard the ladies whisper about him and knew he had dalliances with several. It hadn't concerned her or bothered her in the least; actually, she had found it funny. But she had seen him glance at Adela whenever she was unaware of it, and that expression on his face, a bit lost and bewildered and filled with boundless affection, had stirred a feeling in her that she hadn't been able to understand at all. Now she knew. Oh, what was she going to do?

Rosewater, Wheat Powder, and Kohl

1089 Blois

"Stay still," Adela snapped. "You need to learn this."

Adela was showing Giselle how to use face powder to lighten her complexion. "They grind wheat into this fine powder," she said. "See, we mix it with a bit of rosewater and spread it on the face."

Giselle tried not to squirm. It gave her a strange tingly warm feeling to be the focus of attention and to have someone touch her cheeks with a soft little brush. Would her mother have done this if she had lived? She sneezed. "Why not leave me as I am?"

"You want to appear polished and beautiful, don't you? Well, that's how you do it."

Adela went on to show Giselle how to add red highlights. "See, this is from dried safflowers."

"Why paint me all white and then add red for some color?"

"Stop arguing and watch."

Adela held up the oval piece of silver so Giselle could see what she was doing.

Perplexed, Giselle gazed at a stranger with curly hair, large dark eyes, pale skin, and glowing cheeks.

"And now I'll show you how to use kohl."

Giselle groaned inwardly. It was as if she was at the mercy of a relentless tutor. Adela appeared to enjoy instructing her about everything, Giselle's inadequate wardrobe, her tendency to slouch, her ways of expressing herself.

"It all matters." Adela dipped a small stub into a bowl filled with dark powder and proceeded to darken Giselle's eyebrows with firm strokes. "You want to run your father's estate? Trust me, the way you comport yourself will help you when you assert your authority."

They could not have been more different. When Adela had attended classes at the abbey, Giselle had run wild in her father's vineyards. When Adela watched her mother talk to visiting scholars, Giselle had spent time with the manor cook. When Adela had received lessons in the art of hunting with birds of prey from her father, Giselle had learned how to prune grape vines.

Giselle didn't think she had missed that much. To be sure, unlike Adela, she had grown up with little learning and with a father uninclined to provide his only daughter with fine clothes or other trappings of a gentlewoman. But she had been happy.

She tried to explain this to Adela, who asked her at length about her years of growing up at La Vallée des Sources. Talking about it filled her with longing.

"I loved my father," Giselle said.

Adela didn't comment.

"My mother died when I was still a child, and my father and I became close," Giselle said. "He taught me everything he knew about growing wine."

They were sitting in the great hall. Adela had a way of listening without reacting or showing what was going on in that mind of hers. William sat on the floor, surrounding by his wooden toy horses. He hummed to them and made them move around as if they were jumping over fences or ditches.

As Giselle spent more time with her hostess, she realized that perhaps things had been missing in her childhood. She watched Adela write letters and talk about affairs of state with ease. Once the countess realized she had a willing audience in Giselle, she explained much about England and Normandy, even the work of administering Blois and all the other estates. She called in the steward and questioned him about matters in the castle. Visiting knights found themselves not reporting only to Count Stephen-Henry but also to his diminutive wife, whose questions were incisive and with an astounding grasp of the state of affairs in Blois, Chartres, and other holdings. It made Giselle feel ignorant and a little envious. Sometimes Adela read from a manuscript someone had sent her and talked to Giselle about it until it made her head spin.

"I don't understand any of this," Giselle protested. "I didn't attend an abbey school like you did."

"Well, then pay more attention." Adela picked up another parchment. "Listen to this letter from the bishop of…William!"

Adela leaped up from her chair, scattering the parchments on her lap onto the floor. Her son was edging closer to the fire in the hearth and tentatively sticking his hands toward the flames. She grabbed his tunic and pulled him back, shaking him. "What are you thinking?"

Startled, the boy turned his face toward his mother. "Pretty," he said, pointing at the flames.

"Oh, William." Adela shook her head and gestured to a servant to take the child outside. With a sigh, she sat back down, rubbing her back with one hand.

Giselle was on her knees, gathering the pieces of parchment. When she straightened up, she noticed Adela wiping her face with her sleeve. She'd been crying.

"Something is not right," Adela muttered. "He is almost four, and he acts like a baby. I never know what he is going to do from one moment to the next."

Giselle wasn't sure what to say. Adela had seemed tired and strained ever since she had given birth to her second son, Odo. And now she was pregnant again. It didn't make Giselle look forward to having children herself.

Perhaps it wasn't surprising that Adela was tired. She traveled all over her husband's domain from the east to the west and from the north to the south, sometimes with Count Stephen-Henry and sometimes by herself. She was always working, studying manuscripts, writing notes, and poring over maps. She never said anything about the conflicts between her brothers, William Rufus, the new king, Robert, the new duke of Normandy, and Henry the youngest. Henry had been left without any inheritance to speak of and was like a detached limb, vacillating between the two older ones while trying to improve his financial standing. Adela received letters from him. But she kept her thoughts to herself.

Giselle shivered and drew closer to the fire. It was already November. Another year had gone by, and she was still trapped in Blois, afraid to return home and unsure of her future. Cerdic had spent a lot of time away, traveling at the behest of Lord Stephen-Henry and also returning to his own estate, Les Tilleuls. He had made a point of regularly stopping at her home and checking on her steward. She missed him when he wasn't in Blois, and yet his presence was an agony of another sort. She avoided him, especially when he entered the great hall to talk to Adela. She tried not to look at him, afraid of her face revealing too much. Meanwhile, apparently, Count Clement still dropped by regularly, asking when she would return. She pulled the shawl more tightly around her shoulders.

"You know you will have to marry eventually." It was as if Adela had read her mind. "Not all men are like this Count Clement."

Giselle lowered her eyes. She was annoyed at herself for still having a reaction of utter revulsion whenever she remembered Count Clement. The mere mention of the name evoked the acrid sour smell that seemed to hang in the man's clothes, his heavy breathing the last time he had marched into her father's study and hovered over her, urging her to agree to the marriage, the dampness of his hand he had run over her arm, and the beads of sweat on his forehead.

"Anyway, it's not as if women get much choice in this," Adela said. "I had none. But you might be surprised once you are married."

Giselle looked up. Adela had a satisfied expression on her face, smiling as if she remembered something delightful.

Giselle had come to respect and even on occasion to like Adela. But would she ever understand her? She was such a strange mix—deeply devout, yet fun loving, controlling and impatient, but also kind and generous. Always sure of herself, determined, even harsh at times, she was also observant and quick to read other people's feelings.

Adela loved to talk. She wielded words like others might wield a sword with skill and ease, using vivid words and colors as if she was painting the world for the listener, but that didn't mean she revealed what she was thinking. Talking together with posture, demeanor, and dress was part of a performance that never ended.

Giselle didn't like to talk. Often she felt it was unnecessary to say anything. And unlike Adela, Giselle was filled with doubts. It was odd. When she was a little girl, she had never feared anything or anyone, convinced the world was a good place and that she fit well into it. Now, she wasn't sure. All she knew was that she had feelings for someone who barely noticed her or, worse, thought of her as a child and that she was desperately homesick.

"Don't fret," Adela said, apparently putting her own interpretations on Giselle's silence. She studied Giselle with a strangely calculating expression on her face, as if an idea had just occurred to her. "Really, don't fret. Something good will come of this."

An Excellent Arrangement

"No." Cerdic shook his head. "Absolutely not." He stood up. "I'll take my leave now."

"Think about it," Adela said.

Cerdic bowed, refusing to look at her, and went outside. Curtly, he ordered the stable boy to bring his horse. He flung himself onto the mare's back and rode out of the castle courtyard, the clattering of the hooves on the flagstones like a drumming in his head, no, no, no.

Ever since he was a little boy, he had been at the mercy of others sending him here and there, separating him from his mother and his home, sending him away from Caen, and trying to arrange his entire life for him.

And now, to have to endure this sort of manipulation? He was willing to put up with any number of indignities for Adela's sake. But this was too much.

In the last years, Adela had grown in stature. In part, this was due to the change in her husband's state. After his father's death in 1089, he had inherited Blois. He turned over many of his responsibilities to Adela, who took to traveling regularly through their domains. *Domina*, my dear," he'd say, smiling at her with a mix of pride and affection, "you can handle this." When Adela addressed people, giving orders or reprimanding, the authority in her voice was unmistakable.

Cerdic understood that, and he was proud of her. But now she wanted to tell him whom to marry and to organize his entire life. For the first miles, as he rode towards Les Tilleuls, he hardly noticed anything around him.

Gradually, he calmed down. His eyes took in the patches of snow from the first storm in November and the wisps of golden leaves still hanging off the branches of beech trees that lined the road. Their silvery gray trunks gleamed in the sunlight. It was high time that he talked to Auberi about pruning the lime trees. He tried to work out the details of his plan for a drainage ditch near the kitchen garden, which tended to get flooded during storms. Also, he needed to check on Giselle's steward before he went on to Châteaudun, bearing a gift from Adela for the abbey of l'Église de la Madeleine. The abbey had embarked on a building project, and Adela sent a grant of money together with an embroidered altar cloth.

Lately, Giselle had been avoiding him, clearly uncomfortable and lapsing into silence when he entered the great hall. He couldn't understand this. A few months ago, when they walked to the market together, she had been relaxed and happy. She had even laughed at him, teasing him about his frayed hose. He smiled when he thought of her deep voice—so incongruous for such a small round person, neat and trim like a little wren.

Maybe Adela was right. This might be a good idea. He didn't have much to offer to a future wife, but he could keep Giselle safe. And the two estates bordered on each other. It would give him the status he craved. Then he got furious all over again at Adela's presumption. "Of course, you and your wife will spend time at Blois," she had told him as if sure that he would do exactly what she wanted. "And I know my husband requires your loyal services."

Clearly, she had it all worked out. The fact that it was a good idea made the sense of being manipulated even more grating.

By the time Cerdic was on his way back to Blois, he was reconciled to the scheme.

To his surprise, Giselle was at first shocked and almost angry when he approached her.

"Was this your idea?" There was not a hint of a dimple on her cheeks, and her voice even gruffer and deeper than usual.

"Well, my lady and the count agree that it would be an excellent arrangement; and I need my lord's permission to marry."

This seemed to make Giselle even angrier. She frowned at him.

"Look," he added. "I can help you take care of your father's vineyard. You'd like Les Tilleuls. You and I have been friends for so long. I thought you'd be content."

"Content," Giselle said slowly, the corners of her mouth turned down. She pulled and tugged on the loose end of her robe's sleeve in her hand as if trying to get it off.

Cerdic recognized the robe. Adela had worn it last year. He remembered sitting next to her in the courtyard. She had been in tears over the loss of her baby and worried about little William. "He's still not talking properly," she muttered. "I'm afraid for him." He had briefly put an arm on her shoulder to console her. It was odd seeing Giselle wear it.

Then Giselle raised her head and straightened her shoulders. "Very well."

Cerdic looked at her searchingly, assailed by doubt.

A smile transformed Giselle's upturned face, dark curls framing the dimpled cheeks. For an instant, Cerdic was transported back to that moment of noticing an urchin in the tree above his head, grinning impishly at him. It tugged at him, and he felt disoriented.

"You are sure about this?" He remembered how Giselle had felt about Count Clement.

Giselle took his hand in hers, stood on her tiptoes, and kissed him on the lips. "Your lime trees and my vineyard will be one, and we will be content."

Honey And Grapes

And the angel thrust in his sickle into the earth, and gathered the vine of the earth, and cast it into the great winepress of the wrath of God. 20 And the winepress was trodden without the city, and blood came out of the winepress, even unto the horse bridles, by the space of a thousand and six hundred furlongs. (Revelation 14:19-20).

"What do you mean?"

Bemused, Cerdic stared at his wife. He didn't know whether to laugh or to get angry. She had tied up her kirtle with a rope from the stable, baring her legs, and had donned a badly worn pair of leather shoes that looked like they had belonged to Thomas at one point. Curly tendrils of her hair escaped from beneath the headdress, and her arms were filled with a pile of dried branches.

"What do I mean?" Giselle tossed the branches on the ground. "You tell your Auberi to stick to his own work. What does he know about growing wine? He wants to make a bonfire near the lower field where the new white grapes are growing. How often do I have to tell him that smoke is bad for the grapes?"

"Now, Giselle," Cerdic responded, trying not to lose his temper. When he had agreed to the marriage, he hadn't expected anything like this. Giselle should be more grateful to have the weight of responsibility for her father's estate lifted from her shoulders. Admittedly, he also hadn't expected her to be as knowledgeable about growing wine as she turned out to be. What made this even more galling was the fact that he had so much to learn about running an estate, while his termagant of a wife had grown up with it. And in the last month, it seemed as if both their tempers had reached a boiling point. Perhaps he should spend some time at Blois. "Auberi is just trying to help."

"Help is fine. But not when he starts telling me how things should be done. He should worry about the bees."

"Perhaps, if you looked more the part of a lady of the manor, he might listen to you," Cerdic snapped.

"Oh, such a fine manor," Giselle scoffed. She brushed her hands against her tunic. Then it was as if a storm cloud was swept away. The red spots of anger on her face faded. She grinned at Cerdic. "Last time I checked, the roof still had holes in it."

Cerdic grinned back, relieved. "Indeed. It's the next thing I need to address." Then he noticed how pale she was. Her eyes had dark circles underneath. Was she ill? He reached out and tugged at a twig that had gotten stuck on her tunic. "Come, my dear." He slung an arm over her shoulders. "Let's go inside and rest for a while. Then we can settle everything to your satisfaction."

Later, they sat over a meal of bread and cheese and talked.

"I don't understand why you get so upset with me," Cerdic said carefully, loathe to cause another fight. "I thought you'd welcome more help with the vineyard."

Giselle munched her bread, her cheeks expanded. "Mmmm, this is good. I was so hungry." She swallowed. "You must understand, I've been on my own for so long. And you won't always be here. I hate being dependent."

"Oh." Cerdic cut off a slice of cheese and handed it to his wife. "I hadn't thought of it like that." Then he smiled. "But I am dependent on you, especially when I have to be away. I need you to watch over Les Tilleuls."

Giselle sniffed at the cheese. Then she leaped up and ran outside. Bewildered, Cerdic followed her to the courtyard and found her retching on the flagstones.

"What's wrong?" Cerdic watched her helplessly.

Giselle wiped her mouth with her sleeve and turned to look at her husband. "I am expecting," she said. "You are going to be a father."

"Why didn't you tell me?"

"Because I was afraid." Giselle frowned at him. "Don't you see? It would make it harder for me to do my work."

"It will be fine." Cerdic smiled at her. He couldn't understand what was worrying her. He was elated.

A few weeks later, the summons came.

When Cerdic saw the seal on Count Stephen-Henry's missive, he was excited. He would be back at court once again, entrusted with important tasks and able to watch Adela's eyes as she thanked him for his service. At Les Tilleuls, he had to confront his ignorance about running an estate on an almost daily basis.

"I have to return to Blois," he told Giselle. "It won't be for long."

Giselle pressed her lips together.

Over the next few days, while Cerdic was getting ready, his wife didn't say much to him. Her withdrawn demeanor puzzled him. *Perhaps she won't miss me. Perhaps she'll be glad to have full charge of everything while I am gone.* He thought of her pale face and her eyes that had persistently turned away from him ever since he had announced he was leaving, and he was filled with doubt. When he took his leave, his escort already waiting in the courtyard, Giselle clung to him for a moment. Then she pushed him away and went inside without looking back.

Several months later, he returned home. Maria encountered him as he entered the manor. She was carrying soiled linen in her arms.

"Where is my lady?"

"In bed, resting," Maria said, eyeing him anxiously. "The baby came too early and didn't live."

Cerdic ran up the stairs to Giselle's chamber.

Giselle lay propped up by blankets. Her eyes were red rimmed. "I am sorry," she whispered. "I fell over a dog in the stable, and then the baby came."

"Don't talk now." Cerdic kneeled next to the bed. "It's not your fault."

"It was a girl. Little Marguerite. She was perfect." Tears were rolling down her cheeks. "Thomas is making a coffin for her."

Cerdic felt his eyes sting in response. "I should have been here with you." He put his head down next to his wife. "Please forgive me."

Giselle didn't say anything. He heard her breathing.

"We will have a mass read for her soul." Cerdic stroked Giselle's hand and stayed with her until she fell asleep.

Giselle recovered, and to Cerdic's relief, quickly regained her cheerful and pragmatic demeanor even if she was quieter than before.

When Giselle became pregnant again, Cerdic was delighted. This time, he would definitely stay home until the baby was born. *Adela can't expect me to come under these circumstances.*

SUMMONS

Cerdic was in the courtyard, trying to determine what to do about a new leak in the stable, when the messenger came.

He recognized Adela's seal and opened the rolled-up parchment with misgiving. "Please come as soon as you can." Her handwriting was unusually untidy, with words scratched out and blots on the parchment. "You are the only one I can trust."

For a reason he couldn't quite define, he was glad Giselle had gone to the vineyard to check on the pruning work. It would give him time to decide what to do.

Strangely, Giselle didn't seem surprised when he told her later. She didn't even look up from her needlework. "Of course, you must go."

Cerdic set out the next day. Perhaps his wife had finally accepted that he had other responsibilities, certainly more important than a struggling vineyard and a handful of beehives. She had been so pale and sickly during her first pregnancy. This one seemed easier for her; she was plump and glowing. Women gave birth to children every day without ill effects. It wasn't as if his presence would make any difference. It wasn't as if Giselle was helpless when he wasn't there.

By the time he finally approached the great hall in Blois, he had abandoned these thoughts; he was filled with anticipation about the task Adela had for him. When he reached for the handle on the big oak door, he heard Count Stephen-Henry's raised voice.

"I know Henry is your favorite. But those brothers of yours have been at loggerheads for decades now. Why can't you let them fight it out among themselves? Why do you always feel you must intervene?

Cerdic didn't hear Adela's response. Of course, she had always been close to Henry. They were only a year apart in age and spent much of their childhood together. They were even somewhat alike in temperament and equally well educated. Adela had resigned herself to her brother William having taken on the mantle of kingship only reluctantly. She was convinced that Henry would be a better king.

"Look, my dear." The count spoke with a note of irritation Cerdic hadn't heard from him before. "Henry has been roaming the woods doing God knows what for the past two years. I am sure he will land on his feet. He always does."

"He shouldn't have to be in this position to begin with. My father arranged matters so awkwardly, basically leaving Henry with nothing. Anyway, I am not intervening." Adela's voice sounded hoarse and as if she had been crying. "I just want to give Henry a little support."

Cerdic decided he couldn't keep listening. He knocked and entered. Count Stephen-Henry and Adela were sitting in front of the fireplace; they turned when they heard Cerdic, and both welcomed him with a smile.

"Ah, Cerdic," the count said. "We have been talking about the task with which we'd like to entrust you."

"I am so glad you've come," Adela interjected.

Count Stephen-Henry frowned at his wife. "Let me explain," and went on to outline the current situation.

Cerdic listened politely, but with only limited attention. He knew already much of the sorry history of the back and forth of fighting, betrayals, and broken promises between the brothers. In the last years, deprived of all lands and sources of power by his brothers when they were temporarily united in thwarting their youngest brother's ambitions, Henry spent some time roaming all over French Vexin and the border of Normandy, while reestablishing his network of supporters. He used the town of Domfront as his base.

Cerdic knew all this, at least for the most part. His gaze was fixed on Adela's changing expressions, from frustration to worry and pleading in her glowing eyes.

"In short," the count continued, "Henry is in need of funds."

"Yes," Adela broke in. "We have received a message from him. He indicated a place and a date for a rendezvous and appealed to me to do what I could."

"Of course, the area is awash with marauding troops from both Robert and Henry." The count glanced at Cerdic as if taking his measure. "It will be a challenge for you to arrive safely at the agreed upon rendezvous."

"I am honored that you trust me with this." Cerdic bowed.

A few days later, he was riding through a forest near the Normandy border on a sturdy if plodding bay, the money Adela wanted him to bring to Henry secured in a leather pouch underneath his tunic. He wore nondescript clothes so as not to attract unnecessary attention. His large cloak covered the sword and hid his long limbs and muscular build. Several times, robbers assaulted him and found out, to their chagrin, that their chosen mark turned out to be an experienced and lethal adversary.

He was humming to himself, trying to capture the tune of the song performed by a minstrel in Blois. This journey through the woods offered an unexpected sense of freedom from responsibility. The task set for him didn't appear especially challenging. Right now, Cerdic was merely a messenger.

What if something happened to him here? Would someone let Giselle know? For a moment, her face, devoid of expression when he took his leave, appeared in his mind. It was odd. Despite the years of their marriage, he still couldn't always tell what she was thinking. Adela he could read perfectly well—irritation, anger, impatience, affection, amusement, determination, relentless sense of purpose, even a certain ruthlessness—he knew all those and others. Perhaps that openness was why she continued to hold such sway over him.

The point of rendezvous was at the border between Vexin and Normandy. Cerdic avoided riding at night, and for the most part, stayed on well-traveled roads. It was late in the afternoon, and the sunlight had already softened and begun to glow. It was time that he find an inn for the night. He moved at an easy pace, always listening for potential danger behind or ahead.

But he hadn't bargained on a thin rope strung across the way.

Cerdic's horse lost its footing, and he was thrown over its neck and onto the ground. His face was crushed into a pile of wet leaves, and for an instant he thought of oak barrels filled with wine. Then everything went dark.

He woke up with his head aching. Where was he? The sound of a fire crackling made him try to open his eyes, even though it made the headache worse.

"You lead a charmed life, my friend."

Cerdic peered up at the speaker. In disbelief, he closed his eyes again. "Count Robert?" His mouth was parched, and he could barely get the words out.

"The very same. Here, have some water. It will help."

Robert held the beaker to his lips, and Cerdic drank. It helped him to clear his mind. Slowly, he moved his right hand underneath the coarse blanket to feel along his side for the leather pouch.

"You are looking for this?" Robert reached across to a table behind him and held up the leather pouch.

Cerdic sank back onto the pallet. His head ached even more now. He had failed.

Bright Pledge

"Shall I make some assumptions here?" Robert tossed another piece of wood into the hearth.

Cerdic struggled to sit up. He might as well face what was to come. He raised himself, even though his head was swimming, swung his legs onto the floor, and sat up straight. Little lights flickered in his eyes. He blinked to clear his sight.

Robert had aged since Cerdic last saw him when he visited his sister in Blois shortly after her marriage. His clothes were of good quality, but he looked unkempt, and his hair was long and scraggly. Cerdic remembered King William's voice, chastising his oldest son for his slovenly appearance. "You can't even make sure that your clothes and your gear are in good order. How do you expect to rule a county, never mind a kingdom?" The king had spoken in a raised voice so that all around him heard. Cerdic couldn't help but feel pity for Robert, the disinherited one, the man who had been betrayed over and over by his own brothers, the impetuous son of an impetuous father.

And yet, Robert had moments of nobility. Cerdic remembered Robert's reaction when coming upon his father in battle at Gerberoy, thrown onto the ground by his horse and helpless. Robert had helped the king remount and let him ride off unscathed.

Cerdic had heard of the siege of Mont Saint Michel, a stronghold off the coast of Normandy where Henry had been holed up. As an island fortress, it was easily defended, but it did not have its own source of fresh water. William, for a brief moment united with Robert in the fight against their brother, had wanted Robert to withhold water from the besieged castle. But Robert chose otherwise, and water and supplies continued to reach the fortress. Eventually, Henry abandoned Mont Saint Michel. Meanwhile, William berated Robert for his actions, and the brief alliance between the brothers was at an end.

"How did I come to be here?" Cerdic's voice was still raspy.

"My men have made a habit of watching the roads in and out of Normandy; sometimes they manage to capture a fat prize—or at least someone who might bring a decent ransom. Of course, it is unusual to have someone carry his ransom on his own body." Robert poked at the leather bag as if it might contain a dead mouse.

Cerdic stayed silent. He wasn't going to admit to the source or the intended recipient of the money.

"I take it you are here on my dear sister's behest," Robert said, as if he was reading Cerdic's mind. "And presumably you are once again being coerced to act as a delivery boy."

Cerdic flushed.

"Oh, yes, I remember. My mother made you bring me some sorely needed funds many years ago." Robert stood up. "This is getting tedious. You will find your horse outside. I instructed my men to let you pass through. I'll leave you now." He sketched a bow and went toward the door. Then he turned around again. "Before I forget, you'd better take this." He grabbed the leather bag and tossed it into Cerdic's lap. "Do give my regards to my brother."

Fortunately, Henry had been patiently waiting at the point of rendezvous when Cerdic finally reached him.

"I thought you wouldn't come since you missed the rendezvous by several days. But I thought I'd wait a while. I had no pressing matter elsewhere."

Cerdic briefly explained what had happened.

"My brother has all the knightly qualities, but no sense. I almost pity him." Henry laughed. "Please tell my sister how much I appreciate this."

By the time Cerdic reached home, several months had passed. He rode into the courtyard with trepidation. Would Giselle be angry about his long absence? The first person he saw was Auberi, who was conferring with the cooper.

"Ah, sir," Auberi called out. "It's good to see you back." He beamed at him.

Cerdic nodded and went inside. Giselle sat in a patch of sunlight near the window. Her dark shiny hair was draped loosely over her shoulders. On her lap, she cradled a baby wrapped in a soft blanket. She was humming to it, with her head bent. When she heard his steps on the wooden floorboards, she beamed at him.

"Cid." She shifted the bundle on her lap and gently lifted one corner of the blanket. "We have a son." She looked happier than he had ever seen her.

He peered at the little red face inside the folds of the blanket. His eyes stung. He wondered what his mother would have thought. "I am sorry I couldn't be here sooner."

For an instant, it was as if a shadow passed over his wife's face. But it was already gone. She dropped a kiss on the baby's face and then laughed at him. "Don't you want to know your son's name?"

Giselle had refused to think about that before he left. The loss of little Marguerite was still too raw in her mind. She felt it was a bad omen to pick a name for an unborn child.

"Well, what is our son's name?" Cerdic asked, swelling with pride at being able to say these words.

"Guisbert."

"Guisbert? As in Bright Pledge? I like it. Can I hold him?"

Giselle handed the baby to him. Cerdic was surprised to feel the solid weight in his arms and the warmth that seemed to seep through the blanket. The little face frowned at him and yawned. "Welcome to the world, Guisbert."

Pilgrim From The East

For to you more than to other nations the Lord has given the military spirit, courage, agile bodies, and the bravery to strike down those who resist you. Let your minds be stirred to bravery by the deeds of your forefathers, and by the efficiency and greatness of Karl the Great, and of Ludwig his son, and of the other kings who have destroyed Turkish kingdoms, and established Christianity in their lands. You should be moved especially by the holy grave of our Lord and Savior which is now held by unclean peoples, and by the holy places which are treated with dishonor and irreverently befouled with their uncleanness.
Pope Urban II, Council of Clermont, 1095

Oh, what a noble and beautiful city is Constantinople! How many monasteries and palaces it contains, constructed with wonderful skill! How many remarkable things may be seen in the principal avenues and even in the lesser streets! I would be very tedious to enumerate the wealth that is there of every kind, of gold, of silver, of robes of many kinds, and of holy relics. Merchants constantly bring to the city by frequent voyages all necessities of man. About 20,000 eunuchs, I judge, are always living there.
Fulcher of Chartres, 1097

1095 Blois

"The man smells," William exclaimed, his childish voice bouncing off the stone walls of the great hall.

"Be quiet," Adela hissed, tugging sharply on his tunic so that he lost his balance and smacked his head against the wooden armrest of her chair. "You are almost ten. You have to learn to behave." Then she made a sign to her maid to take the boy outside.

The man did smell. Giselle found herself wishing once again that Adela wasn't so harsh with her eldest. William didn't understand what he was doing wrong. It hurt to see him flinch at his mother's reprimand.

The other children, arrayed on a long bench in the great hall, gaped at the man with rapt attention.

The servants whom Adela had ordered into the great hall to listen to the holy man watched him with blank faces. Probably, they were simply tired from the extra work of feeding the many people currently at Blois.

The pilgrim had just returned from the Holy Land. His brown, travel worn tunic smelled. He ate with his hands, ripping the chicken bones away from the skin, with the juice dripping down his grimy neck and onto his tunic. He never stopped talking.

The long journey, the hunger, the mosquitoes, the treacherous streams and implacable mountains, the thirst, the rampaging illness that affected everyone, the marauders, the strange beasts, the cold, the heat—he droned on and on.

"Thank you, my lady," he mumbled, his voice muffled by the food in his mouth. He tossed a bone over his shoulder, gulped, and licked his lips. "Thank you for your kindness. I'll be sure to remember you in my devotions."

"Tell us about the humpy beasts," Theobald piped up. The boy was tall for his age and stood out among the other children. His brother Stephen was blinking and rubbing his eyes as if about to fall asleep. Their little sister, Lucia-Mahaut, was still in the nursery. Giselle almost sighed with relief that Guisbert was at home, safe in the keeping of Thomas and Maria. He didn't need to hear all this.

It was bad enough that the preacher at home kept echoing the pope's words at every opportunity, relentlessly enumerating all the horrible things the people in the East had done to Christians. With spittle flying off his lips, he screamed at the congregation that those "evildoers devastated them with the sword, rapine, and fire. Some Christians they carried away as slaves, others they put to death. They destroy the churches or turn them into mosques. They desecrate and overthrow the altars." Giselle shuddered, but at the same time her skeptical nature questioned some of this. She couldn't imagine that they would literally pour the blood from Christians they had mutilated into the baptismal fonts or tie their entrails to a stake.

"Never mind the humpy beasts," Odo exclaimed. "Tell us more about the jewels."

"Rivers of jewels." The man wiped his face with his sleeve. His chin was shiny with grease. "I tell you, rivers of them. I saw a church in Constantinople with a dome covered in gold. Women wear jewels in their hair."

Giselle could hear Cerdic mutter to himself. "A pilgrim," he scoffed. "So much for forswearing all worldly goods."

Duke Robert, Adela's older brother, watched the man talk, an intent expression on his face. Giselle didn't care for Duke Robert. His intense, abrupt mannerisms and his ill-concealed arrogance made her feel uncomfortable.

Count Stephen-Henry beckoned a servant to bring more ale. His cheerful, ruddy face didn't reveal anything other than the demeanor of a polite host.

Giselle glanced at Cerdic. She couldn't tell what he was thinking. He had already spent hours closeted with Count Stephen-Henry, Duke Robert, and several others. There was a restlessness among the men in Blois that seemed to spread to everyone. Giselle gripped her needlework tighter until her fingers cramped. Going on a crusade to the Holy Land? This pilgrim didn't give the impression of someone moved by his spiritual experience. He seemed to care more about the visions of wealth than his brief stay in the holy city. He complained about the accommodations. Presumably, he attended a prayer service and visited various holy sites. But he didn't talk about that.

Would Cerdic go with them? She winced; she had stuck her palm with the needle.

They had been happy in the last years since their marriage.

Of course, at first things had been difficult.

Giselle knew that in Cerdic's eyes she was still the urchin spitting cherry pits at him from her perch in the tree. She knew Adela was never far from his thoughts, and it tugged at her as if there was an iron band tightening around her head. It hurt most of all whenever Adela requested that they spend time at Blois, so that Cerdic could fulfill his duties as a vassal of her husband. But whenever they returned home, the world righted itself again.

Cerdic had made a practical decision when offering for her hand in marriage. Giselle knew that. Everybody did that. For that matter, she had done the same—it was a way to keep her father's vineyard safe from the clutches of Count Clement. Only her feelings were engaged.

When agreeing to the marriage, Giselle made a promise to herself. She knew how Cerdic felt about Adela; her love for him made her clear-sighted. But she made a secret vow never to challenge him on this matter. But it was hard. She felt trapped, struggling with insecurity, jealousy, and an overwhelming fear of becoming dependent on a man who was liable to leave at any time.

It didn't help that she felt shy with him for a long time. Sometimes she envied Adela, who was comfortable in her marriage, so assured in her womanly charms.

When Giselle grew up, she was always aware of her father's secret disappointment that she wasn't a boy. He had wanted a son so badly, and he didn't trouble to hide that. He also would talk about her mother, saying that she was the most beautiful woman he ever knew. It made Giselle cringe. She was merely a girl, small and sturdy, with a mess of hair and a short nose. She certainly wasn't beautiful. As she got older, she forgot to worry about this, too busy with taking over more and more of her father's responsibilities while he spent much of his time dreaming about what might have been.

Life in Blois had been a revelation on so many levels. She had learned more from Adela than she had ever expected about the world of politics and letters. She had even learned to care about her appearance. "You must make more of an effort," Adela said one day, when Giselle had once again turned down an offer for a new gown. "It's not about being beautiful, although that helps as well. It's about having respect for yourself and a certain amount of discipline."

Giselle nodded, though she understood this only to a point. She still was most comfortable when out in the vineyard, with her hair tied back with a scarf, her tunic pulled up with a string so it didn't drag on the ground, and wearing a comfortable set of old leather sandals.

"Look, Giselle," Adela had told her a few weeks before the wedding in 1090, "men are like that." She had sat her down in her private room and explained things to her. "Your mother would have told you all this," Adela said, smiled at the younger woman affectionately. "But that's not to be, so listen to me. It will be fine, I assure you."

Giselle listened, too uncomfortable to respond. Doubts flooded her thoughts. All she knew was that she loved Cerdic, and she loved the land she had inherited from her father. But she was afraid. Imagining closeness and warmth was easier than being confronted with the reality of it. She also feared another person taking charge of her life. She had been alone for so long that she didn't know how to settle into this new state of affairs.

During the first years of their marriage, Giselle and Cerdic lived in her father's manor at the Valley of the Springs. It bordered on Les Tilleul, and as Adela and Stephen-Henry had intended, they worked on uniting the two estates. Her steward Thomas had at first been hesitant, especially since Cerdic brought his own steward from Les Tilleuls over for frequent consultations. For a long time, Giselle resented Cerdic's and Auberi's suggestions; it was odd to have someone else stepping into the role her father used to have and that she had come to consider her own. She fought with Cerdic over this; he didn't understand, but at least he tried to listen. Eventually, it got better. Also, Auberi and Thomas came to trust each other and settled into a comfortable working relationship. The elderly Thomas was content to cede more and more of his authority to Auberi. It helped that Thomas's wife Maria was fond of Auberi's son, Jacques. Giselle had retained her maid servant Janine, the daughter of Thomas and Marie, a cheerful and energetic girl. Janine often forgot her status as a servant and was quick with her words, at times treating Giselle as if she were her sister. But she always did her work, and Giselle trusted her.

At first, everything imaginable had gone wrong, from collapsing floor boards to rain pouring into the great hall to a storm knocking down many trees. A sudden downpour flooded the yard and stables, and it stank for weeks of refuse and animal wastes.

Count Clement had been harassing them for months after news of their marriage had become public. A shed had burned down mysteriously; fencing around a pasture broke down, and the cows scattered all over the county; the supports of a crossing over a shallow stream were sawn off, and people walking towards Les Tilleuls fell onto the rocks and got soaked. Initially, they had ignored these events, believing them to be coincidences. Then they hoped that perhaps the count would tire of this. Then they discovered a family of turtles in the freshly stocked fishpond.

"They will eat all the fish if we don't get rid of them." Auberi reported this latest disaster, as if he was afraid he would get blamed for it. "I can't imagine how they got there. We never had turtles in this area."

"Oh, I can," Giselle said. She glanced at Cerdic with a rueful expression on her face. "I think this was another little gift from Count Clement."

"This is too much." Cerdic stood up. "It's time I paid Count Clement a visit."

Giselle stared at her quiet husband in amazement. Usually, his lanky frame was relaxed, and he was quick to smile. Now Cerdic seemed much taller and angrier than she had ever seen him. He turned and left the room. Within minutes she heard him run into the yard, shouting for his horse to be saddled and pulling on some of his knightly gear that he usually only wore when going to Blois or riding about the country on Adela's or Count Stephen's behalf.

He returned the next day.

"What happened?" Giselle asked when he found her in the vineyard, inspecting the new growth on the vines.

"I don't think we'll have any trouble from that quarter." Cerdic grinned at her.

"How can that be?"

"Let's say I gently reminded him of some of his financial obligations. Bluntly put, he owes a lot of money to Count Stephen. Count Stephen had told me about this after we got married. I also pointed out that Count Stephen had been interested in the fact that our properties border on each other."

"I see it all." Giselle laughed. "I guess he now lives in terror of the Count of Blois coming to relieve him of his tenure."

"Well, I offered him a bottle of our wine to reinforce the point. He was quite impressed with the vintage and most polite until I left. I never even mentioned anything about the little gifts he had been leaving for us."

In those years, they laughed a lot.

She had shown him a private place at the river where she used to swim when she was a child. "I dare you to strip and go in right now." Cerdic grinned at her. But before he knew it, she was already in the water, splashing him.

She showed him how to tie up grape vines properly so that he could better inspect the work done by the serfs. He struggled with his hands, awkward and unused to this type of work. She laughed at him.

"You try working with the accounts," he protested. "You won't laugh at me then."

He took her to view the beehives. Foolishly, they had gone without protective clothing. Giselle bumped against one of them, unsettling the bees. Cerdic and Giselle ran as fast as they could to get away from the aggravated bees until they fell down in the field, out of breath and laughing until tears ran down their faces.

The first time Cerdic had to go back to Blois and leave Giselle alone had been a bitter shock. Giselle was pregnant with their first child. By the time Cerdic returned, she had miscarried. Miserable and angry, she felt unmoored and didn't know how to talk to her husband about anything. She was afraid of lashing out, unable to forget her disappointment that he hadn't been there when she felt most alone. But gradually they clawed their way back to some of the contentment that had marked their lives together.

Eventually, Giselle found she was pregnant again.

"I will be here when the baby comes," Cerdic assured her again and again. Then, yet another summons came from Blois. Cerdic was distraught when he came to tell her. "My dear, I must go."

Giselle didn't raise her head from her needlework. *It's always going to be like this. I knew this when I married him. I am stronger now. I can manage.* "Of course," she said after a moment, but without meeting his eyes. "You must go."

Their son Guisbert was born while Cerdic was riding around on behalf of Adela. The little boy was healthy, and by the time Cerdic returned, the baby was already sleeping through the night, and Giselle was so happy to have a living child that everything else seemed to fade away in importance. She could greet Cerdic with a smile on her face when he returned to Les Tilleuls.

Cerdic spent a lot of time poring over the accounts. He tried to put to use everything he had learned from watching Count Stephen-Henry. He worried because neither the vineyard nor Les Tilleuls had been particularly productive in the last years.

"You will hurt your eyes," Giselle chided him when she walked into the great hall with candles and some supper on a tray, the baby clinging to her back.

"There is so much to do." Cerdic rubbed his face.

"Well, say good night to your son." Giselle shifted the boy around, and he stretched out his arms and yawned.

"Ah, Guisbert, my 'Bright Pledge.'" Cerdic stood up and took his son in his arms. "Your mother picked a fine name for you!" He grinned at his wife over his son's still bald head, crowned with the merest dusting of hair.

"Well, mine means 'pledge' as well, or 'hostage.' Sometimes I don't know what I am." Giselle grinned back ruefully.

"You are my hostage," Cerdic said and laughed. "And so is this piglet of ours."

Yes, they had been happy.

Now, it might all come to an end. Sitting in Adela's great hall, Giselle watched the pilgrim and the avid eyes of his listeners and shivered.

Leaving For The Holy Land

Set out on the road to the Holy Sepulchre, take the land from that wicked people, and make it your own.
Pope Urban II, Council of Clermont, 1095

1095 Les Tilleuls

"Why do you have to go?"

It was hot, and Giselle had covered her head with a veil. She was inspecting the grape vines and testing the firmness of the young grapes. They were growing a new variety of grape, one that they hoped to turn into a good vintage of white wine.

Lately, she had discovered to her surprise that she loved wearing colorful clothes. Now that the estate was doing better, she could indulge in new attire. Today, she stood out like a flower in a butter-yellow gown. But she had hiked up her tunic, tying it at her waist, and had kicked off her sandals. Her feet were brown from the summer sun.

"Your elegant gown is enhanced by your bare legs." Cerdic grinned at his wife. He reached for a bunch of grapes.

"Stop that." Giselle slapped his hand away. "It's too soon. They are still sour."

"You know that we have perfectly qualified vintners who can check on the vines, don't you?" Cerdic tugged on her veil, adjusting it to protect her neck. "You don't have to be out here in the sun."

"Of course, I know that, but my father always said that an estate is only as good as its master. If we want things done right, we need to pay attention to everything. I was the one who noticed water standing at the lower end of this field. If I hadn't done that, the vines would be rotting at their bases right now." She straightened up, brushing a lock away from her damp face. "But you didn't answer me. Why do you have to go?"

"To Marmoutier? I told you. Adela and Stephen-Henry are planning to make a major grant for a new priory. It's commendable. They want me to come along to help work out all the details of forest and pasture rights with the monks for the rural settlement."

"Oh, very commendable." Giselle rolled her eyes. "I am sure the monks will be happy to pray for Count Stephen-Henry's safe return from the crusade."

"You know, prayers and good deeds can't exist without a foundation," Cerdic said defensively. "A well-functioning enterprise will create a safe environment for the priory."

"Oh, naturally. And my lady and Count Stephen-Henry will certainly enjoy the customs fees that they'll be able to assess on all that the monks produce."

"You are too harsh. The grant comes out of her dower properties. And she is using her own funds to help pay for the crusade."

"Of course, I don't doubt her charity and her piety." Giselle knew she shouldn't have spoken so openly. She had promised herself to refrain from making snide remarks about Adela. It had slipped out. "I wasn't thinking of your going along to Marmoutier. I know you have to do that. I was thinking about the crusade."

After their last stay in Blois, Cerdic and Giselle had been permitted to return home once more, but now the entire county was in an uproar.

The pulpits everywhere had been ringing with Pope Urban's words, exhorting all faithful to venture forth to the Holy Land. Giselle listened, unable to turn away. It frightened her, this fervor that so many seemed to embrace. In all the lands, people were getting ready, setting their affairs in order, selling their property so that they would have funds for the long journey, hiring guides, and searching for maps. How many wanted to go for the adventure, the dream of glory? How many dreamed of riches? How many were seeking power? Certainly, many truly dreamed of praying at the holiest of holy sites of Christendom. Giselle knew that. Adela was among those, intensely devout and ready to embrace the crusade, ready to contribute her wealth to outfit her husband in his venture.

Cerdic rolled a grape around in his hand, his eyes on it as if it were a precious jewel. Then he tossed it into the grass. "You are right. It's still too sour."

Giselle refused to be distracted. "Will you have to go?"

"You know that I have no choice in this, don't you?" The frown line on Cerdic's forehead accentuated his long, narrow face with its jutting nose. "I owe my allegiance to my lord."

"Of course, you do." Giselle shook her head in frustration and turned her face to look across the field toward the woods. "I am just afraid." She couldn't say what she was thinking. *It's like a fever sweeping through all the lands. So many people won't come back.*

"Everything will be fine," Cerdic said. "I have already arranged everything with Auberi and Matthias. Please don't worry."

That's not why I am afraid, you silly man, Giselle almost blurted out. But she didn't say that either. "Oh, Cid, you are so loyal; they should emblazon it on your shield." She put her hands on his shoulders. "Make sure you come back."

Land Flowing With Milk And Honey

I have said I will bring you up out of the affliction of Egypt to the land of the Canaanites and the Hittites and the Amorites and the Perizzites and the Hivites and the Jebusites, to a land flowing with milk and honey. Exodus 3:17

1097 Nicaea

"Dratted quills." Count Stephen tossed the frayed goose feather into a corner and grabbed another one. "I should have asked Father Alexander to sharpen more for me." He dipped it into a pot of ink and continued writing. Scritch, scratch.

Count Stephen to Adela, his sweetest and most amiable wife, to his dear children, and to all his vassals of all ranks, his greeting and blessing.

You may be very sure, dearest, that the messenger whom I sent to give you pleasure, left me before Antioch safe and unharmed, and through God's grace in the greatest prosperity. And already at that time, together with all the chosen army of Christ, endowed with great valor by Him, we had been continuously advancing for twenty-three weeks toward the home of our Lord Jesus. You may know for certain, my beloved, that of gold, silver and many other kind of riches I now have twice as much as your love had assigned to me when I left you. For all our princes, with the common consent of the whole army, against my own wishes, have made me up to the present time the leader, chief and director of their whole expedition.

Cerdic sat on a stool in Count Stephen-Henry's tent in the encampment outside of Nicaea. His head itched. He would have to check his gear for lice. All the men were infested with them. He could hear them through the tent walls—an unceasing cacophony of shouts, angry voices, muttered curses, and occasional bursts of laughter.

Count Stephen-Henry's tent boasted a Persian carpet, a comfortable pallet, a working area with a folding table, and several travel chests. The count had sent many gifts he received from Emperor Alexios home to Blois, entrusting them to a small contingent of his retinue, but some he was loath to let out of his grasp. And Cerdic had heard him dictate a letter in which he had gone on and on about his delight in the many presents he had received from the emperor.

The count was once again writing to his wife. Usually, he had his chaplain, Father Alexander, take dictation, but today he had dispensed with his services.

Cerdic liked Father Alexander. Tall and slender, with a face that seemed to be carved out of oak, full of crags and sharp corners, he never seemed to lose his calm.

Count Stephen and his contingent had arrived in Nicaea after the siege had been going on for several weeks. Emperor Alexios Komnenos had been solicitous and anxious to show his support by providing Count Stephen and his army with food. However, he was not eager to accompany them. Constantinople had already endured the presence of Peter the Hermit and some 30,000 men earlier. While the city felt relatively opulent and Count Stephen was treated like a favorite son by the emperor, Cerdic got the distinct impression of a populace that could hardly wait for the disappearance of their unwelcome guests.

The count wrote slowly. Cerdic wondered whether he missed the ease with which the chaplain wrote in flowing, beautiful Latin.

"You should write to your wife." Count Stephen-Henry lifted his quill and blew on what he had just written. "She'd be delighted, and if she doesn't read, my lady would be happy to assist her."

"Oh, she reads," Cerdic said slowly. It hadn't occurred to him to do this. It felt almost presumptuous. Writing letters seemed something reserved for lords and kings. But he asked for some parchment. The count handed him a few sheets. "Don't worry about the writing on the other side; we no longer need it. It's from a manuscript I had cut up to use." Armed with this unexpected treasure and several quills, he retreated to the tent he shared with other knights. It felt almost cozy and peaceful to sit there, leaning against his baggage roll, with the shield propped up on his legs as a table.

Through the open tent flap, he could see knights arguing over a bag of supplies. A squire was tending a fire and occasionally stirred the contents of a large cast-iron pot. Two paupers that stood close by, trying to see what was in the pot. "Get away," the squire shouted. "This is not for you."

Cerdic lifted his quill. Then he stopped. What could he write? He couldn't write about what he had seen in Nicaea.

Food among the soldiers besieging Nicaea was scarce. Soldiers looked haggard, and the neighboring villages feared their presence. He couldn't tell Giselle about the miserable men and women wandering about in rags, many without shoes. Nor did he want to talk of the knights marauding in the villages. And it wasn't only food that they stole. Cerdic hadn't envisioned the misery a crusading army would bring to a region. Nor had he expected the degree to which people in the army and the various leaders bickered among each other.

He would have liked to write about Father Alexander. Cerdic had watched him comfort a dying foot soldier. During the siege of Nicaea, that poor man had endured a spear thrust into his shoulder. He lived to walk back to the camp, only to writhe in pain a day later. He was feverish and vomiting until he brought up blood, while blood and excrement had smeared his hose. Oblivious to the stench, Father Alexander kneeled next to him on the ground and held his hand. Cerdic couldn't hear what he said to him, but the man seemed to grow calmer. Father Alexander took out a small flask and gently anointed the man's hands and forehead, marking the sign of the cross. His voice was steady and clear as he spoke the act of contrition. The man mouthed the words, his eyes on Father Alexandre's face, and then he was silent. Father Alexander took his hands and crossed them on his chest and spoke another prayer before rising up.

Cerdic hoped that when his time came, a priest might be there to comfort him. So many had already died on the journey, and what he had heard didn't make him feel confident about the future. He couldn't talk about any of this to Giselle.

And what about Count Stephen-Henry? For all that Cerdic had initially been happy in Blois, he had resented this man after his marriage to Adela. This was Adela's husband? This corpulent older man who seemed unaware of his young wife's many stellar qualities? He was so self-assured and content, patting his young wife on the back as if she was his new dog, beaming at everyone. It hurt Cerdic to watch. It also hurt that Adela had begun to change so quickly he hardly recognized her anymore. Her presence, her clear voice, her musky scent disturbed and unsettled him. He hated himself for harboring such thoughts.

And yet, over the last years, he had become fond of Count Stephen-Henry, and not because he was grateful to the count for his generosity.

The other day, the count had told Cerdic that the other leaders had chosen him to be in charge of provisioning for the army. "I'll need your help more than ever," he warned Cerdic, evidently proud of his new role. "We'll need to make some lists, and there will be many details we'll have to consider."

Cerdic could see that this was a good choice. It was the kind of work Count Stephen-Henry excelled at. The count wasn't comfortable with the martial aspects of the crusade. He certainly looked the part when riding into battle, dressed in the finest gear that a man of his stature could acquire, but he was not eager to charge into the middle of a melee or to take command of a lagging troop of warriors. Religious fervor didn't fuel his motivation to join the crusade. He didn't speak of his doubts about this venture, but his reluctance was evident. Count Stephen-Henry was not a warrior.

He could hardly write about any of this to Giselle. What if she showed Adela his letter?

Nor did he want to talk about meeting Peter the Hermit, the leader of an increasingly unruly band of paupers. This strange, intense priest with eyes sunk deep into bony sockets had taken Cerdic's hand and held it in his hot, dry claws as if he was about to speak a blessing. Then his eyes lost their focus. He dropped Cerdic's hand and walked away. Cerdic had heard such tales about this man that he could hardly grasp them with his mind. Apparently, he had instigated and participated in the torture and slaughter of scores of Jews in towns in the west, such as Colognes, Worms, and Mainz. And his roving bands of paupers seemed little better than a mob, killing and scavenging at will. When Cerdic had tried to question Count Stephen-Henry, the count had waved a hand dismissively. "He is a holy man; he is doing the Lord's work."

"To Giselle, from Cerdic, Nicaea 1097, I miss you," Cerdic wrote slowly. Count Stephen called his wife "my dearest" and "my most amiable wife." Cerdic felt awkward at using such words; his marriage had been a practical solution, a way out of a quandary for both. It felt like a lie to write to Giselle as the count wrote to his beloved Adela. Cerdic pictured Giselle's cheerful grin and her laughing eyes, framed by an unruly mop of hair, because she often forgot to cover it. He did miss her, he realized with a pang.

Then it was easy. He told her of the long journey east. "You would like the wild forests and mountains around the Danube. That river makes the Loire look like a trickle in a meadow." He described Constantinople and his amazement at the density and the splendor of the buildings. "We don't see Duke Robert often; he is mostly with the other leaders like Raymond of Toulouse, Godfrey of Bouillon and his brother Baldwin, Bohemond of Taranto and his nephew Tancred. But, short and slight as Robert is, he is truly a brave and valiant knight, always ready to launch himself into battle. He is much happier here than he ever was in Caen." Not having his father criticize him must have a lot to do with that. Cerdic told Giselle about the honor to Count Stephen in being put in charge of organization and supplies. "You'd be amazed if you saw the script of the Turks. It must be difficult to learn. They have beautiful names; the Sultan is called Kılıç Arslan, which means 'Sword of the Lion.' They are fierce fighters, and they ride fast on small, sturdy horses, shooting while in full gallop; but we will prevail." Cerdic thought about the battle scenes he had witnessed; no, he couldn't write about this. "You like numbers, I know. Can you imagine how much food is needed for 60,000 people? That's apparently how many there are in this crusade. Some say that there are many more."

Cerdic didn't write about the starvation among the men or the illnesses that raged through the camp. He didn't talk about the gut churning fear he felt or his yearning for home. "I am well," he wrote laboriously. "We eat a lot of figs with cheese; you would like that, but perhaps not the salted meat which makes us thirsty. They use honey in everything: bread, pastry, even tea. There is a fruit here that can be dried and eaten like that. It's called an apricot. I will try to bring some back with me. I like the way meat is roasted on thin skewers. But I miss your fish, baked with herbs and leeks." Should he tell her that mostly they ate an unappealing porridge made of wheat or chickpeas and were grateful to have that? He ran his tongue over the sores in his mouth, trying to think of what else to write. He talked about plans for their fields and for the vineyard. He asked whether Count Clement had been annoying her. "It might be a good idea to send him a reminder. Perhaps outfit one of my men with a shield and a helmet and send him to Count Clement with my greeting and a jar of honey. He will get the message. How is my little 'pledge?' When I come home, I will start teaching Guisbert how to swim." Carefully Cerdic wrote his name and folded the vellum. He would send it with Count Stephen-Henry's messenger. It would be a long time before he would get back. He found himself longing for home with an intensity that hurt.

Domina

Predecessors of sharper memory more experienced in literary work commended monuments of things accomplished to the notice of their successors inspiring by this example lest they slothfully neglect something worthy of memory to future times. We, thinking to our and our successors' benefit, since while we know the beginning we do not know what the end may be, lest acts well and piously done be confounded by oblivion through time, let us take care to recall them in memory with virile writings.

Adela of England, Countess of Blois, Chartres, and Meaux,
letter to Public, 1101

1097 Les Tilleuls

"Why do I have to go to Blois?" Giselle muttered to herself. "I hate it."

"You always say that." Janine was holding a pile of clean linen sheets in her arm. They smelled fresh. She grinned at her mistress. "But then you end up enjoying your time there."

Giselle frowned as she watched Janine walk out with her pile of linens and pushed an unruly curl out of her face. That girl was getting too fresh, too opinionated. She relied on Giselle's affection for her father Thomas, who lately spent many days sitting in a sunny spot on a bench in the courtyard and rubbing his swollen hands and knees. And yet, Giselle had to admit the girl had a point.

Giselle held up a formal gown, with fine gold threads woven into dusty red wool, her face flushed from bending over. It probably wouldn't fit anymore. Angrily, she tossed it onto the pile on her bed.

Of course, she hated being called to heel like a dog by the countess whenever Adela desired some company. She hated leaving her little boy. And this was a bad time to be away from home. There was so much work to do in the vineyard. She knew perfectly well that she could rely on Auberi and was grateful to him for his tactful handling of old Thomas. Still, she was anxious when she was not here to supervise the harvest. Most of all, she was homesick whenever she was in Blois. During those times, she longed for Cerdic even more than when she was in her familiar environment.

It was odd, that feeling of missing him. It was almost as if it was easier for her to think of him now when he was far away, farther than she could have ever imagined. She pictured his lanky limbs, the musky smell when he came to her at night, and his quirky smile when he teased her, and she missed him so that her heart ached. Proximity held more traps for her. The reality of his presence made her feel awkward, choking out her feelings of yearning. Her shyness only abated when she was busy with chores and when they were working together. It was worst of all when Cerdic went out of his way to be loving and helpful. It made her blush, and she got all tangled up inside. Adela probably never had that problem. And there, once again, her thoughts had wandered back to Adela.

Despite everything, Giselle had come to like the woman, and life at the court in Blois had changed her more than she expected.

Giselle remembered a lengthy poem by Abbot Baudri of Bourgueil that Adela had shown to her. In minutest detail, the abbot described a beautiful chamber he envisioned as belonging to Adela and covered from ceiling to floor by tapestries with depictions of the creation, allegorical tales, representations of her father's conquests, and even the constellation. In his vision, even the bed hanging was richly embellished with images from the arts and sciences, healing herbs, and mysteries of medicine.

Of course, it was an elaborate flight of fancy, and yet, for Giselle, spending time at Blois and with Adela was a bit like entering a marvelous chamber that filled her with wonder. Giselle shook her head, tempted to laugh at herself for indulging in such notions.

It would be interesting to see how Adela handled her time alone.

Two weeks later, Giselle sat in the great hall of Blois watching Adela discuss a problem that had arisen with the delivery of logs for construction of an abbey she was supporting with the steward. The man standing in front of the countess was shifting from one leg to the other and twisting his cap in his hands.

"My lady, there were several mishaps causing a flatboat to capsize and blocking the progress of the other boats. Someone failed to secure the logs properly, and that caused the balance to shift. There weren't enough people working on this."

"And whose fault was that?" Adela spoke with a soft voice.

The steward flushed.

"Do I need to remind you that I told you to check with me when you do not have enough help for a task?" She quickly scribbled something on a piece of parchment. "Here, talk to this man regarding more help; also don't forget to send a messenger to the abbey informing them of the delay. I want this matter sorted out quickly."

The steward bowed and left the great hall.

Giselle took a deep breath. Count Stephen-Henry called Adela *Domina,* which meant a female lord. And she certainly acted like one.

"Aren't you glad you came back for a while?" Adela grinned at Giselle, in an instant transforming from the authoritative lady to a young woman. "Sometimes I think that we women might be better at this sort of thing than the men. My lord doesn't like to pay attention to details; he simply expects everything to be done according to his wishes. It doesn't always work."

Giselle lost track when trying to comprehend the range of things that Adela's regency included. In one of her acts, she granted monks the right to build a new church. She helped to set up a charter of rights and obligations. Another time, Adela wrote a stern missive to one of Count Stephen-Henry's retainers, instructing him to send more knights to help settle a dispute with King Philip I.

Among her regular correspondents were several bishops.. The other day, she had found Adela chuckling over a letter from Bishop Ivo of Chartres. "Can you imagine? He wants me to advise him on how to control a group of misbehaving nuns."

Giselle had to smile at the images this evoked and could barely disguise her amazement at the light-hearted tone with which Adela talked about the bishop.

"What do you think about this?" she asked Giselle one morning, holding up a manuscript with the writings of St. Augustine. "Do you think infants are already guilty at birth? He seems to argue that infants inherit guilt from Adam."

Giselle shook her head. "I wouldn't know. He was a saint, right? But it is hard to accept that my little Guisbert was born with guilt."

"That's what I think." Adela put down the manuscript. "I will have to reread this and think about it some more. Perhaps I'll write to Bishop Ivo and get his opinion."

She talked to Giselle about her life in Caen and about her school. "I learned so much from my mother. She wanted to make sure my sisters and I were taught as much as my brothers. I want to do the same for my children."

Giselle didn't understand how Adela could be so stern with her children. There was no doubt that she loved them dearly. "He has to learn," she said when Giselle found William crying again. The younger brothers Theobald and Stephen seemed to have an easier time of it, and when they got in trouble, they quickly laughed it off. Once, alerted by the tutor, Adela sharply reprimanded William for his failure to write his lessons on his slate. Distraught and frightened, he ran away and fell out of an opening on the upper level onto the flagstones of the courtyard. Fortunately, he had braced himself with his arms. He had broken one of his wrists, but that was all.

"Oh Giselle, I don't know what to do anymore," Adela said, apparently close to tears, after the boy's wrist had been bandaged, and he was in bed. "William is the oldest, and yet he often acts as if he was younger than my little Lucia-Mahaut." She wiped her face with her long sleeve. "I worry about what's going to happen to him."

What could she possibly say to that? "Maybe he needs more time."

Adela nodded. But she had already resumed the face of calm control she normally showed to the world.

The next day, letters arrived.

"Giselle, I have something for you," Adela called out, waving several pieces of parchment in the air, when Giselle entered the great hall. Theobald and Stephen were pulling on her tunic. William was trailing behind, an uncertain smile on his round-cheeked face.

"You promised you would play ring toss with us," Theobald shouted.

"I will." Giselle smiled at the boys. "Let me talk to your mother first."

"Don't be too long," Theobald said. "We have our lessons later. But we'll get the spikes and the rings, so we are ready for you when you come out."

"Children, I expect you to speak more respectfully to Mistress Giselle," Adela admonished. "You may go now."

Chastened, the boys trooped out.

"It's time for them to go to school," Adela said.

"I enjoy your children; I really do. And I remember playing *quoits* as a child. You should join us."

Adela shook her head. "I have more important things to do. I have received a letter from my lord. And you have a letter as well."

"A letter for me?" Giselle stared at Adela. She had never received a letter in her entire life. Adela had previously read aloud some excerpts from a letter that Count Stephen-Henry had written to her, and Giselle had been filled with envy. She couldn't imagine Cerdic writing to her, much less to address her as his sweet, amiable wife. Count Stephen-Henry had written at great lengths about the honors and gifts he had received from the Byzantine emperor. Giselle had almost started giggling when Adela had read this portion of the letter to her, evidently pleased with the accolades heaped upon her husband. Giselle couldn't help but think of her little Guisbert, proudly displaying the wilted flowers from the field he had collected for her. But she had nodded and said how wonderful it was that the count wrote letters home. And now, Adela was holding out a crumpled piece of parchment, sealed with a wafer that displayed Count Stephen-Henry's coat of arms. She could make out her name written on the outside.

Giselle took it and nearly dropped it in her excitement. "May I be excused, my lady?"

"Of course," Adela said abruptly. She seemed disappointed that Giselle didn't open the letter right away in front of her.

Giselle backed up and quickly walked out of the great hall.

In her room, she broke the seal and carefully pried open the tightly folded parchment. "To Giselle, from Cerdic," she read. She recognized the handwriting from the ledgers at home. "I miss you." Her eyes blurred. "You would like…" she read and then found herself weeping. He was talking to her as if he was sitting in the same room. He missed her.

"You should write to him," Adela said the next day, when Giselle had related some things Cerdic had described. She didn't show the letter to Adela; she had hidden it away in her chest.

She shook her head. "I wouldn't know what to write."

"I am sure you will think of something once you start. Sit here. And we can send it together with my letter."

Giselle sat at the table, staring at the blank piece of parchment. Then she smiled. "Dear Cerdic," she wrote laboriously. "You have another son. He was born five months after you left. His name is Yves because when I look at him, so sturdy and strong, I think of the yew trees on the hill behind Les Tilleuls."

PARBOILED THISTLES

And now, everything which could be procured for food being destroyed around the city, a sudden famine, which usually makes even fortresses give way, began to oppress the army; so much so that the harvest not having yet attained its maturity, some persons seized the pods of beans before they were ripe, as the greatest delicacy: others fed on carrion, or hides soaked in water; others passed parboiled thistles through their bleeding jaws into their stomachs. Others sold mice or such like dainties to those who required them; content to suffer hunger themselves, so that they could procure money. Some, too, there were who even fed their corpse like bodies with other corpses, eating human flesh, but at a distance, and on the mountains, lest others should be offended at the smell of their cookery. Many wandered through unknown paths, in expectation of meeting with sustenance, and were killed by robbers acquainted with the passes. (Siege of Antioch, William of Malmsbury, *Chronicle of the Kings of England from the Earliest Period to the Reign of King Stephen*, p. 208).

1097 ANTIOCH

"400 towers," a squire whispered to Cerdic, when he and Count Stephen-Henry arrived outside the city of Antioch several weeks after the others in the late fall.

"400?" Cerdic repeated in disbelief. "It looks well fortified."

Count Stephen had been loath to leave Constantinople, basking in the cordial hospitality of Emperor Alexios.

Cerdic stared at the city walls. On one side, the city was framed by the Orontes river. Of the six gates to the city, three were along the northern wall, and one each in the south, east, and west, where steep slopes complicated any approach. The crusaders' camps were on the northern and western sides of the city. Count Stephen-Henry, together with Adela's brother Robert Curthose, Robert of Flanders, and others were in the west, close to the heavily fortified Iron Bridge across the Orontes.

At least, the local Armenians were willing to provide the crusaders with supplies for men and horses, even though at extortionate prices. But this source of food was soon depleted. Crusaders had to forage farther afield and risk being attacked by defenders in nearby garrisons while leaving the camps outside of Antioch more vulnerable. Over the winter, hunger set in. Men died. Only 700 horses were left. In January 1098, some knights and soldiers began to desert.

By the spring, the besieging army, broken into various camps alongside the river, made Cerdic think of badly soiled and disintegrating stork nests, occupied by tousled and malnourished birds, all screaming at each other.

Even though the food situation had improved slightly with more supplies arriving from Constantinople in the early spring months, the atmosphere among the besieging crusaders was fraught with mutual accusations of treachery and cowardice. Bohemond of Taranto tried to exert pressure on the other leaders by insisting that Antioch should be granted to him in its entirety. Raymond of Toulouse and Godfrey of Bouillon resisted this pressure even while Bohemond was successful in getting some support from others for his plans.

Now it was already almost the end of May, and the besieging crusaders faced a new threat. A Turkish army under the command of Kerbogha, the feared ruler of Mosul, was descending on the exhausted crusaders. It was an immense fighting force. Kerbogha had joined forces with the Seljuk leaders Ridwan of Aleppo and Duqaq of Syria, and there were also troops from Persia and from Mesopotamia.

Resting on his pallet, Cerdic tried to move as little as he could. Whenever he took a breath, it felt as if there was a sharp dagger poking into his ribs. The sling around his arm itched at the neck, and he could hardly restrain himself from ripping it off. He was lucky to be alive. A broken arm and broken ribs were a small price to pay. He knew that perfectly well. A week ago, he had ventured close to the city, intent on joining other crusaders on a daring attempt to break into the city. They had tried to climb up the ramparts, using ladders they had leaned against the heavily fortified city walls. A defender above hurled a spear in Cerdic's direction. Some instinct made him flinch and step to the side. He toppled into the ditch behind him, falling onto his own sword.

Angry voices in the distance made him open his eyes. Cerdic was so tired he could barely stand. But he knew that there was no choice. He needed to find out what was happening. He got to his feet with a groan and stumbled outside toward the tent where the leaders of the crusade were engaged in a heated discussion.

"If we want to survive, never mind reach Jerusalem in this age, we must take the city before Kerbogha gets here," Robert Curthose shouted.

Cerdic had never much cared for Adela's eldest brother. Robert was impatient, abrasive, quick to anger, and without any sense of humor. But despite all his faults, an unimposing stature, and with a permanent scowl on his dark face, he inspired loyalty and admiration in his followers. While he, along with others, had suffered during the months of deprivation and bore several blood-encrusted wounds on his face and arms, it was as if he fed on war with all its horrors. His eyes gleamed, even though they were bloodshot and sunken in his skull. He glanced around with a furious exuberance, as if he was happy, relishing the opportunity to act in this protracted fight against the infidel. Perhaps he was happy. Again, Cerdic felt a twinge of pity. It could not have been easy to be the king's son. Here he was free to act, not at the mercy of an irascible father's harping and his undisguised disappointment in his eldest son. Away from all that, Robert was a happy warrior, fierce, brave, and riding on a swell of religious fervor.

Count Robert had raged along with the leaders of the crusade about Bohemond's greed and attempt to manipulate them for his own gain. Cerdic sniffed at that thought, but tried to keep it to himself. Weren't they all greedy? For wealth and power? Certainly for glory in the eyes of God. At least, Count Robert appeared genuinely driven in this fight to regain the Holy Land for Christianity, willing to risk his life at every chance.

It was odd. Some crusaders seemed to thrive in this setting. Not so Count Stephen-Henry. At Blois, Cerdic had watched his calm and evenhanded way of dealing with everyone who came through the castle gates and his skill with merchants and at the bargaining table. He seemed to carry a detailed map of the complicated web of trade in his head and always knew when to act swiftly to secure a good deal. He laughed easily, always ready with a glass of wine and a good meal for his guests. Now, he bore little resemblance to the portly man he had been in Blois, even though, given his position, he hadn't suffered as much as the soldiers and servants had. Like the other crusaders, the count had stopped shaving, and the dark beard obscured the hollows in his cheeks.

The count didn't join in the heated discussion. The crusaders were talking over each other, hardly hearing what the others were saying. Bohemond, still intent on his goal of securing the city to himself, claimed he had a deal with an Armenian inside the city walls who could provide access. He insisted that he would reveal this only if the crusaders made him Prince of Antioch.

"Absolutely not; we had agreed that the city would be handed over to Emperor Alexios," Raymond exclaimed. "We can't go back on that."

Count Stephen-Henry listened without comment and then walked away, shaking his head.

Cerdic stayed until the end of the talks and went back to the count's tent to tell him the latest news. He was probably writing. That man wrote too many letters. A few months ago, Cerdic had listened to the count dictate to Father Alexander.

Count Stephen to Adela, his sweetest and most amiable wife, to his dear children, and to all his vassals of all ranks, his greeting and blessing.

We found the city of Antioch very extensive, fortified with incredible strength and almost impregnable. In addition, more than 5ooo bold Turkish soldiers had entered the city, not counting the Saracens, Publicans, Arabs, Turcopolitans, Syrians, Armenians and other different races of whom an infinite multitude had gathered together there. In fighting against these enemies of God and of our own we have, by God's grace, endured many sufferings and innumerable evils up to the present time. Many also have already exhausted all their resources in this very holy passion. Very many of our Franks, indeed, would have met a temporal death from starvation, if the clemency of God and our money had not succored them. Before the abovementioned city of Antioch indeed, throughout the whole winter we suffered for our Lord Christ from excessive cold and enormous torrents of rain. What some say about the impossibility of bearing the heat of the sun throughout Syria is untrue, for the winter there is very similar to our winter in the west.

Cerdic pushed the flap to Count Stephen-Henry's tent. Surprised, he gazed at the scene inside. The usually well-organized interior looked as if a storm had ripped through it. Chests had been opened. A candlestick had been knocked over, and a glob of wax puddled on the carpet. Documents were strewn all over the desk. The seal with the distinctive bar of the House of Blois had rolled onto the floor.

The count wasn't writing letters. He moved around the small space, picking up clothing and other items and tossing them onto a large pile between his desk and his pallet. "Oh, Cerdic. There you are." His voice sounded hesitant. He waved his hands with an uncertain gesture, as if to apologize for the mess in the tent. "So, what have they decided?"

Cerdic explained the plans laid out by the leaders on how to meet the oncoming army without exposing themselves too much to sorties from the defending citadel and town.

"They are fools. They'll all die. I'm done."

Cerdic stared at the count. "Done?"

"Yes; I'm leaving. Tonight. I have already given the order to my squires. Several knights are coming with me. And you, of course."

A Crusader's Homecoming

Stuffed Pigling

Let the pig be killed by cutting his throat and scalded in boiling water and then skinned; then take the lean meat and throw away the feet and entrails of the pig and set him to boil in water; and take twenty eggs and boil them hard and chestnuts cooked in water and peeled. Then take the yolks of the eggs, the chestnuts, some fine old cheese and the meat of a cooked leg of pork and chop them up, then bray them with plenty of saffron and ginger powder mixed with the meat; and if your meat becometh too hard, soften it with yolks of eggs. And open not your pig by the belly but across the shoulders and with the smallest opening you may; then put him on the spit and afterwards put your stuffing into him and sew him up with a big needle; and let him be eaten either with yellow pepper sauce or with cameline in summer. The French Medieval Household Book *Le Ménagier de Paris* (The Goodman of Paris)

1098 Blois

Cerdic couldn't bear thinking of that night when they snuck out of the camp. Perhaps 'sneaking' was too harsh a word.

"I told the others that my health was failing and that I must return to my wife while I still can," the count had said when confronted by Cerdic's silence at his announcement of an imminent departure.

Whatever the count told them, they left quietly when night fell. They wrapped cloths around their gear to muffle the sound and led their horses so as not to attract attention. And then they traveled north as fast as they could.

Two days later, they encountered Emperor Alexios at the head of his army. He was moving toward Antioch in the hope of providing assistance to the crusaders. The emperor and Count Stephen-Henry spoke for a while, out of earshot of the others. And when they broke camp again, the emperor turned around and joined them on the journey north and west.

The news from Antioch reached them a few weeks later. After Cerdic had listened to the messenger, he walked out of their temporary encampment in search of solitude, but could not escape the feelings of bitterness, misery, and shame. The remaining crusaders had breached the city walls, helped by a traitor inside. Sixty knights broke in and opened the gates to the others. Thus, they managed to repel the oncoming Muslim army under the command of Kerbogha. While Count Stephen-Henry was telling the emperor that it was hopeless and urging him to turn back, the crusaders conquered the city of Antioch.

During the long journey home, Cerdic sometimes glanced at the count from the side and wondered what he was thinking. He was certainly pleased with the cartloads of treasures he was bringing back from the east. Whenever they stopped for the night, the count placed guards near the carts.

On the road, they encountered others trying to return home from the crusade. The count and his men still had supplies provided by the emperor. Most of the lone travelers had nothing left. Dressed in rags, they were limping along and starving.

"Can't we help?" Cerdic felt wretched as he watched them.

"If we give succor to them all, we'll have nothing left for ourselves. Let's ride on." The count turned his head away from the pitiful sight and spurred his horse into a trot. This was a side of the count Cerdic hadn't witnessed before. He understood the reasoning, but he started to carry bits of food with him that he could drop quietly as they rode past another miserable soul.

Then it turned out that the count wanted to ride to Chartres first.

"Why now?" Cerdic asked. "Going north will make our journey even longer."

"We need to take some things to the cathedral. My wife told Bishop Ivo that we would do this; it's the least I can do," the count said, a curiously plaintive note in his voice.

In Chartres, Bishop Ivo was delighted. His eyes gleamed as he fondled the jewelry and the elaborately wrought silver chalice with a fine gold rim from Constantinople. "Please don't forget to express my profound gratitude to the benevolent lady, your wife," he said over and over again.

"I am the one who brought all this back from the east," Count Stephen-Henry grumbled out of the bishop's hearing, "and he thanks my wife."

Finally, they resumed their journey, heading south.

"Stay in Blois for a while before you return to your wife," the count suggested. "A few weeks more or less won't make a difference. And my lady will be pleased to see you." It was almost as if he was pleading.

Reluctantly, Cerdic agreed to go to Blois first before returning home. He had missed the blooming of the lime trees. He had missed two harvests. He had missed the birth of his son, Yves. Yves was probably already walking, and Guisbert was running everywhere and making mischief. He missed Giselle. And yet, the idea of going back to Blois filled him with exhilaration and trepidation. He wanted to see Adela again.

When they arrived in Blois in the summer of 1099, Adela was expecting them. Alerted by a messenger, she stood on the steps to welcome her lord. Dressed in a shimmering russet gown trimmed with gold, she looked splendid. "Welcome home, my lord." She sank into a deep curtsy. "A feast has been prepared for you. It will be ready in a while." She turned to go inside. Glancing back over her shoulder, she nodded at Cerdic. "You will excuse us; it has been a long time since I have seen my lord."

Cerdic watched the two disappear into the great hall. Count Stephen-Henry walked gingerly, with his shoulders slightly hunched.

Dinner was a strange and awkward affair. Aside from Cerdic, only two of Count Stephen-Henry's retainers were present. Adela was the only woman; she presided over the table with a broad smile fixed on her face. One dish after another was brought in. After months of deprivation followed by rough fare on the journey home, it was disorienting to be poking around in a dish of fresh lamprey in white sauce, spiced with ginger, cinnamon, and cloves. The lamprey was followed by small quail and thrush, roasted with slices of sausage and bay leaves under their wings, stuffed with rich cheese and beef marrow, and served with fine salt and a pasty. There were honey-sweetened almond fritters, stewed pears, and nuts. The sweet, spiced wine made Cerdic sneeze. His stomach hurt. It was all more than he could bear. He wished he were sitting next to Giselle on the stone bench in the courtyard at Les Tilleuls, munching on grapes and eating bread with cheese.

The next weeks were the most uncomfortable Cerdic had ever spent in Blois.

When he met Adela the next morning in the courtyard, she greeted him warmly and kissed him on both cheeks. Her scent of roses and mint enveloped him like a cloud. She wore a gown of soft green velvet that accentuated her fuller body, and her hair, tucked underneath the white headdress, had been brushed until it was shiny; tendrils of it caressed her brow. She was nothing like the slight young girl who had ridden into the courtyard of Blois years ago. Her ripeness disturbed him and left him unsettled.

"It is good to see you, Cerdic." She beamed as she studied him with her large blue eyes. That's how she had looked at him sometimes in Caen. Then she frowned. "Why are you not with your wife? What are you doing here?"

Cerdic flushed and stammered something about returning to Les Tilleuls soon. He was bewildered by the attack and felt the sting of rejection. He couldn't very well say that Count Stephen-Henry had pleaded with him to stay in Blois for a while.

Adela had suffered a loss while her husband and Cerdic had been sitting in the camp outside of Antioch. Her son Odo, who had not yet reached the age of ten, had fallen grievously ill and died within a few days. Count Stephen-Henry had wept when he heard the news conveyed to him in a letter.

"I am so sorry about Odo," Cerdic said now, speaking hesitantly, because he wasn't sure whether it was his place to mention this.

"Thank you." Adela lowered her eyes. "He was a dear boy, and we miss him, but he is with God." She shook her head as if to brush off all thoughts of him. "I must think of my other children now."

Some discussions in the great hall that Cerdic was privy to involved the usual wrangling over Adela's brothers. The count was not particularly communicative about Robert, who was still in the Holy Land. He was evidently uncomfortable about bringing up any mention of the crusade. Adela and the count had clearly differing views about Henry and William Rufus, who had wasted no time to grab the crown of England for himself after the king's death in 1087. Robert had never yet accepted the loss of what he perceived as his birthright as the eldest son. And Henry, adrift and landless after the death of his father, had eventually allied himself with William Rufus.

Adela disapproved of William Rufus. She was appalled by the stories that had reached them in Blois about his excesses and also his long-standing feud with Archbishop Anselm of Canterbury.

"But he has been an effective ruler," Count Stephen demurred. "You have to admit that under his rule, the realm has been strengthened, and he has repelled various rebellions."

During a light-hearted exchange, the count described arriving in Chartres and delivering the treasure he had brought back from Constantinople. "Bishop Ivo was delighted. In fact, he could hardly contain himself." The count grinned at his wife. "You should have heard him sing your praises. If he weren't the bishop of Chartres, I might begin to worry."

"That was well done, my lord." Adela beamed at him, unfazed by the teasing. "We must do everything to support the church and its good deeds." Then she frowned, bending her head over her work.

Count Stephen stood up and muttered something about having to see his steward.

But these discussions were not what made Cerdic uncomfortable. No, it was the whispering he heard when he happened to be in the great hall and the raised voices that seemed to pierce the walls. Whenever he spent time with the count and his wife, the air seemed to crackle between them. Adela glowed; her color was heightened, and her eyes were brilliant. Cerdic watched her when nobody paid attention to him and was perplexed. She seemed like a young bride. The count had regained much of his bulk and his easy-going demeanor. He couldn't keep his eyes off his wife whenever she was in the vicinity, clearly happy to be with her. And yet, there was something almost furtive in his expression.

Once, he pulled out one of the maps he had brought with him. It was beautiful. An image of the sun appeared on top of the map, while the moon was pushed to the margin below. The holy city of Jerusalem was at its center. The waters of the seas around were green, and the rivers were blue. "This is known as the Red Sea." The count placed his finger on a large blob in red ink. "And this is Paris." He pointed to a densely drawn area toward the bottom. "And see, the sun rises in the east; that's why it's at the top." The sun was a lovely butter-yellow circle with flames shooting out on the sides.

Cerdic stood next to Adela, glancing over her shoulder at the parchment.

"Where did you get this?" Adela bent forward to get a better view.

"It was a gift from Emperor Alexios," the count said proudly. He slid his finger along the red bulge that he had called the Red Sea and then placed it on a spit of land. "This mount is called Djebel Mousa; at its base, there is the monastery of St. Catherine. They say it was built at the site of the burning bush Moses saw in the desert. I wanted to go there to pray; but it wasn't possible."

Cerdic glanced at Adela. She had grown still. Her soft mouth had transformed into a thin line, and her posture made him think of one of her father's falcons, having sighted a prey in the distance. Unspoken words hung in the air. *If you hadn't turned back, you might be praying in the chapel of St. Catherine right now.* Count Stephen-Henry's face was flushed. He busied himself with putting the precious map into a safe place among his other manuscripts.

Cerdic excused himself; neither Adela nor the count paid any attention to him as he walked outside. He heard Adela whisper. It sounded like a hiss until he reached the door. Then her voice rose. Cerdic could hear her even though he had already closed it behind him.

"I could understand how some people gave a lot of wealth to others to go to Jerusalem and pray for their souls because they weren't able to go themselves." Adela spoke rapidly and as if barely allowing herself to catch her breath. "I can respect that. But you, a leader among leaders, left them when they were about to go into battle. You made a promise to the pope. You cannot renege on that obligation."

Cerdic could only make out an indistinct murmur as Stephen responded before he could get away.

Another day, when Cerdic was on his way to the stable to check on his horse, he encountered Adela in the courtyard. She beckoned to him.

"I want you to explain something to me." She glanced around to make sure they were alone. "What is all this I hear about starving crusaders and misery on the journey? It's not as if my lord had been a lowly pilgrim with limited resources traveling in a strange land. You had porters and foot soldiers and all sorts of comforts carried along for you."

"I am trying to picture this in my mind." Cerdic laughed and then grew serious again. "Those comforts you are talking about… most disappeared during the journey before we ever reached Constantinople." He struggled to explain what it had been like, hampered by not wanting to terrify her with details she could not possibly comprehend. But he felt he owed it to the count. "And after we left Constantinople, sickness and hunger ravaged all of us. There was no food to be had."

"But you had your faith to sustain you." Adela's thick eyebrows were drawn together.

"Faith became a brittle vessel for many when faced with something they had never imagined." Cerdic hesitated. "I am sorry to be so blunt. You don't know how unforgiving it is out there. We were hardly the only ones to decide to go back. On our last day in the camp at Antioch, most horses were dead, and the proud army had been sadly reduced."

"If one's faith is shaken by circumstances, then it can't have been strong to begin with." Adela squared her shoulders. "Thank you for telling me all this. I understand better now, but it doesn't change anything. I will have to pray."

Cerdic watched her go back into the castle. He shook his head. More than ever, he wanted to return home. Perhaps Count Stephen-Henry would finally grant him permission to leave.

Les Tilleuls

1098

"Papa is home!" Guisbert almost fell into the solar in his excitement. "I heard the horses. Come and see." The boy pulled on Giselle's gown, dragging her toward the staircase.

Giselle picked up Yves, who was crawling around on the floor. He was heavy in her arms. Her stomach cramped, and her temples throbbed with apprehension.

Almost a month ago, a messenger had ridden to Les Tilleuls with the news that Count Stephen-Henry and his knights had arrived in Blois. The other crusaders remained in the east and were even now on their way to Jerusalem. After the messenger left, Giselle heard the servants whisper to each other. "The count ran away." "Our master wouldn't run away," another voice interjected. "He's no coward." But that wasn't what made Giselle reluctant to move forward.

Cerdic had been back for weeks now, and he hadn't bothered to come home. It was going to start all over again. He would always find a reason to return to Blois. Adela crooked her little finger, and he would drop everything and go to her. Giselle would never be free of that woman.

It had been a hot, dry summer, and September had brought no relief. The courtyard was dusty. The dogs were sleeping on the flagstones, their ears twitching against the flies. A cooper was hard at work in the corner near the stables, getting oak barrels ready for the upcoming harvest. Giselle could hear Maria shouting in the kitchen. "Jacques, get back here. Look at me when I am talking." Giselle couldn't make out Jacques' muttered response. Auberi's son was hardly a child anymore. He was never going to be tall, but he had filled out—almost a young man now. Cerdic wouldn't recognize him. For that matter, he hadn't even seen his youngest son yet. It had been almost two years since he had ridden east in the train of Count Stephen-Henry.

Just then, Cerdic rode into the courtyard. She stared at him, unable to take her eyes off his long-limbed body and his easy manner of directing his horse. Yves whimpered, and she realized that she had been squeezing the little boy too hard.

"Papa, Papa!" Guisbert ran forward.

Cerdic dismounted and swung Guisbert up in his arms. He hugged him fiercely and then put him down. "Let me greet your mother."

Giselle stood frozen on the manor's stone steps. He looked up at her with a tentative smile.

Giselle couldn't speak. Cerdic was so changed. It was as if he had aged by a decade, his hair lighter than the warm brown she remembered, fine lines around his mouth, and his eyes sad. Then his slight smile turned into a chuckle as he reached for Yves. His hands touched hers as he took the little boy from her, and she wanted to clutch them fast to her breast. He was back. He had come home.

"Is this Yves?" He held the boy firmly in his arms, and Yves gazed back at this stranger in consternation. Cerdic tickled him and pulled on his plump legs. "You named him well." He smiled at Giselle. "Those sturdy legs will surely hold him up in any storm. I liked your letter."

Giselle felt her cheeks get red. "Thank you," she whispered. Cerdic couldn't have said anything that would have pleased her more.

They sat together in the great hall after the children were already asleep. Guisbert had been giddy with excitement over the strange wooden toy Cerdic had given to him. It consisted of two disks with a string wrapped around the middle.

"What's this?" he asked, his small face wrinkled in his consternation.

"That is a *joujou*." Cerdic grinned at his son. "Do you want me to show you what it can do?"

"Yes, show me." Guisbert hopped up and down in anticipation.

Cerdic took the odd device and held it in his hand, with one end of the string wrapped around his finger. Then he let it go, so it seemed to roll down along the string. With a flick of his hand, he made it roll back up; then it rolled down again and up in a single fluid motion.

Guisbert was struck dumb, staring with open mouth at this performance. Then he shouted, "Let me try, let me try."

Yves screeched along with his brother, even though he wasn't sure what the excitement was all about.

"Here you go." Cerdic handed it to Guisbert. The two boys disappeared with their prize.

"Now, it's your turn. Let me show you what I brought." Cerdic reached for his stained and mud-spattered bag. He rooted around it and finally pulled out several small pouches.

"What do you have there?" Giselle forced herself to pay attention. She just wanted to gaze at his sweet, familiar face, moved to tears by his evident delight in having brought presents. She resisted the urge to reach out and hold him.

Cerdic opened one of the pouches and pulled out several tube-like pieces that looked like tree bark, "This is cinnamon. It is used for sweets and in some other dishes. I have even tasted it in some hot drinks."

"Oh, I have seen this only as a powder in the kitchen at Blois." She breathed in the familiar scent. The reddish-brown tubes were about the length of her hand. "Where does it come from?"

"Nobody knows. A trader in Constantinople claimed that it came from a place known as the Red Sea, but I don't think he knew himself. He said that one has to shave it into fine slivers or grind it into powder."

"And this?" Giselle pointed at three nut-like balls.

Cerdic shook his head. "The trader called them nutmeg. He didn't want to tell me where they came from. Perhaps he didn't know himself. He said that they are precious and come from far away in the east."

"But what is it good for? One little ball like that?"

"The trader said one nutmeg is supposed to last you a lifetime. You rub some of it into stews or mulled wine. They showed me. It's a strange mix of woody, sweet, and pungent."

"How odd." Giselle rolled one between her fingers. "It seems like nothing. I can't even smell anything."

"Wait, I have something else." Cerdic dug around in his bag. "Where is it? I know I had it. Here it is." Triumphantly, he held up two more small pouches. "Saffron. And this is turmeric. I have no idea what you do with these. I know that in the east, the people put it in many dishes, soups, and stews, and on meat. You try it."

Giselle made a face. Cooking was not her favorite activity. Most days, she happily relied on Maria to help her. She was more interested in the fabric used to make the pouches. She rubbed it between her fingers. "What is this?"

"That? It's called *qutun*. The Muslim traders sell a lot of this fabric. Apparently, there are places in the East where the stuff for it is grown and then spun and woven. Before I forget, I have something else." Cerdic tugged at something in his bag and pulled out a strange long gown. It had an embroidered opening in the front and no sleeves.

Giselle fingered the fabric's thick weave, marveling at the pattern of stars woven into the dusky red cloth, shot with gold threads. "Does this come from the Holy Land?"

"No, a merchant came into camp when we were besieging Antioch. I hope you like it."

"This is for me?"

"Yes. Perhaps you should wear it when we are alone."

Giselle felt her cheeks get hot.

Later, when Giselle was beginning to adjust to having Cerdic back, she asked about the crusade. "We didn't expect that you and Count Stephen-Henry would come back already. Adela was sure he would go all the way to Jerusalem."

"Yes, that was the plan. The count even wrote to Lady Adela from Antioch that he expected to be in Jerusalem in another six weeks." Cerdic poked at the embers in the fireplace and added another piece of wood. "But it didn't turn out that way."

Giselle watched him surreptitiously while pretending to keep her eyes on her needlework. He seemed so tired. She shivered at the thought of all he had seen to leave him with such drawn and sunken eyes, cheekbones standing out starkly, and deep lines on his forehead.

Speaking haltingly, Cerdic told her what had happened. It was not a pretty story. Cerdic didn't elaborate on the horrors of the campaign and the months of deprivation outside the fortified walls of Antioch. But he said enough. "There were times when we welcomed the occasional sorties by the defenders even though it meant than some of us would die." His voice was flat. "It broke up the hopeless sense of waiting and starving."

Cerdic scratched himself absentmindedly. Giselle wrinkled her nose; she had heard how many crusaders had struggled with lice; hopefully Cerdic hadn't brought any little invited guests back with him. The scar over his eyebrow still had a reddish tinge.

He described the discussions among the leaders about the impending arrival of the enemy and the plans for storming the city. But when talking about the last day in Antioch, his voice faltered. "Count Stephen-Henry decided to leave; so we did."

So, Count Stephen had run away. She bent her head over her sewing and said nothing.

"He is a good man." Cerdic tossed more wood into the hearth. "He really is."

"It's late." Giselle put down her work. "Let's go to sleep."

It wasn't finished. Giselle knew that. Adela was not going to let this go. And if Count Stephen-Henry had to go back to the crusade, Cerdic would have to go with him. But not yet. For now, he was home, and she was glad of it.

Cerdic stood up and held out his hand to his wife. "Tomorrow, you will show me everything you have done."

Part III - Tapestry Of Power: Unraveling

A Messenger

He treads the winepress of the fury of the wrath of God Almighty
(Revelation 19:15).

1100 Les Tilleuls

The messenger from Blois arrived on a sunny day in October.

Giselle watched him ride into the courtyard. Guisbert and Yves had been playing with a puppy. Shrieking with delight, they pounced on the new attraction. It's time for them to start working with a tutor. They were thinking up too much mischief. She sighed and shifted away from the window, rubbing her back.

Two months ago, she had lost another baby. She didn't dare ask whether it would have been a boy or a girl. Her belly had started aching when she had been carrying the baby for a few months. The pain was so sharp that she lost all sense of where she was.

"There was so much blood," Cerdic told her later. He had found her in the courtyard, slumped over a basin she used for laundry. Maria had helped to bring her inside and to tend to her. She didn't know what they had done with the baby and was too despondent to ask; she imagined it, small enough to fit in the palm of her hand and perfectly formed. In her fevered dreams that haunted her for many nights, she heard it cry and felt a tiny finger hold on to her in the dark. For several days, she refused to get up, too tired to face her usual work, and angry with Cerdic for leaving her alone. Didn't he care? Eventually, her rage consumed her and drove her out of her room to search for him.

She found him finally at the stream, idly tossing pebbles into the water. She grabbed his arm and opened her mouth to scream at him. But then he raised his head and stared at her, his face gray and his eyes so lost and bewildered that her rage drained away. He was grieving, too. "I am sorry," she whispered.

Cerdic stood up and placed an arm around her shoulders.

"I placed a stone with a cross on the grave," he told her. "It was a girl. Now she is with our Marguerite."

Giselle clung to him and cried. "Thank you," she whispered.

They didn't talk much in the following days; it was as if they were walking around in the dark surrounded by shards of pottery, and finding words was too much trouble, but they were gentle with each other. If only they were left alone. But it wasn't to be.

Of course, the messenger had to come just when they had completed the harvest. The men were about to start crushing the wine. And once that process was completed, the entire mess of pulp and juice went into the winepress in order to separate out the skins and solids from the must. Every vintner worth his salt knew that this work could not wait. Yesterday, Cerdic and Auberi had worked for hours to fix the wine-press. Several wood staves of the basket had broken and needed to be replaced so that they could withstand the pressure when the heavy disc was pressed down onto the grapes. Giselle loved the smell of the grapes as they surrendered their juice and was always eager to bind up her long tunic in order to be able to help add more grapes to the basket and to pour the squeezed juice into casks.

Rubbing his hands and brushing sawdust of his tunic, Cerdic walked out from the winemaking shed and welcomed the messenger.

He took him inside for a glass of wine.

The man apparently enjoyed his wine; he stayed with Cerdic for at least an hour. Giselle entered the great hall after he was gone.

"You have to go back to Blois." It wasn't a question.

"Yes. I will leave in a week." Cerdic avoided her eyes. "Also, they are preparing another crusade."

Over the next days, Cerdic continued to process the grapes while also making arrangements for his departure.

Giselle said nothing. Her thoughts were a tangle in her mind. She was angry and afraid. Sometimes she pitied Cerdic for his blindness, and then that pity turned to bitter resentment for his unshakeable fealty to Adela. Of course, as soon as that woman sent word, Cerdic would rush to do her bidding. And if the count had to rejoin the crusade, Cerdic would go with him.

It was bad enough that Cerdic never felt completely at home in France; his heart remained for ever split in two as he dreamed of the land of his childhood, his onetime home, the place where he had last seen his mother. She knew his yearning for England never left him.

But there was always something that interfered with his wish to visit England.

Cerdic had known the new king of England when he was a mere boy in Caen. He was the youngest brother of Adela and, according to Cerdic, also her favorite. Giselle didn't care about the king of England, or Normandy, for that matter. It was far away. But Cerdic thought that with Henry as king, his chances of traveling to England had improved. "Maybe, one day Adela or Count Stephen-Henry will have a commission for me so that I have to travel to the court of King Henry," he said. "I have to be patient."

Some parts of the story she heard from Cerdic felt strange and sad. King William II, whom Cerdic called William Rufus for his red hair, died in England during a hunt in early August 1100. Henry, who happened to be on the spot, wasted no time to rush to Winchester, where he successfully argued his case and seized the throne. All this happened while the eldest brother Robert was still on his way back from the crusade and in dire straits financially. Thus, he was in no position to do anything about the crown being snatched away from him once again. The unseemly haste with which Henry had made his move hadn't bothered Cerdic. "I believe he will be a good king," he said pragmatically.

Cerdic had once described his journey across the waters from England when he was a little boy. Giselle shivered whenever she thought of the gray roiling waves, picturing the child buffeted by the sharp wind at the railing, with salt spray on his lips and frosting his hair.

Giselle didn't want Cerdic to go to England, and she was distraught at the thought of his rejoining the crusade. But she didn't say any of this to him, just bent her head and did her work.

What was she going to do?

Crusade Of The Faint Hearted

Crusader's Farewell by Thibaut, King of Navarre (1201-1253)

"Take me with you," Giselle said.

They were in the great hall, and Cerdic was talking about the work that needed to be done in his absence.

"To Blois?" Cerdic wasn't sure what to make of this. Ever since the messenger had come from Blois, Giselle had been abstracted, even distant with him. "I thought you disliked spending time there."

"While you were away, I spent some time with my lady. It was pleasant to speak to a woman who is about my age."

"Perhaps." Cerdic frowned. It sounded as if she meant it. "What about the boys?"

"The new tutor is working out well. They will be fine under his care."

"Very well. We will leave the day after tomorrow."

The next month in Blois was one of the most disorienting times Cerdic had ever experienced.

"Cerdic, Giselle, I am glad to see you," Adela exclaimed when they came into the great hall. Out of earshot from Count Stephen-Henry, she whispered, "it's been difficult here. Did you hear that my lord has been excommunicated by the pope? We have had to hire a new tutor for the boys; the other one said awful things to them about their father."

They arrived in the midst of heated discussions between Count Stephen-Henry and some of his most trusted advisors.

There was a new pope. Pope Paschal II had been consecrated as pope in August 1099 after the death of Pope Urban II. A new fervor had taken hold of church leaders, inflamed by the pope's words.

"He certainly is singing a different tune," Count Stephen-Henry muttered.

"You mean Pope Paschal's urging crusaders to reach and claim Jerusalem?" asked a senior advisor who hadn't joined the first crusade. He didn't appear enthusiastic at the prospect.

Cerdic stayed silent. Pope Urban had definitely talked a great deal about the need to support Emperor Alexios in Constantinople in his fight against the Seljuk invasion, while Jerusalem had received less attention. Now the new pope was whipping the faithful into a frenzy to conquer Jerusalem. But Cerdic didn't want to comment on this; it would draw attention once again to the count's dealings with Emperor Alexios and his dissuading the emperor from coming to the aid of the crusaders in Antioch.

"Don't sound so cynical." Adela frowned at her husband. "It should be the most important goal of any crusader to reach this holy center."

Pope Paschal had been preaching energetically, calling for a crusade of the penitent and admonishing all who had abandoned the crusade. Some had already heeded his call. The archbishop of Milan was drumming up a small, disorganized army of poor people.

Duke William of Aquitaine also was eager to join.

"I suppose he thinks that now that he has an heir, he can take the risk." Adela sniffed.

Cerdic tried to suppress his grin at her expression of distaste. He himself had been nearly dizzy at the contortions the duke had engaged in to raise money. The duke had mortgaged Toulouse, which he had originally taken over from his wife's uncle Raymond. And he did so, while Raymond was away, by the expedient of mortgaging it back to Raymond's son Bertrand.

"His willingness to join the crusade is praiseworthy, but it hardly mitigates his unsavory dealings. First, he steals the father's property and then makes the son loan him money on that same property!"

"Yes, to be sure, it looks a little questionable," Count Stephen-Henry said placatingly.

"Oh, you think it's clever, don't you? But that's not the worst." Adela was stabbing a needle into her work with quick jerking motions. "He is also not faithful to his wife."

"He does write beautiful music though," another knight said.

Adela shook her head.

Then there were knights who had also abandoned the crusade and were now trying to raise the funds for another attempt. Hugh of Vermandois, the French King's brother, was among them.

"At least, you are not the only oath breaker," Adela muttered, but loud enough for both Stephen-Henry and Cerdic, standing in front of the large hearth in the great hall, to hear. The count flushed.

Meanwhile, Adela's surviving brothers were once again at loggerheads. Robert Curthose, upon his return from the crusade, goaded by several Anglo-Norman barons, had embarked on an attempt to oust Henry by invading England. But this proved to be fruitless, met with a decided lack of enthusiasm by the English. He was eventually forced to renounce his claim to the English throne.

"At least, he has improved his financial situation somewhat," Count Stephen-Henry said. Robert had recently gotten married to Sybil of Conversano, the daughter of a wealthy Norman count. According to rumors, there were times when he was so poor that he had to stay in bed because he didn't have any clothes. When joining the first crusade, he had mortgaged his duchy to his brother William.

"There is no call to be so snide." Adela frowned. "He's had bad luck, and I believe he loves his wife very much." She glanced at her husband and added, "Besides, he fulfilled his vows and reached Jerusalem."

"To be sure, I never questioned his military skills. He is a great leader," Count Stephen-Henry said quietly.

In the courtyard the next morning, Count Stephen-Henry joined Cerdic to inspect a few horses that had been brought up from the south and to discuss a delivery of timber with a merchant. After some negotiations about the price, he signed the order. The merchant was beaming as he bowed his way out of the courtyard.

"I gave him a good price; I was feeling lenient today." He ran his hands over the timber—straight, strong oak beams. They had traveled along several rivers from the high north close to the Baltic Sea before they were loaded onto Loire river boats. "You know, Cerdic, sometimes I wish I could have been a merchant or an administrator." He sounded sad and defeated. "This is what I do well."

"I learned a lot from you," Cerdic said. Why was he called upon to make this man feel better? "It has helped me at Les Tilleuls."

Cerdic hated all this. Of course, Count Stephen-Henry would have to go back to the Holy Land soon. Adela wasn't about to let up on her efforts to get her husband to return to the crusade. She was radiant and yet with that sharp edge Cerdic had never noticed before —a watchful, almost calculating expression, a look of determination, and stern glances she sent at her husband, who shrank from them as if burned. Sometimes he could still see glimpses of the girl who had befriended him. Mostly now he hardly recognized her; she was beguiling, beautiful, and filled with a nervous energy that made him uncomfortable.

Shortly after this exchange, the count informed Cerdic that he had decided to rejoin the crusade. "I want you to stay in Blois in my absence," the count told him. "My lady will value your support."

"No, my lord, I want to go with you. I have sworn an oath as well."

"Very well." The count sighed. "In truth, I'll be glad to have you by my side."

Cerdic nodded. Should he tell the count of the conversation he had had with Adela? "Go with him," she had said, her eyes pleading. "I can trust you to do your best to protect him." But he decided to let it go.

Over the next weeks, Cerdic helped the count prepare lists of supplies. He inspected armor and weapons, worked with the blacksmith on necessary repairs, reviewed the stock of available horses, and assembled carters, cooks, and wheelwrights.

Giselle had been acting oddly. She didn't like Blois, and yet she had insisted on accompanying him. She was holding him at arm's length as if she was angry at him. He couldn't understand this. The other day, to his surprise, he noticed her go up the stairs to Adela's solar. He wasn't sure how he felt about Giselle becoming closer to Adela. Perhaps it was a good thing. She would need friends when he went away to the Holy Land.

Spears, Axes, and Maces

1100 Blois

"I want to go with them," Giselle said abruptly. "Will you help me?"

Adela's solar was a comfortable room above the great hall. Its large window offered a view onto the castle's kitchen garden and orchard with a glimpse of the Loire in the distance. A fire was lit in the hearth and beautifully carved oak panels gleamed in the light of the flames. Adela sat at a table with a tapestry behind her on the wall that depicted a fountain with three ladies sitting on the rim. The fruit trees behind the fountain were laden with red apples, and small hares and birds sat on the grass next to the ladies' feet. It was a peaceful and lovely scene, and for a moment, Giselle thought of home. She felt a lump in her throat.

"Giselle." Adela looked up from the needlepoint work in her lap. "How nice of you to visit me in this room. It's my favorite place."

Giselle ignored this subtle reprimand. Of course, it was rude to dispense with formalities, but she didn't care. "I will go, even if you don't help me." She spoke faster. "In fact, I am ready to walk all the way to Jerusalem."

"Why?" Adela frowned. "Why do you want to go with them?"

"I let Cerdic go alone before; this time I won't do that. He doesn't know. He won't want me to go along, but I will."

"I understand," Adela said. "You are not the first wife planning on joining her husband. But what about your sons?"

"I was hoping to entrust them to your care. That is, they would remain with their tutor at Les Tilleuls. But if something should happen," Giselle swallowed before continuing, "would you see to their wellbeing?"

"Of course you can trust me." Adela smiled at her. "I will see to their education and their future. But you will return. I have no doubt about that."

Giselle nodded, overcome with gratitude. She had spent so much time heartily disliking this woman, and she had always been jealous of her. Adela occupied a place in Cerdic's heart that would never be hers. And yet, here she was, willing to help her.

They talked for a long time.

"There are women who have traveled to Jerusalem with their husbands. I have heard of this. Some have even taken up the sword and fought in battles against the infidel."

"No, no. That's not what I want to do." Giselle shook her head in dismay. "I need to be there so I can help if he gets hurt and make sure he gets back safely."

"I thought that would be the case. So how do you want to do this?"

"I don't know yet." Giselle was amazed to find that she had an ally. "I can't let Cerdic see me. He would force me to go back home."

Adela studied Giselle, frowning slightly. "You are slim enough to pass for a young man."

"You want me to pretend I am a man all the way to Jerusalem?" Giselle laughed. "How could that possibly work?"

"It might be safer than traveling as a woman."

"Oh, I hadn't thought of that." Giselle stood up and twirled around in her long gown. "I'd be a very short man."

Adela smiled. "We will have to outfit you. Also, it would be good for you to have an ally." She placed another stitch in her needlepoint work. "I might have an idea for you."

The idea turned out to be Josse, who was in charge of the younger soldiers and the support staff.

"Why would he do this?" Giselle asked a few days later.

"He owes me," Adela said. "I helped him with his family, and he always asks for ways to repay his debt to me."

"And would he know I am a woman?"

"No, much better if your disguise is complete. I told Josse that you grew up in a monastery. Your name is Gilles, by the way."

"Oh, that's a good idea," Giselle responded. "That should help to explain any inexperience on my part."

"I wish I could come with you," Adela said wistfully when Giselle came to see her before departure. "I dream of going to Jerusalem to pray at the Church of the Holy Sepulchre. But my duty is here. Now you can be my eyes and ears. I will pray for your safe return. And promise me to pray for my soul when you reach Jerusalem."

Giselle thought about this again and again on the long journey east. It had never occurred to her that Adela might feel trapped in her role.

Four months had passed since her conversation with Adela in her solar at Blois. It might as well have been a lifetime.

Giselle rode in the back of the train of crusading knights with their squires, foot soldiers, porters, cooks, and other laborers bringing up the rear. Her hair was hidden underneath a tight cap, and she wore a dark tunic and hose. A gray wool mantle was rolled up and tied behind her saddle with other necessities for travel. Mounted on a sturdy bay from the stables of Count Stephen-Henry, she was overcome by a memory of following her father into the vineyard when she was small. Maria, who had been told to watch the girl, hadn't paid attention, and Giselle made her escape. That same feeling of trepidation mixed with triumph filled her now.

What would her father say if he saw her now—lean and strong, with muscles in her legs and arms? She already had to tighten her belt twice. She was so used to the feeling of the belt riding on her waist that she almost missed it when she took it off at night. Her horse flicked his ears and continued to trot along with a steady gait, content with his rider and the road.

Josse was almost as old as Count Stephen-Henry and perennially grumpy. But he was true to his word and kept a casual eye out to make sure that Gilles was managing without too much trouble. That callow and weak young man was dear to my lady's heart, even if he was hopeless at handling weapons.

To Giselle's chagrin, Josse insisted on including her in weapons training during rest stops on their journey east. Most of the knights had expensive armor and a set of weapons, especially swords and shields. But others looked as if they had just marched off their fields, armed with shovels, axes, and clubs or anything else they could grab from their toolsheds.

"You'll spend much of your time in the back, providing support services for the army. But you need to be prepared."

He held up a coarse brown tunic, waving it in the air for all to see. "How would this hold up if a spear hit it?"

The men shifted from one foot to another and stayed silent.

"Exactly. Not at all. So, I want you to find some material over the next weeks that you can use as padding. It won't be as good as a knight's armor, but better than nothing. Of course, it can't be too heavy. You want to be able to move."

With the point of his spear, he sketched the kind of armor favored by Seljuk warriors; it was made of overlapping rows of small iron plates. "Of course, you won't be able to find iron plates like this, but thick leather would already help a lot."

Josse described the circular shields carried by mounted archers, and the spears, crossbows, and bows used by the infantry. "Muslim warriors are tough and fast. Never underestimate your enemy. They are infidels, but they are brave and well-trained."

Giselle tried to hide her shiver. Would she be called upon to fight in battle? Then she squared her shoulders and turned her attention back to Josse. She'd better learn everything he could teach her.

Over the next weeks, Josse made them handle spears, axes, and clubs.

"Spread your legs; brace yourself when you want to hurl something."

"Watch who is behind you or next to you."

"Have your eyes point at your target; and the spear will follow it."

"Practice ducking. There is nothing shameful in avoiding a weapon thrown at you." He walked back and forth among them, adjusting their grip, punching them when they weren't paying attention, and demonstrating the proper stance for throwing a spear.

"Hey, Gilles, don't close your eyes," he barked. "Have your eyes point at your target; the spear will follow it."

Giselle gritted her teeth and tried to copy the others; however, she avoided the heavier weapons like swords and maces.

"You're a weakling." The others teased her. "You still have your mother's milk behind the ears."

Giselle learned to laugh at them, grateful that her voice was relatively deep.

At night, Giselle tried to bind up the blisters on her hands; but gradually the soft skin of her palms got tougher.

Her biggest problem was her monthly courses. She was grateful when Josse assigned her duties of fetching water and helping with the preparation of meals, because it afforded her occasional moments of privacy. She could blend in among other porters and servants. Nobody paid any attention to them.

She watched Cerdic from a distance. He usually stayed close to Count Stephen-Henry. He was easy to spot because he was so tall. But he never looked in her direction.

"Are they all that ill-equipped?" Giselle blurted out her amazement when chatting with one of the squires. She was watching a group of peasants who had joined them when they passed into the mountains of the Byzantine empire. Some didn't even have shoes.

"What's wrong with you?" The man stared at her with a frown. "Have you been living under a rock? Most of us don't have any funds to support us on this journey like that fancy lord over there." He raised his chin, pointing toward Count Stephen-Henry. The count was riding in the front, surrounded by some of his knights, including Cerdic. "You are not so ill-equipped yourself." His glance slid over her soft leather boots and her serviceable woolen coat. "I'd keep them on at night, if I were you. They might walk off all by themselves."

Giselle flushed, awkwardly trying to pull her feet back out of the squire's line of sight. Adela had found this pair of boots for her, ignoring Giselle's protests. "You will be glad of these."

Perhaps her faith was not strong enough for all that she prayed devoutly and attended mass regularly. It would not occur to her to walk barefoot all the way to the Holy Land. For that matter, she wasn't sure what drove some of the crusading knights to embark on this arduous journey. What did they really want? Count Stephen-Henry certainly was an unlikely crusader; he liked his comforts, not to mention regular lavish meals. How had Adela convinced him? The image of the count's wife running after him with a raised broom to make sure he traveled east as fast as he could was irresistible. *Your imagination will get you in trouble one of these days*, her father had often said. Of course, Adela would never run around with a broom. She'd probably waved a heavy silver candelabra at her husband. Giselle looked down to hide her grin. It wouldn't do to have others around her ask what she was thinking. Then again, her own motives would hardly hold up under closer scrutiny. She wanted to do everything in her power to bring Cerdic back alive. That's all that mattered.

Now, there was something else that would hardly bear scrutiny if she had to go to confession. After months of travel, she discovered a happiness she'd never known.

Of course, she was tired to the bone, gritty, sticky, with blisters and splinters in her fingers, her nails torn, and bruises all over. She dreamed of taking a bath in the privacy of her solar, steaming and scented with lavender, with a fresh towel readied for her. She missed home and yearned for her boys. Trying to sleep at night, she couldn't erase the image of soldiers who had died on the journey. The idea of forthcoming battles terrified her.

And yet, she was happy. Nobody paid attention to her anymore. She performed her duties and rarely got teased for being a weakling. With a scarf wrapped around the lower portion of her face, and a makeshift helmet Josse had found for her, crammed on her head, dressed in her stained and torn men's clothing, she was unrecognizable, and she was free.

DEUS VULT

Giselle sighed with pleasure. Her bare feet were submerged in the clear water of the mountain stream, and her hair, for once, was free of its covering. She wiggled her toes in contentment.

She hadn't realized how tired she was from all the weeks on the road. Where were they now? Somewhere close to Constantinople.

The leaders planned to rest for a few days, replenishing their supplies and repairing their gear. Replenishing their supplies? Giselle made a face at that notion. The journey east had been instructive in ways she had never imagined.

She hadn't foreseen nor could she have imagined the amount of destruction the crusading army left in its wake as it traveled farther and farther east and south. The knights regularly raided villages and towns they passed through. They called it foraging. Of course, Count Stephen-Henry's army was well supplied with funds, and knights often paid for the pigs, chickens, and grain that they needed. But in many areas, supplies were scarce, and villagers were struggling; they had already been at the mercy of Peter the Hermit's army of paupers that had swept through the Balkans on their way to Constantinople. When knights, with long swords banging against their armor, offered to buy food stuff from desperate people, it didn't seem much better than outright theft. Giselle couldn't forget the sight of children crying in front of their homes, women pleading with crusaders to leave them be, destitute people wandering from village to village in search of food. It was far from glorious. It was grimy, cruel, pointless, and often inspired by greed.

After his return from the crusade, Cerdic had told Giselle about the excesses of Peter the Hermit that he had witnessed. A band of mostly unruly paupers under his leadership had pillaged recklessly in villages and small towns all the way to Constantinople and slain whoever stood in their way. They had even killed Christians in one town. "By what right do we do this?" Cerdic had asked her, his face drawn and shadowed. She had no response then and none now. "*Deus Vult,*" Pope Urban II had said—God wills it. It frightened her.

But for now, she wanted to put it out of her mind. She reveled in the mountain sanctuary she had come upon.

Josse had warned her and others not to wander off by themselves. "That's asking for trouble," he said. But when Giselle found out that they would stop for a while, she snuck off, looking back several times to make sure she wasn't being followed.

The valley, framed by snow-capped mountains, was lined with oak trees and black pines; the stream had widened to form a little pond on one side. Giselle rinsed some of her clothes and laid them out to dry on the rocks. With a comb, she gently untangled her locks and then ran it across her scalp. She sat back against a large boulder and closed her eyes, relishing the feel of the sun on her face.

Something tickled her. Startled, she opened her eyes. An oak leaf had touched her face before fluttering to the ground. The sun had passed its zenith. It was time to get back.

With a sigh, Giselle gathered her things and made her way back down through the forest. She hadn't yet covered her hair, enjoying the unaccustomed feeling of the wind. It was quiet on the path, and the ground was soft and springy under its thick layer of pine needles.

Rustling and cracking of branches made her glance at the thicket to the right. She shivered. Who would be watching her here in the woods? Quickly, she bound up her hair, covered it with the cap, and wrapped the scarf around her neck and the lower part of her face. She would have to be more careful in the future.

"Who is that?" Giselle asked Josse the next morning. She pointed toward a tent from which emerged a tall blond man dressed in a bright red linen tunic with odd embroidery along the neckline and the sleeves and an elegant blue woolen overcoat that would have fitted in perfectly at the court of Blois. His leather boots were in excellent condition. He glanced at her and smiled. Giselle flushed.

"That man?" Josse shrugged. "I've seen him in Blois. He is a timber merchant from up north somewhere. Gustav something or other."

"But then, what is he doing here? He doesn't look like a crusader."

"No, indeed. He joined us a few days ago for protection on the road. He probably has his carts full of goods he wants to trade in the east."

"Timber? That would take up a lot of room."

"No, of course not. He merely arranges for timber shipments. I have heard that he carries small wares like amber, tin, wool, furs, and feathers. One of his servants boasted that his master has several reindeer antlers. I bet he is searching for new markets and uses all this stuff to sweeten the deal."

Amber, fur, and feathers? Giselle would have loved to see some of it. But she had become wary of this man. A few times when he passed her, she noticed his curious gaze. Once, he walked behind her and chuckled. She avoided him after that as best she could. From a distance, she watched him chatting with the crusaders; she could hear laughter coming from people standing around him.

To her delight, the count insisted on a stay in Constantinople for a few days before carrying on. She wandered around by herself. It was unlike any city she had ever seen. She gaped at the hippodrome and was fascinated by the row of towers that surrounded it. The streets were crowded, and she was overwhelmed by all the sights and sounds, dodging carts pulled by donkeys and vendors hawking their wares. Apples, quinces, figs, honey, spices, grains, fish, onions, peppers, olives, and large jugs of olive oil—there seemed to be no end to what was offered. One had a collection of bird cages filled with chirping, chittering, and trilling birds in all colors of the rainbow.

On the last day, before they were about to set out, she walked into a covered market. Carpet sellers displayed their goods on the floor for everyone to walk on. Tables were buried under piles of silk. Oil lamps, silver chalices, fine pottery, precious glasses, and jewelry. She lost herself in all the sights.

"How about some company?" A smooth voice behind her startled her out of her absorption. It was the blond merchant. He brushed his long locks out of his face as he smiled at her. "Come, my dear." He grasped her arm. "Perhaps we might find a more comfortable place to chat. This public market is hardly suitable for a young lady."

Giselle shrank back in shock. "This is outrageous," she said, trying not to stutter. "You are mistaken. Let go of my arm."

"You think all men are blind?" He laughed at her. "I saw you come back from your little excursion into the hills. You had forgotten to hide your lovely hair."

He was already forcing her out into the street and led her down into a quiet alley behind the marketplace.

Desperately, she glanced around. Was there anyone from her group within reach? Sweat trickled down her back. She struggled to control her breaths, loathe to show this man how afraid she was. Exposure was inevitable now.

He pulled her into a small courtyard. Pigeons were playing near a fountain; there was nobody in sight. "Isn't this pleasant?" He beamed at her as if he had invited her into his palace. He still had a firm grasp on her arm.

What did he want? Then she realized how stupid she'd been. Of course, she knew what he wanted. "Let go of me. I am one of Count Stephen-Henry's servants. He would not like this."

"Don't be naïve. Do you think he'd care? For that matter, does he know about you? He'd probably whip you all the way back to Lyon or wherever you've come from." He laughed. "But come, let's enjoy this. I'll reward you well." He tried to pull her closer.

Giselle could smell the man, oily, perfumed, and with a hint of sharp sweat. It made her want to retch. *Think*. What had Josse told them? "Sometimes you are better off to stop resisting. Once you do that, you have leverage. And then, this is what you can do." He had demonstrated the next moves. "Anybody want to try?" Within minutes, several people were on the ground, moaning. "Don't worry; it will pass, even if it hurts like hell right now."

Giselle stopped pulling back and instead moved her foot forward. "That's more like it." Gustav bent his head closer and relaxed his grip. With a swift movement, Giselle lifted her knee and hit him right in the center, as Josse had demonstrated. She was stunned by the effect. Gustav screamed and fell down as if struck by a hammer.

Giselle ran off as fast as she could. That night, she couldn't sleep. What if Gustav went to Count Stephen-Henry or another leader of the crusade and exposed her?

When they left for the harbor the next morning, Gustav was nowhere to be seen. "What about that merchant?" she asked Josse.

"Oh, him?" he responded dismissively. "He is not one for getting into fights. Wheeling and dealing in a city like Constantinople is more in his line. I doubt we'll see him again anytime soon."

Giselle turned her face away so he couldn't see her smile.

The Battle Of Mersivan

The crusaders reached Nicomedia in May 1101.

One disaster after another sapped the army's strength and eroded their resolution.

An attempt to besiege the city of Gangra failed; they marched on to try their luck at the city of Kastomonu, where they could barely hold their own against attacks from Seljuk Turks. They lost an entire party of soldiers that had gone out to forage.

After every skirmish, Giselle was among the silent workers who scoured the field, searching for survivors. She had to hide her trembling hands when called up to help carry men who had lost limbs or had incurred grievous wounds in their torsos; the worst was finding corpses with their heads cut off. Then she found she was not the only one to vomit or to wake up drenched in sweat. Oddly, that helped.

The crusaders were intent on rescuing Bohemond of Hauteville, a renowned leader of the crusade, who had been captured and imprisoned in Danishmend territory.

"Who are these Danishmend?" Giselle asked Josse.

"I don't really know," he answered. "All I know is that they are Turkmen who rule in a region of central and northeastern Anatolia."

In the end, it didn't really matter who they were. The crusaders soon realized that they were faced with a formidable foe. Their leader, Kilij Arslan had learned his lesson about the benefits of alliances. In a three-day battle, the crusaders met not only the

Danishmends but also Kilij Arslan's cavalry and the soldiers under the leadership of Ridwan of Aleppo.

Giselle tried to rest whenever Josse insisted on a break. "A good soldier must learn to rest whenever the opportunity arises," he told them. But for Giselle, sleep was impossible. When she closed her eyes, she immediately conjured the sight of Muslim riders on their small, slender horses sweeping across the open land, with incessant rhythmic shouting that sounded like an invocation and swinging their scimitars, the curved blades glinting in the sunlight.

The crusaders were exhausted by the time they set up camp near the foothills of the mountains of Paphlagonia in northeastern Anatolia after weeks of harassment from the enemy in unceasing small skirmishes. When the battle of Mersivan began on the hot, dry plain under a merciless sun, the crusaders had already run short of supplies.

Every morning, Giselle scanned the crowd of crusaders to catch glimpses of Cerdic. She often lost sight of him in the melee and said many silent prayers for his continued survival. He had taken to sporting a panache of multi-colored silk ribbons on his helmet in the colors of her father's crest, blue and white for the springs in the valley and yellow and black to represent the bees from Les Tilleuls. Tall as he was, it made it easier for her to make him out. He stuck close to Count Stephen-Henry.

"I want you to be ready," Josse told them at first light, as he always did when a battle was anticipated. "Be prepared, pack up everything, so when the call comes, you can be on the move." And he eyed the younger members of his small troop with a frown. "And I don't want to see you out there. Your job is here, and it's as important as swinging a mace around. Don't you forget that."

That first day, by sundown, the beginnings of the disaster were apparent. Not only were there many dead out on the field and others, still alive but in agony, laying there in the rapidly cooling evening air, but they also were surrounded. The next day was no better. Conrad, constable to Emperor Henry IV, led his Germans to try to break through the Turkish lines. They got out with tremendous losses, but the crusaders were still hemmed in from all sides, while the Germans couldn't rejoin them.

"Who knows where they are now—probably holed up somewhere." Josse cursed. "A pointless venture if ever I saw one. And we are isolated as a result."

Finally, on the fourth day, after an anxious if relatively quiet day, the crusaders marshaled all their forces in a desperate attempt to break free.

Biting her lips and holding her horse's lead in a tightly clenched fist, Giselle watched from the hill where the main portion of the crusaders' encampment had been holed up for the last three days. The plain below was churning with men and horses in a hopeless melee; clouds of dust parting like veils to reveal occasional glints of weapons. Cerdic's panache was down there somewhere. For a moment, she glimpsed a blue shield with the white stripe, the distinctive coat of arms of Count Stephen-Henry. No. It was a mistake. And no flamboyant panache, waving cheerfully with its yellow, black, blue, and white ribbons. She gripped the leather lead until her hand hurt. *Oh, God, please keep him safe.*

Along with others under Josse's strict command, she had rolled up her pack and saddled her horse. But there were many in the camp milling about as if nothing untoward was occurring on the plain below. Some were sitting in front of their masters' tents. A few women who had attached themselves to the army, despite all orders by the leaders to send them away, were darning clothes and minding children. A priest stood on the side with a view of the battlefield. He was praying; Giselle could see the rosary beads in his hands. Repeatedly, he made the sign of the cross. Her stomach ached as she watched the children drawing stick figures in the sand. Why were they here?

Screaming below. People on foot running in all directions. Who was that crusader standing on a rock? Besieged from all directions, his shield stuck with spears that quivered like quills. A knight charged across, followed by another with a colorful panache, who grabbed the man's arms and helped him swing up behind him. In a mad dash, they raced away, sweeping attackers out of their way by swinging their maces. A third crusader had joined them.

"Get ready," Josse shouted. "They are heading this way."

In the camp, panic had set in. Men, women, and children ran around heedlessly, dragging some possessions. Men fought with each other over the few horses that were left. Others sat on the ground without moving, as if frozen.

Giselle didn't look in that direction. Instead, all her attention was on the three crusaders below, one with a rider clutching to his back. Now they galloped up the hill.

A Turkmen had noticed and turned his horse around to pursue them.

Unheeding, the crusaders raced past Josse and his men. "Go," they screamed. "The enemy is upon us."

Cerdic's horse reared, dislodging the crusader in the back and tossing him onto the ground. Cerdic got the full brunt of the horse's neck in his face and slid off the side. Stunned and blinded, his nose already swelling up, he was on his knees in the dust, while the other crusader was trying to get back on his feet. The Turkmen had come up right behind Cerdic and leaned down to swipe at him with his sword.

Giselle screamed and grabbed the mace from the man next to her. Nearly blinded with fright and rage, she jumped forward and swung the mace at the rider as hard as she could. A crunching sound made her gag, but she didn't stop and swung the mace again and again. The Turkmen fell off his horse, groaning in agony.

Count Stephen-Henry had doubled back. He grabbed the hand of the crusader and pulled him up behind him. "Cerdic, get back on your horse," he shouted and watched as the younger man remounted. "Thanks, lad," he added, nodding toward Giselle. "You'd better move."

Nearly blinded by the dust kicked up as they cantered off, Giselle heard the drumming of their horses' hooves on the rocky ground as if it were an echo of her heart hammering in her chest.

"What are you waiting for?" Josse exclaimed. His horse was dancing back and forth as he tried to mount. "That direction might be our only chance to break out." Just then, a spear thrown from one of the Turkmen coming up the hill pierced his side. Josse let go of the reins and sank to the ground.

Giselle rushed over to him. "Let me help. You can still make it once you are astride."

"No," Josse whispered, feebly waving her away. "Ride." He lay on the ground in a widening pool of blood; he propped himself up with one arm to keep the spear in his side from going in further. "I am done for. Ride!"

A young squire who had befriended Giselle over the last months dragged her away. "You heard him," he hissed. "We need to reach the harbor of Sinope." He threw her onto her horse.

The horse was already moving when she pulled up and tried to turn it around. "What about the women and children?"

"It's too late." The squire slapped her horse on its rump with his sword so that it jumped forward. Grabbing the reins, Giselle bent low over the horse's neck and galloped in the wake of others fleeing the camp. She glanced back. The Muslim soldiers were swooping down on the camp, slaying all who were still alive. Screams from the tents and the camp fires rose up and then dwindled away. Giselle couldn't bear it anymore and turned away. Gritting her teeth and with tears streaming down her cheeks, she clung to her horse as it traveled north.

Later Giselle could not remember at all the ride to the harbor of Sinope. She was numb when she followed other survivors to board one of the small sailing vessels that would take the remnants of their army across the sea to Constantinople. They were crowded together in the damp and musty hold, the air fetid with the smells of blood and sweat and festering wounds. Dazed, she listened to the moaning and whispering of others around her.

"Do you have any water?"

"No, none. Sorry, brother."

"So many dead."

"It was a slaughter. No other way to put it."

"I think maybe two hundred survived."

"Probably those who were killed immediately were lucky; I hear that others end up being enslaved."

Giselle covered her face with her hands. That crunching sound when she hit the man with the mace—she wished she could forget it. She shivered at the memory of the blinding rage that had overcome her. It was as if another being had burst out of her body. Had she done this? Had she maimed a man brutally? And when she closed her eyes, over and over she saw Josse bleeding out on the ground. He had looked out for her for all those many months. He had been her friend.

"He owes me," Adela had said blithely, when she delegated Josse to watch over Giselle. Would she even care how he met his death? Giselle chided herself for being so bitter. Adela did what was necessary. She would have been a good commander of an army, willing to send people to their death without blinking an eye.

Giselle wept for Josse and for all the others who had died. She wept for herself, racked with guilt at what would have happened to her children if she had died at Mersivan. She wept, overcome with horror at the days still ahead. With just a sliver of her mind, she clung to the sight of the colorful panache that had fluttered in the wind when she and the others had reached the harbor. Cerdic was safe. For now.

Oaths Kept and Oaths Broken

1101

The smelly pilgrim who had graced the table in Blois was right. Accommodations in Jerusalem left a lot to be desired.

Giselle spent her nights in an empty building that smelled of horses, crowded into a few bare cells together with carters, cooks, servants, and foot soldiers. At least, the stone floor was cool and swept free of dirt.

The city was hushed, many areas seemingly devoid of life. But there were a few market stalls, and she could hear hammering and sawing when she walked up the hill toward the Church of the Holy Sepulchre. A squire, who had been here before, told Giselle that it had been completely destroyed almost 100 years earlier. Only some portions of the church had been rebuilt in 1048.

That same squire told her what had happened after the crusaders had vanquished the enemy and marched into the city. "The streets ran with blood." His eyes were blank as if the mere memory of the sight had blinded him. "They killed all the Muslim and Jewish people still living there."

"Women and children as well?"

"All of them. None were left alive."

Giselle shivered when she remembered this. She still could hear the screaming of the women and children in the camp at Mersivan. At night she woke up, drenched in sweat. Had she moaned in her dreams? Fortunately, the men with whom she shared crowded shelters slept so soundly that nobody heard her.

After a brief respite in Constantinople, the crusaders had boarded another vessel that took them to the port of St. Symeon. Throughout the long ride from the port to Jerusalem, Giselle thought about what had to happen once they reached the holy city. She knew what she had to do. Three hundred miles to Jerusalem, she muttered to herself. It should be a song. She distracted herself by taking in the unfamiliar landscape, in turns arid and desolate and then again green and even luscious near springs where olive groves and fruit trees thrived.

Avoiding Cerdic had become more challenging since their once proud army had shrunk to a sad remnant after the battle of Mersivan. She missed Josse's steadying presence; all of those who had been under his command seemed adrift now. There were fewer people among whom she could hide. At least Count Stephen-Henry had apparently forgotten about the 'lad' who had helped during the battle. On the journey to Jerusalem, even though she stayed far in the back, several times she felt Cerdic's eyes turned in her direction as if something puzzled him. He couldn't see her face since she made a point of wrapping a cloth over the lower portion. Most of the others did this, so it didn't make her stand out, and it helped against the dust and the sun. Exposure would be awkward.

Meanwhile, now that they had reached Jerusalem, the time had come for her to give up her disguise. She knew this. She had dreamed of this moment. She craved gazing into Cerdic's face and hearing his voice up close. She wanted to feel the strength of his arms around her and the length of his limbs stretched next to her. In any event, she couldn't go to the holiest of holy places in all of

Christendom while living a lie. But she was afraid. She feared Cerdic's reaction. It didn't help that she felt a sense of regret before she had even shed her man's hose and tunic. It meant losing a part of her that had become precious.

In Jerusalem, she was relieved to find a small market stall selling shawls and gowns. After glancing around to make sure that nobody was paying attention to her, she quickly bought what she needed and, aside from a puzzled look from the vendor, walked away without drawing undue attention to herself.

A few hours later, Giselle, robed and with a shawl around her head for protection against the sun, walked toward the Church of the Holy Sepulchre. She had found a bathhouse set up by the crusaders soon after they had come to Jerusalem. When she emerged, with her hair still damp, refreshed and replete with a sense of wellbeing, she relished the feel of the soft woolen fabric on her limbs even while it also made her feel insecure. Slowly and decorously, she made her way along the pale cobble stones, warmed by the sun. Men glanced at her curiously. There weren't many women in Jerusalem, and Giselle felt exposed and vulnerable. Then, after yet another instant of glancing away from someone's stare, she straightened her back and raised her head. She was strong and lean. She had traveled hundreds and hundreds of miles. She had fought in battle. Let them stare.

Giselle entered the church. Its bare stone walls moved her to tears. There were only a few others kneeling quietly on the cool flagstones, with their heads bent and their hands folded. This was the site of the crucifixion, and close by was Jesus Christ's tomb. It was impossible to grasp; it was too big. So she kneeled and prayed, humbly and devoutly, overwhelmed with gratitude that she had been allowed to reach this holy place. She prayed for Adela. She prayed for her children and for Cerdic. And she prayed for forgiveness for all that she had done.

At peace with herself, Giselle walked outside, blinking in the bright sunshine until her eyes adjusted.

On a stone bench across the plaza, a man sat with his back turned. He was tossing a lemon up and down. Pigeons walked around on the cobblestones in front of him. Cerdic.

"Aren't the lemons here wonderful, Cid?"

Cerdic whipped around and gaped at her. "Giselle?" He stood up, dropping the lemon; it rolled on the cobblestones. The pigeons pecked at it and then wandered off, disgruntled. "What…" He fumbled for words. "You are here?" He raised his hands as if to put them on her shoulders. Then he dropped them. "I can't believe it. I thought I saw you the other day, but it wasn't possible."

"You did see me." Giselle hesitated, then spoke in a rush. "I have been there all along, all the way from Blois. I rode in the back."

"Why?" Cerdic raised his voice. "Why did you do that? Anything could have happened."

"I wanted to help." Giselle's voice cracked. Somehow, her reasons for doing this no longer seemed convincing. She trembled. It was strange to be so close to him after all these months. She wanted to reach for his hands, but was afraid. "At least I did help once—at Mersivan when you fell off your horse, and a Turkmen was attacking you from behind."

"That was you?" Cerdic's face was flushed. "Count Stephen-Henry mentioned a boy who had come to my defense." He stared at her in dismay. "Come," he muttered finally. "We can't talk here."

They walked silently to the citadel where the crusaders had their headquarters. They talked, sitting awkwardly in the cell the count had assigned to Cerdic as one of his senior advisors. Giselle could feel the anger barely suppressed in Cerdic's voice and clenched hands as she described her journey.

"Do you want me to bring my things here?" Giselle finally asked in a low voice. "If it is easier, I could stay in the place I have stayed before with the others."

"No, you can't. That's done with." Cerdic shook his head in frustration. "Of course, you have to join me here."

Giselle winced when she heard the angry "have to" in Cerdic's response. She chided herself for having expected a different reaction.

Later, they sought out Count Stephen-Henry.

"Well, my dear, so you have been with us all along." Count Stephen-Henry smiled at Giselle. "I salute you. Let's see if we can make your return journey a bit more comfortable."

A few days later, they left for Jaffa, where they planned to board a ship for home.

The last evening in Jerusalem, Cerdic and Giselle went once more to the Church of the Holy Sepulchre to attend the evening prayer. Along with crusaders, wearing their long robes, they kneeled for the prayers. Giselle glanced at Cerdic from the side. They were stiff and awkward with each other, and she was helpless in the face of his rigid expression. She bent her head and folded her hands. Was it wrong to pray for Mother Mary's intercession and protection for Cerdic? How could it be wrong? She prayed as hard as she could and asked for forgiveness and acceptance of what was to come. Then the knights began to sing.

Hail, holy Queen, Mother of Mercy,

Hail our life, our sweetness and our hope.

To thee do we cry,

Poor banished children of Eve;

To thee do we send up our sighs,

Mourning and weeping in this valley of tears.

The knights' deep voices reverberated in the cavernous space, and the words were somber bells in her mind. *Do not forget*, they seemed to say to her. Giselle mouthed the words *poor banished children…mourning and weeping in this valley of tears*. When they walked out into the night, her face was damp, and she was licking salty drops of her lips.

Then Cerdic reached for her hand. He held it for a moment before letting it go again. Giselle took a deep breath. Suddenly, the night seemed lighter.

On the journey to Jaffa, the wall between them was back.

Giselle struggled to adjust to riding while wearing a long gown; for comfort's sake, she had donned the hose underneath the gown so that her limbs wouldn't be exposed. She tugged at the folds of the gown so that they wouldn't bunch up underneath her thighs.

Unhappily she watched her husband, who was in the front with the other crusaders planning to sail home. Cerdic kept his distance from her, riding with his usual straight-backed grace, but staring rigidly ahead and never looking in her direction.

"I have been thinking of your father a lot these days," a familiar voice boomed in her ears.

Startled, Giselle raised her head.

Count Stephen-Henry had slowed his horse to ride alongside her. "He would have been proud of you."

Giselle flushed. "You don't think he would have been shocked?"

"Your father?" The count laughed. "I remember how he used to describe your exploits when you were a little girl, beaming with pride in your courage. He would have wanted you to do this. He was a lot like you when he was younger."

Her last memories of her father were those of a sad and broken man. The image of a young man, not bent by sorrow, and proud of his daughter, gave her the same feeling she got as when she walked out into the fields after a sudden rain and the air was fresh and invigorating. If only Cerdic would stop being angry at her.

As if he had read her mind, Count Stephen-Henry glanced at Cerdic's back. "It's easier for a father than for a husband."

Giselle pretended to be absorbed in adjusting her reins.

"Husbands generally don't like to feel less strong than their wives."

Giselle bit her lip. What could she say? She had heard the edge in Adela's voice when talking to her husband. She had observed Adela's attention to every detail in the weeks prior to their departure for the Holy Land, as if she wanted to make absolutely sure that he wouldn't have any reason to turn back. The count had lost the haunted expression that had been on his face before the battle of Mersivan. He hadn't regained all the weight that had characterized him before. But his face had smoothed out, and he appeared content and self-assured.

"Have faith. Everything takes time." He smiled at her and then spurred his horse to move to the front of the line again.

When the crusaders reached Jaffa, they were pleased to find a sailing vessel in port ready to take them home. It was larger and more comfortable than the one that had transported them from Constantinople to the port of St. Symeon. It also pitched less in the waves.

Giselle sat next to Cerdic in their allotted berth as the ship worked its way out of the harbor. She tried to think of home, but Cerdic's silence next to her made her tense and unhappy.

The wind picked up. The ship's wooden boards creaked and groaned. In the dark hold, they could hear sounds of shouting and running back and forth on deck.

"They are probably securing everything," Cerdic said.

Now the wind strengthened, and the howling and whistling made Giselle bite her lips. The big vessel that they had boarded with such confidence now seemed a mere nutshell being tossed around in the waves.

Hours later, the storm abated. People in the hold sighed with relief.

Then the captain came down to speak to them. "I am sorry to tell you that the ship has had too much damage. We can't risk going on and must turn around."

With tattered sails and a leaking bottom, the ship limped back into the harbor at Jaffa.

THE SHORT STRAW

1102

Less than three weeks later, Giselle sat in a small room of a hostel used by crusaders in Jaffa, biting her nails, stunned at the reversal of fortune. Occasionally she got up to go to the sun-drenched courtyard where she paced up and down, unable to sit still for long.

King Baldwin had received news of an invasion by the Fatimids from Egypt. "It's only an expeditionary force," he told the crusaders assembled around him. "We defeated them once before. We'll do it again as long as we don't waste any time to confront them."

"We talked for hours," Cerdic told Giselle after the meeting. His eyes glittered as if he had a fever, and his voice was hoarse.

Giselle gripped her hands, trying to stifle their trembling.

"The king persuaded Count Stephen-Henry to join him. Hugh of Lusignan, the Count of Burgundy, and Conrad Constable of Germany are also coming with their knights. We leave at first light."

"Why do you have to go?" Giselle could barely maintain her composure. "Why? Haven't you done enough?"

Cerdic shook his head. "You don't understand. I owe him."

Giselle wanted to scream at him. *You think you owe him because of what you feel for his wife and because he has been kind to you. But you don't owe him anything, not anymore.* But she stayed silent.

How could she say anything? She had promised herself when she got married to never say these things to Cerdic.

She watched them ride out in the gray dawn—a small army, not even two hundred crusaders, and without foot soldiers to support them. They were traveling southeast toward Ramla, where they expected to encounter the Fatimids. And then she waited.

She didn't sleep that night or the next. Finally, on the fourth night, she dozed off, but only fitfully. Listlessly, she sat in the courtyard throughout the next day. It was already dark when she heard hoofbeats on the cobblestones. Dropping her shawl, she stood up.

A rider appeared in the courtyard. He slid off his horse. It was Cerdic. He had no armor or helmet. He stared at her out of red-rimmed eyes. His tunic was torn in places and covered with dark reddish-brown stains.

"They are dead," he whispered. His lips were cracked. "All of them."

"Come inside." She reached for his arm. "You looked parched." A servant took the horse away while she led Cerdic inside. He followed along as if he was blind. "Don't talk," she murmured. "First you drink something and rest."

Slowly, she pieced together what had happened. Instead of a small expeditionary force, King Baldwin's small contingent of knights met a well-equipped army of several thousand at Ramla. Most of their throng got killed that first day; the survivors, including the king, sought refuge in a tower. After a heated discussion, they convinced Baldwin to make his escape in the dead of night while they stayed behind. The king crept out once it was dark, accompanied only by his scribe and one knight. Cerdic didn't know him, only his name, one Hugh of Brulis. Cerdic fell silent while he fingered the tassels on Giselle's shawl. It was as if he had forgotten her.

"And you and the others?" she asked finally.

"We drew straws." Cerdic's voice was so low that Giselle had to move closer to hear him. "We spent another day in that tower, while the Fatimids were setting fires below and attacking the walls with battering rams. We knew the end was coming. They were all calm and undaunted. You should have seen them. We decided that one of us had to try to get away to carry the news. I drew the short straw. I refused. 'I need you to do this," the count said. 'Not for yourself, but for me.' He smiled at me as if he was sitting comfortably in his big chair in the great hall at Blois. 'I need you to bring the news to my wife. You must understand how important that is to me.'"

Giselle watched him, at a loss for what to say.

"I should have stayed with them. I wanted to stay." Cerdic rocked back and forth, running his hands through his hair. "But he insisted, and I agreed. In the morning, we broke out to charge the Fatimids. I made my getaway in the melee and hid in an empty pottery shed in a back alley until nightfall before walking out. I stole a horse on the edge of town."

Giselle longed to take Cerdic in her arms and to hold him. But something warned her that this was not the time. "He was a good man." She wanted to say more, but how could she express her gratitude for the count saving Cerdic's life when he was so tortured about it?

In the morning, Giselle and Cerdic walked to the harbor to see about a ship that could take them west. On the way back to the hostel, they ran into a man coming around the corner, dressed in a brightly colored long-sleeved silk robe that make Giselle think of what some of the Seljuk warriors had worn.

"Oh, pardon," Cerdic said politely.

The man glanced at her, and his expression changed; he looked like an angry cat ready to pounce. It was Gustav.

The last time she'd seen him, he'd been rolling around on the ground. No, she'd never be afraid of him again. She gazed at him without flinching. "Well, I see you have found a new perch for trading."

"Indeed, my lady." Gustav smirked. "I am setting up a trading post in Jaffa." He eyed Cerdic with a speculative glint in his eye. "And you, have you found a trading post?"

Cerdic flushed. He heard the innuendo but wasn't sure what to make of it.

Giselle placed a hand on Cerdic's arm. "Allow me to introduce my husband, Sir Cerdic of Wessex. But I am sure you must be busy. We won't detain you."

Gustav stared at her, the smile wiped off his face. His smooth demeanor had vanished. He sketched a bow and walked off.

"That's the merchant that traveled with the army to Constantinople." Cerdic frowned. "Why are you friendly with him?"

Giselle had to suppress a grin. Gustav was hardly going to remember her actions in Constantinople as friendly.

"Yes," she said. "It's the same man." There was something in Cerdic's eyes, narrowed with suspicion, that she hadn't expected. It moved her. "He is not important. Forget about him."

"That man has his grubby fingers in just about everything to do with trade. Of course, it's hardly surprising that he managed to establish himself here. I don't want you anywhere near him."

Again, Giselle had to force her features into an expression of acquiescence. It was odd to feel both pleased by Cerdic's obvious jealousy and irked by his assertion of authority.

A few days later, they boarded a ship bound for Sicily and

Marseilles. At night, in their bunk in the cramped hold, Cerdic clung to her, oblivious to anyone around them. The wall between them had disintegrated. He poured himself into her as if to drown his confusion, his grief, and his shame. Part of her welcomed this, but it also made her sad. Was he even aware of her at all? He would sleep after, exhausted beyond speech, and wake up drenched in sweat from endless nightmares of reliving the scenes of battle.

By the time they reached Marseille, Cerdic had recovered some of his equanimity. Slowly, cautiously, they talked about Les Tilleuls and about their boys. They didn't talk about the crusade or about Giselle's part in it, and they didn't talk about Blois.

During the last week of their journey, storms roiled up the sea, and their vessel pitched and rolled incessantly. Even though Giselle had never been troubled by this before, nausea plagued her. It was worst when Cerdic would bring her a bowl of salted meat. She'd have to rush out of the hold to the side of the vessel, retching helplessly into the spray blowing into her face from the waves. A sailor gave her hard dried bread to chew. That helped.

Jaffa, shimmering white in the bright sunlight of the Holy Land, had been almost sleepy, its harbor with only a few ships at anchor quiet and still in the heat of the day, the scents of spices, camel dung, and donkeys lingering between the warmed white limestone walls of buildings, castles, and churches.

Marseilles was awash with activity. Carefully their ship threaded its path into the bay, passing steep hills on one side, with large rocks poking out of the sea, and the imposing Commandry of the Knights Hospitallers on the other. When they reached the harbor, the sailors struggled to find a berth. Vendors rushed them before they had even properly disembarked, and they were surrounded by a mix of languages, French, Greek, Arabic, Basque, Catalonian, Provencal, and others they didn't recognize.

When they left the ship, Giselle still felt ill even though almost dizzy with excitement about being so close to home. She just needed to adjust to being back on land. But then, once the ground had stopped shifting underneath her sandals, and she was walking alongside Cerdic with renewed energy, she was able to think more clearly.

She stopped abruptly.

Cerdic turned his head toward her. "What's wrong?"

"Nothing." Giselle shook her head. "I had a stone in my sandal." She shook her foot and continued walking. She wasn't ill at all. She finally understood what her body was telling her. She was pregnant.

Giselle's eyes were blank when they left behind the busy harbor and set out on the cobblestone streets of the town. She didn't pay any attention as they walked through the market awash in trade goods from all parts of the known world. She didn't spare a single glance for the stalls heaped with flowers, tables covered with piles of silks inviting one to sink one's hands into soft warm fabric clouds, or vendors with olive oil in ceramic jugs, large wheels of cheese, breads, and barrels filled with dried salted cod. The smell of freshly caught fish brought back her nausea for an instant, only soothed by bunches of thyme and lavender around the corner. The signs of Roman construction in buildings and roads left her unmoved, and she barely registered the new church being built on a hill. The light-colored stone of the walls with their pointed windows glowed in the sunlight. The church tower was going to be tall.

"Come, Giselle, we need to find some horses to hire." Cerdic led her across town.

Gradually, the scents and sounds of a city close to home, the snatches of words she understood, and the familiar sights of the houses and inns soothed her. The initial shock of realization turned into a glowing ember of joy that spread from the center of her being outward. She was pregnant. That's why she had been so tired. She wanted to sing and run and laugh out loud; she was so happy.

Would Cerdic notice? She studied him while he negotiated the hire of several horses and a servant to come along for the ride home. He was no longer a young man. But he still rode with the same grace that had drawn her eye from the beginning. No, she wouldn't tell him yet. It was to be a present once they reached home.

Bearing News

The road north was in dire need of work.

Cerdic sniffed in irritation. How long were people going to be content to rely on what the Romans had left them? Admittedly, ancient Roman construction had held up remarkably well, but some occasional maintenance wouldn't come amiss. Irritation was threatening to flood his every pore. The horses he had managed to hire were long in the tooth; his gelding had a stiff gait that was hard to tolerate. At least the servant seemed competent.

Occasionally, he snuck a glance at his wife. Where was the shy, funny girl from the past? How was he to understand her crazy escapade in following him to the Holy Land? His stomach churned at all the awful things that might have happened to her, decked out in men's clothing and vulnerable to every attack. Why had she smiled at that odious merchant in Jaffa? He was angry at her. Yet, there were moments when he felt like bursting with pride at his brave little warrior of a wife. Then shame flooded him. He'd clung to Giselle after Mersivan, overcome with grief and a feeling of futility, frustration, and anger at her escapade, pouring himself into her warm body as if he could drown out his thoughts. He hadn't been careful or gentle. But Giselle, who had always been reticent, even withdrawn, in the marriage bed, had met him moment for moment. He didn't recognize her anymore.

Now, riding north, Giselle had withdrawn into her shell again. Cerdic didn't know what to make of it. He tried to put this out of his mind and focus on what he had to do.

They passed through Lyons and Bourges. Cerdic soaked in the familiar sights and sounds of villages, towns, and markets, and a luscious green landscape that seemed to welcome them back into its folds. Was it wrong to feel so glad to be alive? His heart ached when he thought of the news he was bringing to Adela. On the last stretch of the road toward Blois, they stopped for a rest in a small village, buying some ale, bread, and cheese. Refreshed, they set out again. Outside the village, where one road led straight north to Blois and another northwest to their home, Giselle directed her horse toward the left.

"Giselle."

She glanced back over her shoulder. "What is it?"

"We need to part here for a while." Cerdic had pulled up. "I want you to head home to Les Tilleuls. Leon shall make sure of your safety. I first have to go to my lady in Blois."

Giselle frowned. "You first have to go home to see your sons."

"They have done fine without me for over a year. A little while longer won't make a difference. I can't let my lady hear the news about Count Stephen-Henry's death from a stranger."

Giselle sat on her horse as if frozen. She stared at him wordlessly.

"You must understand that," Cerdic added. "Send Leon back to his master. And send me a message if you need anything."

Giselle pressed her lips together and gave a slight shake of her head. Then she pulled her horse around and cantered off.

"Follow my lady," Cerdic told the servant. "See to her safety." First she had appeared to be irritated, and now she just rode off without another word. He didn't understand her at all.

At Blois, Cerdic had the steward announce him. He hastily washed himself at the well in the courtyard and straightened out his tunic. Throughout the last days, he had tried to come up with the right words to tell Adela that her husband was dead. His mouth was dry when he walked into the great hall.

Adela sat near the hearth with a baby in her arms, dressed in a loose, dark green woolen gown with wide sleeves. She hadn't pinned her hair back; it fell down to her shoulders like a soft brown shawl. She was humming softly.

Cerdic gaped at her. The child couldn't be much older than seven or eight months. So Adela had been pregnant at the time they left.

Adela raised her head. "Welcome, Cerdic. I am glad to see you."

"My lady." Cerdic couldn't remember any of the phrases he had tried to rehearse.

Adela looked at him searchingly. Then she rose from her chair and beckoned a woman who had been sitting in a corner. "Gertrude, come and take Henry outside." She waited until the doors of the great hall had closed before turning to Cerdic. "You have news for me."

"Yes, my lady."

"Bad news," she stated flatly.

"Yes, my lady." He swayed on his feet. Exhaustion threatened to overwhelm him. "I am sorry to tell you that Count Stephen-Henry died in battle on the 19th of May."

Adela's face was a mask. She went to the table and filled a beaker with wine. "Sit down and drink this."

Cerdic obeyed; he was ashamed at his loss of control. Speaking haltingly in a low voice, he told Adela what had happened.

Adela didn't flinch, her eyes on him throughout. She said nothing when Cerdic stopped, just steadily rubbing the fabric of her woolen gown between her fingers.

"Count Stephen-Henry was at peace; he told me so before sending me away," Cerdic repeated. "He had fulfilled his vows. And he was resolute and brave until the end."

"Thank you for coming in person to bring this news." Adela rose. "The steward will show you where you can stay."

Cerdic stood up; he felt dizzy for a moment. Then his eyes cleared. Adela stood in front of him, unbending and composed, and he was flooded with admiration and with pity for this woman who now had to face the world on her own. In the mere space of seventeen years, she had transformed from a young girl into a mature married woman, she had given birth to eight children, she had ruled with intelligence, courage, and clear-sighted determination, and now she was a widow. And over all the years he had known her, she had often been a true friend to him. He bowed, humbled and moved to tears.

"Tomorrow we will talk more," Adela said calmly.

They never did talk more about the crusade or the details of Count Stephen-Henry's death. The next day, Adela arose early as she always did, prayed in the chapel, and began to work. She had put away the soft flowing woolen gown and had chosen instead a stiff sheath in subdued hues of dark brown, black, and red. Her hair was hidden under a white cap that framed her pale face.

Watching her red-rimmed eyes, Cerdic followed her lead during discussions in the great hall over the next weeks. He was amazed how quickly he was once again drawn into the wrangling over trade, politics, and power plays.

Of course, many discussions revolved around her brothers. Robert still disputed Henry's control of England. The fact that he had been forced to renounce his claim to the English throne after a disastrous attempt to invade England in 1101 didn't stop him from trying to make trouble.

"You'd think that now that he is married and to a wealthy woman to boot, he'd have better things to do," one of Adela's senior advisors said.

"Sometimes I feel sorry for him." Adela picked up a pale green glass goblet and gently swirled the wine around before taking a sip. "And he is my brother, after all." She frowned and added, "even though apparently some of his personal habits don't bear closer scrutiny."

Cerdic had to turn away, tempted to laugh. Rumors of Robert's carousing and wild evenings spent with harlots made the rounds. So Adela knew about those.

When Adela asked his opinion, Cerdic once again argued that supporting Robert against Henry wouldn't be in her best interest. For all that there was a kernel of injustice in the way in which Robert had been treated by his father and by his brothers as well, Cerdic believed that it wouldn't do any good, and Robert had to be brought to accept the reality.

Adela showed him some of the letters she received. "You should read this," she said with an expression of chagrin. It was from one Hildebert of Lavardin, the bishop of Mans. "He is a fine administrator and is working hard at the rebuilding of the cathedral, but this sort of thing seems beyond the bounds of what is acceptable."

Cerdic skimmed the lines.

Poverty has a shameless face; it knows no shame when there might be help. Poverty urges to crime and intercedes for mercy. Forgive therefore if at its urging I ask beyond my deserts. You teach me to hope beyond my deserts who do not fail to give beyond deserts, if you ask what or with what confidence I ask. I need a chausuble. You promised it to me. And I think you will not break your promise who hasten to give even what is not promised. Fare well.

The man went on and on about this chausuble that had been promised to him. Cerdic grinned; it did sound like begging.

"I must admit though," Adela added with a smile, "he writes lovely hymns. *This is true faith, for our keeping. Error bringeth sin and weeping.* I like that."

The next day, Cerdic sought out Adela in the great hall. He needed to go home. When he pulled open the heavy oak door, he realized he'd chosen a bad time. Adela was in the midst of berating William, her eldest. The boy was about seventeen. Heavy-set, with a thick shock of reddish blond hair, and a round face, he looked like an overgrown child. He stood in front of his mother, his head bent and his cheeks flushed.

"You can't keep doing stupid things like this," Adela shouted. Her face had reddened. "You are the eldest. What sort of example are you setting the others?"

Cerdic tried to walk back outside when Adela spoke to him. "Cerdic, please stay. We are done here. William, you may go."

The boy walked past Cerdic, tears running down his face.

"This is what I am dealing with." Adela tossed some sheets of vellum she had in her hands on the table. "My eldest decided to drive a bunch of pigs into the churchyard and from there, all the way into the new cathedral. They had already finished part of the work on the flooring. The bishop wrote to me to lodge a complaint. The pigs did considerable damage. And I got an angry letter from the farmer whose pigs William had stolen in this little escapade."

Cerdic studied his feet. Partly he was amused; he didn't like the bishop of the Cathedral of St. Louis of Blois, a pompous, self-righteous, and vindictive man. He also felt sorry for the boy. Ever since he was born, he seemed to have gotten on the wrong side of his mother and everybody else for that matter, not swift to understand, struggling where his younger brothers excelled, with an uneven temper and a complete lack of direction.

"Perhaps he needs a better tutor," he said carefully.

"I am not wasting any more tutoring on that boy." Adela shook her head. "He hasn't shown himself capable of learning all these years. No, I'll have to think of something else for him. Meanwhile, I'd like to ask you something."

"My lady, allow me to ask you something first."

"Yes?"

"It is time for me to return home. I have been here for over a month."

"I understand. But first, I need to ask you to do something for me."

Caught In The Snare

1103 Caen

"But, my lady, any of your knights could do this."

Cerdic had never yet been so frustrated and angry. Adela wanted him to take her son Theobald to her brother-in-law Hugh of Troyes. And she had mentioned another unspecified task. Certainly, she was a widow, and she needed friends around her whom she could trust. But she had other advisors, and for an errand like this, she surely could find someone else. Was he going to be at her back and call indefinitely?

"Theobald has known you all his life. It would be good for him to spend time with you. It has not been easy for him and his brothers." Adela avoided his eyes. "My brother-in-law is a good man and the right person to take charge of a growing boy, especially now that he has lost his father. Moreover, Hugh and his wife Constance haven't been blessed with children. Theobald is his heir designate. It is time that Theobald learns everything he needs to know for his future station and duties in life."

Cerdic stared at her, at a loss for words.

"I can't and don't want to ask anybody else. I trust you."

Cerdic bowed. In truth, he could hardly go on protesting.

Several weeks later, he was back on the road in the company of a surly twelve-year-old boy. For the first hour, they rode in silence. It was early December, and the first hoar frost had turned everything dull and brown. They had to ride north and west toward Troyes; Champagne was a large county, and it would take them about two days.

Theobald had bowed to his mother and ducked out of her embrace. He had mounted his horse without acknowledging Cerdic. He was slender and fine-boned; it didn't look as if he would have his father's sturdy build as an adult. His curly hair peeking out underneath his woolen cap was dark brown, not the reddish hue of his grandfather and his uncles. He rode with his head bent and his shoulders hunched.

Guisbert was ten, Cerdic thought with a pang, not much younger than this boy. Would he even recognize his father?

The first words they exchanged were when Cerdic's horse started limping, and Cerdic had to stop to check the hooves. A stone had worked its way underneath one shoe. Fortunately, Cerdic could pick it out.

"Tell you what." Cerdic straightened up. The boy's expression was sullen and slightly hostile. "I don't trust this shoe, and I don't want the bay to go lame on me. Let's walk for a bit. The next village isn't too far from here, and we'll find a blacksmith there."

So they walked, leading the horses. "What are the roads like in the Holy Land?" Theobald asked after a while.

Cerdic didn't think that the boy really cared about the roads, but it was an opening. "Would you believe it? Some are a lot better than the roads here. Others again are nothing but sand and rocks."

Theobald was silent. They continued walking.

Then Theobald cleared his throat. "You were with my father, weren't you?"

"Yes, I was," Cerdic responded cautiously. "What did your mother tell you?"

"Nothing." The boy jerked on his horse's rein so that the surprised animal flung his head up and snorted. "Sorry," Theobald whispered to the horse. "My mother told me nothing other than that he's dead. I can't talk to her about it."

Cerdic frowned, inwardly cursing Adela. So, that's why she sent him on this journey. She wanted him to talk to her son for her. "What do you know?" he asked, trying to feel his way.

"Have you heard what they say about him?"

"They?"

"Oh, everybody." Theobald rubbed the sleeve of his tunic over his face. "Children, servants when they think they are alone, the priest. They say he was a coward. They say he ran away. They say he broke his oath. We've been called cowards, shirkers, quitters, and worse—Stephen and I. William too, but I think he probably didn't even notice. Anyway, he doesn't care what anybody calls him."

"Your father fulfilled his vows, and he was brave. Let me tell you what happened." Cerdic chose his words carefully, relating the events of the first crusade and the follow-up venture that ended at Ramla. He didn't dwell on the details, but he didn't embellish anything either. It wouldn't help this boy to lie to him. "Many people broke off their crusade that first time," he said finally. "You have to understand how hopeless it all seemed; people were tired, hungry, and ill. Many had lost their horses. It's easy to judge for those who weren't there. And your father…he was a good man. He wasn't a warrior like your uncle Robert, but he was good and kind. Being brave when you are not afraid, now that's not so hard. But when you are afraid and go ahead anyway, that's true courage. Your father went to his death, knowing full well what he was facing. That's brave."

Theobald didn't say anything for the remainder of their journey. But in Troyes, when the steward came out to welcome Theobald, he turned to Cerdic and bowed. "Thank you."

Back in Blois, Adela put him off when he asked what other task she had in mind for him. "Just give me a few days. I'll let you know."

It was frustrating. It was as if Adela was waiting for something and didn't want to explain what it was. She had been spending more time than usual with the children. One of her daughters, Lucia-Mahaut, was still at home, although she probably would soon be attending lessons at the local abbey. Stephen seemed to cling to her more since his brother closest to him in age was gone. Adela always carried Henry around with her, even though she had been quick to send her other children off with their nursemaids. Sometimes when Cerdic entered the great hall, he came upon Adela, who involved herself in her children's work with their tutors, checking their writing work, and helping them with their reading. Henry sat on her lap, watching everything with interest.

Cerdic was torn. He wished he could simply leave, but when Adela looked at him with her large blue eyes, plaintive and full of trust, he didn't have the heart to do that.

Finally, in the new year, she told him what she needed him to do.

Cerdic stared at her in dismay. "You want me to take Henry to the Cluniac abbey at La Charité-sur-Loire?"

Adela was pale, and there were dark shadows under her eyes. "Yes." Her expression was closed, uncompromising. "Henry will be pledged to the church as an oblate, dedicated to the service of God."

"He is a baby." Cerdic knew it was not his place to protest any of Adela's decisions, but he couldn't help himself. "Can't you do this when he is older?"

"No," Adela said. "It has to be done now."

"You are deciding his entire life for him."

"I am ensuring that for his entire life he will be loved and honored and that he will do his duty to God. That's more than most mothers can do for their children. What greater thing than to serve God?"

"But he needs his mother."

"La Charité-sur-Loire is not out of this world. I will visit him occasionally. Eventually, he will go to Cluny. But for the time being, he will be closer."

Cerdic bent his head. What else could he say?

"Anyway, I have made my decision." Adela's voice was hard. "You will take him."

"Are you coming along?"

"No."

"When?"

"When the weather opens up. I'll get everything ready."

Cerdic bowed, at a loss for words. He tried to imagine Giselle sending one of her children away like this. Why? Why was Adela doing this? Of course, she was devout. But her baby? She had been singing to him. In the last months, he had often watched her with the boy. Henry liked to sit on her lap to watch what the other children were doing. He was round-faced, with pudgy legs and pudgy fists, and his deep chuckle made everyone around him smile.

Cerdic had been at Cluny Abbey. Over the years, it had been gifted vineyards, fields, meadows, woods, watermills, and lands both cultivated and uncultivated as well as serfs to work the land. It was probably one of the wealthiest and most powerful of monastic institutions in the land. Surely, some of that wealth spilled over to the abbey of La Charité-sur-Loire. Henry would not want for anything. But Cerdic couldn't picture this little boy growing up in the stark surroundings of an abbey. What did Benedictine monks know about children? Then he remembered that, of course, they did this all the time. Henry was hardly the first to be dedicated to the church at a young age. And Adela would visit him there.

When the snow had melted and the first buds on the trees emerged, Cerdic set out with several escorts, the nursemaid, and Henry, secured in a pannier. The journey from Blois to La Charité-sur-Loire would take about five days, since they had to travel slowly.

Adela hadn't come downstairs to watch them ride out. The evening before, she had handed him a letter for the abbot and money for the journey. She was pale, and her eyes were strained.

"I'll pray for your safe journey. Please send me a message when you have arrived."

"Yes, my lady."

"I assume you'll go home afterwards."

"Yes, with your leave."

"I wish you godspeed."

Cerdic wondered about that as they rode west. And then, thinking of her red-rimmed eyes, he realized that she couldn't bear taking leave from her beloved son in public. She did love the little boy; that much had been clear. So Henry was the sacrifice. She had sent her husband to his death; sending her last-born child to the Cluniac abbey was her penance.

It made him sad. He hadn't thought about his mother in a long time, but now, he vividly remembered her rough warm palm stroking his face as she whispered in his ear that he had to go with King William. His mother had made a sacrifice as profound and wrenching as Adela, not out of a sense of guilt, but out of sheer necessity. It had been the only way she knew of how to provide him with a future.

What would Giselle think about this? He shifted in his seat; it suddenly felt uncomfortable. He hadn't heard much from Les Tilleuls. Giselle had sent only a few terse messages, telling him that everything was fine. It was as if she was saying, *I don't need you here*. She had run the estate for a long time now. She probably didn't need him.

By the time they reached the abbey, Cerdic was exhausted. Henry fretted and cried at night, increasingly anxious in the unfamiliar surroundings. To give the nursemaid a break, Cerdic had taken to holding the baby and walking up and down in the dark courtyards of the inns where they stayed overnight. Henry would gaze at him intently while resting in his arms. His blue eyes reminded Cerdic of Adela. The little boy already had a full head of reddish-brown curls framing his face. Cerdic tried humming, dredging up memories of childhood songs he had heard Adela and Giselle sing to their children. To his intense relief, Henry would fall asleep, a heavy limp warm bundle in his arms.

When they reached La Charité-sur-Loire, several monks came outside to welcome them. "The abbot would like to meet with you, Sir Cerdic," an elderly monk said. "Frobertus will take the child to the nuns' wing."

Cerdic had been carrying Henry, safely secured in his pannier, for the last leg of the journey. He hesitated as he looked at the flushed little face with its round cheeks in the nest of blankets. With a sigh, he dismounted and took Henry into his arms. "You will be safe," he whispered. The boy gazed at him and smiled.

"It is better to do this fast," the monk said calmly. "The nuns will take good care of him."

Cerdic handed the child to the younger monk who walked off with him. Henry was so surprised that he didn't make any sound, staring at Cerdic over the monk's shoulder. Then he struggled, trying to twist out of the monk's arms and whimpering.

"Come, Sir Cerdic." The elderly monk spoke gently. "The child will be fine. Now follow me; I will take you to the abbot. We will see to your escort and the young woman." The younger monk had already disappeared behind the cloister's arches. Cerdic heard Henry crying, and then he was gone.

The abbot received Adela's letter and a munificent gift for the abbey with suitable expressions of gratitude and assurances regarding the care of her son.

The heavy iron gates closed behind Cerdic with a bang as he rode out of the abbey courtyard. Whenever he allowed his thoughts to wander on the long ride west, he saw Henry's face gazing back at him and heard him crying.

The Music of Bees

This animal is pleased by a good tune: when they are scattered,
therefore, beekeepers clash cymbals or clap their hands
rhythmically to bring them home. This is the only animal that looks
for a leader to take care of the whole community: it always honours
its king, follows him enthusiastically wherever he goes, supports him
when he is exhausted, carries him and keeps him safe when he
cannot fly. It particularly hates laziness; bees unite to kill the ones
who do no work and use up others' production. Its mechanical skill
and near-logical understanding is shown by the fact
that it makes hexagonal cells to store honey.
Geoponika, 10th century Byzantine work on farming.

1104

Voices were coming from the goat shed—high-pitched ones and a deep rumble.

Giselle crossed the stable yard while adjusting the baby in her arms and covering its head with the blanket. She had gone into labor a few weeks earlier than expected, on the night of the winter solstice, and she worried about the frail little being. Her back was sore. The pregnancy and the two days of labor had exhausted her more than she expected.

The children loved the goats. They played with them as if they were dogs.

"And there was the knight, with blood running down his face, and his hands drenched in blood." That was Thomas's gravelly voice. "'What have you done, my son?' The priest was trembling in fright."

Giselle peered through the door. Thomas reclined on a pile of hay, comfortably sucking on a piece of straw as he told his story. The children sat on the ground, Guisbert with a goat kid on his lap. Jacques' little brother was there as well. Yves's eyes were huge, and his little fist clutched his older brother's tunic.

"Children, go outside. I want to talk to Thomas."

"Oh, mother," the children protested but walked away, glancing back at Thomas with regret. "We'll come back later."

"Don't tell them stories like that." Giselle spoke sharply. "They don't need to hear about so much gruesomeness or wickedness."

"Yes, my lady," the old man said with a twinkle. She knew he'd be right at it again as soon as she was out of earshot.

Perhaps she was wrong. The children would have to learn about the dark side of life soon enough—evil knights, faithless priests, treacherous women, suffering, even death. Why not learn it through these stories that they could still shrug off even while it gave them a taste of reality? It was hard to make all these decisions. Guisbert certainly would need proper tutoring soon.

A few days later, she walked underneath the lime trees. The baby had been fretting, and the motion calmed it. Giselle could feel it relax in her arms. It was a mild day. The buds on the trees were ready to burst. She had met with Auberi about speeding up the process of pruning the grape vines. Spring had set in earlier than expected, and this early pruning was critical.

She heard someone shouting around the curve of the road. Her sons' voices came bouncing back from up high. They had been tree climbing again.

Several times already, they had amused themselves by shooting their little arrows at passersby from their perches in the trees. "We are attacking infidels," Guisbert told her proudly. She hastened forward to intervene.

"You think you are the only ones able to climb trees?" The man's deep voice was amused.

Giselle stopped abruptly. That voice. Near a lime tree with large branches reaching down to the ground, a tall man held Guisbert and Yves by their collars. "Shooting infidels? Well, let me assure you, I'm not an infidel."

The boys stared at the tall stranger. Then Guisbert exclaimed, "Father." Yves tried to wiggle free of the hand holding him. "Father," he screeched, not to be outdone by his older brother.

"Hallo, Guisbert," Cerdic said gravely. Then, he bent down to the younger boy. "Hallo, Yves."

He raised his head and let go of the boys. "My lady." He bowed. "And who is this?" He gazed at the bundle in Giselle's arms.

"That is your daughter."

"Our daughter?" Cerdic reached out his arms to take the baby from Giselle. "What is her name?"

"We didn't know when you would come. The priest baptized her already. Her name is Orva."

Cerdic flushed. "You chose my mother's name?"

Cerdic's reaction caught Giselle off guard. Something warm glowed in her chest and threatened to bubble over in delight for all that she was still angry about his long absence. "Yes," she said stiffly. "I learned it means 'brave friend.' And the priest told me it also means 'worth of gold.'"

Cerdic studied the baby's scrunched up little face while supporting her head with his hand. Then he smiled at Giselle.

"Worth of gold, indeed." His voice sounded husky. "And you—you should be called 'brave friend.'"

The first weeks of having Cerdic back at home were filled with unexpected traps. "I am going out to meet with Auberi," Cerdic told Giselle in the morning, getting up from the table where they had shared some bread and ale.

"Yes, I have talked to him about the pruning work," Giselle said eagerly. She also stood and was pulling her shawl around her shoulders. "But we need to do something about some of our hives that didn't survive the winter."

"Oh, I see." Cerdic shrugged. "I suppose you have everything well in hand."

Helplessly, Giselle stared back at him. He had sounded so hurt. She wanted to scream at him for leaving her to handle everything alone for so long, and at the same time she had forgotten how much confidence she had gained over the last years, managing the estate. For an instant she thought of Adela, alone in Blois. Somehow she didn't think that Adela had ever spent a great deal of energy trying to protect her husband's feelings.

"I don't know what to do about the drainage matter," she said hesitantly. "You remember? You had some ideas for that, but then you had to leave."

"I don't know." Cerdic frowned and shook his head. "Perhaps I will just ride around for now to reacquaint myself with everything." He walked outside.

The children were shy with him at first. Giselle watched him take both of them in front of him on his horse to ride all over the estate. By the time they returned, they were squealing with excitement. But Cerdic continued to be aloof and stiff with Giselle. He looked at everything, but he didn't comment. A few times, Giselle watched him stand at the hearth, staring into the flames.

Several days later, after the children were asleep, Cerdic and Giselle sat in front of the hearth in the great hall drinking mead. As usual, Giselle had a pile of clothes she was mending. She was glad of the tall candles that filled with the room with warm light. Fortunately, their hives had produced more than enough wax for candles. In fact, she had begun trading beeswax for other items.

"Giselle, you are right. The drainage on the lower field is a problem. Here is what we could do."

Internally sighing with relief, Giselle listened to her husband describe his plan.

"I saw some clever arrangements in the Holy Land." To show her what he had in mind, he sketched a device for collecting rainwater. "While we don't suffer often from a lack of rain, it seems a pity to let water pool and flood in some areas, doing damage while it could be put to good use if we have a way to catch it in basins."

Giselle nodded eagerly.

When they blew out the candles to go to sleep, Cerdic smiled at her. "It's good to be back."

The next years were the happiest Giselle had ever experienced. They worked extremely hard. The children were growing up. Orva talked before she could walk. Her brothers loved carrying her around like a sack of flour; she never seemed to mind this treatment, instead beamed at them when they picked her up. All her children had dark hair and dark eyes like hers. Only Orva's eyes were different, unlike that of her brothers or either of her parents. They were dark golden with tiny flecks of green. Giselle had a secret name for her daughter; she called her Leonne, the little lioness. From the beginning, she was like a lion, fearless and with a mind of her own, and a curious fierce concentration in her golden eyes. Giselle loved her so much that sometimes fear for her threatened to overwhelm her. It was odd; she had never feared so much for her boys, and yet life was just as dangerous for them. Children died so often.

The vineyard took up most of their time. Cultivating the fields, pruning, harvesting, crushing and pressing, fermenting, aging, bottling, shipping, planting new stock, and preparing casks. The vines had to be pruned regularly throughout the growing season. Serfs did most of this labor. Following a principle employed by her father for effective management of workers, both Giselle and Cerdic often went into the fields to work alongside the serfs. However, for larger tasks, Cerdic and Giselle drew on the work of villeins as part of their dues payable to the landowner. Throughout the year, a cooper repaired wine barrels and built new ones. Cerdic discussed with him what wood he'd need—oak or chestnut or ash, depending on the intended use.

To Giselle's amusement, Orva liked to sit on the ground in the cooper's work area, watching intently as he and his apprentice shaped the staves of the barrel with axes, used drawing knives to trim and shave the staves, and smoothed the pieces with planes before fitting everything together with metal bands. The men gave her bits of wood and a small toy hammer they had fashioned out of scraps and smiled as the little girl copied their moves.

For storage while the wine was fermenting and for transport, they had been using barrels. They had the advantage of not breaking on the road or on shipboard. In the last year, they had begun shipping wine to England. They also bottled some of their wine, using beeswax to seal the bottles.

"What do you think about expanding our pottery shed and kiln?" Giselle asked one day. "We need more jugs and flasks. It would give Thomas something better to do than to tell ghost stories to the children."

Cerdic grinned. "I rather like the stories, especially when Yves retells them to me afterward." He pondered her suggestion. "But you are right. More flasks would be handy for bottling and marketing the wine."

Cerdic experimented with grafting grape varieties onto old rootstock.

"How do you know about this?" Giselle asked when he explained what he wanted to do.

"One of the monasteries I had to visit on behalf of my lady has been doing this for years. A monk explained it to me. That's how they produce different and better types of wine."

"It sounds difficult," Giselle said doubtfully.

"It takes patience. You have to get the timing right, and you have to create a good connection between the rootstock and the graft. Then you bind it up and hope that it takes. You have to practice making clean cuts first before you work with live rootstock. Here, let me show you." Cerdic picked up a few branches he had freshly cut.

"Like this?" Giselle attempted to cut two pieces and then fit them together.

"That's it."

Giselle suddenly had a vivid recollection of her father holding her small hands with the large pruning sheers that felt awkward and too heavy for her and showing her where to cut back a shoot. "That's it," he'd say, his soft, dark voice close to her ears. She glanced at Cerdic and shivered. Everything about her feelings for him felt fragile; the slightest wind storm could knock them over. Would he leave again? Would Adela always be more important to him than anyone else? Then she shook herself. These were good days. She had to be grateful.

The harvest and the pressing of the grapes took place within days of each other, and for this, they had to draw on every available laborer. It was exhausting. At the end of the harvest, Giselle prepared a feast for all to celebrate the completion of this important task. But the work of crushing couldn't wait. It began while the feast was still going on.

The courtyard was a beehive of people sitting everywhere with bowls on their knees and a chunk of bread in their hand, while others walked in from the vineyards with baskets filled with grapes and depositing them next to the crushing tubs. Until last year, they had only used tubs that could accommodate one person at a time. Now two people could fit inside comfortably into the big one. "This is a good change," Cerdic reassured her. "It will make this work go faster." The air was redolent with the sour, tangy scent of the fruit. Children ran around, shouting and giggling. Two boys were testing their skills by aiming grapes at each other's mouth until a man shook them by the scruff of their necks to stop them. A traveling jongleur was playing on a lute and singing a song that had the people near him roar with laughter.

"Maman," Orva exclaimed in her high voice. "Want to go in the tub."

Giselle looked up from the big pot. She had been ladling soup into bowls for people waiting in a row. She turned toward the big crushing tub.

Cerdic stood next to the tub watching two men moving up and down rhythmically as they crushed the grapes with their own weight, stomping on them over and over with their naked feet. Then a dark head poked above the rim between two men in the tub. Guisbert.

"No, get him out of there," she shouted, dropping her ladle and moving over to the tub.

"No harm done." Cerdic laughed and lifted his son out, dripping and beaming with pride. "He does smell a bit fermented, though."

Then there were the beehives.

"Maman," Yves shouted when she walked into the courtyard. "Orva is in the apiary again."

Yves, six years older, had taken it upon himself to watch over his sister, but she managed to escape him often once she figured out the use of her legs.

Giselle followed her son to the apiary. It was in a wind-sheltered meadow on the other side of the fruit orchard and edged by hedgerows. Once again, she wondered how this little boy, so eager and ready to embark on the riskiest undertakings without any care to the consequences, was as cautious and anxious as an old grandfather with his sister.

They found Orva sitting cross-legged on the ground near the straw skeps, with an expression of dreamy absorption. She had stretched out her right arm and was holding it perfectly still in the sunlight while three bees were crawling on the slender wrist. The childish peach fuzz on her daughter's skin glimmered in the light like silk. Perhaps the bees liked that and the warmth coming from the little girl.

Orva turned her head and gazed at her mother with her golden eyes. "They are singing. Listen."

"I can't hear them as well as you can," Giselle said. "Maybe your hearing is better. But don't move too fast. You don't want to get them upset."

"They know me. They won't hurt me." Gently, she blew on them. "Go, fly away, bees." One by one, they lifted off and flew away into the white cloud of an apple tree in bloom.

Giselle thought that the bees brought out their individual characters.

Cerdic was entranced by knowledge, reading everything about beekeeping he could get his hands on. He was enormously proud of the new wooden boxes he brought home. "The monks showed these frames to me. They are so much easier to manage and to keep clean without disturbing the hives."

"All that change." Thomas, still their principal beekeeper, shook his head doubtfully. "Where will it all end?"

"I love the straw skeps," Giselle said wistfully. "They make me think of small hunchbacked persons, and besides, they look warm and cozy."

Despite his father's grumbling, Auberi was pleased when he inspected the wooden frames, lifting them and closing them again. "These should make our work much easier. Did the monks have any other advice?"

For Guisbert, the bees were a source of constant annoyance; he had a harder time than any of them to learn patience when being around them. As the oldest, Cerdic insisted on teaching Guisbert the rudiments of working with bees just as he taught him about the vineyard. For Yves, the bees were an enemy to be vanquished. He was a risk taker and careless. He got stung often, and it didn't bother him. But he learned to slow down.

Giselle, ever practical, was interested in the many uses of honey and beeswax. She had heard of a drink of boiled parsley, honey, and wine as something that was good for the heart. Some crusaders had talked of honey's uses for healing wounds. There was so much more she wanted to learn about this.

"Last year, we produced almost 360 pounds of honey and seven pounds of wax," Thomas reported. Giselle and Cerdic were in the apiary together with Thomas and Auberi to discuss when to take the next load of honey from the hives.

Cerdic nodded. "Even though it wasn't a good year. We lost several swarms." He was studying the five cylindrical straw skeps and also the two new wooden boxes they were testing out as housing for the hives.

The bees needed constant attention. Giselle hadn't realized until she spent time at Les Tilleuls that young bees needed food. Beekeepers filled basins with wine mixed with honey, with leaves floating in the liquid to prevent their drowning. In the colder months, they ground up raisins and savory, mixing this mess with barley cakes. In the early spring, the bees needed the extra food before they could find enough nectar and pollen.

Her favorite time was when the beekeepers drove the bees from their hives to sweep out the cobwebs and clean the hives or to harvest honey. The men lit fires with dried cow-dung to incite the bees to leave their homes. For this they donned wide shrouds with hoods—another new-fangled idea Thomas grumbled about. "Beekeepers get stung. That's the way it is."

Cerdic wanted to try out another method he had read about. To keep away the bees, the men would have to smear themselves with the juice of the wild mallow plant. "You don't think it's a good idea?" He looked hurt when Giselle expressed her doubts about it. Fortunately, since they couldn't find enough wild mallow plants to produce the juice, Cerdic grudgingly abandoned this notion.

When she had time, Giselle liked to watch from a safe distance, fascinated by the peculiar slow dance of the men in their shrouds moving around the fires like ghostly apparitions. And then the bees emerged, soared, and scattered into the wind, disappearing into the nearby fruit orchard. It was like watching wisps of her own thoughts and fears flutter about and take flight.

"I hope they don't take all their honey," Orva whispered, standing next to her. "We don't want the bees to get angry and stop working."

Giselle smiled at her daughter. "You have been listening to Thomas."

"Can we come back when they bring the bees back to their homes?"

"You like that?"

"Yes, the bees like music."

When the hives were ready, the beekeepers walked around clapping their hands and clashing cymbals in a steady rhythm to gather the bees and bring them home.

Giselle wished this would work with Cerdic. Whenever he went back to Blois, dancing attendance on Adela, it angered her. He had done enough; his service shouldn't absorb his entire life.

After all, why should Cerdic have to get drawn into Adela's increasing troubles with her son William? According to Cerdic, Bishop Ivo of Chartres had berated Adela for not punishing William for his adulterous relationship with one of Adela's cousins.

"Maybe Adela feels bad over having been too harsh with William when he was a little boy." Giselle remembered some scenes at Blois and a tear-blotched, miserable child who never had any friends.

"Perhaps," Cerdic said. "But it doesn't matter. William is a fully grown man now, and he is the eldest. I wonder what Adela will do."

There was another instance where Adela was at the receiving end of the bishop's sharp tongue over various misdeeds by some of Adela's men, who had violently seized the annual income of the churches at Châteaudun and at Bonneval. They had also stolen wine from the cellars and committed other atrocities against clerics.

"It's embarrassing for Adela, and she needs the good office of Bishop Ivo. But I have no doubt she'll find an elegant solution to this dilemma."

Giselle didn't say anything, even if she had to admit that usually Adela prevailed in situations like this. She admired her and resented her. Thinking of her was like eating a spoonful of honey followed by bitter gall.

Just when Orva was beginning to toddle all over the courtyard, Cerdic went to Blois for an extended period.

When he talked about it to Giselle upon his return, for the first time in her recollection, he expressed a certain exasperation with Adela. "Would you believe it? She made a gift to a monastery, granting them the use of a portion of land with all the wildlife in it, but she held on to her right to preside over jurisdiction regarding any crimes committed in the area." He frowned. "She is so generous and loving and good, and yet she does this. It's like giving something and taking it away again."

Giselle said nothing, inwardly pleased by this criticism.

"But, of course, ruling her vast domain must be difficult for her," Cerdic continued. "Especially with Robert constantly trying to stir up trouble with King Henry and in Normandy. One can't blame her for holding onto control in areas where she feels she can do good."

"Of course," Giselle said glumly.

Countess And Lord

It is a benefit of grace to give, of justice to restore what has been taken away; the perfection of Christian life consists of these. In one an injury is corrected, in the other, a benevolence is granted. Thus I, Adela, taught by the mastery of Stephen's argument, and at the same time terrified by the heap of my sins, decided to raise and honor the church of St. Satur by restoring what was taken away, by bestowing possessions, by strengthening freedom. Therefore in the dedication of said church, in the year 1104, 12th indiction, 3rd epact, Ides of November, celebrated by Leodegaire archbishop of Bourges, I conferred the bread customs of castrum Gordon that the church had anciently had, on St. Satur with the understanding that after the death of Robert to whom I had given it as his it would freely return to the church and meanwhile he would hold and acknowledge it from said church and at the same time do homage for it to the abbot, would pay the owed service, having removed from the successors of that Robert all ability to reclaim it from them. Moreover, I granted a fair established on the anniversary of the dedication and all the income of that fair to St. Satur, so that no dependant of the count or of any other person, except whom the canons appointed, could exercise power or justice over those coming to the fair. Adela of England, Countess of Blois, Chartres, and Meaux, letter to Public, 1104

Blois 1107

"The pope is expected."

"That's nice," Giselle said absentmindedly. She was inspecting a wax tablet that Yves had filled with numbers. She wasn't sure whether the new tutor was up to the task of teaching the boys.

"Did you hear what I said?" Cerdic asked. "Pope Paschal is going to visit Adela. While he is in France, he is planning to consecrate the Priory of Notre Dame at La Charité-sur-Loire."

Giselle put down the wax tablet and looked at her husband with an expression of resignation.

"Don't you realize what an honor it is that the pope will spend Easter with my lady?"

"Yes, Cid, I do."

"Well, she wants us to attend."

So, once again as so many times before, Cerdic and Giselle set their affairs in order, made arrangements with Auberi and with their children's tutor, and rode to Blois.

They had arrived in time to witness the Palm Sunday procession. Priests blessed freshly cut branches as stand-ins for palm fronds and carried them through town, led by a priest holding a cross. At home, Giselle loved Palm Sunday and always made sure to snag a branch from the procession to take home with her to bring the blessing upon her home and her family for the year.

This Palm Sunday was an impressive affair. Several cardinals had traveled to Blois for the occasion, and the procession involved more clergy that Giselle had ever witnessed in a single place. After that, the cathedral, like churches everywhere in the land, was stripped and cleaned.

Good Friday was a day of mourning. Priests exhorted everyone to remember how unworthy they were; all had to creep on their knees to the foot of the cross and kiss it. Then the priests placed the cross into the sepulchre and extinguished all lights inside the church.

On Easter Sunday, the day of the resurrection, the cathedral was once again ablaze and the air redolent of incense and herbs, and priests had retrieved the cross from its sepulchre.

Pope Paschal conducted the mass surrounded by clergy in their finest vestments. A temporary altar had been constructed in the nave, and the flickering flames of hundreds of candles distracted from the unfinished portions, while highlighting the rich velvets and brocades, the glimmering silver chalices, and the large jeweled cross behind the altar.

Giselle always remembered this day. *I was blessed by the pope.*

Adela was a generous hostess, and the customary feast after the Easter mass was a joyous and sumptuous occasion. Even though Adela, as a widow, refrained from participating, there was some dancing and music as well.

A wandering musician entertained the guests in the great hall after the pope had retired.

"This is a new style of music that's will hopefully please you," the entertainer explained, bowing with courtly grace. "It comes to you from the south, and my lord, the Duke of Aquitaine, composed this piece."

Adela pursed her lips but nodded her assent, and the musician sang while playing a lute.

People in the audience whispered to each other. Giselle could make out some snatches of what they were saying; apparently, the duke was quite wild and had abandoned his wife for another woman. And he had other misdeeds to his name.

Giselle forgot about the duke when she listened to the music. She had never heard anything like this—a clear voice filling the cavernous space of the great hall with ease, soaring over the whispering and muttering and the crackling of the fire in the hearth. The music touched her in ways she would never have expected. The language of the songs was strange. She recognized many words, but the phrasing was unfamiliar. Still, she made out some of it. One song was about an unrequited love. Another was sober and sad, weaving a tale of chivalry, pride, making sacrifices, and the challenge of facing death. She had never thought music could be like this, telling stories and stirring emotions.

The musician launched into another song. Some in the audience listened with their faces rigid and their lips pressed together; others giggled and nudged each other. Giselle blushed when she followed the lines. The singer described a man who feared that he would die if he couldn't learn whether a certain lady wore a nightgown in bed or slept in the nude. Giselle glanced at Adela, whom she knew as pious, serious, and devout, and found that she was laughing. Then Giselle remembered some of her conversations with Adela when Giselle was about to get married. Adela had been frank, surprisingly helpful, and evidently enjoying all aspects of marriage. No, a few innuendos in a piece of music wouldn't trouble her.

After the splendid Easter celebration, Giselle agreed to stay in Blois for a while. She hadn't seen Adela for several years. In 1105, Adela had been gravely ill, and her advisors feared that the fever would carry her away. It had been yet another instance where Cerdic had stayed in Blois for a long time. "But you must understand," he had told her, when Giselle asked when he would come home, "she almost died. She will need some support for a while."

Sitting next to Adela in the great hall, Giselle tried to study her without being too obvious about it. Perhaps signs of her illness would still be visible. But this was not so. While she had filled out, she still moved with grace. Her hair was glossy underneath her white headgear, and her eyes were clear. Giselle noticed the fine lines around the eyes and mouth, but that was because she had seen them in her own mirror. Adela was blooming, a woman in command of herself and her surroundings.

Quickly, Giselle found herself falling back into familiar patterns of spending time in Blois while Cerdic was dancing attendance on Adela by running errands for her and participating in meetings with her advisors. Once again, she marveled at the range of Adela's responsibilities and cares. Literally every day, Adela was discussing the details of various charters that were supposed to foster trade and regulate conflicts in her realm. She constantly involved herself in disputes involving both ecclesiastical and non-ecclesiastical matters. She worked hard at administering and overseeing the foundation work for a priory. Adela was not merely a countess; she was the lord of her domain. But her rule was not trouble-free.

"You should hear her talk about William," Cerdic told Giselle one evening when they had retired to their apartment. "She is so frustrated by his behavior and says that she doesn't know what to do." Adela struggled to keep the tales of his misdeeds from becoming public. It didn't help that Bishop Ivo, among others, was involved in an ongoing correspondence with her about this. "William is her heir-designate. That makes it even more difficult."

"Poor William." Giselle had pitied him when he was a child; and she pitied him now, volatile, with a temper, unaware of the impact of his actions, and somehow very young and helpless; he seemed far younger even than Orva.

Some of Adela's advisors, whispering in the hallways and on the stairs, claimed that she was a harsh and demanding ruler. Perhaps she was, Giselle thought. Certainly, she could be a harsh and demanding parent. William may be too weak to flourish in that context.

Just the other day, Cerdic showed Giselle a letter from Bishop Ivo to Adela. She read it with amazement. The good bishop sounded genuinely irate over Adela's actions toward the canons of St. Mary, even accusing her of perverse cruelty.

We heard that you have by your order forbidden travel, bread, water, and all the necessities of this life which are in your power to our sons, canons of St. Mary. What else is this than to condemn to death without audience or judgment innocent and unarmed men? For hunger and thirst kill as the sword does. What more barbarous edict could barbarous Turks, persecutors of the Christian name, promulgate against the servants of God than to deny them the necessities of life? Wherefore, admonishing I counsel and counseling I admonish your nobility that you commute the unconsidered rigor of your sentence until there is a hearing and not condemn to death with such a severe sentence those who have not been judged nor convicted. We have tempered our sentence out of love for you, though it is just and based on judgment; we have not denied even to their persecutors the sacraments of baptism, confession or penance which suffice for the salvation of souls in need. Act therefore so that the praise of the strong woman whom Wisdom commends may be preached about you, not that the perverse woman's cruelty which Chrysostom hated in Herodiad be spread about you through all our provinces.

While ending with compliments, it was a straightforward a disavowal of Adela's actions as Giselle had seen. Why did Cerdic show this to her? She didn't know what to say.

"See, this is where I can help her," Cerdic said, a note of satisfaction in his voice. "I advised her on how to resolve this matter. Perhaps it is easier for her to listen to the advice of a long-time friend, almost a brother, than to that of her advisors, all of whom are always jockeying for advantages to themselves."

"Ah, she listens to you." Giselle tried to hide the bitterness she felt.

A few weeks later, Adela showed Giselle a letter from Abbot Baudri. "What do you think about this?" Her eyes were crinkled with amusement.

"Hail countess, worthy rather of the name of queen," it began. Fascinated, Giselle settled in to read the entire lengthy emanation that continued over several pages. "Didn't he write some of this before?"

"Indeed, he did." Adela chuckled. "He elaborated on the theme."

Baudri praised Adela for her beauty, dignity, and grace, stating that he was nearly blinded by gazing at her, who has the brilliance of a goddess. Giselle almost giggled when she got to the point where Baudri, referring to himself as a naked poet, requested the gift of a cope and perhaps even a tunic. Giselle ran her eyes over the entire poem. Would a poet and abbot write such a letter or poem to a lady he was not married to, moreover one so much higher in station than himself? His language was more effusive than anything she had ever read. Who would talk about shining Phrygian gold surrounding Adela's cope? She didn't know what Phrygian gold was, but it certainly sounded splendid.

You yourself suggest my song to me, my reed/pen, you will give the breath, you will fill the gaping mouth, you pay the deserved rewards to poets, you who compel taciturn bards to speak. Therefore, countess, look again at your speaking bard, and give, o ruler/lady, the cope as reward to the writer. The cope which shining Phrygian gold surrounds, the cope which honors the breadth of the chest with gems, let the chest have you, the limbs be clothed, the cope which carries the worth of the countess, which deservedly I may be able to call the countess's cope. As you excel queens and countesses, so the mantles of queens and countesses, are excelled by this work, which gives you life beyond the stars. I ask great things, but you know how to repay greater; you scorn the pusillanimous who ask for little. I ask not too high, I do not slip too low. With whatever adornment you should adorn ministers, and enrich the treasuries of churches, it is mine to have sought, yours to offer. So respond to me by right that you may favor both, and make sure the cope is not missing its fringe.

"Oh, certainly." Giselle laughed aloud, "Don't forget to make sure the cope is not missing its fringe."

"It's quite flowery, isn't it?" Adela had a twinkle in her eyes, and her lips were curled in half-derisive enjoyment. "Don't look so shocked, my dear friend. Baudri knows full well what he is about, and so do I, for that matter. But I still can enjoy it, if only for a moment."

Adela had now been a widow for almost six years. How old was she? Maybe already 39 or 40? With a shock, Giselle remembered she was just three years younger than the countess.

She tried to concentrate on her sewing. In her mind's eye, she saw the wan face of Count Stephen-Henry before he rode back into the battle of Ramla.

"You think I don't miss my husband, don't you?" Adela's face suddenly was sad. "I miss him every day. Sometimes I dream that he is riding back into the courtyard, his baggage filled with fascinating treasures from the Holy Land that he thought I would like. I miss his voice. I miss his touch. I even miss the smell of his shirts." She resumed her work, sorting through the documents on her desk. "But I have work to do. I have a responsibility to care for my husband's legacy and to ensure his children will thrive and serve to the best of their abilities.

Sometimes Giselle wondered whether Adela was aware of her reservations and her bitterness about Adela's hold over Cerdic. She always arrived at the same conclusion. Of course, Adela was aware. She was observant, but it didn't matter to her. She needed the services of those she could trust and was willing to ignore all other considerations. Giselle had to respect her for this determination of purpose.

Perhaps they were not that different. Both managed their husbands' affairs, like so many women now. Only Adela's husband was dead. Cerdic at least returned home on occasion.

Would it be like this for always? Would Cerdic's affection for Adela keep him at her beck and call indefinitely? It was especially galling because Giselle had tasted happiness for a few brief years. Contentment in working together and passion in the dark had warmed her. Sometimes Cerdic looked at her with his dark, warm eyes as if he truly saw her and wasn't dreaming of another woman.

It was time to go home. Would Cerdic come with her? Probably not. Her heart ached.

"My lady."

Adela was already absorbed in one of the new reports delivered that morning. "Yes, Giselle?"

"I need to go home. It has been a long time since I have seen to my affairs. And my young daughter needs me."

"Of course, I understand, my dear. I hope you will return soon."

Giselle was determined not to return ever again. But it was better to be courteous and discreet. After all, Adela had the power to hurt Cerdic and thereby his family's prospects.

"My lady, it is always an honor to serve you, but for now, I must be with my family."

She went to find her husband.

"But Giselle, I will come a bit later," Cerdic said. "Adela needs my support in this matter of William. It won't be long."

"You always say that, and then you are gone for a year or two or longer."

"You must understand," he said, almost pleadingly, "she trusts me. There is something else," Cerdic added, almost casually, as if to show that it was just a minor thing. "There might be an opportunity for me to go to England on her behalf."

"Oh, please, don't go. I have dreamed about this," Giselle said, appalled. "You won't return. Please don't."

"It is important to me. You know that. We have talked about it often."

"That doesn't mean I am reconciled to it," Giselle said bleakly. She was beyond being angry. Cerdic had always been torn —between countries and between loyalties and even between the people he loved. She wanted to shake him, to wake him up, to show him what he was missing. She loved him, but she couldn't fight this anymore. "Do what you have to do."

Yearning For Home

1118 Les Tilleuls

Cerdic was tired. More tired than he had ever been.

It was drizzling. He had pulled his hood deep into his face and rode along without noticing much of the surrounding land. Most trees were already bare on this gray November morning; only a few still had golden and brown leaves clinging to the branches.

The road to Les Tilleuls had always elated him when he was a young man. *I have land and a manor; it is mine. It is beautiful. It is home*—this had always been a jubilant beat as he rode toward the lush green valley, framed by gentle hills, passing the river and the watermill where he had once jumped in after Giselle. It turned into a triumphant song as he reached the alley of lime trees.

Now, he just felt old. He was 52. What had he done over the last ten years? Back and forth from Blois, not spending enough time at home. And he had never yet gone back to England. A prolonged absence would have been required for such a journey. Whenever he had asked Adela for leave; she'd put him off. "Certainly, I quite understand that you want to see it again. But now is not a good time."

Adela was always working. When in residence at Blois, her desk was covered with parchments, and she spent her days in endless meetings and discussions with her advisors. She traveled all over her domains, regularly visiting the three cathedral chapters in Chartres, Rheims, and Paris, and communicating with their archbishops and bishops. She penned her name to charters and juridical acts all over her lands and involved herself in the affairs of thirteen Benedictine abbeys and their dependencies. She even patronized several hermits and a hospice for lepers. Her interests and concerns had no limits. Often, Cerdic accompanied Adela on her journeys, and she also frequently delegated him to travel on her behalf.

On occasion Adela had taken his advice. There was that trouble over the monks at Bonneval in 1109. Adela had imposed a heavy tax on the town after servants of the church had killed one of her men. She came to see the error of her ways and relented. She had shown him her letter to the monks. The letter was an attempt to settle the matter, but her frustration and rage over what had happened still leaped off the page.

For at one time I had been angry at them on account of one of my men whom their sergeants had killed and, as if in revenge, I ordered an exaction of money, which is customarily called tallage to be levied in the bourg of Bonneval. The abbot and monks, bearing this grievously, came to me and showed me the testimonies of ancient writings that did not permit tallage to be imposed by me or anyone else. Nevertheless I did not acquiesce immediately, and to the extent that anger was propelling me I persevered in that purpose for some time. However, after they beseeched me with insistent and assiduous prayers that I not introduce a new and harmful custom in their bourg, when finally my anger had subsided and I was led to repent of what I had done, I made the satisfaction the monks sought.

So often, her anger and her temper had led her to react in destructive ways, and then she had to repair the damage. Perhaps that was part of the problem in her dealings with her sons.

William, the eldest, had been at the receiving end of his mother's temper from the beginning. Then again, he also had a history of acting in extreme fashion. Once, while his mother had been involved in a dispute with Bishop Ivo of Chartres, William took it upon himself to inflame the issue almost beyond any hope of salvage by demanding that the burghers of Chartres kill the canons, harass Bishop Ivo, and seize lands belonging to the church.

After this debacle, Adela removed William from all remaining comital duties. She arranged a marriage for him with a wife she chose. Once he was safely settled with his wife, Agnes of Sully, heiress to the lordship of Sully-sur-Loire, and had fathered several children, Adela proceeded to disinherit him, placing Theobald in his place. Ultimately, Cerdic agreed with that decision. Adela had to ensure that a responsible person would eventually take over.

In 1111, Adela allowed Stephen to spend time in England. He became the favorite of his uncle, King Henry I. Cerdic missed him. He was about the same age as Guisbert, born in 1093.

Stephen's older brother, Theobald, sometimes confided in Cerdic. "Do you realize she won't even let me marry?" He was in the awkward position of being the heir-designate to someone completely unwilling to cede control. Patiently, he accompanied his mother on her travels throughout her domains, but was only allowed an accessory role. "Cerdic, could you please try to talk to her? You are one of the few of her retainers and friends to whom she still listens."

"I will try." But he knew that it was nearly impossible to sway Adela in something like this.

Cerdic marveled at her ability to keep it all in her head. She instantly recognized visitors and greeted them by name, even if years might have passed since she had seen them last. She was equally comfortable and self-assured when dealing with kings and popes, as with local squires and retainers. As the daughter of a king, she had grown up with an appreciation for the wide-flung webs of power and commerce. Her predominant concern was the church's well-being, but she was under no illusions about how to ensure this. Church institutions were dependent on trade and on material assets; in turn, they helped to provide safe havens for the people in their domains, supported the improvement of roads and public spaces, and created the underpinnings of a strong economy. This was the world in which she moved with grace and ruthless determination.

But it was not his world. Not anymore. Perhaps it had never been his world. Cerdic wanted to work in the fields and forests of the land granted to him, participate in the pressing of the grapes, and go hawking with his sons. He wanted to sit in the meadow near the beehives with his wife and share a meal of bread and cheese. He wanted to go home.

But where was home now? Cerdic didn't know anymore. At Blois, Adela had granted him the use of a separate apartment, but most of his time he spent traveling throughout her domains on her behalf. England was but a dream, distant, unattainable; and his musings about the land of his birth were filled with sorrow over his mother, dying there many years ago without her son by her side. Les Tilleuls? What right did he have to call it home? Giselle had done most of the work over the last years in his absence.

She had become distant and cool. His sons were grown up. Guisbert was already a knight. Yves still served as a squire. They hardly knew him. Orva was a mystery to him. Sometimes when he had watched her at Les Tilleul, with her curly dark hair unbound and her gown kilted up so that she could run and jump unimpeded, he was reminded of Giselle when she had been a young girl. But Orva was different, a wild thing, almost fey, gentle with all living things, but oblivious to rules and customs, and unaware of evil. Her golden eyes often saw things no one else could see, and she talked to the bees. She was old enough to be contracted in marriage; the very thought hurt.

Before Cerdic left Blois this time, he had gone to the great hall to take his leave.

"Of course," Adela snapped. "You must go." She looked irritated.

Cerdic felt chilled. He had given years of his life to serve her.

Then her face softened. "I do understand, Cerdic." She hesitated and then added, "I will miss you. Please give my regards to your dear wife."

She was almost 50, he realized. He could see the frown lines on her forehead and the rays of lines filling the corners of her eyes. As always, she was exquisitely gowned and surrounded by a faint scent of roses, while her hair was properly hidden away underneath the white wimple. The scent reminded him of all the times when he had been consumed with jealousy over her marriage to Count Stephen-Henry and her evident delight in all that it brought her. She had been ruling her husband's domains for many years now. Did she ever feel alone?

With a pang, he thought of Giselle. She'd been alone for so long.

His horse shook its head and bucked, startled by a fox that had darted out of the bushes. "It's only a fox," he shouted while trying to regain control. It had whipped across the road and vanished into the bushes. When the horse had relaxed and was trotting along peaceably, Cerdic tried to collect his thoughts, shaken by a sudden sense of utter clarity.

It had always been Giselle. He loved her.

Yes, Adela had been important to him. She was part of his youth. He loved her.

But not like he loved Giselle. The little waif. The brave young woman who fought back against an unacceptable fate. The warrior who followed him all the way to the Holy Land. The woman at whose side he had worked, with whom he had laughed, and with whom he had shared passion and tenderness. He loved her. He had never told her.

He glanced around. He was already on his land. There was the alley framed by lime trees. In dismay, he stared at two large trees on the ground, partly blocking the road. They had been uprooted, and their roots lifted up. There must have been a tremendous storm. Nobody had made an effort to start removing the branches.

He continued toward the manor. The courtyard was oddly quiet. He put his horse into the stable and walked inside. An old woman sat near the fire with a baby on her lap. Then she turned her head. "Oh, Sir Cerdic." There was a tremor in her voice.

"Maria?" Cerdic was shocked to see how much she had aged. "Where is everybody?"

"They are all at the cemetery."

At the cemetery. Cerdic wanted to scream, but his throat had closed, and he couldn't breathe. He was too late.

THE CROWN OF LIFE

*Fear none of those things which thou shalt suffer: behold, the devil
shall cast some of you into prison, that ye may be tried; and ye shall
have tribulation ten days: be thou faithful unto death, and I will give
thee a crown of life.* Revelations 2:10

Tears ran down Maria's wrinkled cheeks.

Cerdic shook his head and walked back outside. He couldn't
bear asking Maria what had happened.

It was still drizzling. A crowd of people was moving toward the
manor on the path from the church. As they got closer, he
recognized them, Auberi, Thomas, with a cane, Auberi's son
Jacques, other children, villeins, serfs. Then he saw Giselle. She was
wrapped in a dark shawl that covered her head, and she walked
slowly.

Cerdic took a rasping breath, dizzy with relief and dread. He
stood on the steps and waited as they came closer. Nobody was
talking. As they reached the courtyard, most wandered off in various
directions. Giselle came up the steps with bowed head and hunched
shoulders. Then she must have sensed that she was being watched,
and she raised her eyes. She gazed at him blankly. Her face was
pallid, and she had dark circles under her eyes. It was as if she
hadn't seen him. She went straight past him, her sweep of her gown
brushing over his shoes, and entered the great hall. The fire in the
hearth had gone out.

Perplexed, Cerdic followed her inside. She paced around aimlessly, as if she didn't know where she was. The old woman and the baby were gone.

"Giselle?" Cerdic felt cold. "What happened?"

Giselle's shawl slipped to the floor. Slowly, she turned around. Then, as if something uncoiled inside of her, she rushed toward him and hit his chest with her fists. "She is dead, and you weren't here," she shouted while tears were running down her face. Over and over again she hit him. "You weren't here. You never were here. You don't even know what happened to her."

Cerdic finally managed to hold her hands. "What happened?"

"My little girl is gone. My Orva. She is dead."

"Orva?" Cerdic was still gripping Giselle's hands. There was a roaring in his ears. Desperately, he shook his head. "It's not true," he said. "She can't be dead."

"We buried her on the hill above the church." Giselle looked at him almost mockingly. Her eyes were now cold and calm, studying him as if taking his measure. "And there is something else. She was raped, and she gave birth four days ago."

Cerdic dropped Giselle's hands and stumbled outside. Then he ran. He rushed toward the orchard. When he reached the field, where the bees had hunkered down in their hives for the winter, he dropped onto his knees. With his hands he held on to his head, rocking back and forth and moaning. Buried today. His little girl with the golden eyes. And he hadn't been here. Raped. He began to retch.

The drizzle had turned to rain. It rained over the collar into his tunic. Raindrops ran down his head and mingled with his tears. He rolled himself into a ball on the grass. He wished he could will himself to die right there. He lay there for a long time, his thoughts churning in his head. He was drowning in grief and regret, powerless to do anything about it.

Then, it was as if a voice was speaking to him. Stand up, it whispered. Bear the pain. Giselle hadn't followed him all the way to the Holy Land for him to crumble to the ground in a sodden mess. If he had lost much, she had lost as much or more, and she had to face it alone. Even if it was too late for him to make his peace with Giselle, at least he had to help carry the burden.

He stood up; his joints hurt, and he felt as if he had aged twenty years in the last hours. He brushed off his tunic, pulled the hood over his head, and walked back toward the manor.

When he entered the great hall, someone had lit the fire in the hearth. Giselle sat in front of it, some mending on her lap, and her eyes on the flames. When she heard his steps, she turned her face toward him; but it was devoid of expression, as if she expected nothing from him anymore.

Cerdic gazed at his wife. For the first time in years, he saw her clearly, taking in every detail. In her maturity, she had filled out, but she was still slighter and smaller than most women he knew. Her curly dark hair was flecked with silver and gray. There were lines around her mouth. Only her dark eyes were unchanged.

Cerdic swallowed. He loved her so much. He had been blind, and now it was too late. He walked to where she was sitting and went down on his knees. "Please forgive me." He spoke haltingly. "All these years I have been absent. I know it's too late for us, and if you want me to go, I will." He bent his head.

Giselle was silent. Cerdic heard the fire in the hearth crackle.

Then he felt a hand on his head.

"I am sorry," he muttered. "I am so sorry."

Giselle's hand lay still on his head, so the warmth of it reached him, and for a long time they sat like that, motionless and silent.

"Come with me," Giselle said finally, and stood up.

He followed her to a room in the back, lit by only one candle. There was a crib.

Gently, Giselle pushed aside the heavy covering. "Meet your granddaughter."

"Orva's daughter?" Cerdic asked in disbelief.

"Yes. The priest came to christen her already."

"What's her name?"

"Adelaide."

Cerdic stared at his wife. "You named her for Adela?"

"Yes. I thought it was right."

Cerdic reached down to touch the tiny hand that stuck out from under the blanket. It curled into a fist around his fingers with remarkable strength.

Much later, Giselle and Cerdic went to the cemetery. Haltingly, she told Cerdic what had happened.

Orva had taken to wandering far afield. Giselle was not too worried. Everybody knew her and loved her. She passed through the village, visited the priest, and walked through the fields and woods, singing to herself and gathering flowers and herbs. She was happy. It wasn't that she was simple. Like her brothers, she had learned diligently when studying with the tutor; but she rarely joined in during discussions when her brothers were at home. Sometimes she made a comment that showed she understood perfectly well, but mostly she lived in her own world. Giselle wasn't worried. There would be time enough to find a kind and gentle husband for her who would let her be and keep her safe. She was still so very young.

"You know how she was. Oblivious to danger, never thinking that anybody might hurt her."

One day, she came home disheveled, bruised, and silent. She refused to say what had happened. But they knew soon enough.

Giselle found her throwing up in the mornings. "She was fifteen." Giselle was weeping again. Orva never talked after that. Sometimes Giselle heard her humming to herself. And later it seemed she was humming to the baby in her womb.

"Why didn't you tell me?"

"Oh, Cid." Giselle's voice trembled. "I wanted to write to you. I couldn't find the words. It was my fault. I should never have let her walk around by herself." After a moment, she added, "And I was so angry at you for not being here."

Cerdic nodded. What could he say? He hadn't been there, not really, not for years.

Finally Giselle went on with her tale. When the baby came, Orva had a bad time. It went on for several days. "Afterward she was so weak, and the bleeding didn't stop. And then she stopped breathing," Giselle whispered, clutching Cerdic's hand.

Over the next weeks and months, Cerdic and Giselle adjusted to being together again. The baby thrived. Giselle had found a wet-nurse among the villeins who had just given birth to a little boy. She would live in the manor until Adelaide was weaned. Cerdic created a pouch in which he carried the baby everywhere he went.

And they talked.

Of course, they talked about the vineyard and their honey production and the expanding trade network for their wine. Some of it had been taken as far as Paris and Caen.

They talked about the crusade.

"The crusade tested all of us," Cerdic said. "Certainly there were some whose motives didn't bear closer scrutiny."

"I always felt bad for Count Stephen-Henry. He didn't want to be there."

"Well, he won the crown of life."

"Well, yes, if you put it like that." Giselle grimaced. A long time ago, Adela had shown her a beautifully bound manuscript, the Latin bible. The church that Giselle attended when at home didn't have a bible, only a psalter which was more than what most small churches had. To see the Word of the Lord like that filled her with awe. She remembered Adela's fingers pointing to several lines about the crown of life. They had always stayed with her. "To be sure," she added after a pause. "He persevered under trial, remained faithful to the Lord, and received his heavenly reward. But he didn't have much choice about it."

They talked about Adela.

"I resented her so much," Giselle admitted. "Perhaps, especially since I couldn't help but like her." She smiled at her husband. "She was always better read and quicker in her understanding than I could ever be. Sometimes she made me laugh with her sharp wit." Giselle thought of Adela's self-assurance and confidence in her existence as a woman that always eluded Giselle. "I admire her—despite everything."

For the first time, Cerdic spoke to Giselle without reservation. "I have often resented Adela's hold over me for all that I will forever owe her my loyalty."

"I understand that better now," Giselle said. "She has been central to our lives. But can you imagine growing up as one of her children? It cannot have been easy. All that goodness and all that determination."

"Well, having been at the receiving end of her hawk-like stare when she wasn't pleased about something, I have a fairly good idea." Cerdic laughed.

Oh, to hear that easy chuckle once again, Giselle thought, and to watch that dear, long, narrow face with the deep lines she liked to trace with her fingers at night.

They hadn't been able to laugh together for a long time. Now, after so much loss, there it was again.

"If our granddaughter grows up to be half as strong and determined, we could count ourselves lucky." Giselle said.

"You gave me such a gift in choosing her name." Cerdic smiled at his wife.

For a long time, they were content in their cocoon, working the vineyard and the beehives, watching their grandchild grow. News from the world reached them sporadically, but it seemed somehow far away from their current concerns.

There was a new pope, Pope Gelasius II, who had succeeded Pope Paschal. There even was an antipope to make things more challenging. Giselle shrugged when Cerdic told her about that.

Cerdic didn't spare much thought for the ongoing conflicts in the Holy Land. Crusaders lost towns and regions that they had fought for at such cost, and then they regained some of this bitter ground. It was far away. He took more interest in what was happening in France and England.

A rebellion against King Henry of England had flared up in Normandy. Meanwhile, the ongoing disputes between France and England simmered and finally boiled over. In the battle of Brémule, on the 20th of August 1119, King Henry I prevailed. He defended his holdings in Normandy, and King Louis had to accept Henry's son, William Adelin, as the Duke of Normandy.

"Make no mistake. This conflict has been put to rest only for a time," Cerdic told Giselle.

Adela occasionally sent him messages but was content to let him stay at Les Tilleuls.

"Would you believe this?" Cerdic came to Giselle one morning, seeking her out in the vineyard where she was inspecting the spring pruning. "My lady has decided to retire."

Giselle straightened up from what she had been doing, pleased with the morning's progress. She brushed off her hands. "Rolant has been doing a good job; most of the pruning is done, and his cuts are neat." Rolant was the son of a villein, and Auberi had suggested that he might be a good steward, eventually. Now she registered what Cerdic had said. "Adela is retiring? Where?"

"Marcigny. She is going to the abbey of Marcigny."

"Adela will be a nun?"

"I suppose so."

"Does that mean she'll finally let Theobald take over the reins?"

"Hard to imagine her ever ceding control over anything." Cerdic grinned at his wife. "But presumably this will be the time when such a step becomes inevitable. At least, she might now permit him to marry."

"I would have thought she would go to the Abbey of Sainte-Trinité in Caen where there are sisters of her and nieces."

"Marcigny is more prestigious; she'd definitely consider that factor, and besides, she will be closer to her son Henry at Cluny."

Giselle and Cerdic returned to their work.

In September of that year, after the harvest, they received a visitor.

An Invitation

1120 Valley of the Springs

"Giselle."

That was Cid calling. "Giselle, we have a visitor."

The days were turning cooler, and she had gone to the orchard to check on the apples. Her granddaughter sat in a sling like a big warm bolster on her chest. The little girl was babbling and waving her fat little hands. With a sigh, she returned to the house. When she walked into the great hall, Cerdic stood at the hearth with a young man of fair to middling height, with reddish-blond hair curling over his collar. His sleeves were bright red like his hose, and his sleeveless quilted dark green surcoat was secured with a finely wrought belt of silver and gold. Giselle took a deep breath. Clearly, the outside world wasn't done with them yet.

"Giselle," Cerdic said. "You remember my lady's son, Count Stephen?"

"Oh, of course, Stephen," Giselle blurted out. "I beg your pardon, my lord. It's just such a pleasure to see you." He had been a boy when she had last seen him. He was the same age as Guisbert, so in his mid-twenties. Giselle wondered what it had been like for him, being raised entirely in his mother's household rather than being sent off for training to an uncle or another relative. Like his brother Theobald, he was not yet married. Adela had no intention of relinquishing control over her sons before she absolutely had to do so. At least she had permitted Stephen to spend some time at the court of his uncle, King Henry.

"My lady." Stephen bowed with the perfect grace and courtesy of a well-trained knight. He beamed at her, having lost none of his genial manner that had marked him when he was a child.

"Will you stay for a while?" Giselle smiled at the young man.

"Thank you, gladly for a night."

"Here, my lord." Cerdic poured golden wine into a goblet. "I hope you will enjoy this. It's from last year's harvest."

Stephen took a mouthful. "This is delightful. As good as some of our wines from Sancerre."

"Giselle, my lord has news for us and an invitation."

"Indeed, I do." The young man's eyes were shining with excitement.

It turned out that he and many of his relatives and friends were planning to sail to England in late November, following King Henry, who was planning to return to England at that time. William Adelin would be going as well as Lucia-Mahaut and her husband Richard d'Avranches, William's half siblings Richard of Lincoln and Matilda Fitzroy, and many more.

"My mother mentioned that you had always hoped for an opportunity to spend time in your native land. Do come with us. We would be delighted to have you travel with us."

Long after they had accommodated the young man in their guest chamber, Giselle and Cerdic sat in front of the hearth and talked.

"Of course you must go." Tears were running down Giselle's face. She caught some of them with her tongue. They tasted salty.

"Please don't cry. I have dreamed of this for so long. I might not get another opportunity like this." Cerdic was speaking so fast, he almost stuttered. His cheeks were flushed. "I want to see the place where I lived as a child; perhaps I can find some of my relatives. And I want to go to Wessex, where my father was born, and I want to see Senlac Hill, where my father met his death."

"I know. I understand."

"I won't be gone long," Cerdic assured her earnestly. "And when I come home, I will be home for good."

"I will travel with you to Barfleur. I want to see the harbor."

They rode north in November. Cerdic had insisted on taking two escorts along so that Giselle would not have to make the trip back alone. It was a mild fall, and they took their time. Once they left the Loire behind, the journey took them through Le Mans. Several times, Cerdic managed to arrange a room for them in an inn. Giselle relished the privacy; she clung to Cerdic, soaking in his familiar scents and the sounds he made in the dark.

To Giselle's delight, when they reached Le Mans, there was a large fall fair in progress.

"Let's spend a day here," Giselle said. "We have enough time. I want to see what wine they have here and the price for beeswax." They wandered around, marveling at everything and eating roasted meat on skewers, freshly picked apples, tangy and crisp, and bits of bread dipped in honey.

It was a big affair. A bevy of armed guards provided security, and the Counts of Maine had delegated officials to supervise the merchants. There were traders from all over France and from far afield, offering their wools from England, linen from flax grown in Flanders, precious alum from mines in the east, so important for binding dyes to fabrics, spices and silk from the east, wine and olive oil from Italy and Spain, timber, leather goods, furs, birds of prey from lands in the far north, dried and salted meats, and fish from the coast.

"Business is good," a portly merchant told them, when they inspected his carpets. "These come to you all the way from the Holy Land," he said proudly.

"The crusades are such a boon for trade," Cerdic muttered to Giselle. "Never mind all the people killed along the way."

When darkness fell, they attended evening mass in the massive cathedral, which, like so many other buildings they had seen, boasted giant scaffolding and was in the midst of renovation work. For that matter, it seemed as if building work was going on everywhere. Afterwards, enveloped by the sound of the bells, they wandered along the streets and bought roasted nuts and hot pasties, warming their hands over braziers and chatting to the townspeople.

In the morning, they continued their journey north, following the Orne past Argentan and Falaise all the way to Caen. From there they rode along the coast through Bayeux toward Barfleur.

This was the last leg of their journey. Giselle's throat hurt. Several times, she realized that Cerdic eyed her with concern, because she had grown quiet. She smiled at him then. "It will be good for you to see your homeland." Giselle was trying to reassure him as much as she was trying to reassure herself. "And you will be back home before you know it."

The first thing that touched their senses when they were close to their goal was the sound of the waves upon the rocks along the shore and the scent of the sea that reached them in gusts of wind.

When they entered Barfleur, Giselle wrinkled her nose. "Everything smells of fish," she complained, looking at the rocky shoreline and the gray stone houses with disfavor. Indeed, in the market near the harbor, one of the main wares on offer was fish— herring, salted and marinated, mussels, oysters, bass, pollock, turbot, ray, cod, and bream, and others Giselle had never heard of.

"I suppose we'll be eating herring for supper."

The harbor was dotted with fishing boats.

"There she is." Cerdic pointed at a large long vessel with a beautifully curved bow gently bobbing up and down in the harbor, with portholes for the rowers all along its sleek timber sides. Its square sail was folded about the mast. "It's called the White Ship."

Giselle was comforted by the ship's size and its neat, well-kept appearance.

Men were dragging sacks and trundling barrels along the pier, and sailors lifted them into boats that traveled out to the ship.

They found Stephen at the inn usually patronized by the king and his advisers when traveling to and from England. As the nephew of King Henry, he had a room to himself. Cerdic arranged for their stay in the common room and stabling for the horses. The inn was filled with travelers.

Stephen was delighted to see them. "Ah, Cerdic." He bowed to Giselle. "I am glad you came in time. I was about to set out for the harbor.

Cerdic glanced at his wife apologetically. They had talked about spending another night together in Barfleur.

Giselle was slightly dazed, taken aback by the speed with which everything was happening. The three of them walked toward the harbor. Cerdic had slung a *chanerie* over his shoulder, a small leather bag with some essentials for his journey.

"Did you see the ship?" Stephen didn't wait for an answer, he went on, rushing his words. "Isn't she beautiful? Thomas, the captain, told us that she has been newly outfitted and is very fast. Fifty rowers, supported by that powerful sail, will ensure a swift journey."

Giselle couldn't hear what Cerdic said in response. The wind had picked up, and she struggled with her headgear.

"Here is the boat that will take us to the ship." Stephen pointed at a rowboat next to the pier. "We shouldn't tarry." He bowed again. "My Lady." Then he stepped into the boat, where attendants were already waiting.

Cerdic held Giselle by the shoulders. "I'll be back, my dearest," he whispered. He kissed her on the lips even though people were watching. He stepped into the rocking boat. The boatmen loosened the rope, pushed the boat away from the pier, and starting rowing toward the ship.

Giselle touched her lips with her fingers. Tears blinded her. Then she realized that Cerdic had raised his arm to wave at her. The boat was already moving fast. Frantically, she whipped up her arm to wave back. *God keep you safe, my love.*

QUILLEBOEUF ROCK

*The waters compassed me about, even to the soul: the depth closed
me round about, the weeds were wrapped about my head.*
King James Bible, Jonah 2:5

In the gray evening light, Giselle could barely see the boat anymore. She couldn't make out the figures sitting along the railing. The lanterns on the ship shaking in the wind made her think of merry spirits dancing over the waves. Occasionally, the wind carried the sound of voices across the water.

"Did you hear that the crew pleaded with the captain for more wine to be brought on board?" a man standing next to her on the pier asked another.

"Oh, yes, I heard them," a young man responded, shifting a sack filled with tools from one shoulder to the other. His tunic and boots were crusted with dust from his day of work. "The king's son was talking to the captain and told him to do as the crew wished." He laughed.

"There are many young people on the ship," a heavy-set older man said with a frown. "They will party until late into the night."

The young man laughed again. "I wish I were there."

The wind had picked up. The waves washed onto the rocks, and the spray reached the pier. White crests whipped across the sea like tiny wild horses dancing in the dark. Giselle shivered. She pulled the shawl around her shoulders and decided to return to the inn.

The common room where Giselle spent the night was noisy. People snored and groaned on their pallets, and the air was fetid with smells of unwashed bodies. Two men in the corner argued late into the night in aggravated whispers. Others shouted at them, but they were too intent on their fight to stop. Giselle's pallet was thin, with bits of straw poking through the worn fabric, and she could feel the uneven floorboards beneath her back.

The wind from the harbor howled and whistled around the building. Giselle pictured the ship tilting back and forth in the waves. Surely the sailors had taken all necessary precautions. Perhaps the young people were still drinking and feasting.

Eventually she fell asleep, but it was a restless night, filled with disjointed dreams.

When she woke up, the room was empty. She heard shouting outside and the sounds of people running. "Get to the boats," a voice barked. "Come on, everyone."

Giselle rubbed the sleep out of her eyes, straightened her gown, and fixed her headdress. Outside, people were rushing toward the pier. Puzzled, she followed them. In the harbor, boats plied back and forth on the churning waves. It was still windy, and spray from the sea whipped her face. It was raining again. She glanced out toward the sea. Perhaps the ship hadn't departed because of the heavy seas, and the boats were bringing more supplies. She saw nothing but an endless roiling grey expanse dotted with whitecaps.

Two men standing next to her were pointing at something in the distance.

Giselle strained to hear what they said, but their voices were too low. "What happened?"

"Didn't you hear?" The man glanced at her, his eyes gleaming with excitement.

"What?"

"They say the ship went down, and everybody drowned."

Giselle could smell the ale and onions from the speaker's last meal; it had left a greasy smear on his collar. The gloating tone in his voice made her shiver. People fed on disasters.

It was impossible. Not that beautiful strong vessel she'd admired from a distance yesterday. Rumors traveled so quickly. People loved to gossip and made up their own stories. She walked along the pier. Several boats were just setting out.

"Where are you headed?" a man shouted down to the rowers.

"We are going out to where the ship went down to see if there is anything we can salvage."

Giselle sank down on the wet pier. Her legs wouldn't hold her. It wasn't true. It couldn't be true.

"Someone returned from the ship last night; apparently he got sick and decided against the journey," one man said.

"Yes, it was my lord Stephen," the other one confirmed. "Hey, lady, you need some help?" He reached down and grabbed Giselle's hand to pull her up.

"Lord Stephen went back to shore?" Her fingers dug into his arm. "Did he go back alone?"

"I don't know." The man shrugged. "I heard he is back in the inn and not doing too well."

Giselle ran to the inn. The inn keeper stood outside, watching the people rush back and forth to the harbor.

"I want to see Lord Stephen." Gasping for breath, Giselle could barely get the words out. "My husband had gone with him to the ship yesterday. I need to see him."

The landlord waved her up the narrow stairs.

When she opened the door, she almost recoiled. The room smelled of someone who had been violently ill. Stephen was sitting on his pallet in his nightshirt. His hair was matted, and his face glistened with sweat. A basin next to him contained a green, grayish mass. A bucket stood on the other side. Everything stank. Stephen made a motion as if to get up; but then he sank back down. "Forgive me, I can't," he whispered. "The servant has gone out to get me the wherewithal to wash."

"Tell me what happened," Giselle snapped, forgetting all courtesy to this man, a lord and the nephew of the king.

"You heard then." Stephen fumbled with his blanket, trying to pull it over his limbs. "There was a lot of drinking on the ship; and someone had bought oysters," he mumbled and leaned over to start retching again, missing the bucket. Exhausted, he wiped his face with his hands and gazed up at Giselle out of bloodshot eyes. "People were singing and eating. I started getting sick. I felt so ill that I couldn't stand. I decided to go back. Cerdic went with me in the boat and helped me back to the inn."

"Cerdic?" Giselle stared at him. "He came back with you? Then where is he?"

"I gave him permission to return to the ship." Stephen shook his head. "I am sorry. I know how badly he wanted to go to England. He used to talk to me about it. I told him to go."

"Excuse me, my lord." Giselle was trembling. "I have to leave you." She ran downstairs and back outside onto the street. It was about half a mile from here to the pier. Maybe Cerdic hadn't made it. Maybe he was somewhere still. Perhaps he had hurt himself and could not get back to the boat.

Giselle hardly knew what she was doing. All that morning she walked around in a daze, back to the pier, up and down, watching the boats come back to the harbor. People had found a few bodies floating in the water. They were brought on shore and placed on the pier; from there they were taken to the nearby church. But only a few. The bodies were coated with seaweed and their faces gray. She didn't recognize any of them. She turned away, shuddering.

As many as three hundred people had drowned, the townspeople whispered, crossing themselves.

"They say that there was a fire on board."

"I am sure it capsized because of the storm last night."

"The king's son was just seventeen years old."

"They say nothing is left."

"No, that's not right. Wreckage is floating near the place where it went down."

"Would you believe that the butcher survived?"

"The butcher?"

"Yes, Berold from Rouen. He was on board to collect payment for the meat he had sent."

"I know what happened," one man said. "It traveled too fast because the crew had drunk all that wine, and they hit Quilleboeuf Rock."

"The pilot was probably drunk as well and lost his bearings," another man said. "Of course, he wouldn't have been able to see the rock since it was submerged because of the tide and the storm."

That evening, the escorts sought her out. "My lady, when do you want to return home?" They looked bewildered and afraid.

Seeing their distraught faces, Giselle, for the first time, began to think clearly. These two boys were younger than Guisbert. She'd known them since they were babies. They needed her guidance. She had a responsibility. She couldn't sit here and pretend nothing had happened. "We will leave early tomorrow morning. But we won't return straight to Les Tilleuls. We will first ride to Marcigny. I am planning to ride as fast as possible. We will have to change horses on the road."

She gave them instructions and enough coin to pay for their room and board. "Make sure you have some provisions and are well-rested." Bringing the news to Adela consumed her. Adela shouldn't have to hear about this disaster through rumors. Giselle sat in the inn over a bowl of soup. She couldn't taste it.

In the morning, Giselle went once more to the pier. The harbor was calm. A few fishing boats were setting out, resuming their usual work. Perhaps it was all a dream. It seemed unfathomable that so many people had died that night. She stared at the water lapping the pier and the green algae on the rocks along the shore. Squinting and shading her eyes against the pale November sun, she stared out across the harbor. The churning waves, almost indistinguishable from the clouds scudding across the horizon, were all she could see.

Pulling her shawl tighter, she turned and went to seek out the escorts. Don't think, she told herself. Don't think. Whenever she closed her eyes, she heard Cerdic's whispered goodbye. *I'll be back, my dearest. I'll be back.*

The journey to Marcigny took fifteen days. They rode as fast as they could, stopping only to rest and eat, and getting up early every morning. They changed horses several times. Giselle hardly noticed any of it, so intent on trying not to think and to keep moving.

Marcigny Abbey, the oldest Cluniac monastery for women, was a complex of plain stone buildings in the town of Marcigny. Giselle told the nun at the gate that she needed to see Lady Adela. The nun nodded and beckoned Giselle to follow. She was stiff from the days of riding, and her mind was blank. She tried to straighten out her gown and to tuck her hair back underneath her headdress. Her guide went ahead of her into the cloister walk. A few veiled women, wearing the dark habits of the Benedictines, strolled in the small enclosed garden.

"Sister Adela is in her chamber," her guide said, leading the way up a stone staircase.

Giselle's eyes widened. 'Sister Adela' indeed. No more 'my lady.'

At the top level of the spacious tower, the nun pointed to a wide wooden door. "This is her chamber. Just knock."

The chamber assigned to Adela was hardly a nun's modest cell. It was large and bright, with a big window overlooking the street, pleasantly furnished with wall hangings and carpets and a big writing desk, several chairs, a comfortable bedstead, hung with curtains, and a screen painted with exotic beasts and flowers.

Giselle paid no heed to any of this. Her attention was fixed on the small woman with fine lines marking her face like a map. She sat behind the desk with a psalter open in front of her, the wimple completely obscuring her hair. Her blue eyes underneath the thick eyebrows were turned toward her in a direct gaze, clear and resolute. And in that instant, she transformed into Lady Adela as Giselle had always known her. Never beautiful, but vivid, with a power that emanated from her, an undeniable presence, and a grace that even the nun's habit could not disguise.

"Giselle?" Adela rose and moved toward her with a firm step. "My dear, I am so pleased to see you." She removed a manuscript from a chair and tossed it on the table. "Come and sit down."

"My lady, I better stand."

Adela grew pale, but she stood there, straight-backed and calm, just as Giselle remembered her from countless meetings with advisors at Blois.

"My lady, something has happened at Barfleur. A ship was supposed to sail to England, carrying King Henry's son William Adelin, your daughter, her husband, and many more." Giselle swallowed before continuing. "Your son Stephen is safe, but everyone else is gone. The ship sank shortly after starting its journey, and there were no survivors."

Adela blinked; other than that, her expression didn't change. "Please, my dear, sit down." Her voice had become slightly husky. "I think we both need to sit. Tell me everything you know."

Speaking in a low voice, Giselle related the events around the 25th of November. She faltered at some details. Finally, she reached the end. "I didn't want you to hear the news through a rumor."

Adela hadn't moved. Only the fingers of her right hand stroked the rosaries beads that hung from the belt around her waist, back and forth and back and forth. Then she reached for Giselle and embraced her. "My dear, we have suffered a deep loss, you and I."

Giselle thought that she had no more tears left, weeping all through the nights during the long ride from Barfleur. But now, held in Adela's embrace, she broke down, sobbing until she could hardly breathe. Giselle clung to her arm as if it were a rope in the open sea. "Why?" she asked. "I keep thinking about this and torturing myself. Why, oh why, did Cerdic go back to the ship? He could see the storm coming."

"You will never know," Adela said. "My dear, I am so sorry."

Giselle wiped her face and gazed at the older woman in wonder. Adela had just lost her daughter, her son-in-law, her nephew, and many others whom she knew. Her implacable demeanor hadn't changed. She hadn't shed any tears. Her face was devoid of color, but her voice was calm.

Now, Adela picked up her needlework, a partially finished scene of flowers in a meadow. Giselle's throat hurt. How could Adela do this? Didn't she feel anything at all?

Then she noticed Adela's hands. With jerky movements she picked out threads, pulling and unraveling the work she had done.

Her hands, slightly reddened and with swollen joints, were trembling.

Giselle reached out and covered Adela's hands with her own, warming them and gently rubbing the joints, until the trembling stopped.

The two women talked for a long time after that.

"Let me show you something." Adela rooted around among the pieces of writing on her desk. "Here it is. William of Aquitaine wrote this. He isn't someone I approve of by any means, but still some of his music is beautiful. It's called *Pos de chantar m'es pres talens*. In this song, he was thinking of mortality and all he has given up in his life to save his soul. It behooves us all to think about that."

Giselle shook her head. She couldn't see how this helped. How like Adela to bother her with poetry at this time.

"It made me think of Cerdic." Adela looked at Giselle with a slight smile on her face. "Your Cerdic was always ready to give up so much—for his king, for me, for Count Stephen-Henry, and for you, and for the land of his forebears."

Giselle remembered saying something like this to Cerdic many years ago. At least, he stayed true to himself until the end.

"Loyalty should have been emblazoned on his crest," Adela said. "Isn't it strange that his life with us began with a ship journey and ended in the sea off Barfleur?"

Giselle nodded.

"Do you know how I have found consolation at times of loss?"

Giselle said nothing. What consolation was there for her? She couldn't imagine such a thing.

"I work." Adela pointed at the manuscripts on her desk and the partially finished needlework. "This helps me. It's like praying. To expect something to last beyond one's lifetime is vanity. But it's the doing of it that matters."

Giselle's eyes were red with weeping. She was drained beyond thought.

But Adela wasn't finished. She took the jeweled psalter from her desk and opened it. "Do you know my favorite line in there?"

Giselle shook her head mutely.

The days of our years are threescore years and ten; and if by reason of strength they be fourscore years, yet is their strength labor and sorrow; for it is soon cut off, and we fly away.

"You see, our lives are full of sorrow. Yet that's where we find our strength."

Giselle found herself weeping again, and yet something had shifted. She clung to Adela's hands, receiving her warmth and giving her some of her own.

It was odd to find comfort in the words of a woman whom she had considered with resentment for so many years.

Just as Giselle was about to take her leave, Adela asked, "And Stephen, how long is he staying in Barfleur? I must write to him right away. It is urgent that he travel to England as soon as possible. The king has no designated heir now."

Giselle could hardly suppress a grin as she walked back out onto the street. Of course, in the midst of all her grief, Adela was already casting her thoughts to the future. Oh yes, she would do everything in her power to see to it that her son Stephen ascended to the throne. Of course. There was no one like Adela.

Riding home in the company of her young escorts who treated her as if she was a fragile little bird, Giselle found that the incessant churning of her thoughts, back and forth like the beating of the waves upon the rocks, had stopped, and that calm had returned.

Whenever she closed her eyes, Cerdic was with her. She could see him, with his lanky build and crooked smile. She could hear his deep voice that had always retained a hint of someone from another land. She could also see Orva of the golden eyes and even her father, who had loved her. They were there with her. They would never be gone. Her Cid wasn't gone. He had promised he would come back to her.

"Now you know what has happened."

Adela looked at the young girl, who wore her novice gown like a dust rag for all the attention she paid to it. It was crumpled and stained. Her curly hair had once again escaped from her veil. Her cheeks were flushed. But, Adela was pleased with her young acolyte's progress. In the last months, she had been spending more time in Adela's room, with the approval of the abbess. Adela had insisted on tutoring her in reading and writing and had even involved her in discussions about the state of the world and philosophy. The girl was quick and bright. It was time to send her off, she thought with regret and a wave of sadness.

"I grieved for Cerdic," she said. "He was a part of my life and the only one who remembered how things had been when we were young. He was steadfast and loyal to a fault. I am sorry he lost his life on that ship. I pray for his soul."

"But he didn't die." Adelaide frowned. "He came home. At least, that's what my grandmother always told me."

Adela shook her head. "There were no survivors, girl."

"I just know what my grandmother told me. She always insisted that he hadn't gone back to the ship. In the dark, he had an accident and was knocked unconscious. One of the townspeople picked him up and took him in. They didn't know his name for the longest time.

Eventually he returned home, where he died in her arms after a few years. I was too young to remember, but I always loved how she talked about him."

Adela said nothing. She rubbed her eyes.

"Maybe it wasn't true," Adelaide said slowly. She fiddled with a quill on the lady's desk. "She told that story to me so often that it felt real. I think it made her happy."

"It was a long time ago. If it gave your grandmother peace, then that is all well." Adela put her hands on the small sturdy hand of the girl. "But Adelaide, listen to me. You don't belong here. Not yet. I want you to go back home and live your life out in the world to the best of your abilities. Later, when you are searching for peace, then you come back here."

Epilogue

It has come to us that the canons of St. Calais have misrepresented the tithing from the gift of alms from Francheville which the venerable count Stephen, our associate and I gave to the monks of the major monastery, and your paternity should know that this claim was aired in our presence while I was still acting in the world, and it was altogether settled, so that the said monks should not be further disturbed over it. Whereby those canons immediately renounced their complaint against the monks before us, with many legitimate witnesses. For that reason I beg the paternity of your holiness not to permit said monks of the major monastery to be distressed further in any way over this. Fare well.
Adela of England, Countess of Blois, Chartres, and Meaux, to Geoffrey II, Bishop of Chartres, letter, 1135.

1135 Marcigny Abbey

Adela sighed with relief and put down her quill.

She was satisfied with her letter to Bishop Geoffrey. This dispute had gone on long enough. The canons of St. Calais clearly hadn't reported the tithing properly, causing great distress to the monks of the monastery of Marmoutier. The canons had finally renounced their complaint against the monastery. It was good to settle this matter. She folded it up and turned her attention to some writings on her desk.

Someone had sent her a copy of the latest emanations from the archdeacon Henry of Huntingdon.

Adela shook her head as she read the beginning of his voluminous history of the English people. The archdeacon started out by referencing this year as the 35th year of the reign of the glorious and invincible King Henry. How did the archdeacon know that the 35th year of Henry's reign was the 5,317[th] year from the beginning of the world?

Glorious? Had King Henry been glorious? That was for the world in the future to decide. She had wept for Henry, whom she had loved most of all her brothers. How does Huntington know exactly when the Britons settled in England, or, for that matter, the year of the beginning of the world? And yet, perhaps it was the year of grace after all. The year when her son Stephen would become king.

Adela riffled through the pages. Here the archdeacon was addressing an imaginary unknown reader long after he would have turned to dust. At least he appreciated that any form of fame was meaningful only if it was worthy of praise by the Lord. All else was empty vanity. Adela scoffed and put aside the sheets. She remembered meeting him once years ago when he came to Blois during his travels in France and Normandy. Still a young man at the time, he made a point of demonstrating his erudition to all who would listen. Pompous, self-important little man.

Adela bit her lips, thinking of Stephen embarking on the perilous sea to reach England speedily upon the news of the death of Henry. How could she not remember that other disastrous crossing and the grief that had echoed through all the land? At least Stephen had the help and support of his brother, Henry, the Bishop of Winchester.

Should she worry about the claim to the throne by King Henry's daughter Matilda?

Was it wrong to take pride in her son being anointed king of England?

Adela picked up another page penned by Huntingdon, where he expounded on the passage of time. She squinted at the neat script as she read. He admonished the reader to work hard for glory, honor, goodness, and a myriad of other qualities that would be pleasing to the Lord before the physical body fails and decays in one's tomb.

Adela tossed it back onto the table. Such a prosy man. But perhaps he had a point. Soon it would be her turn to decay in her tomb. She could feel it in her bones. Had she atoned sufficiently for all the pride and arrogance she had so often brought to bear on her actions? What would people say of her when she was gone? She pulled the corners of her mouth down. No doubt about it, quite a few people had reason to hate her. Then she shrugged. What did it matter, after all? She was not important, but her deeds might do some good.

She mustn't forget to write to Theobald about the importance of almsgiving. It wouldn't hurt to remind him that his father and she herself had been making such donations to monasteries whenever it was possible and appropriate.

She reached for a clean sheet. Her hands were swollen again, and she rubbed them before picking up the quill and starting a letter to the new canon at the convent of Chartres.

"I trust this finds you well," she wrote slowly, but with a steady hand. "I have been thinking about a matter dear to my heart and would like to present to you a proposal. It concerns the improvement of the hospital for women and children. I have heard that the water supplying it comes from a source where there is too much runoff from the nearby dairy farm. Tell me what would be needed to ameliorate this situation. I would be glad to contribute to this endeavor."

Several hours later, a young novice entered Adela's room. The old lady was asleep, her hands supporting her head on the table.

Poor old dear. The novice placed a mug with a hot drink of mint and lavender on the table. *I wonder who she is.*

Appendix

Principal characters

Historical figures

Adela of England, Countess of Blois, Chartres, and Meaux (c. 1067 – March 8, 1137), daughter of William the Conqueror and Matilda of Flanders, wife of Stephen-Henry of Blois.

Anselm of Bec (c. 1033/4–1109), Benedictine monk, abbot, philosopher, and theologian of the Catholic Church, who served as Archbishop of Canterbury from 1093 to 1109.

Baudri [Baldric] of Dol, (c. 1050 – January 7, 1130), prior and then Abbot of Bourgueil from 1077 to 1106, then Bishop of Dol-en-Bretagne in 1107 and archbishop in 1108 until his death.

Cecilia of Normandy (c. 1056 – July 30, 1126) a French abbess, thought to be the eldest daughter of William the Conqueror and Matilda of Flanders.

Emma of Blois-Champagne (c. 1080 – c. 1127), daughter of Count Stephen-Henry of Blois and his mistress, wife of Herbert, Chamberlain of Winchester.

Fulk IV of Anjou (1043 – April 14, 1109).

Henry I (c. 1068 – December 1, 1135), King of England from 1100 to his death in 1135, the fourth son of William the Conqueror.

Lucia Mahaut, 1097 – November 25, 1120, daughter of Adela, wife of Richard d'Avranches, 2nd Earl of Chester.

Matilda of Flanders (c. 1031 – November 2, 1083), Queen of England and Duchess of Normandy by marriage to William the Conqueror, mother of Adela.

Odo, son of Adela, dates of birth and death unknown, died as a child or a young man.

Henry of Blois (c. 1101 – August 8, 1171), the last and fifth son of Adela, also known as Henry of Winchester, Abbot of Glastonbury Abbey from 1126, and Bishop of Winchester from 1129 to his death.

Ivo of Chartres (c. 1040 – December 23, 1115), French canon regular and abbot who served as the Bishop of Chartres from 1090 until his death.

Robert Curthose (c. 1051 – February 1134), eldest son of William the Conqueror.

Lavardin, Hildebert of (c. 1055 – December 18, 1133), a French ecclesiastic, hagiographer, and theologian. From 1096–97, he was bishop of Le Mans, then from 1125 until his death archbishop of Tours.

Stephen (1092 or 1096 – October 25, 1154), third son of Adela, King of England from 22 December 1135 to his death in 1154.

Stephen-Henry (c. 1045 – May 19, 1102), Count of Blois and Count of Chartres.

Theobald, also known as Thibaut and Theobald the Great (1090–1152), the second son of Adela. He was count of Blois and of Chartres as Theobald IV from 1102 and Count of Champagne and of Brie as Theobald II from 1125.

Toki (birthdate between c. 1045 and 1060, died c. 1078/1079), son of Wigod of Wallingford (de Warwick), Earl of Wallington.

William (c. 1085 – c. 1150), the eldest son of Adela, Count of Blois and Count of Chartres from 1102 to 1107, and by marriage, Count of Sully.

William the Conqueror (c. 1028 – September 9, 1087), the first Norman king of England (as William I), from 1066 until his death. He also was Duke of Normandy.

William II (c. 1056 – August 2, 1100), King of England from 26 September 1087 until his death in 1100, the third son of William the Conqueror, also known as William Rufus.

FICTIONAL CHARACTERS

Giselle, daughter of Artus

Cerdic of Wessex

Guisbert, eldest son of Cerdic and Giselle

Yves, second son of Cerdic and Giselle

Orva, daughter of Cerdic and Giselle

Adelaide, granddaughter of Cerdic and Giselle

Matthias, squire of King William

Douce and Petronella, students at the abbey in Caen

Sister Leona, at the abbey in Caen

Thomas, steward at La Vallée des Sources

Maria, wife of Thomas

Auberi, steward at Les Tilleuls

Janine, servant of Giselle

Jacques, son of Auberi

Josse, squire of Stephen-Henry of Blois

Gustav, merchant in the East

Count Clement, land owner near La Vallée des Sources

SOURCES

Adela of England, Countess of Blois, Chartres, and Meaux, 1100-1101, letter to Public,
https://epistolae.ctl.columbia.edu/letter/814.html/

Adela of England, Countess of Blois, Chartres, and Meaux, letter to Public, 1104 https://epistolae.ctl.columbia.edu/letter/26001.html/

Adela of England, Countess of Blois, Chartres, and Meaux, letter to the monks of Bonneval (the Bonneval cartulary transcribed by LoPrete, AD d'Eure-et-Loir, H.606, fo.1r-v (!1) date 1109.
https://epistolae.ccnmtl.columbia.edu/letter/75.html

Adela of England, Countess of Blois, Chartres, and Meaux, letter to Geoffrey II, Bishop of Chartres, 1133-37. *Marmoutier Cartulaire Blesois*, ed. Charles Metais, (Blois: E. Moreau, 1889-91), ep.146, p.138. https://epistolae.ctl.columbia.edu/letter/76.html

Aquitaine, William *Les Chansons De Guillaume IX*. (1913) Pranava Books; Classic Edition: 2022.

Baudri, Abbot of Bourgueil and Archbishop of Dol (c.1107 (!2)) letter to Adela of England, Countess of Blois, Chartres, and Meaux, before 1107. Printed source: *Les Oeuvres poétiques de Baudri de Bourgueil,* ed. Phyllis Abraham (Paris: Slatkine, 1926, repr.1974), 196-253. [Description of a chamber purportedly belonging to Adela]
https://epistolae.ctl.columbia.edu/letter/94.html

Baudri, Abbot of Bourgueil and Archbishop of Dol, letter to Adela of England, Countess of Blois, Chartres, and Meaux, before 1107. Printed source: *Le Epistole Metriche di Baldericus*

Burguliensis, ed. M. Teresa Razzoli (Milano: SAE Dante Alighieri, 1936), 69-70, and *Les Oeuvres poétiques de Baudri de Bourgueil*, ed. Phyllis Abraham (Paris: Slatkine, 1926, repr.1974), 153-54. [Request for a cope] https://epistolae.ctl.columbia.edu/letter/95.html

Berg-Manor, Rebecca, ed. *An Anthology of Medieval Literature*. Beautiful Feet Books, 2013.

Berners, Juliana (1388?) and William Blades (1824-1890), author of introduction, etc. *The boke of Saint Albans : containing treatises on hawking, hunting, and cote armour,* United Kingdom: Elliot Stock. July 24, 2023 [Copyright Status: Public domain in the USA.]

Bridgeford, Andrew. *1066: The Hidden History of the Bayeux Tapestry*. Walker Publishing Company, New York, 2004.

Carruthers, Bob, ed. *The Anglo-Saxon Chronicle*. Coda Books, Ltd., 2012.

Chibnall, Marjorie. *The World of Orderic Vitalis*. Clarendon Press/Oxford University Press, Oxford, 1984.

Connolly, Sharon Bennett. *Heroines of the Medieval World*. Amberley Publishing, 2019.

Davies, Brian; et al. (1998), *Anselm of Canterbury: The Major Works*, Oxford: Oxford University Press.

Evergates, Theodore. *Aristocratic Women in Medieval France*. University of Pennsylvania Press, 1999.

Folgore da San Geminiano, excerpt of poem from Rosetti, Dante Gabriel *Dante and His Circle: With the Italian Poets Preceding Him (1100—1200—1300)*. Ellis and White, 29 New Bond Street, 1874.

Fulcher of Chartres, English trans. Martha E. McGinty, *Fulcher of Chartres: Chronicle of the First Crusade*, London: Oxford University Press; Philadelphia: University of Pennsylvania Press, 1941. In Internet Medieval Sourcebook, Fordham University Center for Medieval Studies, https://sourcebooks.fordham.edu/sbook.asp/

Geoponika: Agricultural Pursuits by Anonymous; translated from Greek by Thomas Owen, in two volumes (London, 1806).

The Goodman of Paris. translated by Eileen Power in The Goodman of Paris, (London: Routledge, 1928), and reprinted in Richard M. Golden and Thomas Kuehn, eds., Western Societies: Primary Sources in Social History, Vol I, New York: St Martins, 1993.

Pope Gregory VII, letter to Matilda of Flanders, Duchess of Normandy and Queen of England, 1074. https://epistolae.ctl.columbia.edu/letter/50.html/

Pope Gregory VII, letter to Matilda, Duchess of Normandy and Queen of England, 1080. https://epistolae.ctl.columbia.edu/letter/51.html/

Hildebert de Lavardin, *The Hymn of Hildebert and other mediaeval hymns*: with translations by Benedict, Erasmus Cornelius, 1800-1880, New York: Anson D. F. Randolph & Co., 1868, University of California Digital Libraries.

Hingst, Amanda Jane. *The Written World: Past and Place in the Work of Orderic Vitalis*. University of Notre Dame, 2009.

Huntingdon, Henry Archdeacon of. *Historia Anglorum (The History of the English People 1000-1154)*. Translated by Diane Greenway. Oxford World Classics: Oxford University Press, 1965.

Huntingdon, Henry Archdeacon of. *The Chronicle of Henry of Huntingdon,* comprising *The History of England, from the Invasion of Julius Caesar to the Accession of Henry II*, translated and edited by Thomas Forester, A.M., London: Henry G. Bohn, 1853.

Huntingdon, Henry Archdeacon of (archidiaconi huntendunensis) *Historia Anglorum*, 1084?-1155; Arnold, Thomas, 1823-1900, ed. London: Longman & co. [etc., etc.] Harvard University, 1879.

Ivo, Bishop of Chartres, letter to Adela of England, Countess of Blois, Chartres, and Meaux. Historical context: The letter is about yet another jurisdictional dispute, in which Adela has taken punitive action against the canons and Ivo threatens ecclesiastical sanctions unless she rescinds it. Printed source: PL162 ep.179 c180-81; also HGF15 ep.110 p.141-42, same text with 2 variations in spelling, date 1107. https://epistolae.ccnmtl.columbia.edu/letter/86.html

Joynes, Andrew, ed. *Medieval Ghost Stories*. Boydell Press, 2001.

Lack, Katherine. *Conqueror's Son: Duke Robert Curthose, Thwarted King*. The History Press, 2018.

Lavardin, Hildebert of, letter (1101?) to Adela of England, Countess of Blois, Chartres, and Meaux. PL171 ep.3.2 c284 date 1101 (?). https://epistolae.ccnmtl.columbia.edu/letter/90.html

LoPrete, Kimberly. *Adela of Blois: Countess and Lord (c.1067-1137)*. Four Courts Press, 2007.

Llull, Ramon (1232–1316). *The Book of the Order of Chivalry*. Translated by Noel Fallows, Boydell & Brewer, Boydell Press. 2013.

Malmesbury, William of Malmesbury. *Chronicles of the Kings of England From the Earliest Period to the Reign of King Stephen*. Translated by J.A. Giles, 1847.

Manor, Rebecca Berg, ed. *An Anthology of Medieval Literature*; Beautiful Feet Books, 1978,

Orderic Vitalis. *The Ecclesiastic History of Orderic Vitalis*. ed. and translated by Marjorie Chibnall, Oxford, 1969-1980.

Reichenau, Hermann of (also known as Hermann the Cripple) (July 18, 1013-September 24, 1054), a Benedictine monk and scholar. He has traditionally been credited with the composition of *Salve Regina*, sung by the crusaders in the Church of the Holy Sepulchre.

Runciman, Steven. *A History of the Crusades*. London, 1990.

Spencer, Charles. *The White Ship: Conquest, Anarchy and the Wrecking of Henry I's Dream*. London: William Collins Books, 2020.

Stephen-Henry de Blois, letters to his wife. *Recueil des Historiens des Croisades*, Historiens Occidentaux, (Paris: Imprimerie impériale, 1866), v.3, 887-90. Translation from Translations and Reprints from the Original Sources of European History, 1.4, *Letters of the Crusaders written from the Holy Land*, trans. Dana Carlton Munro, Philadelphia: University of Pennsylvania, 1902, pgs. 5-6.

Taylor, Edgar. *Lays of the Minnesingers and Troubadours*. Longman, Hurst, Rees, Orme, Brown and Green, 1825, p. 262.

Thatcher, Oliver J. and Edgar Holmes McNeal. *A Source Book for Medieval History*. Boston: Charles Scribner's Sons, 1905. (Speech of Pope Urban II at the Council of Clermont, 1095).

Thibaut King of Navarre, *Crusader's Farewell*, translated by Edgar Taylor, *Lays of the Minnesingers and Troubadours*. Longman, Hurst, Rees, Orme, Brown and Green, 1825, p. 262.

Pope Urban II (1088-1099): Speech at Council of Clermont, 1095, in Oliver J. Thatcher and Edgar Holmes McNeal, (Ed.), *A Source Book for Mediæval History: Selected Documents Illustrating the History of Europe in the Middle Age* (New York: Charles Scribner's Sons, 1905), 518-52.

Le Viandier de Guillaume Tirel dit Taillevent, le Baron Jérôme Pichon et Georges Vicaire, Paris, 1892 (reprint by Slatkine Reprints, Genève, 1967).

Wheeler, Bonnie and John Carmi Parsons, ed. *Medieval Mothering*. Routledge, 1999.

Note to Reader

Adela, Countess of Blois, daughter of William the Conqueror, presents us with an interesting dilemma. She was recognized as an important historical person and considered a saint in the Catholic church. We know a fair amount about her and even can read some of her letters exchanged with her husband as well as other historical figures. Yet any writing about her life must still be based on a great deal of conjecture.

Kimberly LoPrete, Adela's foremost historian, pointed to the dearth of details about Adela's life. We don't know what Adela may have looked like. We do not even know with any certainty the precise year of her birth or the year of her marriage. We don't know for a fact how many children Adela had. The numbers range from 8 to 11. It is likely that some of the women referred to as her daughters may have been stepdaughters. Several of her five sons appear in this account, her daughters only in passing. Meanwhile, Kimberly LoPrete refers to her as "Countess and Lord," and her husband, Count Stephen-Henry of Blois, called her *Domina*, female lord. That says a lot about who this amazing woman was.

Compared to most women and men of her time, Adela was well educated—far more so than her father William the Conqueror who could not write. Her learning and her familiarity with Latin is reflected in the letters she exchanged with various clerical figures such as Bishop Ivo of Chartres. Apparently, in this she outdid her husband, who relied on her knowledge of Latin in many instances of meeting with prominent church figures. Her husband Stephen-Henry of Blois was significantly older than Adela, who was about fifteen at the time of her marriage. Meanwhile, it appears to have been a good marriage based on respect and trust. She ruled her husband's estates during his prolonged absence while on crusade and after his death. She was deeply religious and expanded considerable capital on helping the church. Apparently, she was close to her youngest brother, Henry. Two of her brothers ruled as kings of England, and eventually her son Stephen became king.

We don't know how she felt about the disputes between her brothers over the control of Normandy and the English crown.

Various accounts describe Adela's displeasure when her husband Stephen-Henry returned from the crusade after abandoning the other crusaders and without fulfilling his vows. However, we do not have any document or writing that reflects her thoughts. We only know that within a short time period, her husband rejoined the crusade. He eventually lost his life in Ramla, either in battle on May 19, 1102 or in an execution shortly thereafter. Once again, there are conflicting accounts of this.

We can only guess at her feelings when her husband did not return from the crusade; we do know that she pledged her youngest child Henry, conceived just before Stephen Henri reluctantly departed again for Jerusalem, to the church as an oblate when he was two years old.

For years into her son Theobald's maturity, she continued to maintain control over her husband's estates while also preventing Theobald's marriage. Even after she retired to the convent at Marcigny, she continued to exert pressure on her children and on ecclesiastical leaders of lands that had been part of her domain, sending letters of instruction and admonishment and reminding them of their duties to the church.

We have no accounts describing her reaction to the White Ship disaster in 1120. Approximately 250-300 lives were lost that day, including Adela's daughter Lucia-Mahaut and her husband, Adela's brother Henry I's heir William Adelin, other cousins, among a total of 140 noblemen and 18 noblewomen, and about 92 servants.

Adela lived to see her son Henry of Blois ascend to the bishopric of Winchester. She was still alive when her son Stephen became king of England in 1135, but died before the open eruption of what came to be known as the years of anarchy, when his cousin Matilda, the daughter of Henry I., challenged Stephen for the throne.

We know of a number of women who joined the crusades. Some women fought in battle. Their presence on occasion resulted in banishment from the army, since it was feared that they would corrupt the men. This applied particularly to women in menial positions. We don't know whether any women joined the crusades in disguise. But it seems to me entirely plausible.

I certainly don't claim, nor did I wish to cover all of the historical events and developments relevant to Adela's life.

Needless to say, accounts written by historians are not necessarily a reflection of what actually happened, but more often than not inspired by the particular perspective of the writer; in other words, history itself is a construct of a multitude of accounts, some of which may be slanted or distorted in one direction or another.

For instance, one might take a look at Orderic Vitalis (1075-c. 1142), the monastic chronicler and author of texts on the history of Normandy. His work is a contemporary commentary on the social, political, and ecclesiastical affairs of his lifetime. Orderic Vitalis is extremely critical of Robert Curthose while largely complimentary in his comments about Robert's brother, King Henry I. Some of his descriptions border on gossip-like enjoyment of bizarre details that might well be taken from salacious publications like the National

Enquirer. For instance, he offers an unflattering description of Adela in her attempts to cajole her husband to return to the crusade, not hesitating to use her sexual prowess to emphasize her arguments. His descriptions and portrayals do not always gel with those of other sources, which suggests that one should be open to reexamining his work as well as modern interpretations that reference his views and perspectives.

If I have exceeded my mandate in providing "an imaginative reconstruction" of Adela's life and some of her contemporaries, I apologize to the reader. I wanted show her essential humanity as a complex individual with flaws and strengths in order to bring to life the historical image we have of this remarkable woman.

I took some liberties with regard to several items where the dates are uncertain at best, in particular:

A letter from Hildebert of Lavardin (1101?) to Adela of England, countess of Blois, Chartres, and Meaux (post date it to 1103/note to reader) Printed source: PL171 ep.3.2 c284 date 1101 (?). I decided to date this letter to 1102, since its exact date is uncertain.

A letter from Adela of England, Countess of Blois, Chartres, and Meaux, to Geoffrey II, Bishop of Chartres, letter, written between 1133-37. I decided to date this letter to 1135, since the exact date is uncertain as well.

There is some uncertainty regarding the birth date of Henry, the last son of Adela. In some sources, it states he was born in 1096. Most reports indicated that he was conceived in the year when Count Stephen-Henry was at home before returning to the Holy Land. Thus, I place his birth in the year 1101.

While we have no certainty where Adela's brother Henry spent much of his childhood, I decided to place him for part of those years in Caen. It is possible, if not probable, that he spent his first years there, working with a tutor.

Note: Regarding the spelling of *sepulchre,* I chose to retain the English spelling; it appears like that in the original documents. I have also refrained from adjusting grammar and spelling in those documents cited throughout the text.

ACKNOWLEDGMENTS

I have been fascinated by Adela for years. In fact, when writing my first historical fiction novel, *The Falconer's Apprentice*, I named a young peregrine falcon Adela in her honor. Falcons are fast, focused, determined, and courageous. It seemed a fitting name. On an entertaining personal note, Gilbert von Studnitz, a relative of mine on my mother's side of the family (née von Studnitz), shared some of his family research with me. As it turns out, my 29x great-grandparents were Count Friedrich im Moselgau and his wife Irmintrud v. der Wetterau, who happened to be Adela's 2x great-grandparents. Perhaps, an echo of that distant link drew me to Adela. Writing a fictionalized account of Adela's life is an act of the imagination given the reality of how little we really know about this remarkable woman. I ask for clemency for liberties taken with her life. Any errors are mine and mine alone. Meanwhile, a lot of work of research went into the writing of the manuscript. I am forever grateful for my local library that diligently and tirelessly obtained materials for me from other libraries and also helped to point me in new directions. Barbara Henderson of the History Quill provided me with detailed and thoughtful feedback on the first draft of the book. Julian de la Motte Harrison made many helpful suggestions along the way. I am happy that the book found a home with Historium Press and beyond grateful to Dee Marley for all her work and her experienced advice. A renowned author in her own right, she is an editor with a passion for and extensive knowledge of historical fiction. Moreover, she addresses literally all aspects of getting a book ready for the road. Dee Marley also founded the Historical Fiction Club, a group of authors and readers. As a result, I have been introduced to many wonderful books with an amazing range of historical periods and approaches for weaving history into one's writing and bringing it to life. I have found my tribe.

My son has patiently watched me travel down one research rabbit hole after another. Repeatedly, I would forget the time when working on yet another draft. His support and encouragement mean more than I can express.

Thank you for your interest. If you enjoyed this book, please consider leaving a review on Amazon or another site where you like to purchase your books. If you would like to learn more about my work, I invite you to check out my website at:

https://www.malvevonhassell.com

I would love to hear from you.

ABOUT THE AUTHOR

Malve von Hassell is a freelance writer, researcher, and translator. She holds a Ph.D. in anthropology from the New School for Social Research. Working as an independent scholar, she published *The Struggle for Eden: Community Gardens in New York City* (Bergin & Garvey 2002) and *Homesteading in New York City 1978-1993: The Divided Heart of Loisaida* (Bergin & Garvey 1996). She has also edited her grandfather Ulrich von Hassell's memoirs written in prison in 1944, *Der Kreis schließt sich - Aufzeichnungen aus der Haft 1944* (Propylaen Verlag 1994). She has taught at Queens College, Baruch College, Pace University, and Suffolk County Community College, while continuing her work as a translator and writer. She has published two children's picture books, *Tooth Fairy (Amazon KDP 2012/2020)*, and *Turtle Crossing (Amazon KDP 2023)*, and her translation and annotation of a German children's classic by Tamara Ramsay, *Rennefarre: Dott's Wonderful Travels and Adventures* (Two Harbors Press, 2012). *The Falconer's Apprentice* (namelos, 2015/KDP 2024) was her first historical fiction novel for young adults. She has published *Alina: A Song for the Telling* (BHC Press, 2020), set in Jerusalem in the time of the crusades, and *The Amber Crane* (Odyssey Books, 2021), set in Germany in 1645 and 1945, as well as a biographical work about a woman coming of age in Nazi Germany, *Tapestry of My Mother's Life: Stories, Fragments, and Silences* (Next Chapter Publishing, 2021), also available in German, *Bildteppich Eines Lebens: Erzählungen Meiner Mutter, Fragmente Und Schweigen* (Next Chapter Publishing, 2022).

A letter from Baudri, Abbot of Bourgueil and Archbishop of Dol (c.1107 (!2)) to Adela of England, Countess of Blois, Chartres, and Meaux, before 1107. Printed source: Les Oeuvres poétiques de Baudri de Bourgueil, ed. Phyllis Abraham (Paris: Slatkine, 1926, repr.1974), 196-253. [Description of a chamber purportedly belonging to Adela] https://epistolae.ctl.columbia.edu/letter/94.html

A letter from Baudri, Abbot of Bourgueil and Archbishop of Dol to Adela of England, Countess of Blois, Chartres, and Meaux, before 1107. Printed source: Le Epistole Metriche di Baldericus Burguliensis, ed. M. Teresa Razzoli (Milano: SAE Dante Alighieri, 1936), 69-70, and Les Oeuvres poétiques de Baudri de Bourgueil, ed. Phyllis Abraham (Paris: Slatkine, 1926, repr. 1974), 153-54. [Request for a cope] https://epistolae.ctl.columbia.edu/letter/95.html

A letter from Ivo, Bishop of Chartres to Adela of England, Countess of Blois, Chartres, and Meaux. Historical context: The letter is about yet another jurisdictional dispute, in which Adela has taken punitive action against the canons and Ivo threatens ecclesiastical sanctions unless she rescinds it. Printed source: PL162 ep.179 c180-81; also HGF15 ep.110 p.141-42, same text with 2 variations in spelling, date 1107. https://epistolae.ccnmtl.columbia.edu/letter/86.html/

A letter from Hildebert of Lavardin to Adela of England, Countess of Blois, Chartres, and Meaux. 1101?.

https://epistolae.ctl.columbia.edu/letter/90.html/

A letter from Pope Gregory VII to Matilda of Flanders, Duchess of Normandy, Queen of England, 1074.
https://epistolae.ctl.columbia.edu/letter/50.html/

A letter from Pope Gregory VII to Matilda, Duchess of Normandy and Queen of England, 1080.
https://epistolae.ctl.columbia.edu/letter/51.html/

For other citations in the book, I acknowledge the following sources:

Saint Augustine, *De Bono Conjugali* (Of The Good Of lMarriage), Source. Translated by C.L. Cornish. From Nicene and Post-Nicene Fathers, First Series, Vol. 3. Edited by Philip Schaff. (Buffalo, NY: Christian Literature Publishing Co., 1887.) Revised and edited for New Advent by Kevin Knight.

Fulcher of Chartres, *Chronicle of the First Crusade*, English trans. Martha E. McGinty, *Fulcher of Chartres: Chronicle of the First Crusade*, (London: Oxford University Press; Philadelphia: University of Pennsylvania Press, 1941), in Internet Medieval Sourcebook. Fordham University Center for Medieval Studies, https://sourcebooks.fordham.edu/source/cdesource.asp/

Pope Urban II (1088-1099): Speech at Council of Clermont, 1095, in Oliver J. Thatcher and Edgar Holmes McNeal, (Ed.), *A Source Book for Mediæval History: Selected Documents Illustrating the History of Europe in the Middle Age* (New York: Charles Scribner's Sons, 1905), 518-52

Folgore da San Geminiano, excerpt of poem from Rosetti, Dante Gabriel *Dante and His Circle: With the Italian Poets Preceding Him (1100—1200—1300)*. Ellis and White, 29 New Bond Street, 1874.

Geoponika: Agricultural Pursuits by Anonymous; translated from Greek by Thomas Owen, in two volumes (London, 1806).

The Goodman of Paris. translated by Eileen Power in *The Goodman of Paris*, (London: Routledge, 1928), and reprinted in Richard M. Golden and Thomas Kuehn, eds., Western Societies: Primary Sources in Social History, Vol I, (New York: St Martins, 1993). Internet Medieval Sourcebook, Fordham University Center for Medieval Studies. https://sourcebooks.fordham.edu/source/goodman.asp/

Hildebert de Lavardin, The Hymn of Hildebert and other mediaeval hymns : with translations by Benedict, Erasmus Cornelius, 1800-1880, New York : Anson D. F. Randolph & Co., 1868, University of California Digital Libraries.

Henry, Archdeacon of Huntingdon. archidiaconi huntendunensis Historia Anglorum, 1084?-1155; Arnold, Thomas, 1823-1900, ed. London: Longman & co. [etc., etc.] Harvard University, 1879.

Huntingdon, Henry Archdeacon of. *The Chronicle of Henry of Huntingdon, comprising The History of England, from the Invasion of Julius Caesar to the Accession of Henry II*, translated and edited by Thomas Forester, A.M., London: Henry G. Bohn, 1853.

Henry, Archdeacon of Huntingdon. archidiaconi huntendunensis *Historia Anglorum*, 1084?-1155; Arnold, Thomas, 1823-1900, ed. London: Longman & co. [etc., etc.] Harvard University, 1879.

Reichenau, Hermann of (also known as Hermann the Cripple) (July 18, 1013-September 24, 1054), a Benedictine monk and scholar. He has traditionally been credited with the composition of *Salve Regina*, sung by the crusaders in the Church of the Holy Sepulchre.

Stephen-Henry de Blois, letters to his wife. *Recueil des Historiens des Croisades, Historiens Occidentaux*, (Paris: Imprimerie impériale, 1866), v.3, 887-90. Translation from Translations and Reprints from the Original Sources of European History, 1.4, Letters of the Crusaders written from the Holy Land, trans. Dana Carlton Munro, Philadelphia: University of Pennsylvania, 1902, pgs. 5-6.

Le Viandier de Guillaume Tirel dit Taillevent, le Baron Jérôme Pichon et Georges Vicaire, Paris, 1892 (reprint by Slatkine Reprints, Genève, 1967).

Citations from the King James Bible:

And the angel thrust in his sickle into the earth, and gathered the vine of the earth, and cast it into the great winepress of the wrath of God. 20 And the winepress was trodden without the city, and blood came out of the winepress, even unto the horse bridles, by the space of a thousand and six hundred furlongs. Revelation 14:19-20. King James Bible. Public Domain.

I have said I will bring you up out of the affliction of Egypt to the land of the Canaanites and the Hittites and the Amorites and the Perizzites and the Hivites and the Jebusites, to a land flowing with milk and honey. Exodus 3:17. King James Bible. Public Domain.

For I am now ready to be offered, and the time of my departure is at hand. I have fought a good fight, I have finished my course, I have kept the faith. Henceforth there is laid up for me a crown of righteousness, which the Lord, the righteous judge, shall give me at that day: and not to me only, but unto all them also that love his appearing. Timothy 4:7. King James Bible. Public Domain.

The waters compassed me about, even to the soul: the depth closed me round about, the weeds were wrapped about my head. Jonah 2:5. King James Bible. Public Domain

www.historiumpress.com